DOUBLE FAULT

"Bickham knows well the ins and outs of telling a story that keeps the reader's interest. He succeeds quite well in doing that with *Double Fault*, mixing an intimate knowledge of tennis with AN ENTERTAINING, ENJOYABLE STORY.

"This book is A DEFINITE WIN for Bickham."

—*Tulsa World*

"TENNIS FANS AND MYSTERY FANS ARE IN FOR A TREAT as Brad Smith for the fifth time walks out onto the tennis courts and into the labyrinths of the CIA.

"This is a skillfully written narrative. Bickham raises his book MORE THAN A NOTCH ABOVE THE COMPETITION."

—*Mystery News*

BREAKFAST AT WIMBLEDON

"An exciting story. THE AUTHOR IS MARVELOUS when he is on the court, getting into the minds of his tennis pros."

—*The New York Times Book Review*

"Quick, spry adventure. The mix of top-flight tennis competition and nicely skewered intelligence communities is ORIGINAL AND ENGAGING."

—*Publishers Weekly*

"A SUSPENSEFUL THRILLER WITH AN ADMIRABLE HERO, and the tennis action is vivid as well. Recommended."

—*Library Journal*

OVERHEAD

"Bickham expertly combines tennis, friendship, espionage and corporate malfeasance in this COMPLEXLY PLOTTED, THOROUGHLY READABLE thriller. Likeable heroes, despicable villains and EXCELLENT SUSPENSE lead to A ROUSING, SATISFYING CLIMAX."

—*Publishers Weekly*

Tor books by Jack M. Bickham

Ariel
Day Seven
Miracle Worker
The Regensburg Legacy

NOVELS IN THE BRAD SMITH SERIES

Breakfast at Wimbledon
Double Fault
Dropshot
Overhead
Tiebreaker

DOUBLE FAULT

Jack M. Bickham

A TOM DOHERTY ASSOCIATES BOOK
NEW YORK

DOUBLE FAULT

Copyright © 1993 by Jack M. Bickham

Cover art by Tim O'Brien

A Tor Book
Published by Tom Doherty Associates, Inc.
175 Fifth Avenue
New York, N.Y. 10010

Tor® is a registered trademark of Tom Doherty Associates, Inc.

ISBN: 0-812-52161-7
Library of Congress Catalog Card Number: 93-1329

First edition: July 1993
First mass market edition: August 1994

Printed in the United States of America

0 9 8 7 6 5 4 3 2 1

Prologue

ALMOST MIDNIGHT, and the snow had been falling steadily on Washington for more than three hours. On the undulating, tree-shrouded grounds of Walter Reed Hospital, Christmas lights on large, ornamental evergreens along the curving sweep of the main road cast fuzzy puddles of red and green on the rapidly deepening white. Nothing moved; many of the windows in the complex of brick buildings had gone dark; the thick, wet snow had already obliterated tracks left by the last vehicle to use the driveway almost an hour before.

A seldom-used side door of one large brick building swung open, briefly spilling interior brightness onto the untouched snow. A figure emerged, moving quickly. He wore only the lightweight pajamas issued patients at Walter Reed, and he was barefoot. He had something metallic clutched in his right hand. Middle-aged, completely bald, a short man whose skeletal frame looked lost in the pajamas, he hurried out into the snow, looking furtively this way and that as the metal door swung shut behind him. Then, seeming to get his bearings, he struck out across a sprawling field of white, hurrying clumsily through the snow toward the shelter of a grove of trees.

Behind him, no alarm sounded.

Moving fast, the man reached 16th Avenue. Crouching in shrubs that provided his last cover, he looked frantically up and down the wide, usually busy thoroughfare. It lay silent, ghostly white under the streetlights. Two cars, northbound from the traffic light down toward the park, moved as the

light changed and trundled up past his position. Idiots, Arnie
Tubb thought, probably headed for midnight Mass. A lone
panel truck went by going south, its tires squishing in the
deep, wet snow.

Tubb left his hiding place and scuttled out onto the
pavement, hurrying faster. The snow stung his feet and his
teeth had begun to chatter. He was freezing. But that was not
why he hurried. They were sure to miss him and sound the
alarm any minute now.

He headed to his right, numb feet scuffling in the deep
snow, headed for the residential area he knew was nearby.
Passing cars on 16th forced him to stop twice and hunker
down behind snow-mounded vehicles to avoid being seen.
Disjointed thoughts darted through his mind, but almost
everything in him focused on the snow, the cold, his aching
feet and hands, the way he hurt—fear of the sounds of bells
or sirens or *something* behind him that would indicate his
escape had been discovered.

He reached the far end of the shrubbery marking hospital
property. Beyond, not far, he came to the first intersecting
residential street. Row houses—flats—packed tightly along a
street so narrow that the cars parked on both sides left room
for only single-lane traffic between them. Lights shone from
a few windows. Most were dark.

Tubb hurried along on feet that felt like stumps, darting
glances at the cars. The third one in line on his side was an
elderly Chevrolet, and he knew he could hot-wire its ignition
in moments. He grabbed the door handle: locked. He moved
on. He would find one. He had to, and fast.

Halfway up the block, just when his desperation had
begun to scream at him, he checked the door handle of an old
Corolla that would work. The latch moved, showing it was
unlocked. *Perfect!* Tubb jerked the door open. The interior
dome light flashed on. He scrambled inside and closed the
door to make it dark again.

Muttering noises to himself, Tubb put his precious pliers on the other seat and set to work with his other stolen tool, a screwdriver.

Inside their apartment, Calvin Jones finished getting all the wheels of the tiny HO-gauge toy train on the track encircling the Christmas tree. He turned to his wife, kneeling beside the couch while she stuffed the stockings. He whispered to avoid waking the kids sleeping upstairs. "Honey, will you pass me that little tunnel thing?"

Smiling, she reached for it. "They're gonna love that train."

"It's going to be a great Christmas."

The unexpected sound of a car engine, being revved hard, came from the street. Calvin Jones turned sharply. "Who's that? Hell! It sounds like *our* car!"

He jumped to his feet, brushing against the Christmas tree and making it sway wildly. At the window he pulled back the draperies. "Shit! It *is* our car!" He turned wide-eyed to his wife. "Somebody is stealing our goddamn car! Call the cops!" He ran for the front door.

Out on the snowy street, Arnie Tubb cranked hard on the steering wheel of the Toyota, spinning its wheels as he gunned the engine to escape from the parking space. He saw the apartment door flash brightly open and someone run out. *Too late, motherfucker.* He got the Corolla into the narrow driving lane, bounced lightly off a car on the far side, and slithered up the street far faster than the snow should allow.

At the corner he took a left. The small car slid again—too much speed—shit—the rear end banged deafeningly into another parked car, but then swung free. Tubb kept going.

Another left turn and a block, and he was back at 16th again. He saw only a handful of distant headlights to the south. They glowed hazily white through the continuing snowfall, and for just an instant Tubb had a flashback: *Jeep lights, or maybe trucks, shining through the dense vegeta-*

*tion surrounding the perimeter; no sign of the fucking heli-
copters, and the stink of mud, sweat, cordite, and death all
around. Dinks out there, close, moving closer, moving
around so you couldn't see where they were at, sending in
mortar rounds. Next to Tubb, not fifteen feet away, a pile of
raw meat and torn rags and strewn entrails that had been
two guys less than five minutes ago. If them lights ain't our
lights, I'm next, I'm a dead man.*

A traffic light changed far up the street, snapping Tubb
back. He turned right and accelerated hard, tires spinning in
the snow. He felt sick from fright, sicker from the radiation.
He wondered if he was going to puke.

Walter Reed: Noon, Christmas Day

COL. LIONEL T. BRACKEN adjusted some official correspon-
dence on his desktop. His hands shook slightly. He hated
showing feelings. He couldn't help it. He struggled to make
his voice sound calm: "I can assure you that every normal
security procedure was in place."

The two men standing in front of his massive desk wore
civilian suits, but they were not civilians. Bracken did not
know their rank, and it hardly mattered. They were some
kind of Pentagon Intelligence people, and the commanding
general had gotten explicit orders to give them anything they
wanted, no questions asked.

Tatwhiler, the older of the two men facing him, perhaps
fifty, with tightly cropped gray hair and a profile like a
hatchet, flipped open a small OD notebook. "Your report
says he escaped between 2300 and midnight?"

"I wouldn't use the word 'escaped,' " Bracken said, desperately quibbling for breathing room here. "He was not
transferred to this facility as a prisoner—"

Tatwhiler's voice whipcracked. "He came from a VA hospital's psychiatric ward! Jesus Christ, Colonel!"

"We had him on extra observation in the oncology section," Bracken protested weakly. He could feel the ground eroding under his feet with every exchange. "There was no way to predict that a man in his weakened condition could do much of anything, much less walk out in a blizzard."

Tatwhiler's lips became a pencil line. "Well, he's done a lot. We think he walked out of here, stole a car right up the street, drove into Silver Spring with it, abandoned it and stole a second vehicle, and got clear out of the area before the second theft was even reported this morning. Now the search will have to go nationwide."

Bracken nervously mussed his papers again. Then he looked up at the two grim men facing him, and the question simply blurted out: "Who *is* this man? What did he do? I've looked at his file, and there's nothing to indicate why he should be—"

"The file you received on his transfer was incomplete," Tatwhiler snapped.

"Incomplete! That's unbelievable! How could—"

"Colonel, it's a security matter. End of subject. Where are those security people who were on duty last night? Where is the chief of oncology?"

"I've sent for them."

"Then where are they? We want to see them now, Colonel. Not tomorrow sometime."

Bracken reached for the telephone and punched the intercom button. "Sergeant Ahles, are Dr. Carpenter and the others here yet? . . . Well, find them, goddammit! I want them here now!"

He slammed the telephone down. It almost made him feel better. It was always nice to have someone else's butt to kick when yours was getting blistered.

But oh, the colonel thought, feeling the chill, unblinking

eyes of the two agents staring down at him—oh, it was really hitting the fan this time. He wondered how it would be, retired, living in Fort Lauderdale.

Boston: December 29

ARNIE TUBB limped down the black, frigid street, his stolen shoes hurting his feet. He was cold and hungry, and felt spooky and dazed, like he might have another case of pneumonia coming on. It was a bad neighborhood: crummy pawnshops and stores dark and vacant behind barred security doors, sooty brick buildings walling in the streets, some of the streetlights broken—maybe shot out—making long parts of each block pitch-dark. A man could get killed here, even a man like Tubb, skulking along in his too-big wool pants and sweatshirt and tattered hat and coat, all stolen from the same store where he had gotten the shoes.

The danger didn't matter. The way he felt didn't matter. The only thing that mattered was the obsession pounding inside his skull.

It was his second night of prowling the neighborhood where the volunteer at the shelter for homeless veterans had told him he might find Purvis.

Tubb was not far now from the area where the highway crossed over the neighborhood on concrete stilts. Up ahead he could see the lights of the cars whooshing along despite the lateness of the hour. Tubb kept walking.

A figure emerged from the mouth of an alley a half-block ahead: a tall man, deeply stooped, some kind of shapeless hat pulled over his head and a blanket wrapped around his body. He seemed to be carrying some kind of plastic bag. He turned away from Tubb, heading toward the overpass area.

It could be, Tubb thought, and hurried.

At the next alley intersection, the stooped figure moved into the darkness. Tubb reached the alley and looked down it. Fifty feet away, a dim security light on the brick wall shone down on two large Dumpster units. The man in the blanket had climbed up the side of the nearest Dumpster and was hanging over the lip, rummaging inside. Tubb saw him find something, put it in his plastic bag, and rummage again.

Tubb hurried forward.

The other man heard his footsteps and hopped down from the side of the trash container. With startling, scared agility, he swung around to face Tubb. The security light shone momentarily on his dark, bearded face.

"Purvis!" Tubb cried out. "Man! How are you?"

Purvis Brooks straightened convulsively, clutching his plastic bag closer to his chest. His voice rasped, "I got a knife! You better back off! I got a knife!"

"Purvis," Tubb said, holding out his hands. "It's me— Arnie Tubb!"

Brooks froze. "Arnie?" he repeated in soft bewilderment.

Tubb moved forward and grabbed the much taller black man in his arms, hugging him fiercely. The joy of finding a comrade made him feel hot with pleasure and dizzy.

Brooks pushed him away, staring down at him with vague, emotionless eyes. Brooks looked like an old man. "Arnie?" he repeated. "How'd you find me, man?"

"I went to that shelter you wrote me about. They said you'd bugged out. They said I might find you down here someplace."

Brooks looked off into space, clutching his sack, and seemed to be thinking about it. "Um," he said finally.

"Purvis," Tubb demanded, "are you *okay?*"

Brooks stirred. "Sure. Fine."

"Where are you staying?"

"I got a nice place to live down under the highway. Cops don't make you move but about once a week." Brooks seemed to remember something, and opened the puckered mouth of his plastic bag. "You want something to eat? I just found some real good stuff. Sandwich. Pizza."

"Screw that," Tubb said impatiently. "Purvis, listen! I

been in the VA hospital. A guy came to interview me a couple
months ago. He's doing a book on *us*, Purvis—our unit in
Nam. He wanted to know some stuff about Quang Xi,
Purvis." Tubb saw the glaze in Brooks's eyes. "Quang Xi,
Purvis! You remember that! You got your Purple Heart and
Bronze Star at Quang Xi."

Brooks stared at him. "So what?" he asked.

"Purvis, he had the names!"

"Names?"

Tubb fought the impulse to grab the teetering giant and
shake him as he would a stubborn child. "The names, Purvis.
The *names*! The guys in the gunship! Purvis, listen. After
that guy came, some guys from the army came. They asked
questions too. I guess they heard the other guy was working
on a book, and they were checking their own info. I didn't
give them shit. But they had a picture of one of the guys. I
stole a copy of the picture. I've got it, Purvis. We've got the
names and I've even got a picture of one of them. We can
hunt for them now. We can finally make them pay."

Brooks stared down at Tubb with liquid brown eyes.
"What you want from me, man?"

"I need you to help me, Purvis. I ran off from the hospital, the latest one they put me in. I've got cancer. They
moved me from New York down to Walter Reed to treat me
for it, and I've had a couple treatments—it makes your hair
fall out and you feel like shit all the time—but they didn't
have good guards on me like in the psych ward in New York,
and I seen my chance and I walked away. That's why I'm here
now, Purvis. You've got to help me. We've got to get some
of the old group together—find these two guys."

Purvis Brooks—winner of two Purple Hearts, the Bronze
Star with a cluster, and the Silver Star, all for heroism as a
combat infantryman in Vietnam—thought about it for what
seemed a long time. His mind seemed to be running in some
other dimension of time, slowing everything down.

Finally he began shaking his head. "No," he said.

"Purvis!"

"No, man." Brooks's voice rose and became stronger. *"No*, man. I don't fight no more. I don't give a shit about Quang Xi or anything else. No. Go away. Leave me alone. That's all I want, people leave me alone." Sudden tear-tracks glistened on his cheeks.

Tubb saw now that his hopes for help here had been groundless. There was no sense arguing. He felt disappointed and infinitely sad.

He reached up and put his hand on his comrade's shoulder. "Okay, Purvis. I understand."

The tall black man brightened and reached into his plastic bag. "You want some supper? I found some good stuff." He pulled out a pie-shaped wedge of pizza. It looked soggy, like it had been soaking in something, and it had coffee grounds on it. "It's pretty good. No kidding. Or . . . lemme see . . . I got part of a sandwhich in here. It's fairly fresh. You want a sandwhich, Arnie?"

Knoxville, Tennessee: January 1

MIKE ROMANOWSKI and his wife, Madge, had just finished taking down the Christmas tree and repacking the ornaments for another year when the telephone rang in the kitchen of their small, white frame house. Madge went to answer it while Romanowski finished taping shut the boxes for the attic. A burly man with a fringe of red hair over his ears, a well-developed beer belly, and a face lapped and overlapped by the sagging tissues of late middle age, he was a welder by trade, and his arms, bared by the undershirt he was wearing, were festooned with old tattoos: an eagle, an American flag, a skull and crossbones, a very large snake, and a cluster of army insignias. He was forty-seven, but felt older.

"Mike?" his wife called from the door to the kitchen. "It's for you."

Romanowski's hands were all stuck up with tape. "Who is it?"

"He didn't say."

Muttering, Romanowski moved ponderously into the tiny yellow kitchen and picked the telephone receiver up off the counter. "Yeah?"

"Mike? It's Arnie. Arnie Tubb."

Romanowski could not have been more shocked. "Holy shit. They let you go? You're okay? Where are you?"

"I'm down at the convenience store two blocks from your house. We've gotta talk. Can I come down?"

"What's happened?" Romanowski demanded. "I thought you were—"

"Mike, listen to me. I'm on the lam. I ran from Walter Reed. I don't know how long I've got. You've got to help me. You've got to hear what I've found out."

"Found out? Found out?" Romanowski didn't want Tubb here. He didn't want to see Tubb or any of his other former buddies from Nam, not ever again. All that was over now. Finally over, finally done with, finally buried. But curiosity made him add cautiously, "What did you find out?"

"I know who the guys were in the gunship, Mike."

"Oh, no," Romanowski groaned.

"What do you mean, 'Oh, no'? Isn't this what we've always wanted?"

"Call some of the other guys. Call Stuhlder. Call Hack. I don't want to do any more. I want out. I just want out."

"I tried Stuhlder." Tubb's voice went shrilled with desperation. *"I tried Ackerman. They're chickenshit. They're assholes. They won't help anymore. They want to forget. You've got to help me find some of the old group that still remembers, Mike. Mike! I even got a picture of him!"*

"Picture of who?" Romanowski demanded in despair. "You're not making sense!"

"The pilot!" Tubb said. He sounded like he was crying. *"He's out there someplace. And I think I know where we can*

*get a lot more information. It isn't over. Mike. You know it
will never be over until we've finished it. Now we can. We
finally can."*

The last thing in the world Romanowski wanted to do was
have Arnie Tubb here at the house. But Romanowski saw
that there was no help for it now. The clammy pain tighten-
ing around his stomach was already almost unbearable.

After all this time, he thought.

If Arnie Tubb was speaking the truth about this, there
was absolutely nothing to do but contact some of the other
guys. The thought made Romanowski feel sick.

The voice on the telephone, shriller: *"Mike? Mike?"*

"All right," Romanowski said. "Come on."

The connection broke. Romanowski moved heavily back
toward the living room, where he found his wife uncoiling the
cord of the vacuum cleaner, ready to take up all the dry
needles as soon as he carried the tree out the front door. It
was their ritual ending of Christmas.

"Madge," Romanowski said, "you'd better go to the store
now, and do that sweeping later."

"I'd like to get it done, honey," Madge Romanowski
remonstrated. "It will only take—"

"No, I want you to go to the store now."

She looked up, frowning at his angry tone of voice.
"What—"

"Just do it, Madge, goddammit! Will you just *do* it?"

She dropped the sweeper cord and fled. Romanowski
stared at the messy living room, seeing instead the mess that
now must lie ahead. Very briefly, a picture of suicide flick-
ered in his imagination. It would be quick—the shotgun
muzzle in his mouth. He had mentally rehearsed it a hundred
times.

He heard the sound of the car being backed out of the
garage, tires on gravel driveway. Then Madge was gone.

Romanowski sat down, locked ham-sized hands, and
waited. The nightmare had resumed.

One

On May 22—my birthday—I got myself shellacked by Bjorn Borg, 6–4 6–4, in a celebrity exhibition match in Seattle, flew back to Montana with my ill-gotten $10,000 paycheck, and drove the Bronco down from Missoula to Bitterroot Valley Resort.

Darkness was just settling in over the mountains when I arrived, and it had started to get cold for the night. I parked in a staff spot near the main lodge building and went inside long enough to find my co-owner, Ted Treacher, to let him know I was home. Then I toddled down the cart path to my cabin in the woods, hauling my rackets and a duffel, with the intention of taking a hot shower, building a big warm fire, sipping a big cold drink, and collapsing before the clock struck eleven. Happy birthday, Brad Smith.

My plans changed less than thirty minutes later when my telephone started quick-ringing the way it does when someone is calling from the resort office.

Still dripping from the shower, I limped into the high-beamed living room and picked up. "Yes?"

"Brad?" Ted's familiar voice said. "You've got a visitor on the way down."

"Down where?"

"Down there. To your cabin."

"For God's sake! Who is it, at this hour?"

"I don't know. He said his name is Frank Simmons."

"I don't know any Frank Simmons. I told you I'm beat.

Why did you just send him down without checking with me first?"

"Brad, I'm sorry. He wouldn't take no for an answer."

"You didn't have to tell him where I was. It's been a long day, Ted."

Ted's voice sounded worried and remorseful. "Well, he says he's a federal agent. He says it won't wait."

"A federal agent?" That sounded fishy. "What kind of a federal agent?"

"He didn't say."

"Thanks a lot, Ted. I really appreciate this."

Ted Treacher is one of the nicest men alive, and he was still apologizing when I hung up on him.

Padding into the bedroom, I toweled off, grabbed my heavy white terry-cloth robe and fleece-lined slippers, and ran a comb through my hair. The face that looked back at me from the mirror was pale after the long Montana winter, and seemed to have some new lines and sags in it. Maybe I was just noticing because of the birthday, and the way the day had gone. I was not feeling very festive.

I had played two sets of early-morning doubles today, and then my match with Bjorn had not been easy because neither of us ever took pleasure in losing, exhibition or not. My most recent knee surgery had put a lot of things back together again after the Wimbledon fiasco, but it would never be right again: I still required the brace and I still hurt after violent exercise. So I was not only tired but in just enough pain that the extra-strength Tylenol was not getting the job done. The last thing I needed was some stranger—G-man of some kind or not—messing up my plans for an early wipeout.

If he walked around the parking lot to the back, then came down the cart path as I had, he would be here in another minute or so. I started out of the bedroom, thought of something, and went back to the end table beside my bed. Somebody rapped on my cabin door just as I opened the drawer in the table. Dropping the little S & W .38 detective special into the pocket of my robe, I returned to the living room, aware that I was probably being very melodramatic. The cold war was over and I was not aware of anyone out there now with a major grudge against me. Still, it didn't hurt to be cautious, and I could console myself with the thought that nobody would ever know about the gun. Unless I happened to need it.

My uninvited guest knocked again, really hammering this time.

"Wait a minute!" I called.

Going to the door, I flicked on the outside porch floodlight, a 300-watter bright enough to blind anybody getting it full in the face. I opened the door with my left hand, keeping my right in my robe pocket.

The man standing there with a hand raised to try to protect his face from the unholy glare was of medium height, slender, wearing jeans and a lightweight jacket. A lot of his dark hair had gone from the temples. He had a thin, hook nose and an even thinner mouth. His eyes, narrowed against the light, looked extraordinarily green. I don't know why, but before he said a word I did not like him.

"Mr. Smith?" he said. "Could you possibly douse that light, please?"

"No. What do you want?"

The green eyes flared with dangerous anger, then as quickly went out. He dug into the inside pocket of his jacket for a billfold which he flipped open at me, very businesslike. "My name is Frank Simmons, sir. Army Intelligence."

I stared at the impressive little gold badge pinned inside the wallet. It had the right words on it, but you can get authentic-looking badges at most novelty shops.

"What do you want?" I repeated.

"If I could come in, sir, there are a few questions I'd like to ask. We're trying to locate a couple of military veterans of your acquaintance."

"Who?"

The slightest frown creased friend Simmons's forehead, showing he didn't particularly like being kept standing on the porch, and probably had a short fuse. But he kept his temper. Taking a small notebook out of his inside coat pocket, he inspected a page. "One of the men is Kevin Green. I believe you knew him in college, and saw him again in Vietnam in 1968. The other man was his helicopter gunship copilot over there: David Wentworth. Perhaps you met him also in Nam?"

"I never heard of any David Wentworth," I told him, "and Kevin was MIA, then a POW, and he died over there in a prisoner camp."

"No, sir," Simmons replied, still ice-calm. "Kevin Green is not dead. I can explain. I believe it would be in your best interests to let me in."

Invariably, when someone tells me I'd better do so and so because it's in my best interests, or if I know what's good for me, I react badly. All the doctors told me to get out of competitive tennis, if I knew what was good for me, after I blew out my knee the first time back in 1976; so of course I blew it out a second time a year later, trying to make the comeback that would prove them wrong. Much earlier, back in the sixties, a college advisor had told me that if I had any sense at all I would hit the books harder; so naturally I hit the books even less, failed two courses, and ended up matriculating not in college that fall, but quite involuntarily in the good old Americal Division, home of such luminaries as one captain named Medina and one lieutenant named Calley. It was while I was in Baker Company, 2nd Battalion, 20th Infantry, 11th Brigade, that I had had my brief reunion with Kevin Green, and met David Wentworth.

Kevin had been two years ahead of me in college, and was gone to Vietnam long before me. He piloted a helicopter gunship, all right, and Wentworth—a fiesty Irishman with a bawdy sense of humor—was his copilot, precisely as Simmons had just said. I had had some beers with both of them in Quang Ngai City once. It had been pleasant to run into the guy who had captained the college tennis team ahead of me, and I had liked Wentworth at once. Both of them had been shaky that evening, having seen some stuff in the province's free-fire zone that they just wouldn't—or couldn't—talk about. They were my kind of people; I had already seen some things that I didn't want to think or talk about, either.

When I heard just weeks later that their ship had gone down during a troop-support mission about fifty miles north, it hit me hard. Later, when they were reported POWs, I took some heart, but not a lot. I had learned by then what the chances were of surviving one of the Hanoi Hiltons.

I felt quite sure Kevin had never come back. So when Simmons said Kevin was not dead, my surprise and curiosity overrode even my usual crabbiness about being advised as to what might be in my own best interests. I stepped back and let the gentleman in.

Simmons walked into the living room with the smooth, careful movements of a man who took good care of himself. He had a tightness about the way he moved. It told me that he worked out regularly, probably with heavy weights. He reminded me of deputy sheriffs I had met in rural parts of Texas when I lived down there: phony-cool, phony-tough. All he needed was the sunglasses with the mirror fronts.

Standing in the middle of the living room, he looked all around with great interest.

"Nice," he told me.

I pointed to the couch. "Sit down."

He took my favorite chair.

I went to the fireplace and kept my back to him while I shoved in three logs and some fatwood starter, and got a nice small blaze started. Then I walked silently around him and went to the Bombay bar on the far wall and poured myself a drink without offering him one. Only then did I go back to the couch, the .38 bumping my thigh with every step, and sit facing him.

He seemed unfazed by my rudeness. His expression had not changed, actually, since I turned off the floodlight. "Nice trophies," he said, looking at the case in the corner.

"Thanks."

"I guess the biggest ones are Wimbledon and the U.S. Open?"

"Actually, no."

"But you won both of those."

"Is this what you came to talk about?"

He looked down for a moment, but not quickly enough to hide the dangerous flare in his eyes. He reeked of potential violence. It occurred to me that if I had been a teenager or college kid he almost certainly would have been making threats by now. "We're looking for information," he told me.

"If it's about Kevin, you've wasted your time. I'm sure he's been dead a long time now."

Simmons crossed thin legs, his pants riding high enough to reveal the tops of gleaming black western boots. "I'll level with you, Mr. Smith. There was a major snafu when Green and Wentworth left the service. The army owes them some back pay—quite a considerable amount—and we'd like to locate the two gentlemen so we can clear the books on the matter."

The story sounded phony to me. "In that case, I'm sorry I can't help you."

He slapped his knee. "I guess we'll just have to keep looking, then."

I didn't give him the benefit of an answer. I was trying to figure out what he might really want with a dead man, or with me.

"And," he said after the silence had extended, "you have no ideas that might help us?"

"If Dave Wentworth is still alive, he hasn't made the fact

known to me. And I still feel sure Kevin is dead. He never came back."

"No, sir, he isn't. We have proof he's alive, actually."

"What?" I asked, and I couldn't keep the skepticism out of my voice. "Did somebody mail you some beat-up, doctored photograph of an old white guy in baggy pants with some barbed wire in the background? Or maybe a tape of a man who heard a man who heard a man who heard a man say he had heard a rumor about a story somebody told in a bar in Hanoi?"

Simmons appeared truly puzzled. "What are you so angry about?"

"I'm angry at you and every other son of a bitch in or out of the government who wants to pretend there are still MIAs and POWs alive over there. I've done a lot of study on this subject, and talked to a lot of people. Kevin didn't show up in 1973 when Vietnam returned prisoners. I watched those lists of repatriated POWs. I even called Kevin's wife one time to make sure I didn't miss his name somehow. He never showed up. He never came back. There aren't any more guys alive in prisons over there now. If they're not back by now, they're *dead*."

"The Defense Department still lists more than twenty-two hundred as missing."

"But only a handful are really still unaccounted for, and you ought to know that. We've already identified more MIAs from Nam than from any war in our history. What's your angle? Why can't people like you let the rest of us forget that damned filthy war?"

Simmons just watched me. My pulse was thumping and I felt slightly out of breath. I was shocked by the bitterness that had just erupted out of somewhere inside me. I had thought I was past Vietnam long ago.

Simmons finally asked, "Are you through?"

I drank part of my drink. My hand shook a little.

Simmons dug into his coat pocket and came up this time

with a small paper folder from which he pulled three five-by-seven photographs. He handed them across the coffee table with great care. "These were made from a TV tape that a news station in Denver shot some time ago. This man back here"—he pointed to a figure a few paces away from the ticket line depicted in the first shot—"was incidental to the story. But someone recognized him and contacted us. We think there's no doubt."

He paused, then added, "Wouldn't you agree?"

It was a bad picture, all right, shot from a videotape playback that hadn't been all that great in the first place. But the man walking directly toward the camera position could not be mistaken. He was closer to the camera in the second and third frames, and my certainty grew. I could not believe it, and I felt a chill of shock.

Part of what I had been saying to Simmons were lies, yes. But the part about Kevin had been the absolute truth about a man I had known and loved like a brother. I had been positive he was dead long ago.

But here in these pictures he was.

Older, yes, and thinner. But two decades had not changed him all that much.

The pictures were of Kevin Green, walking through Denver's Stapleton Airport, lugging a shoulder bag like any other traveler, and certainly not a ghost.

"I assume," Simmons said quietly, "you recognize him."

I licked papery lips before handing the pictures back with studied carelessness. "This guy looks a lot like Kevin, sure. But it isn't him."

Simmons's eyes felt like X rays. "Why do you say that?"

"Kevin was stockier, for one thing. And taller. See how the woman close to him in two of those shots practically towers over this guy?. Kevin was well over six feet. And this person's hair is darker. It's not Kevin."

Simmons carefully put the photos back into the folder. "The man who noticed this sequence on Denver television was a comrade of Mr. Green's in the service. The army sent out a list of men to whom pay was owed several months ago, and the gentleman in Denver was among those who got a copy. When he spotted this TV sequence, he notified the Pentagon at once, and we followed up. The man in Denver is positive in his identification."

"Well, the man in Denver is wrong."

"Do you feel just as sure that Lieutenant Wentworth is dead?"

I shrugged, deciding I could give him a little as long as it wasn't helpful. My instincts told me I certainly wasn't going to give him anything useful. "I spoke to him once about eight . . . maybe ten . . . years ago."

"Do you recall the nature of the contact?"

"Sure. I was playing in a tournament somewhere, and my name was in the papers and wire services. Dave saw it and called me at the tournament site. I think I might have been in Dallas at the time. We had a good long visit and agreed to get together sometime, but then we never did."

"Where did he call from?"

"San Francisco," I said, picking the first city that came to mind.

"And did he give you an address?"

"No, he said he was moving to a new job, and he would get back in touch."

Simmons's mercury eyes watched. "But he never did."

"That's right. He never did."

He leaned back in my favorite chair. "This is very disappointing."

"I'm sorry I can't help. Nobody—with the possible exception of his family—would like to believe Kevin is alive more than I do. And if Dave has money coming, I would be the first to want to help him get it."

Simmons's smallish facial features tightened. He got to his feet. He was very hard to read, but I thought he seemed vastly disappointed.

He reached into a different pocket of his coat and produced a business card. "If you should happen to hear again from Mr. Wentworth, we would appreciate notification, sir."

I took the card. "I'll be in touch if I hear anything at all."

"Would you allow me to use your telephone before I leave?"

"Sure. It's right over there."

He went to the telephone on the table beside the doorway to my bedroom. Turning my back on him, I went to the fireplace and moved the logs around a bit, adding a new one. I needed a moment to regroup. This visit had shaken me.

Behind me, as I messed with the fire, I heard Simmons telling someone that he was concluded in Montana and would be back in Washington after a stopover in St. Louis, as per schedule. I wondered how many more people he was asking about Kevin and Dave. *Kevin is alive*, I thought, still numb with shock. *Good Christ, Kevin is alive.*

"Yes, sir," Simmons said into the telephone. "Good night."

He hung up the phone. I finished at the fireplace and faced him. "Anything else?"

He shook his head. "No, sir. Thank you. I'll be on my way."

I walked him to the door. We shook hands. He went out into the night, walking briskly up the sidewalk through the trees in the direction of the lodge.

I gave him a good ten minutes before I unlocked the little steel box in my bedroom, dug out the list of numbers, and placed my 614 area code long-distance call. As the connection went through and the phone back in Ohio began to ring, I wondered if he was even still there. We hadn't talked in well over a year.

He answered. *"Hello?"* He sounded muffled and sleepy.

"Dave? This is Brad Smith."

He sounded wider awake and glad to hear from me: *"Brad? Are you in town?"*

"No, I'm still in Montana. Listen, Dave, I just had a funny visit from a guy asking about you."

Wentworth's tone changed again, becoming wary. *"Yeah? Who?"*

I told him about Simmons's visit.

"And he asked about Kevin, too?"

"Dave, he had some pictures."

"Of what?"

"Of Kevin."

"You must be mistaken." Wentworth did not sound at all surprised.

I listened to my pulse. "Dave, are you sure? Is it possible Kevin *is*—"

"No." Wentworth's voice sounded tight and angry, maybe even scared. *"Kevin is dead. And you don't know where I am."*

"Okay, Dave. But I thought you ought to know about this guy."

"I gotta go, Brad. Stuff to do. Stay in touch." The connection was broken.

I hung up and stood there a few moments, replaying the sudden brusqueness in Dave Wentworth's tone. Maybe it had been a mistake to call him, I thought. But I couldn't begin to guess what the hell was going on here.

More than puzzled, I built another drink, put another log on the fire, and turned my chair around so I could watch the flames and try to sort out my feelings. I realized I had been more deeply shaken than I cared to admit.

You think you are well past a bad experience sometimes, and congratulate yourself. A death, the end of a relationship, a severe financial setback, a stupid mistake you can never retrieve. You get over the bad feelings, you think, and as pal Kevin himself would have said, you keep on keeping on. But then something else happens, and it's as if you had been jerked back by a giant rubber band to the long-ago, with all the feelings as intense and bad as they ever were. Most of my

unwanted sudden recollections go to my father's funeral or
the later death of my mother, or to Danisa. But like most of
the people who went to Vietnam, I will always protest that I
put all that behind me long ago, and like most of the people
who went to Vietnam, I will always have these rubber bands
when I know it is not behind me at all.

Frank Simmons's visit, the photo, and Dave Wentworth's
odd reaction to my call had conspired to do more than con-
fuse and puzzle me. For a few minutes—maybe longer—they
took me back to Vietnam, and being in a unit in a zone
allegedly so infested by the Vietcong that you were authorized to kill anyone who wasn't clearly a friendly. I remembered some of the killing I had seen, and some of the more
gruesome things Kevin and Dave had vaguely alluded to—
their faces twisted by revulsion—that night in the city.

You never got over some things. Not really. Dave was in
hiding from someone over something, and apparently Kevin
was not dead at all, but in even deeper hiding. The flashbacks
I experienced sometimes, sitting in front of my nice fireplace
in my cozy cabin in the mountains of Montana, must be
nothing to whatever it was in the past that had driven them
to this kind of hiding.

I puzzled over possible theories to explain their behavior,
and whatever might really be behind Frank Simmons's questions. I tried to convince myself that Simmons was on the
up-and-up, and failed. I congratulated myself for having had
the presence of mind to be suspicious and withhold the little
information I might have given him. Wentworth had told me
long ago that he "had a past," and could think of a lot of
people he didn't want to see again.

I had done right, I told myself. No harm.

It was not until the next day that I began to see how badly
I had screwed up.

Two

May 23

THE CUSTOMERS' name was Skurcinski, a middle-aged couple from Chicago on their first visit to the Rockies and staying a week at Bitterroot Valley Resort. I liked them, and wished our spring weather had been just a little warmer for them. Nevertheless, they were out on the courts each morning promptly at nine, gamely shivering as they waited for another lesson and then some doubles, perhaps, with one of our other scarce guest couples.

I rolled out on time Thursday morning despite feeling creaky from yesterday's exhibitions in Seattle and the plane ride home, and the Skurcinskis were already oncourt as usual, waiting for me. Putting some random worries about last night's odd visit out of my mind, I started the day's lesson, working first with her, then with him. They had begun to make some real progress, and they were excited about it.

They had never had a lesson before coming to Bitterroot Valley because, like a lot of people, they thought they were too old or too inept, or possibly because they didn't want to shell out the amount of money and time that they thought a long series of lessons would require.

The progress they had made in a few days sort of amazed them. But the fact of the matter is that a teaching professional can improve the average recreational tennis player's game in a single one-hour lesson. He or she will likely watch you hit a few balls, and quickly make a judgment about which aspect of your game needs help the worst, then work on that without talking about other aspects that might require work later. Fix the most glaring weakness first, or the one they complain most about.

Often that may be the service, but learning a higher, more consistent toss and stronger service motion is one of the tougher things to do, and can be almost out of reach for the older player. Fortunately, most hackers—and I use the term with no disrespect because they're the real heart of the game—most hackers if asked will say the part of their game that needs the most work is their backhand.

That's great because it's one of the simplest things to teach and one of the easiest things to learn. It's the forehand that's unnatural, regardless of how the different shots may feel to you when you're trying to bring them off.

When I had asked the Skurcinskis what they most needed to work on during our sessions, they had both promptly started moaning about their backhands, and proved their case by not having any during our warm-ups. Which of course gladdened my crusty heart, because I knew I could get them showing a tremendous improvement after the first hour oncourt.

Watching them hit a few balls that first day they were at the resort, I saw at once that neither of them knew the correct grip for either the forehand or the backhand, and that on the backhand both of them tried to "wrist" the ball back from a flat-footed stance. It was fun showing them some shortcuts and then seeing the results.

The old advice for taking your forehand grip is still usually the best: Holding the racket with its face vertical to the ground, place your right hand (or left, if you're left-handed, of course) with the palm flat against the strings. Now slide your hand down the handle, and when you near the end, simply close the fingers into a grip.

Mrs. Skurcinski got that part right away, but her husband had been using an awkward western forehand grip, and it took a few minutes to tease him out of it. Once both of them had the correct forehand position, however, it went smoothly when I showed them how to put their racket hand out in front and across their body, bend the racket down to make a "hump" in the wrist, then rotate the hand slightly toward the body until the hump disappeared, and regrip.

With both of them now holding the racket in a stronger position, I had each of them stand sideways to me in the backhand position, with the racket extended partly across the body at roughly waist height and slightly forward. Then I tossed each of them a few balls and instructed them to simply block each one back.

Naturally, with the stronger grip and no attempt to swing the racket, they immediately started making solid contact with the ball. It was a joy to see the look of astonishment on their faces when each ball ponged off the motionless racket with at least as much pace as either of them had ever been able to attain with the wristy stroke.

From there it had been easy enough to get them to take the racket back to their other hand held at about the seam of their left-side pants pocket, then step up to the ball to take it slightly ahead of the body. This all sounds more complicated than it is, and Mr. Skurcinski got the idea almost instantly and began banging back some good ones. Before the end of the hour, his wife was whacking them, too, and grinning like a Cheshire cat.

After that, all we had to add the second day was a little loop introduced by taking the racket back to a higher position on preparation, then bringing it down in a controlled arc and finishing high. Eureka, topspin. I had made two people very happy.

Now, near the end of the week, they had both picked up a few other tips as well. They were playing better than either of them had ever thought they could, and unless they took their newfound skills back to some local country club somewhere and fell in with the wrong crowd, they would stay happy for a long time. I felt good about that because I liked them.

Their good cheer this morning carried through the lesson portion, which included volleying at each other near the net and hitting some forehand drives. They didn't begin to look forlorn until the lesson ended and they looked around and realized that none of the other guest couples had come out to offer doubles competition for them.

"Looks like it's hiking or nothing today," Joan Skurcinski sighed.

"And we have to head home the day after tomorrow," husband Milo said.

Both of them looked crestfallen as they cased their rackets. I had some work to do around the place, but what the hell.

"I need a workout," I told them. "Would the two of you possibly be interested in some Australian?"

Milo Skurcinski looked genuinely surprised. "Us? Play a real set with you?"

"Sure. Why not?"

"That would be great!"

"You two serve first, then, all right?"

Still looking a bit stunned, they took the new container of Penns I handed them and marched off to the north end of the court.

Australian doubles is a game usually played when one of the foursome doesn't show up. One player, defending the singles court, plays against two on the other side, who have to cover the wider doubles area. It's usually seen on public courts, but there's nothing wrong with it as a game just because you'll never see it at the U.S. Open—or anywhere else in a real tournament, for that matter. I didn't mind playing it, and the Skurcinskis were nice people who shouldn't have to take an unwanted hike or go forlornly back to the lobby and watch the Weather Channel off our satellite dish.

Milo served and I sent it back softly. They were nervous and didn't do a lot of the things I had just been trying to teach them, but I worked on placement more than power, and made sure they were in position for a lot of good gets. My sore knee began to loosen up after a while, and they relaxed on the other side of the net, and we were having a nice, easy time of it an hour or so later when Ted Treacher, wearing a worried frown, appeared. He stood just beyond the high fence, hands jammed in the pockets of his windbreaker, and scowled without letup.

"Whew!" I told the Skurcinskis at the end of that game. "I think that will be quite enough for an old man today!"

They both beamed, sweaty and worked up and happy because they had won a lot of points. "I'm going to work on that backhand!" Milo Skurcinski told me.

"You're both getting pretty tough," I told them, and gathered up my stuff to walk to the gate where Ted was still waiting for me.

Ted and I go way back. Roughly my age, he lost his reflexes a bit earlier than I did, but still plays an adequate game. He had been in Belgrade a few years ago when there was still an Iron Curtain and my job was to get someone out from behind it. Ted and his lady made our escape possible through an impersonation act. Later, after he had bought the resort here and nearly lost it and his life because of nasty opposition nobody seemed to understand, I had been able to return his earlier favor by helping him stave off financial disaster. As a result of all that, we now shared ownership of the place: the sprawling white frame lodge, sixteen rental cabins in the woods along with mine, a dozen condominiums (a few of which we had actually managed to sell so far), a beautiful eighteen-hole golf course, fourteen courts, and mortgage, personnel, supply, and maintenance payments that gave us some sleepless nights. But most of the time both of us felt happy. All you had to do to feel happy was look around—at the fir and spruce forests, the rumpled lower hills spiky with lodgepole pine, the higher elevations of the Sapphires and the Garnets, their craggy faces still blinding-white with snow at this time of year.

Sometimes Ted does look worried, of course, but not in exactly the way he did now as I walked over to him, wiping off with a towel as I reached his side.

"Bill collectors?" I guessed.

"Mrs. Washington just came up from your cabin," Ted told me. "She was quite upset."

"Upset? Why?"

"It seems she thought she had broken your telephone."

Annabelle Washington was one of our cleaning people, a lovely black woman of about fifty who made more money than some of our office and kitchen staffers because she was so good at her work, and always went the extra mile to do even better. I liked her a lot. I knew she didn't mess up. "I doubt she could break my telephone, Ted. What's the story?"

Ted dug in his jacket pocket for something. "She was dusting in your cabin. She picked up your phone and wiped it with the dustcloth, and this fell off the bottom or from someplace inside." He found what he was looking for and held it out in the palm of his hand.

I looked down. The object was a small, thin, rectangular chunk of metal or plastic, flat black. It looked like a large computer chip.

"What is it?" I asked.

Ted's angular features drooped. "I thought you would know."

I took the gadget out of his hand and examined it more carefully. It was surprisingly heavy for its size. A very thin, stiff wire extended out of one corner about an inch or two. On the back side of the thing I found some gray gunk, the kind of stuff that would allow someone to stick this gadget on the bottom of a telephone—or anywhere else, for that matter—in a matter of a second or two.

I thought about last night, and suddenly my sweaty body didn't feel warm anymore. "Ted, I need to drive up to Missoula right away."

"I thought so," he said glumly. I could tell he was thinking the same thing I was.

In Missoula there is an old acquaintance who worked for the Company—real work, not like my occasional contract assignments. He had a full and distinguished career before retiring to raise cabbages and such, and shoot an elk each winter. I figured he would know what my telephone gadget might be.

I found him working fresh horse manure into a large compost heap out behind his house in the part of Missoula they call the Target Range. Sandy-haired, vigorous, and roughly good-looking, he dragged a red bandana out of the hip pocket of his filthy army surplus pants before shaking hands.

"Nothing like some good horseshit to open the sinuses," he told me. "What evil mission brings you to our fair city?"

I dug out the little gadget and showed it to him.

His grin faded as he examined it very closely. "Oh, boy," he said finally, very soft. He looked up at me, and it felt like I was being X-rayed again. "Where did this come from, Brad?"

"The maid found it in my cabin. I think it was stuck on the bottom of my telephone."

He rubbed a callused thumb over the goopy stuff on the back side of the thing. "Yep, that would work. This gunk still feels fresh. So it wasn't there very long, I'd guess."

"What is it?"

He handed it back, all smiles long gone. "Transmitter."

"Transmitter?" It was what I had feared but hoped against. "What does it transmit? Voice?"

"I would think probably not. Touchtones, probably. It might transmit a hundred yards or so, probably way up there at UHF."

I stared at him, aware of my own pulse and the smell of the manure and the seriousness of his expression and the dawning realization of just what had happened.

"So," I said numbly, "it might pick up your touchtones when you made a call, and transmit them to somebody outside somewhere with a receiver and a recording device, and they could play the touchtones back and know the exact number you called."

My friend didn't even bother to confirm the obvious. "Are you okay?" he asked. "Are you in trouble?"

Back at Bitterroot Valley, I used a lobby phone to call Dave Wentworth's number again. It rang and rang, no answer.

That was okay, I told myself. Dave worked somewhere. Naturally he wouldn't be home in the afternoon.

Try again after six, his time.

No answer.

Well, maybe at eight.

Mr. Frank Simmons, the probably bogus Army Intelligence man, had certainly gotten maximum cooperation from me. I had had my back turned all the time he made his call. If he actually made a call at all. What he had really been doing was securing this damned thing to the bottom of my telephone and extending the little antenna. *Maybe*, he must have thought, *this dude knows where one of my subjects is. And maybe he'll be stupid enough to call them. So I'll just leave this little giftie and sit out in my car with my handy-dandy receiver on, and take down the numbers of anybody he calls.*

I walked a few miles around my cabin, waiting for another hour to pass so I could try Dave Wentworth yet another time. I again reviewed my conversation with Simmons—or whatever his real name was—trying to figure out what he was up to.

I knew this: I had been stupid not to realize at once that Simmons was almost certainly a fraud. I should have thought

of it sooner: if anyone in Washington had really wanted
something out of me, they would have gone through the CIA
and had somebody like Collie Davis, my old contact, get in
touch with me.

I knew this, too: somebody was serious about something,
here. You didn't impersonate a government agent and throw
around expensive bugging equipment for a lark.

The picture of Kevin Green could have been faked, but
now I didn't think so. Simmons had really wanted information on both men. I suppose I would have been dumb enough
to call Kevin, too, if I hadn't thought for years that he was
dead.

Dave Wentworth, in hiding, or at least not broadcasting
his whereabouts. Kevin Green, evidently alive and in deep
hiding, perhaps even with a new identity.

Why?

To hell with why. When I tried Dave's number for the
ninth time, at almost midnight his time, I knew the vacant
ringing at the other end could mean something really, really
bad.

Don't panic, I lectured myself. This is probably no big
deal.

But what if it was a big deal? People don't hide for no
reason. And people don't pursue them for no reason. I had
given Simmons a gorgeous lead to Dave Wentworth, and now
the Wentworth telephone wouldn't answer.

There ought to be someone I could call in Ohio and have
them check this out, I thought. But I didn't know anyone.
Calling the police—if Dave was safe and still trying to be
anonymous—might only compound my errors by shining a
spotlight right in his face.

By midnight my time, 2 A.M. in Ohio, the telephone still
wasn't being answered and my nerves had gone to tapioca. A
telephone call to Missoula arranged things, and Ted Treacher
frowned with worry, but said nothing, when I told him I
would be gone a day or two, and don't ask where.

* * *

The next morning, Friday, I boarded the early Delta for Salt
Lake. From there another flight took me to Chicago. Two
hours after that, I was walking through the glittery, chrome-
domed airport in Columbus, Ohio. Every step along the way
I was aware that I could be screwing up further here, and so
I did all my pitifully inadequate tradecraft stuff, doubling
back and going through opposite doorways and changing
taxis three times and going downtown and walking all over
the mammoth new Civic Center Mall, just as if I knew what
the hell I was doing and might really elude someone if they
were shadowing me.

The result of the travel, the changes in time zones, and
my pitiful cloak-and-dagger work was that it was very late
when I finally drove my rented car south out of Columbus
along Ohio 33 to the town of Lancaster. When Dave Wentworth had given me his telephone number, with instructions
to pass it along to no one else, he had also given me an
address.

It took a while, but I finally found the apartment complex
on Lancaster's near north side.

It was past 2 A.M. Saturday, and very quiet, with a few
stars peeking out between puffy gray clouds in the night sky.
My footsteps sounded far too loud as I walked between shin-
gle-sided apartment units to an interior courtyard, where
Dave Wentworth's unit was located.

The windows of the unit were dark. A cool, muggy breeze
stirred, bringing with it the sound of a distant hound yodel-
ing at whatever kind of spooks there are that dogs can see in
the night. I reached toward the doorbell button of Dave
Wentworth's apartment, but stopped before touching it.

The front door stood slightly ajar.

Feeling shaky and tight, I swung the door back and
stepped quickly inside, closing the door as quietly as possible
behind me.

It was *black* in here, I mean incredibly dark, a darkness

so thick that you felt you ought to be able to grasp it in your hands. I smelled stale cigarette smoke and maybe the dying aroma of a microwaved TV dinner, and something else—a kind of wet, raw odor that made the hairs stand up on the back of my neck.

"Dave?" I called quietly. Nothing.

Nothing ventured, nothing gained. The darkness was making me skittish. I fumbled around for a lamp, bumped into one, found the switch, turned it on. The sudden light hurt my eyes as it revealed a small, spartan living room: cheap couch and chair, end table, small color TV, a few magazines and newspapers on the floor. There were the remains of two TV dinners on the floor, too, which surprised me because Dave Wentworth had struck me during our brief acquaintance as a very tight, careful, neatnik-type of person.

I moved through the living room into the adjacent kitchen, throwing on a light there, too.

What I instantly saw on the floor in here was infinitely more surprising—and terrible—than a little mess that happened to be in the living room. What I found here was Dave Wentworth.

He did not look much like himself with his head nearly severed from his body. Judging by the viscosity of the incredible pool of blood all over the tile floor—the source of that raw odor I had caught on first entering—he had been dead for almost twenty-four hours, perhaps longer.

Staring down at him in shock, it took several seconds—perhaps longer—for me to notice the other thing about him. That was when I quickly turned the lights out again and left the apartment as swiftly and silently as possible, stifling my gag reflex as I hurried to my rental Chevy and got the hell out of there.

In Vietnam, one of the insanities was how some of the grunts collected grisly "souvenirs" from dead Vietcong—or imagined Vietcong. What they did was cut off one of the dead person's ears. I've seen American soldiers wearing a dozen or more severed ears in a hideous necklace. Once a jeep drove past our position with a major in it, and punched down over the radio aerial like shriveled, blackened potato slices were maybe fifty human ears.

That was long ago, and a time of madness. On a day-to-day basis I've stopped remembering things like that, and have even begun to convince myself that such atrocities were an aberration never to be repeated.

But the memory and the horror were back, very fresh and raw in my mind, as I drove north toward Columbus, leaving the pretty, light-spangled hills of Lancaster behind me.

Dave Wentworth's throat had been slashed wide open. But in addition, one of his ears had been sliced off and taken away.

Simmons—or someone—had moved very fast, once my stupidity had given them a road map.

Three
Elsewhere

Columbus, Ohio: May 26

BUDDY TURNER, his fear like a rat gnawing at his stomach, showered and shaved before dawn in his downtown hotel room. Again he had gotten only an hour or two of sleep, and then his exhausted slumber had been filled with vivid, terrifying dreams: the night the mortar attack caught them on the riverbank and the rounds kept coming in all around him, making the mud quake in the shallow foxhole where he cowered, eyes squinched tight, hands clasped over his ears in a vain attempt to make it stop—just to *make it stop*—and no hope for the choppers to get them out before daylight; the stench in the hooch that other day when he and Brubaker rushed in, expecting to find VC and finding instead the decaying bodies of the man and woman and two children somebody else had already wasted and left to rot where they fell; crimson fire-flashes in the night another time, the sons of bitches all around them, the blinding white flash of incoming shells, Brubaker nearby, waving one minute that he was okay, then another round coming in right on top of him, and when Turner's eyes could see again, nothing where Brubaker had been but a smoking hole in the ground and what looked like hamburger meat; the body bags all lined up in a neat row, like sleepers awaiting inspection, and knowing you were next—your luck had already stretched too thin.

The nightmares were never going to end.

Turner cut himself twice while shaving. He couldn't make his hands stop shaking. He looked at his watch: still seven hours until his flight departed for Omaha. At the time

it had seemed sane and cautious and reasonable to delay
leaving Ohio for a day or two after doing what had to be done
down in Lancaster. A quick trip in and out might have
somehow called attention to his name if authorities scanned
passenger manifests. But now Turner wished fervently that
he had not been quite so bright. Staying around had driven
him to the edge of losing self-control: he had had to flee the
restaurant last night when he caught himself on the brink of
breaking down in tears. He felt like he might fly apart at any
instant. All he wanted to do was get back home and back to
his night-watchman's job and back to his familiar little apartment where nobody ever bothered him.

Turner had *had* it. Nobody could say he had shirked his
duty. He had done his part. Now he was through with it—he
would never take part again. It was someone else's turn.
Maybe at least someday he could stop shaking if someone else
took over and he was simply left alone.

He dressed carefully, dark slacks and a lightweight sport
coat, and left the hotel for a morning walk that might settle
his nerves. He knew no one would pay any attention to him.
People never paid any attention to him. Glancing at his
reflection in the plate-glass window of a hotel lobby shop, he
congratulated himself on being so ordinary: a little man in his
middle fifties, thin, balding, plain. He looked just like what
he was, he thought: a nothing.

It was a beautiful morning. The bells of an old church
nearby began tolling as he started his walk.

He walked along High Street, in the direction of the state
capitol. Despite the lovely day, he had the sidewalk virtually
to himself.

His stomach pain constant, Turner walked several blocks
before stopping at a streetside newspaper rack to pull out the
fat Sunday edition of the Columbus *Dispatch*. Nearby was a
city-bus stop, the waiters' bench vacant. Turner sat down and

started through the newspaper, searching for the item that would confirm they had found the body at last.

He did not have to look far. The story was on page 2:

LANCASTER—The body of a TV repairman was found in his Lancaster apartment late Saturday, his throat slashed by an unknown intruder.

The victim had been dead for some time, police said.

Dead is David L. Wentworth, 45, a Vietnam veteran described by neighbors as a quiet, reclusive man who "worked hard and always had a smile for everyone," according to one person who lived in the same apartment complex with the slain man.

Unmarried, Wentworth came to Lancaster sometime in the early 1980s after being one of the last Vietnam prisoners of war to be repatriated. Records found in his apartment indicate that he was a native of Texas and was a holder of the Purple Heart.

Authorities said they are "pursuing several leads" in the case. Attempts to locate any relatives of the murdered man have been unsuccessful so far, they added.

In a bizarre sidelight, police reports indicate that one of the victim's ears had been cut off.

"There were no signs of burglary," Police Chief Dayton Hostedter said. "We intend to find the perpetrator and bring him to justice."

Turner winced at the concluding paragraph. But then he told himself to cool down. They had about as much chance of finding "the perpetrator," he reminded himself, as of solving the Berneen job back in 1979 or the Leveridge operation in 1983.

It hadn't seemed quite so horrible back then, doing those jobs. Those had been more clearly necessary—sheer revenge, and almost a pleasure. And so many more guys had been involved back then. You didn't feel like you stuck out. Now so few remained as part of the group; some had died, more had drifted away, lost contact, refused to be a part of it anymore . . .

Turner nervously left the bus bench and walked again along Columbus's main north-south downtown street. He passed the capitol grounds. Big dark doves and the inescapable throngs of pigeons walked around on the sidewalks and flitted from tree to tree. In front of one of the building entrances stood the bronze statue of a World War I soldier, your classic doughboy with the tight pants and the little pie-plate hat. No goddamn statues for Nam, Turner thought, and the embers of the old, impotent rage puffed up into a brighter flame inside him for a moment, then guttered out.

Turner found a sidewalk telephone. He put in his change and dialed his collect call to Knoxville. Mike answered and accepted the charges.

"*Are you all right?*" Mike asked. He sounded nervous.

"It's all fine," Turner told him, watching a city bus snort up to the curb nearby and disgorge a few passengers. "I'll be heading out."

"*You're going home now?*"

"Yes. And I forgot to mention: I got the souvenir."

There was a pause. Then: "*All right.*"

"I threw it in the river."

"*All right.*"

Turner hesitated. "You'll pass the word?"

"*Yes.*" Another pause. "*Buddy?*"

Turner waited.

Mike sounded as sick of it all as Turner felt. *"Good work."*

"I'm never doing it again," Turner said.

"There's just the one to go now, Buddy. Just the one. We got all of them who wouldn't go on after the kid. The only one left is the chopper pilot."

"I'm through!" Turner said, and hung up.

Knoxville

MIKE ROMANOWSKI padded back to the kitchen table and sat down in front of the dregs of his morning coffee. Light rain pattered at the windows. The briefest flashback darted through his mind: a field radio, broken; the choppers overhead somewhere, stuck up there beyond the low scud and smoke, the drizzle falling just like this. Then the deafening, concussive *whap! whap! whap!* of the chopper blades, and then moving on, and the first explosions and screaming.

"Honey?" Romanowski's wife called from the other room. "Who was that?"

"Nobody," Romanowski called back. "Just a wrong number."

"I'm getting in the tub."

"All right."

He waited until he heard the water running in the bathroom. Then, feeling goaded, he went back to the telephone and punched in the number of the boardinghouse. The woman manager sounded crabby, but went to get Arnie Tubb. Romanowski waited, his heartbeat so irregular it made him feel sick.

"Yes?" Tubb's voice said.

"He's heading home," Romanowski said.

"What about the other one? What about Green?"

The tumult in Romanowski's chest intensified. Was it never going to be over? "Arnie, haven't we done enough? Can't we let it go? Do we—"

"You know better!" Arnie Tubb's voice shrilled. *"He's the one we've been looking for all these years!"*

Romanowski swallowed bile. "I'll get back to you."

"I need some more money. You said you'd get me some more money."

"Arnie, I'll get back to you." Romanowski quietly put the telephone back on its wall cradle.

He felt like he was suffocating. He didn't want any of this. He had thought they were done. Now it was all happening again.

Romanowski thought again about simply calling the local FBI office and telling them where Tubb was living. But he knew instantly that he could not do that. Tubb was insane. He might escape again—come here—exact his revenge for the betrayal. Or word might leak to some of the others.

Romanowski was sure of only two others now—Buddy Turner and Jack Maxwell. But there were others who had been involved before and might be pressured into getting active again. Tubb might locate one of them and have *them* pay Romanowski a lethal call.

Romanowski could not take the chance. He was trapped. He had to follow through.

The realization gave him another tiny flashback: *stink of river mud, the body lying there in front of him with no face, just the maggots.* Then it was gone and he was back in his kitchen again.

In spite of his yammering nerves, Romanowski tried desperately to be logical. Their other leads had led nowhere, he thought. The tennis player out in Montana, Brad Smith, had known where Wentworth was, and had fallen for it when Jack Maxwell visited him and planted the bug on his phone. Maybe this man Smith knew where Lieutenant Green was, too—might even be in contact with him. Somebody *had to watch Smith for awhile, hoping he might tip off knowledge of Green's whereabouts.* It was possibly their only hope of locating Green and having this over once and for all.

But Jack was in a panic now. He had already said he would not go back and try to watch Smith again, because the danger was too great that Smith might recognize him—grab him—spoil everything. Racking his brain, Romanowski could not think of anyone else who was left to do that job.

He was, he saw, left with no choice. Arnie Tubb would never stop bugging him—might even attack *him* if he didn't stay in the game. Somebody had to watch Smith for awhile, and with none of the old group available, there was only one choice left.

Romanowski thought of how much it would probably cost him. The numbers added to his despair. But he had to follow through. If he had to secretly destroy their life savings, he had to keep going now until it was over for good.

The sounds of running water had ceased in the back of the house, and Romanowski knew his wife was deep in her bubble bath now, luxuriating. She would soak another ten minutes, at least, so he had that long. Pulling out his battered billfold, he dug a scrap of paper out of the card compartment and refreshed his memory about the number on it. He reached again for the telephone.

Missoula, Montana

FRED SLATER had intended to sleep in until at least nine o'clock this Sunday morning, but the jangling of the telephone took care of that.

Sitting up in his rumpled bed, he found the phone and picked it up. "Fred Slater speaking."

"*Mr. Slater?*" the nervous-sounding male voice said. "*This is Mike Roman, down in Knoxville. You remember me?*"

Slater rubbed his eyes. He recognized the burly voice now, and remembered quite well. This fellow Roman had paid him $400 for one of the easiest jobs Slater had ever done since retiring from the Missoula police force and setting up shop as a private investigator. All he had had to do was drive down south of Lolo, visit that resort down there under the guise of looking for a condo, and verify the whereabouts of one of the owners, the tennis player Brad Smith. It had to do with some kind of a divorce investigation, Slater recalled.

"I remember you, Mr. Roman," he said, switching on the bed lamp.

"*So you remember the man we asked you to locate for us?*"

"Sure do."

"*Mr. Slater, we need some continuing surveillance on that man. About a month. Can you take that on for us?*"

Visions of that new 4 × 4 danced in Slater's head. "I could do it, Mr. Roman, but a job of that duration would cost you a great deal of money."

There was a pause. Then: "*We don't have a lot. I don't know what we could work out. How much are we talking about, here?*"

Slater did some fast mental gymnastics. He didn't have a damned thing going right now except that one child custody case and some courthouse work on a land deal. He tried to figure the least he might do it for. "At a minimum, three thousand dollars. That's for a month. Plus expenses."

The line fell silent again. *Too much.* Slater thought. *I blew it.*

The voice on the phone said, "*We don't have anything like that much.*"

Slater tried to recoup: "Tell me what kind of information you're looking for. Maybe we could work something out."

Again a pause, then: "*I guess really we just want to know if he makes any trips. Any unscheduled or long-distance trips. And if he does, you try to follow him and report back where he went—who he saw.*"

Slater's mental calculator went into high gear again. "Maybe I could do it for less. But I'll have to drive down there and register as a guest—really stay close. All my other pressing business will have to be put on hold. I guess I could do that for four hundred a week. But you would have to pay for my expenses down there. A room and meals down there don't come cheap."

The voice crackled with tension: *"You'll report by telephone at once if he sets up any trips, does anything unusual?"*

"Yes, sir."

"How much would you have to have in advance?"

Again Slater balanced his greed against realism. "A thousand now, the remainder billed out by the week."

The pause this time was longer. *"We can send the thousand in the morning. Federal Express, like before."*

Slater felt intense relief. Another pudd job, great! "That will be satisfactory, sir. You have the office address?"

"Yes, yes. When can you start?"

"Tomorrow afternoon."

"Plan to do it, then."

Slater hung up. Whistling, he went to the bathroom and brushed his teeth before coming back to his bedroom telephone and placing a local call.

Bill Wynn, his sometimes associate, sounded sleepy, too. He began to sound more alert the moment Slater said he had an assignment for him.

"How much?" Wynn asked suspiciously after Slater had outlined how he should go to Bitterroot Valley, check in as a guest, and watch Brad Smith.

Slater knew Wynn had been out of work for a long time, and could hardly say no to any offer. But Slater felt he could afford to be generous. "Forty a day. And expenses."

"I'll do it," Wynn said without hesitation.

"Call me after lunch tomorrow to confirm, and plan to head out in time to register for tomorrow night."

"Wilco."

Slater hung up and went in to shave. "Wilco" indeed, he

thought ironically. Once an old airplane jock, always an old airplane jock.

Slater felt good. One-twenty a week for doing nothing was the kind of work he could use a lot more of. He wondered how messy this divorce case was going to be, and how long the people back in Knoxville might be willing to keep him on the job. A long time, he hoped—a very long time.

Hays, Kansas

JACK MAXWELL, beginning to breathe hard now, chuffed along the country road on his way back in from his six-mile morning run. The flat prairie stretched out in all directions, making him feel like he was running on the surface of a billiard table.

Maxwell had needed the run more than usual this morning to burn off some of the nervous tension filling his body.

Going up to Montana and pretending to be somebody named Frank Simmons had been a piece of cake. Planting the listening device had taken no particular skill at all, and then Brad Smith had obligingly been a fool and called one of the two men they wanted right away. A piece of cake, all of it.

But Maxwell knew now that Buddy Turner had done his part of the job, and the guy named Wentworth in Ohio was dead. Brad Smith would find out about that, too. Then—if not before—Smith would start adding things up and realize he had been had when Maxwell, alias Simmons, had visited him.

Smith would remember him and be watching for him, Maxwell thought, cresting a slight rise in the road and looking ahead toward the flat sprawl of Hays. That was why Maxwell had told Romanowski he was out of it now, for good. It was too dangerous and Maxwell felt he had done enough. He didn't give a damn about the other name they had finally come up with, Lieutenant Green. He didn't give a damn about any of it. He had only helped with the Smith part because it seemed relatively easy, and out of a sense of loyalty to the old unit.

But now Maxwell was starting to be more worried about the part he had played. He hoped he could remain clear just by staying away and doing nothing more. He hoped Brad Smith wouldn't give anybody his description. If things got tight, Smith knew what he looked like, and that could mean trouble.

For now, Maxwell had decided to lay low and mind his own business. But he knew Romanowski would keep him updated. If at any point it looked like Smith might become a danger to him, Maxwell thought, then he might be forced to get back in the game. But maybe that would never happen. Maybe he was out of it for good. He hoped so.

Four

"Son," Avery Whitney told me as we pulled our golf cart up beside the No. 18 tee at Bitterroot Valley, "if I was a better person, I'd probably feel real bad about taking all this money from you." The gangling old coot wiggled a shelf of eyebrows. "You ain't concentrating today."

It was June 8, exactly two weeks since I had found Dave Wentworth's body in his Ohio apartment, and I hadn't been concentrating very well on anything else since then. "Avery, I'm sure you feel terrible about it."

He climbed stiffly out of the cart, a tall man, past sixty, well over six feet tall, wearing bright red knickers and a vivid green pullover sweater, a tam-o'-shanter, and white hose and golf shoes. The white hose on his skinny legs made him look like a stork dressed up for a Halloween party.

"Oh, it's not that I worry about skinning you for all your money," he told me, extracting a jumbo metal driver from his black kangaroo-skin bag lashed onto the back of our cart. "I mean, I know you're a rich man, to own a place like this. But I could use a little more competition." He paused and made his eyes wide as he stared at me in exaggerated innocence. One of his eyes didn't quite track with the other. "If you know what I mean?"

Avery had owned Bitterroot Valley before we did, and he knew *exactly* how close to the financial edge we had been ever since we bought it. I said, "I appreciate your compassion, Avery."

He teed up a Titleist, looked down the tree-lined fairway

with cool enmity, and then turned back to me. "You wanna press here on eighteen?"

"Forget it, Avery. Hit, Avery."

He addressed the ball, took the club much too far back, and then swung so hard his tam fell off. The ball took off like a gunshot.

"My, my!" he cried happily. "Will you just look at what I did!"

His gorilla tee shot landed about 250 yards out, and the slight draw on it made it leap forward with overspin, bounding out another thirty or forty long paces.

"I'll bet you five dollars you can't—"

"Forget it, Avery," I said, and sailed my ball deep into the woods.

"What you need to do, son," he lectured mildly as we drove up the fairway, "is learn to relax. Now, having your lady-love way out there in California, that is not a good thing. No, sir. Not a good thing at all. And going off alla time playing these exhibitions, that might not be a good thing, either. What you need to do, son, is find you a local girl, like I did. I mean, you *know* my Melody is not your basic genius, and sure, it sometimes gets real tiring, explaining to her what war we ended by dropping the bomb, and who came first, Teddy or Franklin D." He stopped the cart at the edge of the fairway where I needed to start my expedition in search of my ball. "But if you don't mind a little fatherly advice, son— which, even after you lose this hole won't cost you quite as much as if you'd gone up to Missoula and hired a shrink— what I think you really need is—oh-oh." He stopped abruptly.

Hopping out of the cart, I glanced at his face. He had turned from me and had one big hand up to his forehead, shading his eyes as he stared upslope toward the No. 18 green.

A figure stood beside the trap up there: medium height, slender, his hands jammed in the pockets of his windbreaker.

I recognized him by his stance, if nothing else: Collie Davis, a man I considered a friend despite some hairy situations he had gotten me into on behalf of the CIA.

He had taken long enough, I thought.

Avery said, "Ain't that your friend up there?"

"Might be," I said, and climbed back in the cart. "Listen. I'll concede the hole. That ball is lost anyway. Go ahead and hit yours."

We reached the green. Avery's second shot lay hole-high, thirty feet from the pin on the right. I went over and shook hands with Collie and then we both waited while Avery putted out. Naturally—after pacing around endlessly, hitching up his pants, smoothing his white hose, readjusting his tam, removing his glove and stowing it in a hip pocket, doing the pendulum alignment thing from behind his ball, and twitching and fidgeting over the putt for what seemed like six hours, he ran it straight into the middle of the cup for a birdie three.

"Fabulous," he grinned, lighting a cigar as he came over to us. "Howdy, Mr. Davis. That's your name, ain't it? I never forget a name. Faces, I'm horseshit with. Well, son, it looks like you owe me an even twenty dollars. Cash, please. I don't take credit cards."

Pulling off my glove, I stowed it in my golf bag and pulled my wallet out of another bag pocket. Avery Whitney had shot an even 80, not bad for him this early in the season. I had been 85 on the last tee, thinking maybe I could break 90.

Avery was speculatively eyeing Collie Davis as I walked back with the money. There were people who thought Avery Whitney was eccentric, and they were right, although he liked to say that he never did anything *he* considered odd. There were others who thought he was stupid, and they were very, very wrong.

"Haven't seen you around here for a spell," he told Collie.

"I was nearby, and thought I'd drop by for a chat," Collie told him.

Avery took my money. "Yeah," he snorted at Collie. "Right."

Collie grinned at him. "You don't believe me?"

Avery put a fatherly hand on his shoulder. "Mr. Davis, pardon me for saying this, but I know what you do, and I know who you do it for. Every time you've showed up at Bitterroot Valley to see the boy, here, the tapioca has promptly hit the Mixmaster." Avery stopped and looked quickly all around, his eyes sharp. He turned back to the two of us, standing side by side.

He added, "It don't matter to me if the CIA is violating its charter and meddling in some domestic matter again, Mr. Davis, and it don't matter to me if old Brad helps you again. Actually, I'm kind of relieved to see you here. Maybe now he can straighten out whatever's been bothering his mind the last couple of weeks. He hasn't been fit company for a grizzly lately, and on the golf course, well, he's been just pitiful. Just plumb pitiful!"

Before either of us could say anything to that, he turned and climbed into the cart beside the green. "I'll locker your clubs, son. I expect the two of you want to walk back to the clubhouse while you have a confab."

Collie watched the golf cart scoot up the path through the trees. "He doesn't miss much."

"What took you so long?" I demanded.

"I had a lot to do since you first called me. Like answering another fifteen calls from you, none of which were necessary."

We started up the asphalt path, my cleats clicking on the hard surface. "You could have let me know how you were doing," I told him.

"I'm here now. Give me a break, for Christ's sake!"

"Have you got something for me?"

"I think so."

."What?"

He looked ahead at the pro shop building. "Change your shoes and let's have some coffee."

"What have you got, Collie?"

He gave me a narrow-eyed stare. "Will you try to calm down? Isn't it enough for you that we might be violating the charter, even trying to get hold of another agency's reports? I don't think I should even be here, Brad, but this is a very unusual situation—very unusual. So just give me a break and go change your shoes, and buy me a cup of coffee, okay?"

"Okay," I said, feeling foolish for having pushed him too hard.

I changed shoes quickly inside the tiny pro shop locker room, rejoined Collie outside, and walked on up the hill with him to the lodge.

It felt odd, being with him again on business. He had been my contact ever since I quit the tennis circuit and thought that signified the end of my occasional little errands for the CIA.

In my playing days I had never done anything interesting—just pick up an envelope here on the tennis tour and then leave it or hand it to someone else somewhere down the line, or maybe take a couple of pictures of something or someone like any other innocent tourist.

After my knee injury and slowing reflexes took me off the tour, I didn't hear from anybody in the Company for a long time, which is what I had expected. Then, about four years ago, it had been Collie who appeared with a request that I help out on a job in Yugoslavia. He had shown up a couple of other times since then, and the result had always been the same: an assignment that sounded simple but wasn't—and gave me still another opportunity to prove my ineptitude. I had been lucky, though, and had managed to help sometimes. That always made me feel good. I have this curious, old-fashioned notion that all of us owe our country far more than we can ever repay, and if we're asked to do something, we ought to do it.

Please understand: the occasional little jobs did not make me anything more than I am: a beat-up former tennis champion with bad knees and not a hell of a lot of courage. There are people at Headquarters who consider me a loose cannon at best, and the only reason Collie had ever come to me was the fact that my tennis background and part-time work as a free-lancer for the tennis magazines gave me ideal cover for something they needed very badly to get done. I don't think they would have ever asked me to do anything if they could have thought of anybody else with the same background credentials.

Now, with the cold war done and my reputation with Langley in worse shape than it had ever been, I didn't expect ever to be asked to do anything for them again. This time I had been the one who made the contact; I had come back to Montana and immediately put in a call to the number where Collie or a secretary would answer, day or night. He had been in a meeting—they're always in a meeting when you call—but he had called back, giving me my chance to tell about the visit from a man who said he was in Army Intelligence, the discovery of the telephone bug, the trip to Ohio, and what I had discovered in Dave Wentworth's apartment.

Stateside murders—obviously—were not in his bailiwick. But the Vietnam connection seemed to interest Collie, and he had promised to ask a few questions, although he couldn't guarantee anything.

A day after that conversation, my retired friend from Missoula had showed up and said he had instructions to get the telephone bugging device from me. I gave it to him, he went away, and nothing more happened for several days. Then Collie called back with a few additional questions, and promised to get back to me. Since then I had been biting my fingernails until last night, when Collie telephoned again to say he would be around in the next day or two.

We walked onto the lodge deck and found a table on the north edge, far enough from the building to catch the late-morning sun. None of the other tables nearby was occupied.

I gave one of our waiters the high sign for coffee and then leaned over toward Collie. "What did you find out? Was anybody able to find anything in his apartment? Did that number this guy Simmons gave me check out? Has somebody picked him up yet?"

"Calm down," Collie said, reaching for cigarettes.

"Go to hell. Give me one of those."

He extended the pack. "I thought you quit."

"I thought you quit, too."

He produced an ancient Zippo which flared and fluttered wonderfully in the very slight breeze, lighting both our cigarettes. Then he leaned back in his metal chair and studied my expression. When Collie is really alert and controlled, his eyes have the dull silver color and sheen of liquid mercury. They looked very much like mercury now. "I suppose it had to be a shock, finding the man there like that."

"It was my stupidity that got Dave Wentworth killed."

"It could have happened to anybody."

"It happened to me."

Collie gave me a long, stony look.

"All right," I said. "I'll try to stop whining."

He inhaled smoke. A young couple strolled by, and his eyes followed the brunette's pretty legs. I knew a little about the wreck of his marriage not all that long ago, and it was nice to see a sign of life in his eyes again.

He turned back to me. "You couldn't be sure this guy Simmons wasn't legitimate, and you certainly had no reason to suspect a device on your telephone. Maybe when you rushed off to Ohio that was kind of dumb, but you got away with it, and you couldn't have saved Wentworth whatever you did, once they had his telephone area code and number to trace down."

"You said 'they,' " I cut in. "Who are 'they'?"

The waiter interrupted, coming to our table with cups and saucers and spoons, sugar, sweetener, and cream, and a large insulated silver pot of coffee. I nodded him away. Collie waited until the waiter was well away from us before replying.

"We don't know who they are," he told me. "But we would very much like to find out. So would the Department of the Army, the Bureau, and a lot of other people."

"Why?"

"For one thing—from the CIA's standpoint—because the other man you said this Simmons character was interested in, Kevin Green, has never been accounted for since the war."

"He isn't MIA, Collie. I saw the pictures of him."

"I didn't say MIA. I said 'missing,' period."

"I don't know what you're trying to say."

Collie poured coffee for both of us and then stirred a sickening amount of sugar into his. He sipped it and nodded, seeming to pronounce it good, before looking back at me again.

He said, "Kevin Green was a POW."

"I know that."

"Back in 1973, after the fighting was over, his name, rank, and serial number showed up on one of the first lists of prisoners that North Vietnam said they planned to return to us."

"And?"

"Let me talk. Don't butt in. When the guys were turned over, some of them were in bad shape. There was a head count and a cursory roll call. Lieutenant Green was checked off as answering the roll, and the total number of names on the Vietnamese list checked against the number of men bathed, deloused, and put on a plane for Hawaii."

"Then—"

"Will you just shut up a minute and let me finish? When the plane landed in Hawaii and the Americans were taken by buses to the hospital, initial screening began and the head count was repeated. At that point, the number of men in the ward totaled one less than the number on the return list, and friend Kevin Green was nowhere to be found."

I stared at him in disbelief. "You mean they *lost him* somewhere?"

"He was checked off as being one of the returnees in Vietnam. He was missing when IDs were next verified at the hospital."

"How the hell did something like that happen!"

"You tell me."

"He just vanished?"

Collie sipped coffee before answering. "We've queried the army. Things like this can fall under our jurisdiction. They say there was a search, but he was never found and nobody knows what happened."

"This is unbelievable," I protested. "Listen. I called Kevin's wife once. She said the army had notified her that he was presumed killed in action. She was still clinging to the hope that he was still only MIA, and might turn up somewhere, but I felt sure then he was dead."

"He was listed presumed dead after he vanished from that prisoner return group."

"But dammit, if he was alive, and returned to us, how can he be listed as presumed dead?"

A bleak amusement made Collie's lips twitch. "What would you have had the United States Army do? Create a new category, 'Returned to Our Side, but We Lost Him'?"

"So he was returned, he got lost in the shuffle somewhere, and the army changed him to the 'presumed dead' category to cover its own ass?"

"I'm sure the administrative procedure could be described more kindly."

"But in a nutshell—"

"Yes."

I thought about it. "Then you don't think I'm crazy, believing those pictures Simmons showed me."

"No," Collie replied. "Not at all. Kevin Green probably isn't dead. We just don't know where the hell he is—or how he got wherever he is—or why one or more unidentified persons seem to want him dead, just as they wanted this Wentworth character dead."

My coffee cup made a clattering sound in the saucer. "Then I wasn't out of line, calling you."

Collie's eyebrows canted. "Hardly. A lot of people are interested in this, it seems. We've run into a lot of locked, classified files nobody will open for us. We're interested because of the Vietnam angle, and part of our charge is to check out all reports of MIAs who might still be alive somewhere. The army is still interested—to what extent it's hard to say. The FBI seems to be interested, too. Maybe some other agencies are. That's part of the reason I'm here."

"I don't know what you're saying."

"You were asked about this Kevin Green. We're interested in him, too. His is the only name of a potential target that we have. For all we know, he may be the only target remaining . . . the only man still alive who might be able to tell us truthfully what this has all been about . . . over the years."

I felt a chill despite the sunlight. "Are you saying there have been others like Wentworth?"

"Yes," Collie said matter-of-factly, and raised his coffee cup again. "There have been seven others that the FBI knows of, apparently. And they might have missed a few. But Wentworth is the first in almost ten years—the violent death, the Vietnam connection, the missing ear. Which makes the whole thing even more puzzling. Maybe you can provide some answers. Why Wentworth? Why Green? What did they have in common with the earlier victims? How did someone know to come to you for information? What the hell has been going on here?"

I refilled my cup while I thought about it. "I can add a couple more questions to that list, Collie."

He watched me with that tight, bulldog look he gets sometimes.

I said, "How many murders might have gone unnoticed?"

"That's—"

"Let me finish, okay? What if they've managed to find Kevin by now, and he's dead, too? What if there are a lot more candidates out there, and you just don't know about them? What if 'they'—whoever they are—are working for Vietnam or China or North Korea or some other foreign power for reasons we haven't begun to guess, and for stakes a lot higher than we've figured out yet? Or what if you're dealing with only one person here—a real loonytune—the guy who visited me, and what you've got is a serial killer on your hands?"

Collie leaned back in his chair and turned away from me for a moment, looking out over the lawn toward the woods, and the creek valley beyond that, and the hazy white of the mountains far beyond that.

When he spoke again, I had the eerie sense that he was reciting a prepared text: "You're right. Many angles, Brad. You understand that our charter clearly places stateside investigation of a matter of this type outside of our jurisdiction. You are to consider my visit here at this time a personal one, with no official authorization. We may informally compare notes and exchange information about matters of interest, but this in no way signifies official action by me on behalf of the Agency. Understood?"

My face heated with frustrated anger. "Dave Wentworth is dead—my fault. Kevin is out there, and he may be next. Am I supposed to just—"

"It is possible," Collie interrupted with a look of intense impatience, "that another organization or agency of the executive branch might contact you about this matter after you and I have had our informal, personal talks. If this should happen, you should not infer that the Agency had anything to do with arranging such subsequent contact. Is that understood and agreed?"

Prickles of understanding filtered through my nervous system, and I finally had the good sense to shut my mouth. I understood at last. The CIA could not get involved directly in this one. But it could farm me out to some other organization in our government, if I would help.

Collie was watching me, waiting for my slow-mo brain to get done with its figuring. "Understood?" he repeated. "Agreed?"

Ted Treacher and Bitterroot Valley needed me full-time, especially right now with the first real influx of summer patrons. My date book had several exhibition matches penciled in over the next few weeks, and I couldn't afford to cancel any of them. Beth—my lady in California—would go bananas if she learned I was involved in anything like this again. I didn't want to face the kind of horror I had found in Dave Wentworth's apartment, a scene that had already filed itself in the catalogue of brief, bright, ugly nightmares which sometimes came to me in the night when I least expected them.

But I already had the guilt of having caused Dave's death by my stupidity, and maybe—just maybe—Kevin would be next unless I could help somehow.

I saw that I had no choice.

"Understood," I told Collie. "Et cetera."

"Good," he murmured, reaching forward to pour himself more coffee. "Now let's talk some business."

Five

THE LAST known ritual execution prior to Dave Wentworth's had been in 1983, Collie told me. The FBI had thought they were over by now, but a description of the killing in Ohio had tripped commonality triggers in Bureau crime-comparison files.

The earlier killings had also involved Vietnam veterans. The grisly removal of an ear was a common theme. But there was a lot more commonality than that, and some of it explained the CIA's keen interest, even if it could not get directly involved in the present circumstances.

All the known victims had been in the army, and all had been in the America Division. All had seen combat. All had served in Quang Ngai province in 1967 or 1968. All—except Dave Wentworth and Kevin Green—had been infantrymen.

The units the victims had served in were all in combat operations at about the same time, and may have taken part in joint operations; records were unclear on specifics about that. When the third murder took place in 1975, the army noticed and began investigating. Later, attempts were made to contact all surviving veterans from the victims' former units in an effort to figure out what common denominator might link the crimes. As a result, Collie said, there were dozens of fat investigative files in Washington, but none of them helped at all.

Some of the division's combat units had suffered unusually high casualty rates, Collie told me. Two platoons in particular, the 2nd and 3rd of Baker Company, had suffered attrition as high as eighty percent during one period in 1968. Of those who had survived, some remained today in VA hospitals and had not been able to help army investigators with the murder puzzle. Others, crippled by posttraumatic stress syndrome, were lost entirely—street people without names, wandering wrecks society chose to forget once they had been used to help fight an unpopular war. In toto, the army's investigation apparently hadn't uncovered much.

After we had talked about that, I suggested we go to my cabin; more guests were appearing on the deck and I felt uncomfortable. Collie agreed and said he had to get something from his car first, but would meet me in a minute. I went on down, and when he appeared at my door, he had a small, soft-plastic case under his arm.

"What's that?" I asked.

"Hang on, my good man," he said coolly.

He put it on the kitchen table—a case about the size that would be right for a cassette tape machine—and unzipped compartments. He took out a black metal or plastic gadget with several switches and diodes on its face. When he flicked a couple of the switches, some of the diodes began to blink red, yellow, and green. He pulled a short antenna out of one end of the box and it kind of spread itself out into the shape of a small fan.

Without explanation, he began walking around the cabin interior, pointing the gadget this way and that, and intently watching a meter under a row of the flashing diodes, all of which happened to be green at the moment.

While he checked, he kept up a string of idle conversation, whether to help his instruments work or because of our old friendship I'll never know. He asked how the resort was doing, and I told him we were keeping our head above water, sometimes higher than the nostrils. He seemed interested, so I explained the old debts we had inherited from the early months of Ted's lone ownership, when so many things went wrong and so much had to be repaired or rebuilt. He asked if the future looked brighter, and I said we hoped so: business was up so far this year, and an early spring had helped us get the golf course ready a month earlier than anticipated. There were actually months now when we made ends meet and didn't dig ourselves into a deeper financial hole.

"And you're not limping," he observed, standing on a chair to run his gadget's antenna along the wall behind the telephone.

"When I blew it at Wimbledon, I thought I was done," I admitted. "But they've got some new surgical techniques now."

He got down off the chair and moved toward my trophy case. "Is that so?"

"They moved ligaments around and sewed them different this time. I think it's going to be better than it's been for years."

"That's great." He headed for the kitchen. His voice came back, "And how's Beth?"

The question felt like it does when you wake up in the morning and don't remember something really bad that's happened—and then do. "She's fine," I said instantly. *Leave it alone, Collie.*

"She's still working in L.A.?"

"Yes." *Please leave it alone, Collie.*

"She get up here very often?"

Leave it alone, goddammit, just leave it alone. "Once in awhile."

He picked up something in my tone and poked his head around the partition. His forehead wrinkled. "Problems?"

"Problems."

"Like . . . ?"

"She's got her career in California, and it's important to her. I've got the resort here, everything I have tied up in it."

"I'm sorry to hear that. She's a neat lady."

"She's a great lady. She's a beautiful lady. She's an ambitious lady."

He went back to poking around with his gadget. "I guess I was hoping, since you hadn't done anything for us for awhile, any trouble you might have had would iron itself out."

"Look," I said, "would you like a drink?"

"You mean would I change the subject?"

"Yes."

"Okay. I'll have the drink, too."

He worked for awhile without talk, the only sound the shuffle of his feet and an occasional little grunt as he stretched or bent to check a place where some sort of electronic device might have been hidden in the few seconds or minutes I had had my back turned to the estimable Mr. Simmons. I built myself a manhattan—Scotch-rocks for him—and thought about Beth, and why things seldom work out the way you expected them to.

I still missed her, badly. But we hadn't even discussed our differences in a long time now. Every time we had tried to discuss the issues, all we found were stone walls.

I don't think either of us had quite given up yet. I didn't intend to, as long as there was an atom of hope left for us. But that's about how much hope remained—an atom.

Sometimes it seemed I had a talent for screwing things up with women. There was Elizabeth, my first wife, who left me. There was Danisa, murdered because of me, and radiant memory of her still haunts me. Now Beth.

I knew it was not all her fault and not all my fault, the way our lives were drifting apart. Maybe, I told myself often, the rational thing to do was to write it off and try to forget.

But it hurt sometimes, wanting her.

Well, Smith, you're whining *again*. Shape up. Get with the program.

My father's ghost-voice in my mind. Right, as usual.

Collie seemed to be putting his gear back into the small bag.

"Anything?" I asked.

"Think we're clean."

"Now what?"

He dropped onto my couch. Handing him his drink, I noticed again how tired he appeared.

"Wentworth," he said. "Is there anything more you can tell me about him?"

I had expected the question and had been thinking about it. "I don't know anything about his family, if that's what you mean. He was from Illinois originally, somewhere around Peoria."

"That's right."

"Then you know just about as much as I do, Collie."

"Did he ever say anything at all that might give you any clue about anything he might have been involved in in Vietnam that could make him a candidate for killing? Drugs, for example? A black market operation of some kind?"

"Are you kidding? Dave was your all-time down-home kid. He probably still believed in Jack Armstrong and the Easter bunny."

"Did you ever talk with him about the war after it was over?"

"No. We just had a telephone conversation, maybe two."

Collie sighed and lit a cigarette. I took one, too. He produced the old Zippo. "Is there *anything* about this Simmons character you didn't tell me?"

"Collie, I think I told you everything, moment by moment."

"Well, the number he gave you was a fake, so he didn't expect you to get in touch with him again. His sole mission was to set you up to call either Wentworth or Green."

"Which I conveniently did. God!"

"No more breast-beating, okay? Now about Kevin Green. Do you have any ideas about him?"

"I don't know what you mean."

The mercury eyes were watchful. "No thoughts about where he might be hiding out?"

"None. I just hope he's still alive."

"Simmons wouldn't have asked otherwise."

"Collie, isn't it time you told me what you—pardon me—what some other department might have in mind for me? How I might help?"

"It's a long shot, but worth trying. There's a chance that persons unknown not only set you up and bugged your phone, but put a tail on you."

"On me? Ridiculous. I would have noticed by now."

"Right," Collie said, his voice heavy with sarcasm. "You know the complete background on every guest in this place, and every person you've hired in the last three or four months. You are so brilliant, skilled, observant, and intuitive that you would know instantly if a real professional was watching you."

My face felt hot. "You're right, of course. I'm officially classified in the files at Langley as an idiot, so I couldn't be expected to notice someone following me."

"Let's not rake over dead coals, Brad."

"The coals aren't quite dead. I was pronounced incompetent and taken off the job halfway through the Wimbledon assignment last year. I've kept the letter listing all the reasons my contract was terminated. Do you want to see the letter?"

Collie's face splotched with sudden anger. "You can sit around nursing your old hurt feelings, Brad, or you can help on this. Just let me remind you of one thing, though. If somebody is watching and tailing you—and you could lead him into the open enough for our pals in the Bureau to grab him—it wouldn't just be a nice gesture from you to us old meanies. It might ultimately save your friend Kevin's life."

"Damn you. That's way below the belt."

"It happens to be the truth, too."

I thought about it and gave up. "So that's it, then? Somebody wants to dangle me?"

Collie ignored the question and asked his own. "What was Kevin Green to you?"

"He was the captain of the tennis team when I was a freshman in college. He sort of took me under his wing—practiced with me, taught me a lot. He put me in there on the varsity as his doubles partner far sooner than my ability or savvy really justified. Later, when he graduated and headed off to the service, he urged the rest of the guys on the team to make me captain, even though a senior usually got that honor." I paused, remembering tall, good-looking, longish-haired Kevin Green, moving around the court like a shadow, hammering everything back at impossible angles, hitting all the lines and making chalk fly. I remembered him serving as best man at my wedding. I remembered the last time in Vietnam, too.

"He was a good friend," I added. "A good guy."

"Then you won't mind if somebody wants to dangle you."

"How?"

He got up abruptly and started pacing back and forth, clearly uncomfortable with this. "Since I have no official capacity here, I can only speculate—"

"Yes, Collie. Right, Collie. Get on with it!"

"You might be asked to go see his wife."

"Kevin's wife?"

"Yes."

"Surely she's remarried by now."

"No."

"That's hard to believe."

"She knows a little about the prisoner return screwup—not much, but enough to make her cling to hope he might still be alive. She thinks there might be other MIAs being held captive somewhere. She won't give up."

"God! After all this time!"

Collie's mouth tightened. "Of course the recent evidence indicates that she might just be right about her husband. She isn't just another of those pitiful cases, clinging to absolutely impossible hopes. There aren't a lot of others to hold out hope for, Brad. You know that."

I knew he was right. They had let me in on a number of things back in Virginia when all of us were younger, the cold war was still very real, and they hadn't yet decided I was a screwup. It was during this time that I had been briefed on what an incredible and comprehensive effort had taken place to account for every American lost in battle—during the war itself and since that time.

Back then, all the data on missing military were kept at what they called the JCRC at Nakhon Phanom Air Force Base, Thailand. I don't remember if the initials stood for Joint Casualty Recovery Center or Joint Casualty Resolution Center. Either way.

Every MIA report, mostly airmen, went into a computer. Lists were spit out periodically and sent to CIA operatives in deep cover around the countryside. They would study maps and find locals willing to hike to suspected crash or death sites and ask seemingly innocent questions of the locals who might have seen something. If anything at all turned up, a chopper was sent in, plopped down in a hole in the jungle, and its crew sent out to check further. Col. Charlie Beckwith, of later Delta fame, ran the operation. Beckwith did not run sloppy operations.

Everyone who could have been accounted for in the Vietnam theater had been accounted for. *Maybe* a few had been taken to Russia or somewhere, but damned few. Present-day relatives who still held out hope were deluding themselves; no war had ever seen anything like the scope and accuracy of our efforts to account for everyone lost in Vietnam.

I said, "Barbara Green knows Kevin was listed as a returnee who then didn't show up in Hawaii?"

"Right."

"Then it's easy to see why she won't give up. She is one loyal, wonderful lady."

"So much the better," Collie said.

"Why 'so much the better'?"

"It makes it easier for us to use her."

"Use her?"

"Send you out to visit her. Dangle you. If anyone *is* watching you, they're bound to follow you right to her doorstep, thinking they're about to discover something helpful. But the FBI is tailing you, too, and maybe our tail pounces on theirs."

I thought about it. "All of which only works if I really am being watched."

"Of course."

"What do I talk about with Barb?"

"Old times. Kevin. Her hopes."

"That's cruel as hell, if the dangle doesn't work. All I might accomplish is stirring up old hurts."

He shrugged. "Can't be helped."

"Collie, you have to watch that soft, sentimental streak of yours."

He gave me a hard look. "You might also actually learn something from her—taking advantage of your old friendship. Some clue earlier interviewers might have missed. Something that might be followed up on in an attempt to track him down."

"But the dangle is the main thing," I said.

"Yes. I believe you can count on the usual per diem for this, incidentally."

It occurred to me to bawl him out for speaking as if I would be doing it for the money. But that would have been too stupid and self-indulgent even for me. Collie knew me better than that.

So instead I said, "She's still in California?"

"The L.A. area. I feel sure someone will be giving you an address and sticking to you like glue. But there's no reason why you might not grab the chance to see Beth while you're out there."

"See Beth when I'm on another job? Have you forgotten

how she hates your ass and everybody else associated with my doing this kind of work?"

Collie's face became a mask. "She wouldn't have to be told."

"Right. And I'm acting as a decoy, putting her in possible danger by seeing her, and she doesn't have to be told."

"It was just a thought." He was irritated with me.

I asked, "Is there anything else I ought to know about all this?"

"No," he said, and I knew instantly, by the smoothness of his tone, that he was lying.

But Kevin was out there, whether Collie was lying or not. That much was real, and so was the thing that had happened to Dave. *Hell, they never tell you everything anyway, so what else is new?*

I said, "So if I understand you right, I'll be contacted by somebody else soon?"

"Yes."

"Can I get a cash advance?"

"Is it necessary?"

"Yes, dammit, or I wouldn't ask."

"Then you shall have it, Brad. No problem."

I could remember at least two earlier occasions when he said something would be no problem. I still carried scars from one of those jobs. The old wounds ached in cold weather sometimes, made me feel like a gimpy old lady instead of just a middle-aged jock who hated sleeping alone, and sometimes saw ghosts.

Collie was waiting.

"What?" I said.

"Any more questions?"

"None that I think you would answer."

He relaxed a bit. "How about another drink?"

I fixed them.

Six

COLLIE SAID he could not speak officially and he was only speculating, etc., etc., but he imagined I would be contacted by someone within a day or two, and I might want to start planning my trip to Los Angeles.

"This contact," I said. "I want him to present verbal bona fides. I've already been stung once by an imposter."

Collie looked pained. "I was about to say something about that before you interrupted me. *Assuming* someone were to contact you, Brad, they would mention the aspens, you would say something about fishing, and they would mention white water rafting."

On that basis, I made a call Saturday evening and booked a morning flight out of Missoula for the next Wednesday morning.

I didn't hear anything Sunday, and by Monday afternoon I was beginning to get antsy. When I put on my sweats and went into the lodge workout room during men's hours Monday afternoon, I was starting to wonder if something hadn't fallen through the cracks.

The workout area had cost Ted and me a bundle, but it was popular, especially during the morning hours. Located in the lower level, it had everything: Nautilus equipment, a treadmill, some NordicTrack stuff, and an adjacent sauna, whirlpool, and showers. I was somewhat surprised to find only two other users on hand when I went in to continue the rehabilitation work on my knee.

I was doing leg lifts on one of the Nautilus machines when

another man strolled in, lean and youthful, not a blond hair out of place, in immaculate gray sweats and Nikes that looked new. I had casually noticed the newcomer when he checked in late Sunday because he was by himself and looked unlike most of our guests. Most arrived rumpled and tired and usually wearing casual clothes. He had been wearing a pale tan suit as flawlessly unwrinkled as the ones you see on mannequins in department store windows. His dark brown tie was knotted fashion-ad tight, and his collar had so much starch in it that it looked like celluloid. Standing a shade under six feet tall, he was office-pale, with a small straight nose, tight small mouth, and eyes that looked studious behind round-rimmed eyeglasses. His sandy hair was cut rather short, and he came in carrying an overnight bag and a slim black attaché case. I had taken him for a salesman of some kind, looking for business from us, but he had registered and gone up to his room without a word that might hint of a business intention.

Since then I hadn't given him another thought.

Now, walking into the little gym with a towel over his shoulder, he looked around a moment as if memorizing everything. Then he walked over and bent over to make a resistance adjustment on the weights of the machine next to mine. Adjusting himself in the machine's embrace, he started doing energetic curls. Obviously he did a lot of working out. He worked the machine perfectly, and his lean, hard muscles hadn't gotten that way from sitting in front of a TV.

I returned my attention to flexing my leg upward from the knee against my machine's resistance. It made the knee ache, but the work was good for it. I resumed keeping count on my repetitions.

Which was when he spoke.

"Mr. Smith?" he said softly, maintaining his steady rhythm on the machine.

I glanced at him. "Yes?"

He didn't miss a beat, didn't look my way. "Please continue your exercise routine, Mr. Smith. Please do nothing to call untoward attention to our conversation."

That was what he said—"untoward" attention. I was not sure I had ever heard the word spoken before, although it's fairly common in print. But this guy *talked* like he was in print: precise, every word measured and spaced equally from every other, without a trace of human inflection. He was here to try to sell us something after all, I thought.

I resumed my leg lifts. "I hope you're enjoying your first day at Bitterroot Valley," I told him without turning his way.

His machine kerchunked and retracted with metronomic regularity. "Allow me to introduce myself, sir. McDonald. Reese McDonald. I believe that a mutual friend has spoken with you recently. On that occasion, I believe, you expressed interest in meeting me prior to the instigation of an endeavor in Los Angeles which we hope will be mutually rewarding."

Despite myself, I glanced over at him in surprise. He was looking straight ahead as if unaware that I existed. He had already begun to work up a healthy sweat that partially fogged his eyeglasses. In his gym clothes, he looked about thirty, going on fifteen. A big droplet of sweat dripped off his small, pointed nose. *My God*, I thought, *they sent me the agent's kid*.

Aware of my inspection, he twitched his facial muscles in irritation. I was supposed to be pretending I didn't know he was here. I resumed. My machine began to creak and groan again as I went back to hurting myself.

He said, "The aspen are very pretty here."

It was kind of stupid because pines and firs dominated the local landscape, and the aspen only showed in the fall, when they turned. But I went along: "I like to fish when they're in their autumn colors."

He said, "I imagine the white water rafting is good then, too."

"All right."

"Anterior to this familiarization, Mr. Smith, there will be

little further discourse between us. I will contact you privately to provide a briefing, and explain the circumstances under which I would expect future reports from you. It is extremely unlikely that you will again be aware of my presence at any later time. I am a trained professional whose proximity will not impinge upon your consciousness. But I do wish to assure you, sir, that I will have you under scrutiny as often as deemed mandatory by circumstances as they may develop."

I kept pumping, wondering if McDonald was for real. If he hadn't already demonstrated a knack for reaching out after a big word and grabbing one that meant the exact opposite of what he intended, I might have looked more closely at him to see if I could detect any flashing diodes or ill-concealed gear mechanisms in him anywhere. Androids acted like this on TV.

He was also younger than I wished, and his disconcerting calmness—as if every move had been programmed in advance—made me wonder how good he would actually be if things started going sour and spontaneous on him.

He seemed to read my mind: "My specialty is surveillance, sir. You needn't be concerned."

"So what have you noticed so far?" I asked.

"Sir?"

"Is somebody else watching me at the present time?"

He seemed slightly surprised and possibly irked by my question, which gave me a little perverse pleasure. "Mr. Smith, if I had uncovered another surveillance personage at this point in time, he—or she—would most assuredly be already in custody and undergoing questioning."

"Okay, fine. So what's next?"

"Have you booked passage for Los Angeles?"

"Yes. The early Continental flight on Wednesday."

"Excellent. I shall plan to be on the same plane. However, I will check out here and depart an hour prior to your departure for Missoula, in order to assure that no one connects us at that time."

"I haven't told you yet what time I plan to leave."

His machine kerchunked and wheezed on. "Hardly necessary. I can anticipate your tendencies with a degree of accuracy that might amaze you."

He was starting to irritate me with his damned calm self-assurance. "Is that so?"

"Yes. I have carefully timed the drive between here and the Missoula airport. Taking your flight time, I add the driving time plus an hour and a half."

"An hour and a half?"

"Yes. You should be at the airport at least thirty minutes prior to departure. However, you are a precise and careful individual who, judging from everything I have read in your file, could be expected to build in plenty of additional time to cover such exigencies as a possible flat tire or a traffic tie-up on the highway due to a wreck, something of that nature. Therefore I have predicted that you will walk to your Ford Bronco at 6:15 A.M., give or take fifteen minutes."

Damn. I had made a mental note to leave at exactly 6:15, no later. I had to start trying to change my ways. I was becoming far too predictable in my old age.

Beside me, McDonald kept on pumping. At least he was breathing slightly hard now. He said, "I will be on the same flight you take to Denver, but we will not be ticketed on the same connecting flight into LAX. Not to worry. I will arrange to arrive ahead of you and be waiting to pick you up visually the moment you step off your plane. You will not see me but I will be there. You may rest assured that I or a colleague working in my relief will be nearby at all times."

Before I could ask, he went on, "My colleague is six feet one inch tall. He is slightly heavyset and wears a closely trimmed reddish beard. Like myself, he wears glasses. He will be dressed casually—sport shirt and lightweight slacks— unless the occasion obviously demands more formal attire.

Like me, he is excellent in his work and you are extremely unlikely to see him. Further, he will be on duty only at such times as I may require a bit of rest."

"You do sleep, then," I said.

"Pardon?"

"Nothing. What's your partner's name?"

"You have no need to know that, sir."

"Thank you. Anything else?"

"Only two stipulations, Mr. Smith. I realize that most of this is new to you, and may be frightening. Try to remember that you are in good hands. You have nothing to worry about. Just act normally and all will be well."

"Thank you for the reassurance."

"Not at all. One additional note of importance. You are a dangle in this operation and you must not at any time take any action that might involve you in any other way. Remember that we are trained professionals. We can meet an exigency which might arise. Even the most well-intentioned attempted intervention by an amateur like you would only complicate matters and make our job more difficult. I'm sure you understand. . . . ?"

"Sure." My leg was beginning to kill me. I climbed up off the machine bench and stood beside it, toweling my face. "I see you must have read the part of my file that says I tend to go off half-cocked and disobey orders."

He glanced up at me for the briefest instant. "We try not to overlook anything, Mr. Smith."

I walked over to the Roman chair and started doing a few bent-leg lifts while supporting my weight on the parallel sides of the contraption. Reese McDonald kept right on with his curls. He and the machine looked interchangeable, both new and not used much yet and quite perfectly maintained.

A little Pacific cold front moved in late Tuesday night, and I left for Missoula a half hour earlier than planned, worried about the snowflakes mixed in with the cold drizzle that had started about 3 A.M. McDonald was long gone, having checked out a bit earlier than he had said he planned, too. He had outguessed me again.

I didn't see him at the airport until just before boarding. Then, standing in line to be admitted to the jetway and thinking he had screwed up, I saw him standing well back in the boarding area, a copy of the day's *Missoulian* partly concealing his face. Our eyes met over the top of his newspaper. He looked away instantly. He seemed to be functioning perfectly, by the book, as usual. For some reason I did not feel reassured.

Seven

Elsewhere

Langley, Virginia: June 12

THOMAS DWIGHT and J. C. Kinkaid were sipping rancid black coffee in Dwight's metal-walled office cubicle deep inside the Headquarters building when Collie Davis, scowling, poked his head in the door.

"He's headed out," Davis said dourly.

Dwight nodded. "Good. Forget it. He's out of our control now. Come in."

Collie Davis entered the cubicle, pulled the only other metal chair up beside Kinkaid's, and sat down. His angry expression persisted. "Have you got those other files?"

"Have some coffee," Dwight urged amiably, pushing a red-capped aluminum thermos jug halfway across the paper-littered surface of his desk. "You look strung out, my man."

Davis used the plunger on the top of the jug to spurt some evil-looking coffee into a Styrofoam cup. "I get this feeling we're screwing him again."

"Nonsense," Dwight replied. A thin, pale, ascetic-looking man, possibly forty-five, with light hair receding at the forehead, he had removed his suit coat and half rolled the sleeves of his white dress shirt, which made him look more like an accountant than the middle-level supervisor he was at Headquarters. He had the kind of cool, detached manner that you had to have if you were to survive long in the rat-warren maze of frustrations that characterized his level of management at Langley. "It's not our operation," he reminded Davis. "He isn't our man. The chances of anything at all coming out of it are about ten thousand to one anyway."

Davis sipped the coffee and grimaced. "This stuff is terrible."

Dwight allowed himself a ghost-pale smile. "I don't know how you can say that, Collie. I made it myself just last weekend."

Davis refused to be put off. He turned to Kinkaid, sitting in the other office chair beside him. "Have you seen the other files?"

Kinkaid, slightly younger than Dwight, darker-colored, of medium height with wide-set eyes the color of asphalt, nodded almost imperceptibly. "Just did."

"You seem to have a severe hang-up about those old files," Dwight noted.

"I didn't feel very good about walking Brad into this without having first read those old files myself."

As if Davis had not spoken, Dwight opened a folder and poised a yellow No. 2 Ticonderoga pencil over a notepad inside. "Will he call you back?"

"At some point, I feel sure. Can I see those files now?"

Dwight jotted a note in his tiny, meticulous handwriting. "Just make sure there's no provable link to us."

"I know, I know. Where are the—"

"You verified that the Bureau picked him up?"

"Sure. Of course. Where—"

"It might be the best break we ever had, somebody contacting Brad. His description of that visitor who bugged his phone was excellent. I was surprised."

Collie Davis's face flushed. "Why should you be surprised? He's done some damned fine work for us in the past. He isn't an idiot."

"He screwed up the last one."

"He didn't screw up on the last one. Jesus Christ! He kept the stadium from being wrecked! He just didn't do it by the book."

Dwight inclined his head as if in assent. "Whatever. Even

a loose cannon shouldn't be able to mess this up. And it might even work, who knows?"

J. C. Kinkaid reached over to pour himself more coffee. "My only problem with it is that I wish we were doing the surveillance ourselves."

"Well," Dwight retorted quietly, "you know that's out of the question."

"Yes. But do you get the same feeling I do? That the Bureau isn't giving us everything they have?"

"Maybe. But the DCI went straight to the top on this, right to Risenhof himself. They're aware of our interest."

"About the files," Davis cut in doggedly.

"In a minute. When did Brad plan to see Mrs. Green?"

"Tomorrow, I imagine. With the FBI information we were able to give him on Mrs. Green's usual schedule, he ought to be able to make it look like a chance reunion then."

Dwight jotted another tiny, perfectly formed note. "Okay, good." He closed the folder. "Now, there are some other matters we ought to go over, since the three of us are together anyway."

"I want to see the files," Davis insisted.

Dwight sighed as if bored with the whole matter. "Oh, all right. There are only two, an old one closed in '80 and the new one with just a couple of cross-indexed entries in it." He moved papers on the top of his desk, revealed two thin filing folders that had been there all the time. "Nothing to be excited about," he said, sliding them across to Davis.

Davis reached eagerly for them and opened the top one on his knees. Dwight joined Kinkaid in pouring more coffee. The only sound in the cubicle was that of Davis's flipping pages. Many of them represented bureaucratic busywork, and he moved ahead swiftly.

After a minute or two he came to a page where he stopped and scanned intently.

"Hell's bells," he muttered.

Dwight and Kinkaid exchanged glances, but did not comment.

Davis flipped two more pages, skimming. Then he looked up with a blank expression of astonishment. "We knew all this shit in 1980?"

"It doesn't help with the current case," Dwight pointed out. "That's why it's in the inactive file."

"But we knew all this about the Vietnam end of it all the way back in 1980?"

"Obviously. The dates are right there in front of you."

"It looks like we could have at least given Brad some of this information going in."

"The army doesn't even know we have some of that. Why should any of it go to Brad Smith unless things change, and he might have need for it?"

Collie Davis sighed and resumed reading. Twice he stopped and read slowly, grunting in surprise.

Finally he finished. He looked at Kinkaid, then at Dwight, with a puzzled, half-angry expression. "Does the FBI have all this?"

"We don't know," Dwight said.

"Obviously," Kinkaid put in, "the army doesn't want it out."

"Obviously. Jesus Christ!"

"You can see that Brad doesn't need any of that information at the present time. All he has to do is go see Mrs. Green in Whittier and hope the Bureau can pick up a tail somebody put on him."

"You don't think maybe he should have been told what happened to this guy Army Intelligence sent out on what they thought was a hot lead in 1986?"

"That has nothing to do with this."

"Except," Davis retorted, "that the guy ended up on a mortuary slab with part of his head blown off."

Dwight had not had enough sleep lately, and when he leaned forward toward Davis, it was obvious that his veneer had cracked. He stabbed the air with an index finger as he made his points. "Number one: we didn't twist Brad Smith's arm. Number two: if this killing doesn't provide a solid lead, there may never be another chance. Number three: the army isn't going to help and it isn't going to share information. Number Four: as long as Brad has no reason to expect an attack on him during a seemingly innocent bit of business, he'll act normally and have the best chance not only of netting us a suspect but of surviving. Don't give me a hard time, Collie. J.C. and I have been up all night on the Guatemala thing, and I'm not in the mood for any horseshit."

"It still feels like we're hanging him out to dry."

"Well, I don't think so. But if we are, we are."

Knoxville

SITTING IN front of the TV set in his rented room not far from downtown Knoxville, Arnie Tubb dozed. But it was a light, troubled sleep; he had not been able to sleep normally for years, and the sounds of traffic on the Kingston Pike nearby penetrated his room and his consciousness, making his face twitch painfully, his shoulder and arm muscles tighten and spasm in time with the recurrent dream.

Nam. Jungle on one side of the mud road, kid in a rice paddy on the left. Ear-hurting gunfire constant off to the right someplace, the kid standing there up to his knees in the brown water. Kid holding hands above head—looks harmless enough—no way to tell. Raise rifle, kid panics, starts to run, splashing in the mud. Fire once, twice, three times. Kid blown forward from shots in the back, plunges into the water, vanishes.

Going into the village. More than half the guys go the wrong way. Hear the shooting start. Hooches burning, old people and women screaming, running out, everybody shooting. Old woman begs, Hunstable kicks her down, puts rifle at her head, blows her off. More shooting—up ahead, every-

body running, great excitement. Hey, Tubb! Get your ass over here and help with this! *Guys standing beside a ditch, ditch filled with crying, pleading slopes, women and little kids, babies. Guys firing down into the ditch. Bodies thrown around, blood splashing, the captain standing there. Goddammit, nothing to do but finish it now, they're probably all VC anyway.* Look out, Tubb! That woman! Behind you! Stop her! *Turn. Young woman, almost naked, black hair streaming back. Fat, bloated, funny—Geezus she's pregnant—fire. Down she goes. Flopping around in the dirt— godalmighty, godalmighty—*Finish her, Tubb, you stupid—! *Captain Aldrich runs partway after her with his M-16, hoses her down. Bullets tear her to pieces and you can see the smashed-up baby slide out of her belly with all the other shit. Captain comes back, his eyes are crazy. Has Mabry take his M-79 grenade launcher and fire it right into the trench. Ka-ploom, pieces and stuff flying out—got to finish it, got to do them all now—sons of bitches, probably all VC, just like the man said. Why do they hate us? What's wrong with these people? Blood all over, and where are the rest of our guys? What's that noise—incoming—!*

Tubb jerked wide awake with a convulsion so violent he almost fell out of the chair. His breath whistled in his lungs. His heart felt like it was going two hundred a minute. Coppery taste. Soaked in sweat. Smell of his fear-sweat thick in the room.

Tubb saw the TV set and remembered where he was.

Moving spasmodically, he lurched up out of the chair and into the tiny yellow tile bathroom. The shiny, hairless face that leaped out at him from the mirror was puffy, haggard, the eyes wild, red, crazy.

Tubb wet a washcloth in cool tap water and mopped his face, bare skull, and neck. Then, still shaking, he pulled his tee-shirt off and dropped his pants and underwear so that he stood in front of the mirror in only his shapeless brown socks. He began mopping over his whole sweaty body with the washcloth. He tried not to look at himself in the mirror as he bathed. But the moving image was there, repellent and fascinating as a snake.

He looked.

The figure in the mirror was almost totally hairless, just fuzz coming back in now. He looked soft, puffy, white, like an enormous maggoty slug just crawled out of some jellified, putrescent thing. The new body fuzz was almost invisible. Looking at himself, Tubb shuddered.

The chemo did this to you. Every hair fell out. You went pasty white, and everything you put in your mouth seemed to turn to instant fat at the same time you felt like they had used the big needles not to inject the plastic bags of poison into your bloodstream, but instead had somehow used them to suck your muscles right out of your body. What the needles didn't do, the radiation did, burning your flesh inside and out.

Tubb was months past due now for additional treatments. At first he had started to feel better. Now he felt worse. The lumps had come back . . . were growing. He could feel them in his groin and armpits. He needed more chemo. But he couldn't get chemo without turning himself in. The lumps were going to kill him if he waited much longer. His only chance was to finish this thing once and for all, and then turn himself in before it was too late.

They were so close now. Just find Captain Green, and it would be over. They would finally have their revenge and at the same time make sure no one was left who might tell what had taken place.

Then, Tubb thought, sponging his flabby legs, it would be over completely. For all of them. There would be no one else left out there who might ever tell. And Captain Aldrich, and all the others, could rest in peace.

He would be able to rest then, too, Tubb thought. In his mind he had built a convincing theory that the dreams and flashbacks would stop once April 6, 1968, had been put fully to rest—buried forever, done with. Then, with rest, his body could fight the cancer, too. They had given it to him with Agent Orange—he was sure of that despite all their lying denials, because he knew too many others who had met an identical fate—so they would treat him again when he went back, get him well again.

And then it would all be over at last . . . as soon as Captain Green was dead, and one of his ears taken, just like the others.

A knock on the door of his room made him jump sharply. Naked and moist, he padded out of the bathroom and leaned close to the flimsy frame door. "Yes? Who is it?"

"Mr. Jones?" It was the apartment manager's voice, and Mrs. Kloscis sounded irritated. "You have another call on the office phone downstairs."

Tubb modulated his voice, making it soft, obsequious. "Thank you very much, Mrs. Kloscis. I'll hurry right down."

"Well, see that you do," the crabby voice came through the door. "We're trying to run a business here!"

Hurrying into pullover sweats, Tubb thought that he really ought to get a telephone installed in the tiny apartment. But that would require better ID than he had yet . . . probably some references . . . no telling how much extra danger of capture it might bring. Still, maybe he could carry all that off, assuming he could get the needed money out of Romanowski.

Tubb almost felt sorry for Romanowski, having to give him all this financial help. There were so few of them left now—not many to share any money burdens. So many of the original group dead. Agent Orange the culprit in many cases . . . suicide in a few, natural causes in two or three others. Just himself left now, along with Romanowski, Turner, and Maxwell. But that was enough. They could do it.

Tubb padded down the wooden staircase in his bare feet and reached the frosted-glass door of the rooming house office. He tapped diffidently. Mrs. Kloscis's crabby voice called for him to enter. He went in and found her fuming at the window, the telephone on her desk off the cradle.

"Thank you very much," Tubb murmured, and picked up the phone. "Yes?"

"*Arnie?*" Mike Romanowski's voice said.

"Speaking." Tubb watched Mrs. Kloscis's broad, angry back, and could tell she was listening to every word.

"*Slater, the private detective, called from Missoula. Smith got on a plane, ticketed for L.A. I had to authorize Slater to ticket his man to follow. I don't know what it means yet.*"

Hot excitement flooded Tubb's veins. Maybe this was the break. "You'll call the others and let them know, right?"

"*Yes.*"

Tubb hung up and turned to Mrs. Kloscis, who had swiveled her head to stare at him. "Thank you very much, Mrs. Kloscis. I can't begin to tell you how appreciative I am of your patience with me."

She scowled again. "These calls are disruptive, Mr. Jones."

Tubb made his tone even softer. "I'm terribly sorry, Mrs. Kloscis. I'll have my own telephone soon, I assure you."

"Well," the woman said, looking hopeful and unsure. "All right, then."

Tubb climbed the stairs to his room. He would either have to move or talk Mike into getting him a telephone, he thought. The damned woman was acting too crabby and snoopy. They were so close now, after so long. Nothing could be allowed to screw it up.

The Pentagon

THE SECRETARY of defense walked into the meeting room. The two generals and a colonel who had been waiting nervously for him got quickly to their feet.

The secretary of defense walked to the head of the walnut

conference table and sat down, staring at his officers across an expanse of burnished wood that looked big enough to land an airplane on.

"Any new leads?" the secretary demanded.

"Not yet, sir," the older general, a two-star man, said quickly. "However, we have reason to believe he is in the Knoxville area, and it's just a matter of time now."

"Gentlemen," the secretary said, with that icy control capable of making most men wince, "the Department of Defense cannot allow much more. If you and your people can't get the job done, we're going to be looking for someone else who can. Do I make myself clear?"

"Sir," the older general said into the vast silence, "I have every confidence we can expedite this matter."

The secretary's voice rose. "Expedite? Expedite, you say? Goddammit, General, he's been on the loose for more than five months now! There's been another goddamned murder! Do you want all that old history to come out? Are you prepared to deal with that kind of publicity just at a time when Congress is looking at our budgets again?"

"Sir, we—"

"Just find him! Put more people on it!" The secretary turned and stormed toward the door.

It slammed behind him. The three military men were left staring at each other—and ruin if they couldn't deliver soon on their promises.

Hays, Kansas

JACK MAXWELL returned to his room after work and found two messages on his answering machine. The first wanted to sell him storm windows. The second was a tight, familiar voice that jerked him to attention.

"Jack, this is Mike. Our friend up Montana way is off on a trip. It wasn't on his calendar. Don't know what's up. We've arranged to have an escort for him, if you know what

I mean. No need to worry. I've let the other guys know. I'll call you back when I know more. Maybe it's a break."

Maxwell played the message back twice. His nerves grated against each other. Did Smith know something he hadn't revealed when the tap was on his telephone? Maxwell did not believe it.

Then why was he making an unscheduled trip—one their snitch had not copied off his datebook in the lodge office?

Maxwell did not like it. It scared him. He almost wished now that he had gone ahead and taken steps to put Smith out of commission permanently. Maybe, Maxwell thought, he would still be forced to do it. He felt hounded by the knowledge that Smith knew what he looked like. As long as Smith was alive, he was in danger.

Just wait, he told himself, trying to calm down. *Nothing to panic about. Just wait and see.*

It was hard to do. Maxwell felt very near the breaking point. He knew what the breaking point felt like; once before, feelings similar to these had put him in the psych ward at the VA hospital in Kansas City. He did not want to go back there. He did not want to feel this way. He had to hang on.

Eight

THE COSMIC question (*Brad Smith Faces Life*, Chapter 600) was answered for me when my flight into Los Angeles was delayed several hours and I didn't clear the airport until almost 1 A.M.: I would not call Beth tonight.

In the morning there was nothing much to do around my motel in Burbank, and I could have called her at her office. I didn't, and this time there was no handy excuse. She would ask why I was in L.A. and I didn't like lying to her, but telling her the truth would only restart the disagreement that had already begun to feel old.

There would be time to call her later during my visit, I told myself.

Whether I would do it or not was a question still occupying a part of my mind early that afternoon when I drove toward Whittier and the tennis club where the FBI report said Barbara Green always played tennis on Thursday.

It was a hot day and the air quality wasn't very good. I couldn't see the mountains. The sun looked like a big silver cottonball through heat haze. Traffic on the freeway was dense as always. I watched my mirror, but saw no signs of being followed. In the traffic, that meant nothing. This entire mission seemed to me today to be a classic waste of time. I tried to convince myself that I was just feeling sorry for myself because of the simmering anger at Beth, the continuing erosion of hope.

The Redlands Racquet Club turned out to be a medium-sized facility parked behind the palm trees and lush grass of

a municipal golf course. The builders had tried to make it
look like San Simeon, or maybe an old-time movie theater. I
found a parking place among the glittering Toyotas and
Volvo station wagons—mommy's day at the club, children—
and went in with my racket bag slung over one shoulder and
my duffel over the other.

I hoped for an observation deck, the better to spot her
and stage our "accidental" encounter, and I was not disappointed. Walking out onto the utility-carpeted upper deck, I
had a nice view of the sixteen courts, cement with green
plastic paint, all in use. For a few seconds, scanning, I didn't
see her.

Then I did: out on Court 8, two women slugging it back
and forth in a singles match far more vigorous than any of the
games on nearby courts: a tall, lithe, leathery blonde in pink,
blasting every ball with a controlled ferocity, and Barbara—a
slender, pretty brunette with a red headband and graceful
oncourt movements that made it appear she never had to
hurry to make a return. Thank you, FBI. You have done
good and now my deception can begin. I looked for the
staircase that would take me down to court level.

It was about thirty minutes until her match ended with
the angry-lipped blonde gladiator hitting a smash to the backhand, then rushing the net like Martina, only to watch help-
lessly as Barbara whistled a backhand crosscourt for the
conclusion of the breaker. The blonde shook hands with what
I considered not very good grace and hurried to collect her
stuff. Barbara took a bit longer to towel off and was alone on
the court when she collected her gear, walked toward the gate
where I had stationed myself, and looked up and saw me.

Her eyes went wide with startled recognition. "*Brad?* Is
it really you?" Her smile became radiant. She hurried
through the gate, dropped her rackets and towel, and gave
me a big, sweaty, hugely enthusiastic hug. "What in the
world are you doing here!"

"I can't believe it," I said, grinning down at her. "This is great luck."

"You mean you didn't know I was here?"

"No! I came by on the chance I could get a game and loosen up after some business downtown, and there you were."

She held me at arm's length and kept on beaming. She looked good, really good. Time had put some experience in her face, but she still had those fine gray eyes and sturdy, handsome features. In her brief tennis dress it was obvious that the lady still had those legs, and maturity had filled her out in ways that were most pleasant. "What in the world brings you to L.A.?" she demanded. Then she immediately waggled a finger. "Never mind! You're here and that's all that counts. This is wonderful, Brad!"

I chuckled with genuine pleasure and bogus surprise. "I couldn't believe it when I walked out onto the deck to get the lay of the land and spotted you out here. It's great to see you after so long, Barb."

"Hey, it's a miracle, is what it is." She bent to retrieve her stuff, and that was when she noticed mine, dumped on the pavement by the fencing. "Have you got a game yet?"

"No," I said. "But I don't—"

"Let's see if we can get a court. My time is up on this one." She paused, looking dubious. "Unless you want a tougher workout than I can provide."

"I watched for awhile just now, and you'll give me more than I can handle, lady."

The old imp danced in her eyes. "I show no mercy."

"Fighting words, ma'am. Which way to the pro shop?"

Thoroughly delighted, she linked arms with me and led the way behind the row of courts toward the small white building that housed the pro shop. She said she played two days a week there and had been a member for years. She said she still lived in the same house about five miles away and worked three days a week plus two evenings as a marriage and family therapist in an office she shared with another licensed social worker. I pretended that this was all news to me. She wanted to know where I lived now, and what my business there was all about, and how long I planned to be in town. Thanks to the briefing given me by super-efficient Reese McDonald back in Montana, I looked surprised at all the right times and had my lies prepared in response.

She was obviously in glowing good health, successful, and happy. The lady was also even prettier than I remembered. She looked fine and substantial and honest, with none of the phony quality of some of the club's middle-aged mommies, with their eternal hair-teasing and tummy tucks in a desperate fight to retain that teenage Barbie Doll look.

I liked her. I always had.

We entered the pro shop. She introduced me proudly to the young guy behind the counter, whose eyes got a little bigger as he pumped my hand and said it was a real pleasure.

"My God, I was watching a highlight tape on ESPN just last weekend," he told me, "and they ran that sequence of you at Wimbledon last year when you blew your knee out again. My God, the way that knee bent on you! My God, I think you could have taken John that day if your knee hadn't gone out again. My God! It's great to have you visit us, sir!"

Ah, when the young studs who would have eyed you with killer intent only a few years ago now start calling you "sir," you know it won't be too much longer before you can get your AARP card. But he seemed like a genuinely decent chap, so I told him thank you kindly for the nice words, but McEnroe probably would have taken me anyway.

He wanted to talk about that, but Barbara stamped her tennis shoe on the tile floor in mock impatience. "Jerry, do we get a court or not, darn you?"

Jerry swallowed, smiled, and assigned us Court 10. Down that way the two of us sallied, Barb still prattling about this and that, and young pro Jerry scuttling along discreetly behind us, whispering to a few members as he progressed, so that by the time Barb and I walked out and started warming up, there were thirty or forty people lined up behind the fence, and a couple of matches on adjacent courts momentarily at a standstill while participants gawked.

Barbara courtesy-served the first ball right into the net. I could see her blush all the way from the backline. I felt for her; playing before an audience of any size or kind was not in her experience, and we were drawing more people all the time.

So I made an exaggerated swish at the next ball she sent my way and moon-balled it eight feet beyond the backline at her end, which she looked surprised at, then turned to study my grin, then grinned herself. After that she started to relax.

After a few warm-ups my knee loosened and the first sweat came. The day had gotten hazier and warmer, one of those southern California days when you couldn't be happier unless you allowed yourself to think about that pretty purple haze up there and what kind of chemicals might have contributed to it. I hadn't brought my newest knee brace because no heavy-duty tennis was contemplated, but the leg felt good and strong. We ceremoniously spun the racket and Barb called up, and up the label was, and she served.

I enjoyed it. She was good enough to make me work. There was a pleasure for me in watching her strong brown legs pump as she ran down balls, and her hair fluff up as she went for an overhead. I let her take the first set, 6–4, and then put a few more out of her reach in the second, making the second set 6–3 me, to even up the match.

Through it all, as much fun as it was, part of me was reviewing my plan, not liking me very much for being such a dishonest bastard, and planning how to get maximum information out of her even if information was a secondary goal here, and my primary mission was to be followed and give the renowned professional, Mr. Reese McDonald, a chance to show his stuff.

Even the choice of my motel location in faraway Burbank

was dishonest. The idea was to mention at some point how far away my room was, and that might (a) get me a dinner invitation, and if things went extremely well, (b) an offer to let me spend the night on her couch or studio bed to avoid the long, late drive back. If that worked out, so the theory went, my FBI tail would have considerably more opportunity to watch for the *other* tail—if any.

· The whole thing made me feel oily and unworthy of the lady's trusting friendship. Allegedly the ends justified the means here. Maybe. I have never been good at making such judgments.

Anyway, we finished the second set, our court time was up, Jerry the pro called eagerly for us to stay on as long as we wished, Barb looked slightly tired now, and I pleaded achy knee. We headed for our respective showers then, promising to rendezvous in the bar in about thirty minutes.

Showering gave me time to think. I was curious about several things, notably what she thought about Kevin's fate these days—whether she still put faith in the fact that his name had once appeared on a POW return manifest. I wondered, too, if she had heard about Dave Wentworth. Nobody had told me what to ask her about, but my own mental list was growing.

When I strolled into the bar twenty-five minutes later, she was already waiting for me. No endless primp-and-admire, she. Her hair, still damp, hung in tight natural ringlets. A dab of lipstick and a plain cotton dress with scoop neckline, and nobody could have looked better perched on one of those tall bar-table chairs.

"Hi!" she grinned. "You hurried."

A waiter, Johnny-on-the-spot, reached our table before I could answer. I looked questioningly at Barb.

"Diet Coke," she told him. "Lots of ice."

"Same," I said, and he went away.

"That was fun out there!" she told me. She looked almost as pink as her dress, flushed from exercise and a shower and excitement. She had always had an enormous zest for life; it hadn't diminished.

"I enjoyed it," I said. "You're still a dynamite player."

"And you took it easy on me."

"Hey, I'm just recovering from knee surgery again. You gave me all I wanted."

The waiter, a boy who seemed to work faster than your comic book character's speeding bullet, hustled back with our Cokes in tall clear glasses brimming with shaved ice. He presented them on paper napkins with a flourish befitting a Dom Perignon, gifted us with a small silver bowl of peanuts, and went away again.

Barb sipped greedily, holding the little red plastic swizzle stick to one side with a tapered index finger. "I got a little dehydrated out there."

"You used to like gin and tonic after tennis, I seem to recall."

A pale shadow scudded behind her eyes. "No more."

"Oh?"

"No. There was a while there . . ." the shadow moved again ". . . when I was always thinking about Kevin . . . always bitter and mad at the world and thinking our government could get him back if it really, really tried—" She stopped and looked down, turning the swizzle stick in her Coke. "Well. Better I stick to soft drinks. I don't want to go back *there* again. Ever."

"I still think about Kevin," I told her.

"Do you?" She searched my face.

"He was the best friend I had once."

"He isn't dead."

"You still believe that?"

"He isn't dead," she repeated with emphasis.

I said carefully, "I thought he was listed as presumed dead long ago."

She stubbornly shook her head, making the wet-ringlet ends bobble on her shoulders. "No."

"You *know* that? How?"

For an instant her eyes changed again, becoming vacant and lost as she looked backward in time. Then she seemed to rouse herself, and was back with me again. "I had a notice years ago that he was among the men who were scheduled to be repatriated, he was on a Vietnamese list. Brad, I was so excited and happy I think I could have *flown*. I waited by the phone. I frantically cleaned house. I had my hair and nails done. I made plans. I bought . . . I bought some new lingerie, and a present for him. His mom and dad came down from Seattle. We had a party."

Her throat worked and I thought she might cry. But then she got control again. "I saw pictures on TV of the released prisoners going into a hospital in Hawaii. I watched for Kevin. I didn't see him. Then we all waited for a call. There wasn't any call."

She paused again, and her breasts heaved. "I—a few days later, a man appeared at the door. He was a sergeant, or whatever they call them in the army these days, and he was all spit and polish and young and handsome, and before he said a word, I knew what he was going to say. He said it had been a mistake. He said Kevin had not been among the prisoners. He said the army's new information said Kevin had died in the POW camp. He said the army was going to list him now as KIA—killed in action. He said Kevin was going to be given a medal posthumously—"

She stopped there, and her control cracked a little. The old grief and rage swept up and made her eyes glisten. Feeling helpless and awkward, I reached across the table and grabbed one of her hands.

She pulled away as if angry with me, too. "I'm sorry—shit—" she sniffled and dug in a small purse for a Kleenex.

I sat there mute, feeling not only inept but more dishonest. She didn't need this crap from me. She didn't need me or anyone else raking up the old agony. She was still a good friend, a great lady, and I was here with her under false colors, doing nothing but causing her renewed pain. *Wrong!* the rational part of me yelled back in the face of my feelings. *This is for her and Kevin's own good . . . if he really is alive somewhere.*

Of course that was all perfectly true, assuming we could somehow make this turn out all right. But if memory serves, it was thinking not much different from this—justification for dishonesty—that had gotten me into virtually every serious personal problem I had ever had. Maybe I was doing the right thing here. But it did not feel good.

In a minute or two she got herself back together. She put the soggy tissue away and managed a brief smile. "Sorry."

"Maybe I shouldn't have said what I did the way I said it."

"No." She shook her head vehemently. "But I just don't think he's dead."

"Do you have any reason for feeling that way? I mean—"

She looked around the club bar as if remembering where we were. "This is a heck of a place to be having this conversation. What are your plans, Brad? Do you have a meeting somewhere this evening?"

"No," I lied smoothly, "actually I don't have to be anywhere until the middle of tomorrow afternoon." I paused a beat and then added, "Why?" as if my infinite innocence did not anticipate what she said next.

"Why don't we have dinner?" she asked.

I pretended to be surprised. "That would be great—if you're not busy."

"Not tonight I'm not. I had one client scheduled, but she canceled."

"Great! I can drive back to the motel and change clothes, and—"

"Where are you staying?"

"Up in Burbank."

"Well, you don't want to fight that freeway traffic all the way up there and then all the way back down here, do you?

Of course not. Look. You can just come to the house. That way you won't have to change. I've got some stuff in the fridge I can rustle up."

"That sounds like a lot of trouble."

"Nonsense. It's settled. Where are you parked? Out front? You can follow me home."

"That would be really nice," I said, as if vastly surprised at this turn of events.

And if you're out there, Simmons or whatever your name really is, follow me real nice and close so Reese McDonald can show what a stud he is by picking you up right away. Because I don't know how long I can keep lying to this woman, regardless of how good my intentions may be. I think too many people have lied to her already. Including her own government, the one her husband went to Vietnam for.

Nine

BARBARA'S HOME was a small stucco on a street of small stuccos facing a small, tree-lined municipal park. She pulled her Toyota into the garage and I parked back on the narrow, crumbling pavement of the driveway. Following her onto the vine-shrouded front stoop and into the house, I found myself in an old-fashioned entry hall with featureless wallpaper and rounded-arch doorways leading into a cozy living room and a back hall to the kitchen.

The sixties-style living room had two curtained windows, a fake fireplace with a gas grate in it, a pale green sofa bed flanked by two end tables with small lamps on them, a venerable mahogany secretary, two easy chairs with floral slipcovers, a coffee table, and a modest entertainment center in one corner which included a bookshelf stereo system, small-screen TV, and a VCR. Nothing was new, but all of it was spotless. A few magazines on the coffee table and some fingernail polish and a hairbrush on an end table were the only items that could remotely be called clutter. On the mantel was a framed picture that I didn't have to examine to know it was a picture of Barb and Kevin in days long gone by. They looked very young and very happy.

Barb pointed me toward the couch. "Do you want another Coke while I start dinner?"

"Not a thing. Are you sure you don't want to order a pizza?"

"Not on *my* diet. I've got a lot of quick recipes."

"Can I help, then?"

"Sure. Come on."

The kitchen was tiny, with an even smaller breakfast nook off to the side. The kitchen had old-fashioned painted cabinets and a linoleum floor long since turned a permanent yellow by too much wax and too many years.

Barb noticed me looking around. She said, "I keep thinking I'll move or else redo the house, but I'm a pack rat and moving would be too hard. I got some estimates on remodeling, but that would cost a fortune."

"It looks okay to me."

"Yep. Been here a long time." She dug three large potatoes out of a sack under the sink. "Here. Take that knife right over there and peel these, then cut them into little chunks, okay?"

I set to work at the sink while she bustled around, producing carrots, celery, and some leftover pot roast for the cutting board, plus some other things that I didn't see when she dropped them into a large cooking pot.

"Great," I said. "I like slumgullion."

She looked up, surprised. "Where in the world did you learn that term?"

"My mother used it all the time for a kind of cross between soup and hash that you threw everything but the kitchen sink into."

She grinned and started dicing the carrots. "Kevin used to make stew like this when we went camping. Slumgullion was what he called it. I never heard anyone else use that name for it."

"I guess it's old-fashioned."

She nodded, fingers deftly handling the knife. "Kevin told me once there was a place he liked to go fishing that had a Slumgullion Mountain, or something like that. He said he was going to take me there after the war."

I still felt like a traitor, using her. But there was always the chance it might help. I plugged ahead. "I guess you haven't heard from the army or anyone else about him in a long time now?"

"It's funny you should ask. I've had a slew of visitors. First, last January, a man called and said he was doing a book about the America Division in Vietnam. He wanted to talk about Kevin and some of his army friends. I met him for lunch. He seemed like a nice man. He already had a lot of names of people I had never heard of, other veterans. He kept me there more than two hours, firing questions at me."

My antennae went up. "What kind of questions?"

"My gosh, all kinds. When Kevin went in, where he trained, when he went overseas, what areas I might know he served in while over there . . . let's see . . . what else . . . oh, what kinds of helicopters he flew, how many combat-support missions he flew, if I had any idea who his copilots and gunners were, whether he ever flew the big Hueys to take troops in and out of combat zones, what date he was first listed MIA, how long it took the army to notify me, whether I had heard from any other historians before he interviewed me—I can't begin to remember everything he asked. I remember thinking I was never going to get away from that lunch."

"Did he ask for the names of friends, too, Barbara? I mean, would he have asked about Kevin's college days at all? Take me, for instance. Did you give him my name, by any chance?"

She paused in her dicing. "Yes. He asked about all our old friends. I mentioned your name. It turned out he's kind of a tennis junkie and we ended up talking quite a lot about you and your career. Why?"

"No reason," I lied. "What was this guy's name?"

She frowned. "Newton, or something like that. No, it wasn't Newton . . . Newman? Newberg? Wait a minute. Newberry. I think it was Newberry."

Before I could ask, she put down the paring knife. "I think I've still got the business card he gave me in there in a pigeonhole of the secretary. Hang on a sec. Let me go look. I think I know exactly where it is."

She strode out of the kitchen. I rinsed my hands at the sink and dried them on a paper towel. Had Barb's visitor been my Frank Simmons, pumping her for information that might lead him to Kevin? Maybe I was onto something here.

She came back and handed me a standard-sized buff-colored business card. I read it:

WALTER NEWBERRY
FREELANCE WRITER

7171 Kingsley
Norman, Okla., 73069

The printed telephone number lower-right on the card had been scratched out, and a different one—still in the 405 area code—had been scrawled in with a black felt-tip pen.

"He said he had just changed telephone numbers to avoid crank calls," Barb told me. "He said the book he was working on wasn't going to be very well liked by the army or some of the men who served over there. Did he call on you, too, Brad?"

"I don't remember it," I told her. "What did this guy look like anyway?"

"Tall. *Very* tall. Over six feet six inches, I think. I remember how he ducked his head coming through the doorway at the restaurant. About fifty, I imagine. Thick glasses, bushy gray hair. And very intense. *Very* intense. Like I said, he seemed like a nice, sincere guy. But the way he kept firing questions at me made me feel almost . . . uneasy."

Obviously it wasn't my man Simmons. I didn't know whether to be relieved or disappointed.

"You can keep that if you want," Barb said, eyeing the card I still held. "He said to keep it in case I remembered anything else that might interest him, but I haven't and don't think I ever will."

I carefully pocketed the business card. "You say you had other visitors lately?"

"Yes. Late the same month, a man named Leventhal called. He came by."

"Another writer?"

"No. He said he was a college professor. He said he served with Kevin. He seemed shocked when I said Kevin was still missing, and the army said he was dead. I didn't let him in, though. He was *very* nervous. I didn't get good vibes from him."

"Leventhal, you say," I repeated, so I wouldn't forget.

"Yes. He said some of the old units were planning a reunion, and they were contacting everyone they could to make sure they were invited."

"I wonder," I said, still fishing, "where he got his list of names and addresses."

"I wondered that myself. Maybe the army gave it to them."

I tried to make my voice as casual as possible. "I don't suppose he left a card, too?"

"No. Nothing. I didn't *want* a card from him. He was too spooky."

"Here. Let me hack up that onion. Do you know the trick of putting a piece of bread in your mouth when you slice onion? Your eyes don't water. Do you remember anything else about this man?"

"Not really. He was tallish, gray-haired, glasses. That's about all. I just kept him on the front porch, remember, so he didn't hang around long."

It seemed like good stuff—far more than I had expected to learn. I wondered if the writer was really a writer, and who the second visitor had been. The reunion story sounded phony.

"You *have* had a string of visitors," I observed.

"The worst was in March," she told me.

"What happened then?"

"That was when the army came."

"The army!"

She grinned. "Well, two nice young men in civilian clothes who said they were with Army Intelligence, and had the papers to prove it."

"What did *they* want?"

"They said they were following up on Vietnam MIAs. They tried to ask questions about Kevin, his friends and everything, but I'm afraid I was pretty rude to them. I reminded them that the army said Kevin was KIA, after first telling me he was about to be repatriated, and I wouldn't talk to them anymore."

Curiouser and curiouser. "What did they say to that?"

Barbara shrugged. "They left."

All the information would go to Collie first. I wasn't fond of the idea of turning it over to Reese McDonald; for one thing, I had no instructions to turn anything over to him, and for another, my instincts told me he might bury it in a report somewhere that wouldn't get read for about ten years.

I finished the onion, my bread-in-the-mouth trick working pretty nicely, and Barb sliced up the leftover roast and dropped the pieces into our growing stack of slumgullion stuff. She added water and some chicken broth, which was a new trick to me, and onto the stove it went, medium-high, with a lid. Then she set things out on the tiny round table in the breakfast nook and readjusted the flame under the slumgullion, and we took Cokes into the living room. It was time for the evening local news and she turned it on. The lead item involved a cute girl anchor and two cute boy anchors at a mall somewhere, passing out station logo caps and signing autographs for their adoring public. Barb changed channels at that point, and on the second local station the news team was in the middle of an "exclusive report in depth" on free puppies at the local animal shelter. Barb muted it. Thank

God for the mute button. We sat there and watched the
news-children silently laugh and ad-lib about a background
picture which seemed to show a fatal car wreck, and Barb
asked a lot of questions about what had been happening in
my life. I spared her the details of the long-ago crack-up of
my marriage, how I had met and married Danisa and how she
had been killed, how there was a lady named Beth Miles
somewhere within a hundred miles of where we sat, how our
relationship was going down the tubes from benign neglect
and male-female value systems that didn't match anymore.

"And there are no more tournaments at all, Brad?"

"Only celebrity things, stuff like that."

She seemed to hear something in the kitchen and got up
abruptly. "Excuse me."

In a minute she was back. "It was starting to boil over. I
had to turn it down again. I'm going to give it fifteen more
minutes, and if the vegetables aren't cooked, into a glass
container and the microwave it goes."

"Sounds right to me."

She breathed deeply, the way she seemed always to do
when thoughts of Kevin went through her mind. "I wonder
if Kevin would have been a good player—world-class—if he
had come home."

"I don't think there's any doubt about it," I told her. "He
was more powerful than any of us. More fundamentally
sound. He would have had to get used to the pressure, but he
would have done that, too."

She hugged her arms around herself. "It gets . . . lonely."

"You never thought about remarrying?"

She seemed startled. "After Kevin? What for?"

So she still loved him this much. It made me think of
Beth. Was her refusal to consider living and working in
Montana a sign that her love didn't go deep, as this woman's
did? Or did I still simply not understand what the code of the
New Woman was really all about? Maybe I was the one whose
love was shallow; maybe *I* was the one who should move. I

felt angry with myself for wondering. I thought of Linda, the
lady I had been with in London during the Wimbledon thing.
As hope about Beth faded, I found myself thinking more and
more about Linda. I felt angry with myself about that, too—
like a man losing one woman and pitifully beginning to
fantasize about the next.

I roused myself. "You are one loyal lady," I said.

"Besides," she replied, "I don't think he's dead. I know
he's not."

"How—?"

"I don't know. I've made up a hundred theories. None of
them makes sense. I just know. I feel it"—she pressed her
palms against her breasts—"here."

"I'm sorry."

After awhile Barb checked the slumgullion stew again
and pronounced it good. We carried bowls into the breakfast
nook and it was better than good. I did a bit more poking
around with questions, but couldn't seem to elicit anything
more of value. We talked about other things, her practice
among them. She liked her practice, was proud of it. I liked
her for that along with everything else. She was the kind of
person who would have worked her tail off to be the best, and
like her work, if she had been riding the back of a garbage
truck. Such people are the best, and it has nothing to do with
what they do, only how they do it: well.

It was dark when we finished doing the dishes—no dish-
washing machine here. Then she offered me a cognac, which
I accepted and which she poured from a very old, very dusty
bottle. She didn't have any. I wondered how long she had
been a recovering alcoholic, probably thanks to our quest for
coonskins in Vietnam, but I didn't ask. A little later, when I
made motions to go, it took only one remark about probably
getting lost on the freeways in the dark to get her to suggest
that I should stay over, sleeping on the couch. I remonstrated, but gave in quickly to her wonderful idea.

We said good night early. I cleaned up a little, rubbed my

teeth as well as I could with a finger loaded with her Pepso-
dent, and returned to the living room to find the couch
unfolded into a bed, and sheets and pillow already in place.
She had gotten into a shapeless corduroy robe and had
removed her scant makeup. I liked her even better without
makeup. She had that kind of face.

She leaned close for a split second and brushed cool lips
across my cheek. "I'm glad you came and we ran into each
other, Brad. Old friends shouldn't lose touch. Good night."

Out went the lights, and I could hear her moving around
in the bedroom beyond the closed door for awhile, and then
the house got quiet. I lay awake a long time, thinking about
things better thought about only in the light of day. Then I
slept, and when I awoke with the first light of dawn in the
morning, something made me look out one of the front
windows.

There were three police cars, two TV station remote
units, and an emergency ambulance, along with a couple of
dozen curious neighbors, in the park across the street.

I threw on my clothes and trotted over there. With luck
and some impolite shoving, I managed to get close enough
just as the ambulance guys were lifting the body of a man off
the ground behind some dense shrubbery and putting it onto
their rollered stretcher.

The victim was heavyset, with a closely trimmed auburn
beard. He was wearing rumpled khaki slacks and a sport
shirt. His eyeglasses were still on his nose. There was some
caked blood on the side of his head, but he was alive.

He perfectly fit the description brother McDonald had
given me of his working partner.

I looked around. That was when I spotted Reese McDonald standing on the edge of the crowd. Our eyes met, and he
appeared so shaken that he even forgot to look away instantly. They had blown it. His partner had spotted somebody, all right, but he had gotten too close, and almost paid
with his life.

Ten

BARBARA ATTRIBUTED the commotion in the park to the kind of random violence her neighborhood, like most, had been seeing with increasing regularity. I let her think that.

After coffee I got out of there amid the usual promises to stay in touch. Her smile from the front door as I backed out of the driveway looked sad and thoughtful. If Kevin was alive somewhere, I thought, how in hell could he stand it, knowing this woman was waiting for him?

But now the pathetic charade hatched by either the CIA or the FBI, or both—dangling me in hope of catching someone who might shed some light on the mystery—obviously had backfired. Someone *had* been tailing me, but Reese McDonald's partner had blown it. We had not only missed a chance, but the bad guys were now alerted to our efforts to catch them. They would be more careful in the future. The odds against our identifying them had just plummeted.

Back at the motel, I sent bacon and eggs down to a churning stomach, picked up the weekend edition of *USA Today*, and took it back to my room to sit tight like a good little boy. I would be contacted after this monumental screwup. It was just a question of when.

I had showered, shaved, changed into fresh clothes, and read the newspaper end-to-end, including even the agate-type sports items from every state in the Union, when the telephone finally rang.

"Mr. Smith?" the familiar voice said. "McDonald here. I shall be at your motel in twenty minutes."

"What—" I started to ask, but he had hung up.

He rapped on my motel room door exactly twenty minutes later—not nineteen, not twenty-one. Dark tie cinched tight at the collar, tan summer suit without a wrinkle, every bristle-cut hair in place, he showed no sign that anything might have gone amiss. He had his thin attaché case in hand.

"Good afternoon," he clipped, striding stiffly into the room. He sniffed the air, probably detecting the stale smoke from the pack of cigarettes I had bought after breakfast, and noted the dirty ashtrays. "No maid service yet? Disgraceful." He sat in the only chair, put his case on the floor beside it, meticulously adjusted the crease in his trousers, and gave me a dirty look. "You should not have gone into the park this morning. Unconscionable deviation from your instructions."

I sat on the edge of the crumpled bed. "I humbly beg your pardon, *sir*. I don't remember your instructions covering an FBI agent getting hammered, and half the neighborhood looking on."

He sniffed, withdrew a spotless linen handkerchief from his back pocket, and patted at facial perspiration I couldn't see. "Well, no additional harm done, as far as I can ascertain."

"Is your partner still alive?"

"Yes. He has not regained consciousness yet, but his vital signs are good." McDonald seemed utterly unfazed about this part of it. "He was struck very hard with some blunt instrument, but the physicians believe he will have a complete recovery." He sighed. "For a moment, when I first examined him after securing the prisoner, I feared he might have found the Boojum."

I leaned forward. "Found the what?"

"Oh." He stiffened. "My apologies. That is a private joke between myself and a few associates. When one says one has found the Boojum, it means that he or she has located a truly terrifying monster, as it were. In Hale's case, the monster would have been an untimely death."

"Lewis Carroll would be honored," I said.

His eyes widened. "You recognize the literary referent, then."

"Yes. I've read five or six books in my life, actually."

He missed the sarcasm entirely. "Some of us often privately compare our work with *The Hunting of the Snark*. We are a diverse group, as those hunters were in the poem. And I must say that sometimes our prolix investigations partake of a quality of confusion and frustration eminently analogous to the poetic hunt. What we always wish to avoid at all costs, of course, is a conclusion in which someone locates our investigatory prey, but in the process learns that the outcome is not at all what one anticipated, as the poor soul does at the conclusion of the poem when the Snark turns out to be a Boojum, and devours him."

He had to be the most boring man in the world. I said impatiently, "But the operation did end up sour."

His eyes widened slightly. "Sour? It didn't go sour."

"I saw your partner with his head bashed in!"

"Oh. That. Yes. But the operation otherwise went perfectly"

"It *what*?"

He patted his face again. "Hale assumed surveillance duties at 2 A.M. I retired at a nearby motel. When he spotted our subject in the park shortly before six, he of course alerted me at once via Handie-Talkie. I sped to the scene. The subject appeared to be returning to his automobile preparatory to departure. Hale agreed with my judgment that immediate apprehension appeared mandatory. Approachment of the subject was initiated. The subject attacked Hale and injured him before I could take appropriate action to bring him fully under control."

"You mean," I said in astonishment, "you *caught* the guy?"

McDonald tilted his head, one corner of his mouth quirking with impatience. "Surely you didn't imagine we had botched the operation."

"O me of little faith," I muttered.

He put a cupped hand behind his ear. "Please?"

"Nothing. You have somebody in custody, then?"

"Of course."

"Who is he? What have you learned so far?"

"Mr. Smith, the files of ongoing FBI investigations are closed to the general public. Surely you know that."

My face got hot. "Sorry. I keep forgetting I'm only a part of the general public in this thing. Being the dangle, I tend to assume I have a vested interest in the outcome."

"It's a natural erroneous impression, Mr. Smith. Think nothing more about it."

Knowing how much it would irritate him, I got up to get a cigarette and didn't speak again until the smoke curled between us. "Then you're finished with me."

"Yes. I am authorized to state that you can return to Montana at your convenience." He leaned over to pick up his attaché case and place it carefully across his knees. Locks snapped sharply as he pressed them and opened the lid. "I have copies of the expense claim forms here, and an envelope already addressed and stamped. Please do not fail to submit your expense claim promptly." He handed me the forms.

I took them. "Was the man you caught the one who talked to me last month in Montana? Does he match the description?"

"No. I believe I can tell you that much. This is a different person entirely."

"Then shouldn't I be worried about the other guy? I mean, what happens when he hears about this?"

Snap-snap!, the attaché case locked again. "The question of your possible endangerment was a subject of discussion prior to instigation of the mission, Mr. Smith. After *a priori* analysis of all the predictable outcomes, the judgment was that the risk to you was acceptable."

I stabbed my cigarette into the ashtray. "Pardon me all to hell for saying this, Reese, but what you just said didn't make sense."

"Please?"

"*You* decided that the risk to *me* was acceptable?"

"Permit me to restate. If anyone had been after you personally, they would have made an attempt on your life long before now, in Montana. The computer models for circumstances such as this one suggest with a ninety-seven percent degree of certainty that the additional perpetrator or perpetrators will go out of their way now to avoid any proximity with you, for fear of identification by you, or another surveillance operative working for us. To put it in the vernacular, in my opinion they are going to avoid you like the plague. Trust me, Mr. Smith. I seldom err."

Thinking about it, I saw he was now making good sense. Nobody on the other side—whatever the other side was—would get within miles of me now.

So presumably I was personally safe. And, just as surely, my own chances of figuring anything out had just gone to zero.

McDonald got to his feet and hefted his attaché case. "I assume you learned nothing of value from Mrs. Green."

"It was very frustrating," I lied.

He shook hands with me. "Try not to feel bad, sir. The art of interrogation takes years to master. The woman surely has no useful information anyhow. Good day."

I stood in the room door, watching him get into his Ford, carefully buckle up for safety, start the engine, frown through a meticulous inspection of all the instrument panel gauges, and finally drive away. I closed my door and went back inside.

I called Langley. The secretary said Collie was in a meeting. I left the motel number and my room extension, and said I would be here another hour, and it was important. Then I called the airlines and learned that the best I could do on a decent connecting flight out was tomorrow morning. Which raised the Beth question again.

I was mulling that one when Collie called back.

"What's going on?" he asked.

"You know about early this morning, et cetera?"

"Our friends have sent us a report. It doesn't provide details."

"Well, Collie, maybe you're not authorized to know anything good they might turn up."

"Can you shed any light?"

"Me? Hell, no. I'm the general public."

"I can tell you've been having fun."

"I saw Barbara. She told me a few things that might interest you."

"She did? Holy shit. It never occurred to anybody that you might actually pick up some useful information. What is it?"

I told him about the visit in January by an alleged writer, and the later visits by people saying they represented the army, and then the man talking about a military reunion. I hadn't said much before I heard a click on the line which told me he had flicked on a recording machine.

When I finished, he asked a couple of questions I couldn't answer. Then he said, *"Some of this can be checked into. You're heading back to Montana now?"*

"In the morning."

"Seen Beth yet?"

"No."

"Planning to?"

"I'm not sure."

"See her, man."

"I'm thinking on it."

"We'll get back to you. Unofficially, of course."

"Of course."

After that call I prowled the room awhile and went out for coffee I didn't need. A couple of hours later I was still looking at the telephone and vacillating. Maybe a visit would only mess things up worse between us. But I wanted very badly to see her.

It was late in the afternoon when I finally picked up the phone again.

Eleven

Elsewhere

Missoula, Montana: June 14

FRED SLATER returned to his office on Higgins Avenue at 5 P.M. and found two bulky men in business suits waiting for him.

"Mr. Slater?" the gray-haired one asked. He opened a leather billfold and showed a very official-looking ID. "We have some questions to ask you, sir."

Slater's pulse began to thump. "Me? About what?"

"You have a partner named Wynn?"

Oh my God. Slater maintained a calm expression and tone. "I have an acquaintance who sometimes does work for my agency, yes. Why?"

"Was Mr. Wynn working for you in Los Angeles, sir?"

There was no percentage lying. Slater's feeling of disaster grew. "He was working on a divorce case for me, yes. *Why?*"

"Mr. Wynn is in custody, sir. We have a number of questions we want to ask you about his assignment. Will you accompany us now to our car, please?"

Twelve

June 14

THE WAY things had been going between us, I wasn't at all sure how Beth would react when she got my call. But she sounded delighted. "Brad? You're *here*? In Los Angeles? When did you get in? How long will you be here? Why didn't you let me know you were coming? My gosh!"

Lie time: "It was arranged at the last minute, some investors to meet. I've already got that wrapped up. In early this morning, out tomorrow morning."

"Where are you now?"

"Burbank. At a motel."

"And you have to leave in the morning?"

"Yes."

"What are your plans for this evening?"

"Nothing. I've finished my business—"

"Check out of that place," she ordered crisply. "You're staying with me. I'll meet you at my apartment in an hour and a half."

"Can you get off that early?"

"Dummy," she purred. "Is that anything to ask the woman who loves you?"

You figure it. I had been to the Coast twice in recent months, and she had been to Montana once. Each visit had only seemed to make things worse. Her practice was beginning to thrive. Bitterroot Valley was demanding more and more daily attention from me. Although we hadn't skated the thin ice of talking about it lately, she was still bitter about my last job for the Company, the one at Wimbledon. Yet here she was, saying she loved me, and clearly thrilled I was in town.

I don't know what kind of reception I had expected, but this was not it.

We had met on St. Maarten, in the Antilles, when she was attending a tennis school/resort and I was visiting the same place in search of the truth behind the death of a very dear old friend. I had still been quite crazy over the death of Danisa at the time. Beth had been magic, and healed me. Then, partly because of my own ineptitude, she was shot and almost killed.

That had been when she learned the truth about my occasional work for the Agency. I assured her at the time that it was highly unlikely I would ever be doing any more work for them. But then another contract job had come along, and I took it. Which was when she said she might be able to handle all the job-related separations, but she couldn't deal at the same time with my sometimes-work that might get me killed if I played my cards wrong.

I didn't intend to let her know what I had really been doing in L.A.

I showered again, put on my best bib and tucker, and drove the rental car into anthill traffic on the freeway. Feeling sure it was a waste of time, I got back off and did some things to throw anyone off who might be following me, like doubling back on my route, driving in and right back out of a parking garage, and taking a few alleys. Back on the freeway again, I felt silly because there was no earthly reason to assume anyone was on my tail now, and I knew that my flubby amateur tricks would not throw off a pro tailing me anyway. But I wanted to be just as sure as I could be that by visiting Beth at her apartment I was not leading the wrong kind of character into her proximity. All the maneuvering was added insurance.

Her apartment was in a huge block of two-story apartment buildings that seemed to run from the highway to forever. I parked beside her little Mazda coupe and walked briskly to her door, aware of a faint rising of my pulse and other stirrings which are better left unidentified. I expected control here today: a very controlled, cool, businesslike lady, a "good friend" whose every remark was perfectly proper and gracious—and noncommittal.

As I stepped onto the little redwood stoop at her door, the drawn draperies beside it stirred a fraction. I reached for the doorbell button. The door opened before I could press it. A bare arm reached out, grabbed my sleeve, and hauled me imperiously through a crack in the doorway that opened just wide enough to let me in. Then the door slammed behind me and I became aware of considerable dimness in the living room, the scents of incense, perfume, and girl, and the lady herself quite naked and pressing against me with an urgency that knocked me off balance in more ways than one.

"What *took* you so long?" she whispered fiercely.

"I didn't expect—"

Her eager mouth shut me up for a minute. Then she leaned back in my arms. "What *did* you expect after three months, you jerk? Piety and platitudes? Don't answer. I don't even want to hear about it. Just shut up and let me—dammit, how does this belt buckle work? God, aren't you ashamed of yourself, turning me into a sex fiend?" Her breath caught as I picked her up. "Oh, hey, I think you're getting the idea, darling—!"

She kept jabbering as I carried her into the next room. She let out a little yike of surprise when I dropped her roughly onto the bed, and then I finally managed to make her stop talking.

Later we lazed in the oceans of pillows on her big brass bed, the light of day fading from the window draperies, a pink glow coming from a night-light plugged in near the doorway to the adjacent bathroom. The talk consisted of phrases and fragments that didn't make a lot of sense, but the real talking wasn't in words anyway, but in the touch of palms on sweat-slippery skin, nuzzle of lips against places where pulse throbbed, combing of fingers through hair. There was a time when both of us almost, but not quite, dozed in the warm cocoon of bedsheets and cling of flesh.

It felt perfect. It was perfect. I wished it could go on forever.

It couldn't.

"Oof," she said, sitting up at last, the cover spilling back from her breasts. She ran a hand through her tangled hair. "You made me look like a mess."

"Yeah, you look really bad," I told her. "You must look worse than anyone in the world." I traced a fingertip down the long curvature of her leg.

She shivered. "Ow."

"Stop?"

"No. Ow."

We sat in silence for a while, lightly touching, piled up in the wreckage of the bed. I felt myself coming slowly back to reality, and guessed she was, too. You always come back to reality.

"Brad," she said finally, in a tone that said reality.

"Yessum?"

"What brought you to Los Angeles on such short notice?"

"I told you. Business."

She studied me with great, love-wrecked eyes. "I don't believe you."

I wanted to lie. I had even made up some good embellishments on the basic deception while driving over here. But you start lying to your lady and you're hopping onto a streetcar you may never be able to get back off of until it's taken you all the way to the city dump.

I said, "I'm trying to find an old friend. He goes back to college days. And to Vietnam."

"Is he in trouble?"

"I think he is."

She would not look away from my eyes. "And is Collie Davis in it?"

"Why in the world would Collie be involved in it?"

"Is he?"

"Not officially."

"But unofficially."

"Yes. But—"

I got no further. Abruptly she swung nude legs off the bed.

"Hey, Beth, wait a minute."

Bare legs twinkling, she hurried into the bathroom. The door closed firmly behind her. I heard water running and drawers being opened and closed louder than absolutely necessary. I sat where I was, waiting, trying to convince myself that I hadn't just messed things up again.

After what seemed a very long time, she came out wearing a long, shapeless cotton robe, the cord knotted tightly around her waist.

To add to the shattering of the effect, she flipped a switch. The overhead light came on like an atomic flash.

"Ouch," I said, shielding my eyes.

She might have been able to make a joke about that, but she didn't. No more playing around, Smith. She said briskly, "I guess if we're going out for dinner, we'd better get moving."

"We could just stay in," I suggested, still trying to pretend that our particular Boojum wasn't now in the room. "Maybe order Chinese?"

She refused to look at me. "No."

I held my arms out. "C'mere just a second."

"You're doing another job for them," she said in her courtroom tone. "Right?"

"It isn't dangerous," I said, knowing how much good that protest would do.

"Bullshit!"

I made one more try at reclaiming the nonreality. "Hey, counselor, is that any way to talk in the bedroom? Come over here. I have another motion to file."

"You know how I feel about you doing anything more for those people," she said, flint-hard. "It's bad enough, Brad, us trying to figure out some way to keep a relationship stuck together with postage stamps. Then you do something like this—risk your life again."

"Hey, I'm not risking my life!"

She banged the doors of the walk-in closet open and strode stiffly into it. Her voice came out of there like icicles. "You really don't care much about us anymore, do you?"

"That's a hell of a thing to say. Of course I care!"

She flounced out, carrying a summer dress and some other things over her arm. "I'll use the other bathroom so you can take a shower in here."

"Can't we talk about this?"

She stared at me, blond hair rumpled and eyes bright with rage and something near tears. She had never looked more beautiful, more hurt, or more angry. "Brad, there's nothing to talk about, really. Is there?"

I sat there like a fool with absolutely no idea what to say.

She turned and hurried into the hallway. More bright lights sprang to life, making the whole apartment feel chilly and public. I heard the other bathroom door close—lock—and the water start splashing into the tub.

I sat there a minute, trying to figure out exactly what had just taken place. The bed still looked like it had been wrecked, but the real wreckage wasn't the bed, if my sick feeling was any criterion: the real wreckage was us.

Thirteen
Elsewhere

Knoxville: June 15

ORDINARILY, MIKE ROMANOWSKI would have marked Saturday by playing golf early in the morning and then piling up in the living room for the baseball game of the day on TV. But this was no ordinary Saturday.

There should have been a report of some kind from Missoula by now, but he hadn't heard a word. What was going on out there? Why hadn't Slater called? He had to know how anxious Romanowski was to learn why Brad Smith had gone to Los Angeles, who he had seen. Had Slater's partner bungled the assignment? Had something gone wrong?

There was nothing to do but wait. Waiting always made Romanowski nervous. He had to do something. The only thing he could think of was to clean out the garage. He compulsively cleaned out the garage every time something happened that made him edgy.

Carrying the portable telephone outside with him, he crossed the narrow part of his backyard to the white frame garage. It could not have been a more beautiful day—a few puffy clouds in a brilliant blue sky, the sunshine warm, not a trace of breeze, birds singing somewhere in the fruit trees toward the back of the lot, a distant sound of a power mower. Everything normal, Romanowski thought bitterly. Everything just fine for everyone but him.

He unlocked the side door to the detached garage and went in, turning on the dim overhead light. The garage smelled of mildew, cigars, and gasoline. Propping the telephone, antenna extended, on the back of his workbench, Romanowski flipped on the big fluorescents over the bench. The brighter lights made everything stand out. He looked around for what to do first. Both his pickup and his wife's small Buick needed a wash and vacuuming out. The workbench was a mess, littered with garden tools, half-used packets of vegetable seeds, and the wrenches and sockets he had used to change the plugs in the F-150. The trash barrel was full of wadded paper, discarded oil containers, wrappers from McDonald's.

Romanowski decided to empty the trash barrel first. Getting a black plastic trash bag out of the box on one of the shelves over the parked mower, he flipped it open and started picking stuff out of the barrel and putting it in the bag.

The portable phone made its electronic beeping sound. Romanowski put down the trash bag and walked over to pick the phone up and slide the on switch. "Hello?"

"This is Fred Slater."

"About time you got around to calling," Romanowski grunted. "I didn't think we were paying you to—"

"Listen, mister," Slater's voice cut in sharply, *"my partner is in jail down in Los Angeles, charged with assaulting a federal officer. I just got out of the clink here, and the FBI may not be done with me yet. The only reason I'm calling is to let you know that."*

Romanowski's mind reeled. "Jail? Assault? They arrested you? You didn't tell them—"

"Shut up and listen. I gave them your name. I realize it's probably a false one. But I also gave them this number. I've got an idea you're going to be hearing from them very soon. I thought I owed it to you to warn you, although God knows why I feel that way. If I had known this crummy assignment involved messing with the federal government, you would have never gotten me to do any work for you in the first place."

"But—" Romanowski began.

"Don't ever call me again." The connection broke.

Romanowski stood holding the dead telephone, shock seeping through his nervous system like a numbing anesthetic. Jesus, it could hardly be worse. A trap. They must have set up some kind of trap. And Slater had spilled his guts to them.

Calm down, calm down, Romanowski told himself. *Slater didn't really know anything.*

But he had given them Romanowski's number. They would trace it and they would be coming here.

Hands shaking, Romanowski turned his portable telephone on again and punched in a long-distance number from memory. *Be there,* he prayed. *Just be there!*

A familar voice answered. *"Hello?"*

"Jack?" Romanowksi said, to be sure.

"Speaking. Is that you, Mike?" The voice went tight. *"Is something wrong?"*

"Listen, Jack, and don't interrupt. I may not have much time. The guy our private detective sent to L.A. got picked up by the FBI—"

"Shit! What—"

"—and Slater, our detective, got arrested, too. Slater just called. He gave them my phone number. They'll trace it and pick me up sure as the world."

Jack Maxwell's voice came back shrill with anxiety: *"Don't tell them anything. Don't give anything away. They can't prove anything."*

"I know that," Romanowski grated. "We're all right, it will be okay. But the other guys have to know. I'll call Arnie right after this. You contact Buddy and let him know. Call Stan, too."

"Stan? Why call Stan? He said after interviewing Mrs. Green he was quitting—he'd never do another thing for us—"

"Jack, just call him, okay?" Romanowski could have wept. "We're going to be okay, but everybody needs to know. Goodbye." Maxwell was protesting when Romanowski pressed the button to cut him off.

Putting the telephone on the workbench, he dug in his wallet for the little folded piece of paper with the rooming house number on it. Hurriedly he punched that in.

The woman manager sounded impatient and short-tempered, but went to get Tubb. Romanowski waited, fidgeting, more scared than he liked to admit.

The sound of car tires on the gravel of the driveway in front of the garage made him jerk his head around. Through the dirty little panes of the overhead door he saw two men in business suits getting out of a nondescript gray Plymouth sedan. They didn't see him. They walked up the sidewalk toward the front porch of his house.

Tubb's voice came on the line. *"This is Mr. Jones."*

"Listen and don't talk," Romanowski panted. "The thing in L.A. went bad. The man we hired got caught. Now the FBI has arrrested our detective in Montana. He gave them my number."

"What in the hell—"

"Shut up! Shut up! Listen. I've got two guys in my driveway right now. I think they've come for me—to question me."

"You won't—"

"No. But you'd better get moving. They might have some way of getting records from the telephone company and tracing down your number there. You need to get out."

Arnie Tubb said something then, but Romanowski did not hear it because the side door to the garage swung wider and the first of the two men walked in. His partner came just behind him.

Romanowski clicked the phone off and hastily put it on the paint can shelf beside him.

"Mr. Romanowski?" the first man said politely. "You're under arrest, sir." He reached past Romanowski to pick up the portable phone, turn it on, and press the redial button.

Horrified, Romanowski saw the rooming house number flash on the telephone's tiny display panel.

The agent pulled out a pencil and pad and hastily wrote down the number. He handed it to his partner. "Find out where this number is, Steve. Somebody will want to go over there right away." He turned back to Romanowski. "Will you come along with us now, sir?"

Tubb stood paralyzed at the desk in the rooming house office, the silent telephone still in his hand.

Mrs. Kloscis, the manager, looked up irritably from the small pile of checks and cash she had been counting at her desk. "Well? Are you through? Can the management possibly have back the use of its own telephone?"

Tubb stared at her. They had Mike, or would have him any minute. Maybe Mike wouldn't talk. He had said he wouldn't talk, but he had sounded scared shitless. He might tell them. They might be here next.

Tubb had to run again. *Now.*

He didn't have any money—just the few bucks Mike had given him. Cigarette money. He had to have money.

Mrs. Kloscis was still staring up at him, her expression filled with sarcasm. It looked like quite a bit of cash in front of her, the money paid today by renters who paid by the week.

"Well?" she said sharply.

Tubb hung up the phone and went around the end of the counter. "I'm terribly sorry, Mrs. Kloscis. I can assure you this won't ever happen again." He put the telephone back on the corner of her desk beside a large, old-fashioned bronze paperweight formed in the shape of a seashell.

"Well," his landlady said, a bit mollified, "see that it doesn't. I've told you before, Mr. Jones, that I run a business here. I can't—"

The paperweight slammed into the side of her head with the meaty feeling of a baseball bat when the ball is hit just right. Blood flew. She slid off the chair onto the floor, going halfway under the desk.

Tubb scooped up all the paper money, crammed it into a pants pocket, spied her car keys on the desk beside the checkbook calculator, grabbed the keys, and ran outside.

Hays, Kansas

JACK MAXWELL finished the second of his two telephone calls. Stan Leventhal, up in Michigan, had sounded terrified. If worse came to worst, Maxwell thought, Leventhal's would be the first name he would give the authorities. There had been no reason for Leventhal to back out of everything after interviewing Mrs. Green in California. They were down to a handful now, couldn't afford more losses.

Maxwell thought about the arrest of their detective in Montana. He would tell the FBI—if he hadn't already done so—about being hired earlier to provide Maxwell with information about Brad Smith's schedule so Maxwell could go up there, pull his fake ID, and get the tap on the telephone.

That information would take them to Brad Smith, Maxwell realized. Then Smith would give them a detailed description of him, and he would have the FBI putting his sketch on posters. *Or maybe Smith had already done all that. Maybe Smith had already been working with the FBI, and that was how the man tailing him had been caught.*

Cold sweat burst out of every pore on Maxwell's body. They were going to be looking for *him* now, sure as the world. If they found him, they would drag him in front of Smith, and Smith would give them a positive ID. Then—*God!*—they might start linking him to everyone else—everything else—maybe all the way back to Nam, and how they had taken care of a few potential stool pigeons by arranging their deaths "in combat."

That could not be allowed to happen, Maxwell thought, panic dancing. Something had to be done.

Brad Smith had to be taken out—permanently.

Maxwell couldn't count on anyone else to do it. As badly as the idea made terror shriek inside him, he realized that he had to handle this himself.

Maxwell paced the floor, trying desperately to think of any other way out—anything at all.

He couldn't see any other way out. Smith had to *go*.

Maxwell had to see to it. Now. Right away.

Fourteen

CONTINENTAL ALLEGED bad weather somewhere in their system Saturday afternoon, enough excuse from their standpoint to make me wait eight extra hours in Denver for my connection back to Missoula. It was past midnight when I finally got back to Bitterroot Valley in a not very happy state of mind.

I found the lodge quiet, the lobby deserted except for our night clerk. I checked for messages, thinking that surely by now there would be something from Collie Davis as a result of what I had told him the day before. My call box was empty. I walked down to my cabin in a thin, cold drizzle that matched my mood.

Friday evening with Beth had not been your basic fun time for lovers. We went out to dinner after our one-sided row about my assignment in Los Angeles, and I had tried for awhile to make engaging conversation. I am about as good at making light conversation as George Will is at defending a Democratic campaign platform, so perhaps my efforts were doomed from the outset. At any rate, Beth replied mostly in monosyllables—chill, tight-lipped, polite—about what you would expect from a lawyer with a hostile witness. After an hour or so of this, I quietly lost my temper and gave up trying to make small talk. We finished our meal in stony, preoccupied silence, which made us resemble many of the married couples scattered around the room. You know the type: they've been married about twenty years, and during the last twelve or fifteen of them love and even mutual respect have been long gone; but both parties decided at some point to grimly hang in there anyway "for the sake of the relationship"; he has a girlfriend; she has a lover; their friends say they have a perfect marriage; once a year they take a trip together; they play CDs in their car so they won't have to face the silence on the road, either; *they*, by God, will "never become a divorce statistic."

Maybe ordinarily we would have gone to a club for dancing afterward. But by the time I had paid the exorbitant tab and left a tip larger than necessary because I can never figure fifteen percent in my head, she was already ankling for the exit and I was fighting so hard not to explode that there wasn't energy left for anything else. I drove her home.

We had turned off the main street and were almost there when I gave it one last try: "Are we going to talk about it?"

"No," she replied with no intonation of any kind.

"Fine," I snapped back.

I parked and walked her to her door. She unlocked. Nothing was said about my overnight bag in the backseat of my car, which she couldn't have missed seeing, or about her earlier orders to check out of my motel. She stepped inside her apartment. I tried to kiss her. She turned her head so that my lips brushed her cheek. I wanted to hit her. Instead, I turned and stomped back to the car like a teenager just turned down by the prom queen.

The new motel room I found had a TV set with broken vertical hold, so that pictures flopped by in a multihued blur. By then I had begun to feel like a Steve Martin skit. Not a good night, followed by a late takeoff from LAX, a bumpy ride to Denver, and Continental's cheery *Delayed* on the connecting flight's departure board.

Now, back at home sweet home, I found a note from Ted Treacher in my cabin mailbox, informing me that the swimming pool heater had broken down, that he had called Avery Whitney and even Avery hadn't made much headway with it, and he hoped I could figure out what was wrong and repair it first thing in the morning. I wished for a cat to kick.

After a small brandy and a long, hot shower, I turned in. Slept badly, rain on the steeply pitched roof of my cabin translating itself into whispering voices in whatever dreams I had. When I rolled out early Sunday morning, however, the rain had gone east and the sky was as clear as the finest glass, the sun brilliant on new snow at the higher elevations all around, the temperature a fine, brittle thirty-five.

The schedule book on my bedroom desk had *Kansas City* written in the blank for Tuesday the eighteenth, with a line drawn horizontally all the way through next Sunday, the twenty-third. Despite everything else going on lately, I hadn't forgotten the tournament down there, one I had accepted a bid to five months ago. The field hadn't then and still didn't look very strong, and there was a chance I might get as far as the semis and pick up a nice payday. Thinking about that, I postponed my assignation with a sick swimming pool heater and pulled on sweats for a morning run. Recent events had put me behind on my conditioning and practice alike; Ted would have to give me five hours on the practice court today and tomorrow, before I headed to Kansas City, if the goddamned swimming pool heater never got fixed.

The jog was good for me in more ways than one. By the time I was on the way back, puffing along the far side of the No. 16 fairway, some of the coiled nervous tension had gone out. Near the No. 16 green I startled five deer grazing on fresh, lush dandelions and other weeds thriving in the shady places where the rough met the fir woods. An eagle yelled at me, and moments later a fine little gathering of ducks exploded off the pond at No. 17 as I lumbered uphill toward them. A fat rabbit ducked into high brush as I passed. Squirrels scolded me. By the time I got back to my cabin, panting and sweaty and thoroughly wrung out, with my pulse at 140, I felt considerably better—might have actually felt human again if my thinking while I ran had given me any ideas at all about Beth, or about the mystery of Dave Wentworth's death and Kevin Green's invisibility.

I unlocked the cabin, went back inside, and had just started to peel off my sweats when somebody banged on my door. Wearing just the pants and socks, I padded into the living room.

"Who is it?" I yelled through the door.

"Me," the familiar voice called back.

"Shit." I pulled the security chain off the fixture and opened up.

Collie Davis walked in.

"What are you doing here again?" I demanded. "How did you get here so fast?"

Ignoring my questions, Collie flopped down on my couch. Wearing faded Levi's and a flannel shirt, he looked like one of our guests, except that he had a thin leather folder under his arm. His bloodshot eyes betrayed a lack of sleep. "Have you got any coffee made?"

"Not yet. How did you get here so—"

"Corporate aviation," he said, "is a wonderful thing. You can hire a Lear jet and be anyplace in a few hours. In my next life I think I'll be rich and own a private jet of my very own."

"You flew a charter out here? What the hell for?"

"I needed to talk to you. Obviously."

"Why not on the phone?"

"Because you were jumping around airports and out of touch all day yesterday, for one thing. But more to the point, I've got something for you to read."

"Hand it over."

"Make some coffee, all right?"

"Are you going to hand it over, this thing I'm supposed to read?"

"I need coffee first. I'm dying."

I gestured toward the kitchen alcove. "Then you make it. I need to shower before I cool all the way down."

With a sigh of resignation he climbed to his feet and

shuffled into the alcove. I hurried to the shower, made quick work of it, and rejoined him in the living room after throwing on some clothes. He was sitting in the same spot on the couch with a steaming cup in his hand.

I veered off to the kitchen and found the coffeemaker clean and cold. "How did you make the coffee?"

"I made instant."

Muttering, I started a pot of the real stuff, then went in to face him again. "Now."

He put down his cup. "This is unofficial."

"I know, I know. Go ahead."

"You remember the guy they picked up in Los Angeles."

"Of course. Have they already gotten something good out of him?"

"Not much, at least not that they're telling us. We do know he turned out to be a private investigator."

"Who for?"

"He worked for an agency in Missoula."

"I didn't know Missoula *had* a private detective agency."

"Everybody has a private detective agency. How do you think people check up on their truant children or get the evidence for big divorce settlements?"

"Who hired this guy? Is he the one who came down here and bugged my telephone?"

"We don't think so, so—"

"You don't *think* so! Goddammit, I gave you a good description."

He grimaced. "Well, the Bureau hasn't sprung loose with a picture of him, his boss, or the man in Tennessee who evidently hired the agency to follow you."

"Man in Tennessee?" I detected the early signs of a headache. "What man in Tennessee? What's going on here?"

"The FBI grabbed a man in Whittier who turned out to be working for a private detective agency in Missoula," Collie said with the air of a man explaining to a child. "He gave them the name of his boss. The boss in Missoula gave them the name of a man in Knoxville who paid to have you shadowed. The FBI hurried right along and had the Knoxville suspect in custody by sometime yesterday morning."

"Who is he?"

"They haven't released a name to us yet."

"You guys don't know very much!"

Collie gave me a dirty look. "They aren't telling us very much. They're pretending this is ho-hum, Bureau routine, no concern of ours. And since it's all domestic stuff, at least on the surface, we can hardly roar in with demands for prompt disclosure of information that's properly none of our damned business."

"Is this what you came to tell me?" I asked. "That the FBI is doing something but you don't know what?"

His expression of irritation changed to dull, controlled anger. "Are you going to continue acting like an asshole?"

"Sorry. I haven't been having a very good time. I'll shut up."

He nodded, mollified. "I'll try to make a few things clear. Somehow related to the arrest of this guy in Knoxville is an all-points the Bureau put out within a couple of hours of his arrest. The bulletin is for another guy. They had put out information on this other guy as far back as January, but the new one says he was suspected of being in the Knoxville area, which gives us the hint that the arrest and the new bulletin relate to one another."

He paused, watching me, evidently waiting for me to pipe up with something. I kept my promise and stayed quiet.

He looked almost relieved. "The wanted notice is on a man named Tubb, first name Arnold, who walked away from the oncology ward at Walter Reed last Christmas. He had been transferred there from another VA hospital in New York—the psycho ward."

"He's nuts?"

"He's suspected of murder. Posttraumatic stress disorder. He's supposed to be armed and dangerous." Collie gave me a keen look. "Vietnam veteran. Served with the Americal in the same part of Vietnam you and the late Dave Wentworth and the mysterious Kevin Green served in, and at the same time."

I leaned forward, aware of a slight tingling. "You think he's involved in Wentworth's death?"

"We don't know, and if we did, it wouldn't be in our bailiwick. But it goes back to Nam and some things that happened there which have never been adequately explained, including several MIAs and the Kevin Green case. Those things *are* in our bailiwick."

"Wait a minute," I said. "You said this man walked away from the oncology ward. That's cancer. If he's been on the loose all these months, that means he hasn't had any treatments. Why isn't he dead?"

Collie's forehead wrinkled. "He could be. But the FBI apparently doesn't think so—and we're guessing they're playing the whole thing close to the vest because they think they're onto something big here, and want to make sure the case is all theirs."

"Does this missing vet fit the description of—"

"The man who visited you? No."

"How about any of the people who visited Barbara Green?"

"Unfortunately, no."

"Have you been able to find out anything about that string of visitors Barbara had?"

Collie's mouth tightened. "A request for information on the writer type you told us about was sent through proper channels. Both the Pentagon and the FBI sent back no-info notes on him."

"Then his ID was a fake?"

He looked at me scornfully. "Hell no. All somebody had to do was check the microfiche of books in print at the local chain bookstore to learn better than that. The guy is legit.

He's published two books on Vietnam, and evidently has been working on another one."

"Let me guess," I said. "About the Americal Division."

"Sometimes, Brad, you amaze me."

"Is he a veteran too?"

"No. Bad heart. Congenital. We know that much."

"What else do you know about him?"

"Brad," Collie said patiently. "We don't keep files on—"

"All right, all right. Go on."

"There isn't a lot more to 'go on' about any of the information you gave us. But the Vietnam connection rang a bell." He unzipped his leather case and pulled out some papers. "There's a very old, very puzzling bunch of stuff about one operation back in Nam. The army doesn't know we have any of this information. Most of it was developed through returnee interviews and . . . um . . . other sources. We would still like to know about all this, and it falls under our jurisdiction. The Wentworth death, someone visiting you and asking about Kevin Green, and even this whacko running around with a body full of cancer cells may all relate to it."

He handed over a thin sheaf of typed pages. I immediately saw the blacked-out lines and paragraphs interspersed through the text, and looked up at him questioningly.

He said, "What's left is classified, too, but you're cleared that high. Read it. I think you'll see why we're interested."

The heading read simply, "Incident at Quang Xi 6 Apr. 68." I began wading my way through the pages, trying to make the fragments fit into some kind of cohesive story.

I had to read it twice. This is the best I could do:

One of the platoons of Baker Company, 1st Battalion, 20th Infantry, had been choppered into Landing Zone Charlie, in the Quang Ngai province near the South China Sea coast, on April 4, 1968. A combat mission plan apparently called for additional troops to be put in at the same time. But the weather, already bad, worsened rapidly and most of the Hueys had to turn back.

The company commander, Capt. Roger S. Aldrich, went in with the first and only platoon landed before the weather caused an abort. He was ordered to get his troops out of the landing zone and proceed toward a hamlet or subhamlet called Quang Xi, about four miles to the north.

Halfway to their destination, the platoon ran into a Vietcong ambush and took some casualities. Under confusing circumstances, Aldrich extricated his tiny command and holed up overnight. Reports later said the unit was under sporadic harassing fire all night. Three or four more GIs were killed, and five wounded.

In the morning hours of April 5, choppers managed to put part of a second platoon on the ground in marginal weather before being driven away by heavy ground fire. The two platoons—two-thirds of a healthy 2nd and the remnants of the battered 3rd—were ordered to link up. But the 2nd ran into heavy resistance and bogged down. Helicopters ordered to take them back out were unable to get through the dense rain and clouds.

Meanwhile, the 3rd under Captain Aldrich was not having an easy time. Two more men were killed by some kind of booby trap. A small Vietnamese boy was involved in this somehow. The boy, twelve, was shot. Aldrich would later claim twelve VC killed in this same action, but a unit that went through later would report finding only some old men and women who had evidently been shot and killed while working in a rice field.

Aldrich's radio report at the time claimed additional VC resistance which again claimed lives and put his shrinking command under sporadic fire during another long night. The miserable weather continued into a third day, April 6.

That morning, the small command somehow got split into two groups. The smaller of the two, under Aldrich, entered the hamlet of Quang Xi sometime shortly after dawn.

His radioman reported "heavy action." All the huts in the hamlet were set afire. An unspecified number of women and children were killed, according to later investigators. After about two hours, a few men from the other part of the command reached Quang Xi. These stragglers did not join Aldrich's group when it left the village and crossed over a small stream into rice fields on the east side.

Aldrich's unit claimed Vietcong resistance in the rice fields and claimed another eight VC killed. Reports filed the following day spoke of five small children found shot to death in this area. (Other details of follow-up reports blacked out in my copy.)

At approximately 1100 hours on April 6, Aldrich's command had moved approximately two miles east and north of Quang Xi. There, while helicopter gunships and troop-carrying Hueys milled around above an impenetrable layer of cloud and smoke, Aldrich's group came under intense Vietcong or North Vietnamese fire.

Virtually his entire unit—some of the 3rd and by now some of the 2nd—was wiped out. It was one of the single worst military disasters of the war.

As the sky cleared and the relief choppers could move in, they could easily spot the place where Aldrich and his troops lay dead, the ground shot up all around them and a few small craters still smoking. The enemy, as usual, had struck and melted away.

Neither the handful of badly wounded survivors nor any of the men who had, for unexplained reasons, remained on the far side of the stream south of the devastated Quang Xi hamlet were able to offer any coherent report of what had happened during the action.

An investigation later concluded that the hamlet had been heavily infiltrated by VC, and any actions taken by Aldrich and his men were justified during heavy engagement in a free-fire zone.

In subsequent weeks, the reorganized 2nd and 3rd suffered an extraordinary number of deaths from friendly fire. Reports attributed these accidental deaths to combat fatigue, and by the end of the month all those still surviving were withdrawn from the area for rest and medical evaluation.

Finally finishing with my second reading, I handed the pages back to Collie, who had silently sipped coffee, giving me all the time I needed. The old emotional vomitus had crept back inside me as I read, forming my own conclusions from the stilted bureaucratic language of the report.

Maybe no one really knew any longer what had happened at Quang Xi. The mention of the dead women and children told me as much as I needed to know.

Collie stared hard at me. "What's wrong? You're as pale as—"

"It brought a lot back."

"Are you okay?"

"Sure. Fine." *Just pay attention to what's happening now. That was a long time ago and you weren't involved. You may have a few nightmares from Vietnam that you'll always live with, but you don't have to take this one in and add it to your collection.*

I said, "There are a lot of holes in this."

"We know there are a lot of holes in it. It's a good bet that the army has a hell of a lot more information than we do, but they didn't share anything at the time, and they still aren't."

Our eyes met.

I said, "Reading between the lines. It was a massacre."

"We don't know that."

"It was a massacre," I insisted.

"We don't know that," he repeated firmly, almost angrily.

"Is that why the Agency is involved? To find out, after all this time?"

Collie shook his head. "That's not our business."

"Why, then?"

"During the investigation of MIAs conducted by our people over there at the time—and since then—it became apparent that an inordinate number of cases developed on men who had been assigned to the units involved in this incident at Quang Xi. We know of twenty-seven cases of 'killed by friendly fire' or missing in action—and never accounted for—out of the relatively small number of troops on the ground in the zone when this took place."

"That's—" I began.

"In addition," Collie went on, "there have been a number of violent deaths like the Wentworth case. All of those that we know about—the missing ear et cetera—were men who served with Baker Company—this Captain Aldrich's command."

"My God, Collie!"

"It's hardly a high-priority item at this late date," he told me, "but some of those MIA files will never be satisfactorily finished unless we can get more information." He leaned back and reached for a cigarette. "And just between us girls, the army has stonewalled us ever since day one. I think the DCI is pissed."

"Maybe," I suggested, "the FBI is pissed, too."

He shrugged. "Could be. Some of these murders of veterans in more recent years have fallen on the Bureau's shoulders, and it hasn't made any progress on solving any of them as far as we can tell. Could be that they're wanting now to break this thing and make both us and the army look like bumblers."

"But where does Kevin fit into any of this?"

"Records indicate he was piloting one of the gunships stuck up on top of the scud during the final day's action."

"What does *that* prove?"

"You tell me, and we'll both know. All we know is that he was in the area—him and his copilot. He got shot down the same day, and was a POW. He was repatriated, but vanished in Hawaii. *Somebody*—whoever killed Wentworth—thinks he's still alive, and wants him, too. The Wentworth killing followed the pattern on victims from Baker Company. Beyond that, you tell me. Your guess is as good as anyone else's."

I thought about it, yearning for a smoke but trying to resist. Even a couple days of not smoking would get most of the nicotine out of my system and improve my wind for the tournament down in Kansas City. But the tournament seemed far away and irrelevant. My head was spinning with new information and questions.

Finally, however, all the questions boiled down to one.

"What do you want from me?" I asked.

Collie held up fingers as he counted off. "One. The Bureau is likely to ask you for additional information on the man who contacted you originally, or whatever. We hope you'll cooperate—and if you can get anything back, let us know."

"Fine."

"Two. We want to make sure you understand the length and extent of this conspiracy, or whatever you want to call it. You need to be aware that your own life might be in danger—I know, I know. The danger may be remote. But you ought to think about it."

I swallowed. "All right. I will."

Another finger went up. "Third. This man Mrs. Green told you about. The writer?"

"What about him?"

"If you should by chance decide—entirely on your own, you understand—to go visit him and ask some of the obvious questions—*if* you happened to do that, without encouragement from us, you understand—we would want a complete and immediate report on anything you might learn."

"I've got a tournament in Kansas City this week," I said.

He shrugged again, feigning an indifference I didn't believe for a minute.

"Is the Bureau going to be following me again?" I asked.

"We have no idea."

"What do you think the chances are that this murderer or murderers—whoever is involved in this shit—might take mighty offense at my having led their private snoop into an FBI trap?"

Collie's eyes took on their mercury opacity. "You mean, what are the chances somebody might come after you? It's possible."

"I feel very reassured by your definite answer, Collie."

Spots of color appeared in his cheeks. "It's the best I can do."

I hesitated, walked to the kitchen and poured more coffee, and went over all of it in my mind. I went back in and sat down again. "Okay."

He appeared startled. " 'Okay'? Just like that? No questions about how you're going to be paid, anything of that nature?"

"Let me counter with a question of my own," I retorted. "You think Kevin Green is out there somewhere, hiding?"

He thought about that. "If a man hadn't come to you with a picture that looked recent, and if he hadn't pumped you about Green's possible whereabouts, I probably would bet Green was long since dead and in a shallow grave someplace. But they—whoever—are still looking for him. Therefore, I tend to believe he's still alive and in hiding.

"Furthermore," he went on before I could respond, "if we could find him, he might be able to tell us what all of this has been about. That's a long shot, both finding him and getting all the answers from him. But it's an intriguing possibility."

"Okay, then," I repeated.

"Still no questions about the money?"

"Kevin was my best friend. That wife of his out there is one in a million, and she's still waiting. I'll play. I'll do what I can."

The telephone rang. I got up and went to answer it.

"Hi!" a bright and cheery female voice came back. *"This is Lynette. I'm up at the lodge. Can I come down and ask you a few questions?"*

Lynette Jordan was the bright, energetic young reporter for our local weekly newspaper. She had been a part-timer when I first met her, and then she had gone off to the big time in Denver for a year. Now she was back, having somehow raked up enough cash to buy herself a piece of the local press. She was actually starting to put some news in it, and not just public relations handouts and colorful reprints from a hundred years ago. I liked her a lot, but I instantly worried what this call might be about.

"I'm kind of busy right now, Lynette. What's on your mind?"

"Heckfire!" she trilled. (Lynette was one of a kind; she really did talk like that.) *"You're going off to Kansas City to play in that tournament, right? That's the biggest news we're likely to have for Friday's paper. I want to ask you how you've been training, what you think about meeting Borg again if you get to the semis, all that kind of good stuff!"*

I told Lynette to come on down. Collie got out of there with a few quick closing words, hurrying down the path away from the lodge just like the spook he was. I stood in the doorway of the cabin, waiting for Lynette, my mind teeming with problems that had just gotten more complicated.

Maybe somebody was going to come at me. I couldn't do anything about that. Maybe the FBI would send Reese McDonald or one of his clones back to talk to me again. I couldn't do anything about that, either. I had no way of knowing if the army had really sent people to talk to Barbara Green, any more than I could figure out who one of her other visitors had been, or how to locate him.

The name and address of Walter Newberry, free-lance writer, were the only concrete things I had to go on. Therefore—it now dawned on me—I really had only one fairly simple problem I could actually do anything about: how was I going to work out my schedule so I could get to Norman, Oklahoma, and meet this Walter Newberry?

Fifteen

Elsewhere

Washington: June 16

THE HALLS of the J. Edgar Hoover Building were quieter than usual, even for a Sunday afternoon. No outside sound penetrated the small meeting room on level 3.

Three persons sat at the meeting table. On one side was the deputy director, a graying, deceptively soft-faced black man of fifty-two named Ellis. Facing him sat two of his best in-house special agents: Miriam Gonzales, a tall, lean, handsome Hispanic woman of thirty-three, and Roger Magiris, a bulky white man of the same age who was her coworker on the case at Headquarters. Ellis appeared calm, almost austere, as he flipped through pages of the reports he had already studied in detail. The waxen expressions of both Gonzales and Magiris, with blank yellow legal tablets on the table in front of them, betrayed their tension.

Ellis finished his brief excursion back through the sheaf of documents and looked up at his two aides. "Anything in the last two hours?"

Gonzales cleared her throat. "No, sir."

"Romanowski is still stonewalling us?"

"He claims he never heard of Arnold Tubb, and he has no idea how those other names got in the address book we found hidden in the toolbox in the garage."

"We're still questioning him, of course?"

"Yes, sir. He's scared. But the Knoxville office is not optimistic about getting him to talk."

Ellis's lip quirked in an ironic almost-smile. "Instruct them to proceed tomorrow morning with filing of charges on the machine gun they found during the search. I know the damned thing wasn't in working order, and this Romanowski seems to be a legitimate small-time gun collector. But it was never registered for a federal permit, and that's all we need to hang onto him right now." Ellis turned to Magiris. "Now, what about those other names?"

Magiris moved his legal pad to reveal several small file cards with his neat block printing on them. "There's nothing on Arnold Tubb. We didn't miss him by much at the rooming house we located from the last number dialed on Romanowski's telephone."

"What about the manager of the place?"

"She's all right. Back at work. Five stitches, where he hit her with something."

"And your best judgment is that he's out of the Knoxville area by now?"

"Yes, sir. You know we found the manager's car abandoned not far away. The second car he stole, the Lincoln, has turned up in Nashville. We haven't sorted out all the stolen-car reports in the last twenty-four hours to get a list of what he might have stolen next, but we believe he's back on the road, fleeing to parts unknown."

A scowl knit Ellis's eyebrows. "The other names, then. What about them?"

Again Magiris glanced at his cards. "There were only four that checked out against our files. One of those, a man named Hempstead, died four years ago—suicide. No question it was a suicide. Like the others, he had a lengthy record of minor brushes with the law, and had been hospitalized twice before, following suicide attempts. He was injured in Vietnam, and chronically depressed—"

"If he's dead," Ellis cut in bluntly, "forget him. What about the others?"

"Maxwell, Jack J.," Magiris said, reading from a card. "Number checks to an address in Hays, Kansas. Vietnam, 1967 and 1968. Wounded, discharged 7 August '68. Five arrests in our files: assault on a police officer following a speeding ticket, 1969; suspected of grand theft, released for insufficient evidence, 1971; assault, 1974, served six months; armed robbery, 1975, served seven years, paroled 1982; assault with a deadly weapon, 1985, served four years, paroled 1989. Our file indicates chronic minor problems and nine separate admissions to VA facilities for treatment of psychiatric ailments in the same time period."

"Violent bastard," Ellis murmured.

Magiris looked up, surprised. "They all are, sir."

"Next?"

"Leventhal, Stanley. Ann Arbor, Michigan. Vietnam, same time period. Discharged July '68. Three arrests between February 1969 and March 1972, all assault cases. Hospitalized by the VA, June '72 through January '73. No record since that time. Currently a member of the faculty at Michigan."

"He was in the Americal, like the others?"

"Yes, sir."

"Go on."

"Turner, Raymond 'Buddy.' The telephone number traces to Omaha, and he's listed there in the current telephone directory. Duty in Vietnam in the same time period, discharged 12 December 1969. Thirteen arrests, ranging from assault to bogus checks, but most of them violent. No record of medical or psychiatric evaluation. He—"

"That's enough," Ellis cut in. "And that's the entire list?"

"Turner, Leventhal, and Maxwell. Yes, sir. Add subject Tubb, and you have the four names we've been able to come up with who might be a part in whatever conspiracy that Romanowski has been a part of."

"All are Vietnam veterans, the same era, and as far as we have been able to ascertain, all members of the same unit at one time."

"That's correct, sir."

Ellis glanced at his notes. "And the unsolved murders we've had over the years—the ones where an ear was missing—were all in the *same* unit."

"That's right, sir."

Ellis pulled out a handkerchief and polished his immaculate eyeglasses, held them up to the light of the overhead fluorescents, and put them back on. "Christ. No wonder the Pentagon is concerned about this character Tubb. We have some sort of organization of madmen here. They *must* be involved in those murders, including the one in Ohio last month." He paused and looked from one aide to the other. "What the hell is going on here?"

Neither Gonzales nor Magiris spoke.

Ellis sighed. "The army is still sending over requests for information on our bulletin *in re* Tubb?"

"Yes, sir," Gonzales replied. "Apparently they aren't aware yet of the Romanowski arrest. What do we tell them about that?"

Ellis snorted with surprise. "Tell them? We tell them nothing. We've never had a lick of cooperation out of those people on any of these murders. Whatever they know, they're stonewalling us as badly as Romanowski is down there in Knoxville. Whatever this is all about, the army doesn't want anybody to know anything. Well, that's fine. Two can play that game. The director says we develop our own investigation on this, and tell no one anything until it's all considerably clearer than it is now."

Ellis paused to glance at his notes. "I want the present domicile and location of subjects Turner, Maxwell, and Leventhal verified immediately. This is to be done without approaching them or any friend or associate. We will pick up all three of them the moment we have verification of whereabouts, but we don't want to move too fast and allow any of them to warn the others.

"Other aspects of the operation are to continue as reviewed and approved last night. Any questions? Good. Let's get cracking."

Hamilton, Montana

DARKNESS HAD come on and Jack Maxwell shivered as he climbed back into his car after gassing up at the convenience store. It was going to be a cold drive from here on, and his heater hadn't worked since the damned breakdown near Lima, Montana, had cost him precious hours.

The delay had practically driven him crazy. He had no time to waste. Having made his decision, he wanted it over, done with. Stress was making his mind act funny. *Have to do it, never thought it would come to this, won't ever be over. Too much risk, do it and run.* Then, instantly, he thought about Lieberman, his supervisor at work. Why did Lieberman always bring his lunch to the plant? Did he think it made everybody else look bad, that he never left his desk during lunch hour? Thoughts about the diner. Trudy was kind of cute. Fantasy about Trudy. The road. Why didn't they have a sign pointing to the resort? He had had trouble locating it the first time, when he had to come to question Smith, pretending to be army.

Army. Nam. *Cooper. Terwiliger. Irben. Dead. Shuppman with his legs blown off, screaming—"Hand me my leg, I want my leg back." They're going to get me, too. Going to get all of us. Which way is the hamlet? Lots of VC there.*

Gas prices. Higher again. Maybe get a new car. How? No money. What was Romanowski telling them? Too dark to see the mountains now. How did people live in mountains? How did they breathe when you couldn't see anywhere in any direction because the mountains stuck up? Tubb. Where was Tubb? Wish Tubb had never gotten out. Green. Green left. *I never wanted any of this, Mom. You used to make the greatest cookies.* He could taste the cookies. How much farther? Not far now. Concentrate. Try to think, keep your mind going in a straight line. You'll have to wait until later tonight. What day is this? Is this a workday?

Shivering, Maxwell reached across the seat to the small duffel beside him. His fingers found the hard weight of the gun. He was as ready as he would ever be.

He drove, funny shadows jumping in and out of the cone of headlight illumination on the two-lane road ahead.

Sixteen

June 17

IT TOOK a long time for the very small sounds at my cabin window to awaken me in the dead of night.

Almost too long.

I had given Lynette Jordan her interview about the tournament in Kansas City, then put on work clothes and hotfooted it down to the pool, where I found a sweating, profane Avery Whitney sitting on the damp concrete floor of the filter and heater building, the front of the 350,000 BTU heater unit pulled off and heater parts all around him. It took less than thirty minutes to determine that we needed to replace the thermocouple, but it required almost four hours to get everything else back together again and then reglue some of the PVC pipe fittings Avery had taken apart for no earthly reason.

Avery pronounced me a wizard, and said he would give me a stroke on the five-pars the next time we played just to demonstrate his admiration.

After that, a shower and change of clothes put me on our No. 1 court with Ted Treacher right after lunchtime. Ted gave me a good workout. Leg-weary from getting up and down two hundred times to crawl around in the pool equipment shack, I did not have my timing; the forehand drives went long or else slammed into the tape and fell back; the backhands, topspins and slices alike, flew all over the court instead of where I aimed them. When we walked off at four o'clock, I didn't feel like I had accomplished much of anything.

We walked back to the lodge together, talking about it, where we learned at the desk that Mr. McDonald, Reese, no middle initial, had called from Missoula to request another reservation. He would be in tonight, he had told our clerk.

"It looks like your lucky day," Ted told me with a slanted eyebrow.

"My cup runneth over," I said, and hurried down to the cabin to shower.

I tried not to think about Beth. I was still very angry, and thoughts about Linda kept intruding again. But the idea kept coming back that Beth could not be blamed for wanting to stay in southern California and advance her career. She could not be blamed because she hated my occasional work for the Company, because I had been on a job on St. Maarten when a madman came within a hair of killing her just because she was with me.

I could not blame her for anything. But I couldn't still my bitterness, either.

The late afternoon and evening went routinely, with no Reese McDonald. I felt curious about his motives for coming back here again. I also felt slightly irritated. I would accomplish nothing if he insisted on staying close to me. My tickets for a flight to Oklahoma City Monday afternoon were now waiting for me at the Missoula airport, and the last thing I wanted was company from McDonald.

We had a small dinner party for some of the new guests at eight o'clock. McDonald still hadn't shown up when it was over. I toodled down to the cabin shortly before eleven, thought about calling Beth—got angry with myself for trying to figure out a way to rationalize calling her—and hit the sheets at midnight.

Now, sleeping deeply, I became aware of the small sounds in the cabin, but not as noises external to the dream I started having to explain them. I was standing in a woodworking shop, and a man I didn't know was sawing at a board. He would saw a bit, then stop, frown, put down the saw, pick up a pry bar, and stick the point of it into the sawn crack, trying to split the wood apart. The saw made an odd, tiny whisking sound. The pry bar made a sound like something tinkling against metal.

He picked up his pry bar again and threw his weight against it, and it made a sharper, brighter noise.

Enough noise that I suddenly awoke with a hell of a start, sitting up in bed.

All my nerves yammered like banshees. My heart crashed around in my chest. Something primitive coiled and twisted inside me. The bedroom, as usual, was totally dark. Only the faint orange glow of my bedside alarm clock provided any orientation. The dial said it was ten minutes past three in the morning.

The sound came—a quick, sharp, *sliding sound*, stopped as abruptly as it began. Then came another noise: something creaking.

It came from the front of the cabin and I was hearing it through the doorway to the living room. Another flutter of noises, like muffled fingertips being drummed on a tabletop, isolated the source for me: my front window.

My bare feet hit the floor silently. Groping in the faint illumination provided by the clock dial, I slid the drawer of the bedside table open and got out the .38. I didn't hear anything more from the front of the cabin. I had left my slacks draped over a chair beside the nightstand. I pulled them on, straining all the while to hear another sound.

That was when it came: a quick little whispering sound of something rubbing on something else, no louder than the noise made when you slit an envelope open. But I recognized it and my sudden sweat felt cold: *the front window being slid upward—open—on its sash.*

I felt along the bedroom wall for the telephone extension, found it, picked it up, intending to dial the desk and holler for help. The line was dead.

In the living room, another mouse sound told me some-one was crawling through the window, or about to. I was beginning not to like this very much. My brain started going about a hundred miles an hour, which was not fast enough to keep up with how scared I was getting. The logical thing to do was to step into the living room, switch on the overhead light, and do a John Wayne yell to freeze, pardner, or die. The only problem with *that* was the location of the living room light switch on a different wall, inside the front door; and switching on the bedroom light might illuminate my visitor just fine, but it would also backlight *me*.

I peeped around the corner of the door into the living room. Like the inside of a film-developing bag in there. Another minute sound—shoe leather scraping on the floor, and the creak of the windowsill as weight bore down on it. My time to play Hamlet in this deal had just run out.

I counted to three, stepped into the living room black-ness, flattened myself against the wall, cocked the .38, and reached back behind me and around the corner to hit the bedroom light switch. It came on, throwing enough light into the living room to make my eyes shrink as it threw every-thing into sharp contrast.

Across the breadth of the room, he was half inside, half still out, one leg over the sill and on the floor inside, his torso stuck through and a bit tangled in the brown draperies. Shock twisted his face, but not so much that I couldn't instantly recognize my erstwhile friend from the army, the man who had called himself Frank Simmons. In the nanosec-ond before anything else happened, I registered his Levi's, boots, black sweater, black or navy wool cap, and smears of black gunk on his face like the commandos used to wear to keep white skin from shining in the dark during a raid.

"Hold it right there!" I bellowed, holding my .38 out in front of me and leveling it, hand-under-wrist, the way I had been taught once.

What I hadn't noticed was the pistol in his hand. Maybe

the draperies had hidden it. All I knew was that it appeared in a magic instant, there was a hell of an explosion and flash of light, something made a hot puff of air stab at my ear, and something bashed into the wall about an inch from my head. Pieces of wallboard bee-stung my face. I fired back, but reflex jerk-back from the near miss made my shot go high, shattering glass well above his head.

He threw himself back out through the pried window, vanishing. Without thinking about it, I ran to the door, pulled the chain lock out of its slot, whanged the living room light on, and ran out onto the pavement beside the cabin, feet hitting cold asphalt.

Mistake. Two more brilliant little flashes winked at me from the front corner of the cabin. Another wicked puff of concussive air told me one of the shots had come as close as the first one. I took a nosedive into the ground cover beyond the sidewalk and rolled over two or three times, coming up half under some spreading juniper and with my revolver aimed in the general direction of the last shots. I didn't see a thing. The gunshots had almost deafened me, but through the ringing I heard the sounds of somebody thrashing through the brush on the far side of the cabin.

Anyone in his right mind would have dug a hole or run for the boonies, but I wasn't thinking quite straight. My only thought was that he had damned near killed me, and now it sounded like he was getting away to try again. It sounded like he was heading off the right back of the cabin. So I scrambled to my feet and rushed around the left back side, around the woodpile, my bare feet paying a price in sharp rocks, stickers off pines, and God knows what all.

Reaching the far back corner of the cabin, I stopped, out of breath, listening. It dawned on me that he could be standing just beyond the log joints at the corner, waiting for me to poke my head around so he could blow it off. I couldn't hear a thing except my own breathing and heartbeat.

Some semblance of sanity leaked into my head. I hated to

think about his getting away to try another day, but I hated
worse to think I might make a mistake that would let him
finish the job instantaneously. I took a couple of steps back
from the corner, skulking into the deep black behind the
man-high stack of firewood. *Think it over. Wait. Be smart,
for once.*

No sound came through the woods. All I could hear was
the ringing in my own ears. From my hiding place I could see
the front door of my cabin, light spilling out onto the porch
and pavement. *Where the hell was he?*

Beginning to shake, I moved to my left behind the woodpile. The space between it and the far back corner of the
cabin lay in total blackness, but I knew no one was there
because I had just come from there. I waited again. Nothing.

The clearing around the cabin was very small. The first
couple of ponderosas stood faintly visible in the starlight
about ten feet from where I crouched. From behind the
ponderosas I could look down the other wall of the cabin.
Taking a deep breath, I ran for it.

Just as I got there, something moved *behind me*—coming
around the *other* side of the cabin. I hit the dirt again at the
same time I recognized the shape of a man darting into the
faint illumination thrown from the open front door. He froze
there, both arms extended as he pointed his gun, and the
thought went through my mind that I had royally screwed up
this time—he couldn't be expected to miss yet again, especially with me sprawled in the pine needles between ponderosas that didn't offer cover worth a damn.

I rolled anyway, really cornered now. Two more shots
banged in the dark. Not feeling a thing, I scrambled frantically behind the nearest ponderosa, which was only about six
inches in diameter and about as much help as an umbrella in
a tornado.

Something back there just beyond the woodpile hit the
ground. *What the hell?* Then I heard footsteps, running.

Another figure rushed into view. He had a gun in hand,

too. He hurried forward, bent down to examine something out of my sight behind the woodpile, then straightened up and looked directly my way, apparently unable to pick me out in the dimness.

"Mr. Smith?" the voice called hoarsely. Reese McDonald's voice.

Feeling a rush of hot weakness, I clambered to my feet and started forward. "Here," I croaked.

McDonald appeared out of the brush. His face shone pale under a dark stocking cap. He was wearing dark, heavy pants and jacket, and boots. He had what looked like a Browning pistol in his hand. His chest heaved like a bellows as I stumbled up to him.

"Are you all right?" he asked huskily.

"Did you have me staked out?" I asked, incredulous.

He pointed into the woods. "Bedroll back there. We feared something like this might occur."

"You were almost too late anyway."

His face tightened. "I fell asleep. Disgusting weakness."

I was shaking too badly to say anything clever.

Half turning, McDonald peered down again at whatever he had inspected behind the woodpile before calling my name.

I looked too. My friend "Frank Simmons" lay sprawled in the wood chips, staring fixedly up at the night sky. He looked surprised. Also dead.

"Oh dear," McDonald said softly. "It appears I have entirely vitiated a splendid opportunity for a potentially fruitful interrogation."

Seventeen

TED AND our night security man were the first ones on the scene, and Reese McDonald coolly ordered them to let no one down near the cabin. Ted wrung his hands about upset guests, and McDonald suggested a cover story saying a prison escapee had been apprehended and there was nothing whatsoever left to worry about. With a couple of additional lodge employees stationed on the sidewalk to make sure no curious visitors got close, Ted hurried back to the lodge to put on his no-problem act while McDonald called the undersheriff in Elk City and I fixed a stiff drink. Then McDonald gave me a lecture about being a foolhardy amateur who was lucky to be alive, etc.

By daylight the body had been taken away and McDonald had made some telephone calls full of cryptic yes-sirs and no-sirs and that-was-not-apparent-sirs. I had swollen feet from my running around outside, residual ringing in my ears, and the mother of all headaches.

McDonald duly noted my verification that the dead man was the one who had visited me before. Then he trotted off to his lodge room to make more calls and presumably get new instructions. When he came back in awhile, he said he was ordered to drive to Missoula and meet someone. He asked me my immediate plans and I told him I didn't have any. He "strongly advised" me to stay put until he returned.

Thirty minutes after he drove out of the driveway, I was packed and on my way to the airport for the afternoon flight to Oklahoma City. I had no idea why "Frank Simmons" had come back with the obvious intent of putting me six feet under. I didn't even know for sure if I was out of immediate danger. About all I really knew was that Walter Newberry, boy writer, had asked Barbara Green a lot of questions about Kevin and the units he served with. I wanted to know where he fit into all this, and I might never get another chance to visit him without someone like Reese McDonald tagging along.

It was just dusk, a red sunset flaring across an impossibly flat and distant horizon, when I drove into the city of Norman after landing at Oklahoma City's Will Rogers Airport and renting a compact car. The heat, humid and oppressive despite the lateness of the hour, reminded me of my former home place, Richardson, Texas. So did the traffic, much to my surprise, once I pulled off Interstate 35 and onto Norman's West Main Street. It had been a sleepy little college town when I visited it for a tennis match as a collegian. Now it seemed to sprawl all over the place, and the traffic hinted at a population that had outgrown its streets.

A stop at a convenience store got me directions to Newberry's neighborhood. A call confirmed that he was home. He sounded very surprised and nervous on the phone, and made it clear that we had nothing to talk about. I used the old salesman's trick of not letting him start listing all his reasons for not seeing me, and hung up after saying I was on the way out.

His address was on a curving street attached to another curving street that didn't seem to go anywhere in particular on Norman's near west side. His house turned out to be the smallest on the block, a modest brick-veneer ranch-style with a fine big pin oak in the front and mature abelia bushes that cut off all street view of the wide, useless, concrete-slab front porch. The lawn looked perfectly manicured in the last light of day. The house looked perfectly maintained. I walked up to the like-new front door in the light of a perfectly clean porch light, and pressed the door-chime button. The door opened and Newberry—no one else could be that tall—peered out at me through bottle-bottom eyeglasses. He looked perfect, too—baggy but clean Dockers, pale blue tee-shirt, polished old tan loafers, fresh shave, every hair on his bushy head brushed into submission.

"Mr. Smith," he said politely enough, eyeing me from his six-and-a-half-foot vantage point. "I've followed your tennis forever, and it's a great honor. But I really think you've wasted your time, sir, if you want to talk about that Vietnam book."

"I won't take more than five or ten minutes," I told him. I added, "I would really appreciate it. I've flown in from Denver just to meet you."

His eyebrows almost knit in a quick, worried frown. But then his long, heavy jaw quirked into a quick smile. "I guess if the famous Brad Smith comes to *my* door, I would be an idiot not to take advantage of the chance to visit with him." He swung the screen door open, letting cool air-conditioning gush out. "Come on in, sir." He offered a curiously mis-shapen hand half the size of an old-time racket. "It's a pleasure."

He had a strong handshake, and he had a nice home, larger than it appeared on the outside, furnished in old but beautifully maintained traditional furniture. He led me past a small living room that looked never used, past a doorway into a dimly lighted kitchen, and into a dark-paneled fire-place room at the back. A TV set, muted, glowed in one corner. Bookshelves covered one entire long wall, and over the fireplace hung a framed linen-print layout map of Wim-bledon. I spotted a cased Prince racket leaning against the wall near a sliding glass door to the backyard, and began to feel more at ease. If he was a tennis nut, I might be able to take advantage of that.

Newberry, towering over everything, pointed to one of

the chairs flanking the closed, dark fireplace. "Sit down, Mr. Smith. Can I offer you a drink?"

I was surprised by his courtesy after he had obviously not wanted to see me at all. I told him, "Thanks, but I'll be here only a few minutes."

He sat facing me, long legs all over the place, and leaned forward with another of those quick, tight, driven frowns. "I would like to talk tennis, but I already know that's not why you're here."

"In a way it is," I said.

"Oh? How is that?"

"A few months ago you interviewed the wife . . . or widow . . . of one of the best friends I ever had. His name was Kevin Green."

Newberry rocked back in his chair, nodding with recognition. "Of course! So that's how you got my name and heard about that book project. Mrs. Green. In Los Angeles." The frown of concentration returned. "But I don't remember anything about her husband. And that interview was for the book project I've since abandoned, as I said on the telephone."

"Why did you abandon it?"

He looked briefly down at big hands interlocked between his jutting knees. "I couldn't get the project off the ground. The required research effort was . . . too much. It became . . . overwhelming. I decided to turn my hand to something quicker and easier."

"Mr. Newberry—"

"Call me Walt."

"Okay, then. Walt, pardon me for being blunt, but you don't strike me as the kind of man who would ever quit a project once it was under way. Those earlier books you've published must have been hard, too."

His quick grin came and went, and back in place went the scowl of worried concentration. "Thanks, I think. But that's the truth. It just got too hard. There was too much opposition, too much trouble. I hate to quit on a project. You're right about that. But there are limits."

He was holding something back. I decided I liked him, and felt he was a man who could be trusted. Sometimes— God knows—my instincts play me false, as with the lying Frank Simmons, he of the telephone bug. But I felt surer of Walt Newberry, and I had to take the chance anyway.

I said, "Somebody came to see me a few weeks ago, asking about Kevin. I guess you know we were in college together before Vietnam?"

"Yes. Of course. But he was a pilot over there. I believe you were a grunt."

"So you remember some things about Kevin after all," I said.

He looked embarrassed by the slip. "Oops."

"I'm going to level with you," I said. "I think Kevin is still alive someplace in this country."

Newberry tried to act surprised, but he failed miserably. "Why would you say that?" he asked, his voice weak.

I had to risk it. I told him about the visit from the alleged Frank Simmons, the telephone device, and my trip to see Barbara Green. I left out Dave Wentworth and a lot of the rest of it, but I told him I knew something about Quang Xi and what had happened there. When I mentioned Quang Xi, he went quite pale.

"I don't know anything about any of that," he cut in sharply. "I can't help you at all. I've completely abandoned that project. I'm working on something about the Gulf War now." He spread big, crooked hands and gave me a wan smile. "It's a much more popular war anyway."

"When this man Simmons came to me," I said, "he was looking for a way to track down Kevin. I know a few other things, and they tell me that somebody is going to keep on tracking Kevin until they find him. I know that when they find him, unless I can find him first and/or learn what the hell this is all about it—help shut it down once and for all—Kevin is going to be killed." I paused, watching him closely, and let that soak in. Then I added, "And one of his ears cut off."

You would have thought somebody had hit Newberry flush on the mouth. The violence of his startled jerk backward made his chair groan loudly in protest.

I didn't give him time to regather himself. "If you know anything that might help me, give it to me now. I don't have time to play games."

Newberry stared at me. His eyes, gigantic behind the thick glasses, looked very, very scared. When he spoke, his voice had shrunk to a hoarse whisper. "I'm not working on it anymore. I told you that."

"Files. You must have some files. You must be able to shed some light on some of this."

He got abruptly to his feet, making the chair rock. "Come this way."

Puzzled, I followed him out of the fireplace room and down a short hall evidently leading to bedrooms. He turned into the first door and flicked on the overhead light before I could enter behind him.

It was an office room—his writing office, with more bookshelves, a very old rolltop desk, two utilitarian four-drawer filing cabinets, and two flat worktables with computer equipment and printers all over them. It was fine computer equipment, state-of-the-art. Papers strewn everywhere showed he was working on some book project, if not the one I had hoped for.

He crossed the office to the filing cabinets, opened a drawer, fingered through folders, found one, pulled it out, and handed it to me. "Look."

I opened the folder. Inside were a half dozen color photographs of this very room—but a room in a very different state. The pictures showed it *wrecked*—drawers pulled out of the filing cabinets and dumped on the floor, the rolltop drawers also out and dumped, computer equipment tossed aside and smashed. Nothing had been left intact. Even the pictures on the walls had been pulled down and broken, tossed against the bookcases, which had been stripped of their neat rows of research books.

The photos showed complete devastation.

"Did kids break in and trash it all for no reason?" I asked, already guessing otherwise.

Newberry's jaw twitched again into a quick smile that had no pleasure in it. "No. It wasn't kids."

"Did you catch—"

"No. No one was caught. I know because I was broken into twice. This was the second. The first was a burglary— some files taken, a few things messed up, but nothing like this. *This* visit, the second one, was designed to make sure I dropped the project."

"How do you know that?" I demanded. "It looks to me like this ransacking was just like the other one, only worse."

"I know," Newberry said in a tone that chilled me, "because the other burglary happened while I was out of town. This one took place while I was home."

"Here? You mean you were in the house when it happened?"

"They came in through the back patio doors. I heard them. I started to dial 911, but somebody came up behind me—put a rag over my face. Chloroform, or something like it. Then they wrecked my office, destroyed everything."

"But I still—"

"When I woke up," Newberry added before I could form the question, "they had things as you see in the picture. They had also left me another form of warning." He held up his large hands with the strangely gnarling, crooked fingers. "They broke these."

"Oh, Christ," I mumbled.

"They're getting better now. But I still face one or two more surgical procedures on them."

"*Why?*" I asked, revolted. "What did you have? What were you onto?"

He took the folder back from me, replaced it in the cabinet, closed the drawer, turned back to face me. I saw how more than his hands had been broken.

He said, "I know your name was prominent in some of the notes I took from my talk with Mrs. Green. She talked a lot about how you and her husband were best friends once—even met in Vietnam. Maybe that's how somebody got your name and knew to visit you, from my stolen files. But I don't know what I had that threatened them so badly. And that is the honest-to-God truth, Mr. Smith. But I do know I'm not tired of living."

He paused and sucked in a long, ragged breath that made his whole skinny upper body shake. "What records and floppy disks they didn't destroy, I took out into the backyard and burned in a trash can. Everything—because, you see, I had no idea what might be dangerous and what might not. I gave in. They beat me. I quit. And Mr. Smith, this is the truth. *I don't to this day have any clear idea of what I had.* But I'm never going to look into anything relating to Quang Xi or anything else about *any* of those military units, ever. And I'm sorry, but I don't want to talk to you anymore about it, either. I truly do not know anything. And they might find out about your visit and come back to visit me again."

I had no idea what to say. I felt intensely sorry for him, and even angrier at these faceless bastards who did things like this.

He said, "I'm sorry. But that's the truth."

I hid my disappointment. He had been my next-to-last hope, and my only other clue was so slender that it bordered on the impossible—those casual remarks Barbara Green had made about Kevin speaking of a favorite place near a mountain named Slumgullion. No such mountain was listed in my cabin bookshelf map book. In my interview with Lynette Jordan, I had asked her to look through her reference books at the office to see if she could turn up anything, not explaining why I asked. She had promised. But there are a million mountains, and many of them aren't called their proper name by locals living near to them. Maybe my last real chance had just died.

But I couldn't dwell on that now. There stood the slope-shouldered, sad-faced, skinny giant of a man who had just admitted to me that he had been scared off a project once obviously close to his heart. For a person like him, admission of any weakness was like revealing a cancer. I felt sorry for him. He looked so sad I felt I had to say something positive. "It probably doesn't matter," I said.

His eyes behind the bottle bottoms swung sharply to my face, and the bitterness—for just an instant—flared. "No. It matters. A lot. But I'm a coward."

"You're not a coward, man."

He actually flinched as if I had struck him. I saw that if he said anything else, it would only be to protest that he *was* a coward—that he had fallen miles short of his impossibly high expectations of himself. I hoped he wouldn't do it.

He didn't.

Swallowing, he said, "Well." Then he stopped right there.

He had said it all. The men who had broken into his home, wrecked his office, and broken his hands had defeated him. Maybe he would get over it one day. I hoped so. But only some do. Some carry the unhealed broken bits of themselves around inside until they die.

A few minutes later, I left. Newberry's final words to me were a wistful wish that we might have met under other circumstances—that he might have rounded up his usual tennis partners for a doubles game, and walk onto the court and introduce me as his playing partner for the day. We chuckled together about that. I put my hand on his shoulder and told him if I was ever back this way, we might do it yet.

The last I saw of him, he was still standing in his lighted doorway, waving goodbye. I wished I had time to stay a day and go to some court someplace with him and rally, at least—give him that. But maybe he would not have been able yet to grip a racket properly with those mangled hands they had given him.

Eighteen
Elsewhere

The Pentagon: June 19

THE TWO-STAR general, whose name was Simon Gilette, looked up from his desk at the sound of a discreet tap on his heavy office door. "Come."

His secretary looked in. "Sir, Colonel Hunt and Major Briggs are here."

"Send them in."

Col. William Hunt and Maj. Steven Briggs, stiff and obviously under pressure, came in and snapped to in front of the general's desk, giving him brisk salutes. It showed unusual in-office formality, but the situation was not normal. As Hunt had told Briggs only a minute or two before, "Old Razorblades is pissed. We don't have the right answers for him. If we can't calm him down somehow, both of us might be on our way to Saudi again."

General Gilette returned the salute, his pale eyes bellicose under a shelf of bushy gray eyebrows. "Sit down, gentlemen. What do you have for me?"

"Good news, General," Colonel Hunt said with phony enthusiasm. "The FBI has promised us a complete report explaining why they issued that new wanted notice on Arnold Tubb."

The general's hands formed fists on the desktop. His one-word question dripped venomous impatience: "When?"

"Soon, sir."

"*Soon?* What the hell does that mean? *How* soon?"

Perspiration gleamed on Colonel Hunt's forehead. "The

wording of the memorandum actually said 'as events warrant,' sir."

One of the general's fists hammered the top of his desk like a gunshot. "As events warrant? As events warrant? What does that mean? On what basis did they say this man Tubb was in the Knoxville area? On what basis did they say he is presumed departed from that area? What happened down there in Knoxville that we don't seem to know a goddamned thing about?"

"Sir, we don't know."

"Colonel, we've had a dangerous psycho running around loose since last Christmas. *Since last Christmas!* Why haven't we made any headway on recapturing this man?"

"Sir," Colonel Hunt said huskily, "we just aren't set up for this kind of thing. Our usual—"

"I don't give a flying rat's ass about 'the usual'! Gentlemen, this man Tubb must be half-dead from his cancer by now! He isn't invisible! We have every reason to suspect he was involved in that murder in Ohio. Why aren't we doing anything? Do you have any goddamned idea how much pressure this office is receiving from the secretary about this situation?"

The younger officer, Major Briggs, a few freckles shining through his nervous pallor, spoke up. "Sir, there's no reason to believe that Tubb or any person possibly hiding him would have anything whatsoever to gain by going public with details of anything that happened back at Quang Xi. And, as you said, his cancer must be far advanced by now—he can't possibly live much longer. If we're looking for a silver lining—"

Wham!, the fist hit the desktop again, making both officers flinch. "Silver lining?" the general yelled. "Fuck the silver lining! Gentlemen, I've got to go up and give the secretary a report on this situation this afternoon! What am I supposed to tell him? That we haven't accomplished a goddamned thing and we're all a bunch of goddamned stupid assholes, but he should look for a goddamned silver lining?"

Neither Colonel Hunt nor Major Briggs moved a muscle. They sat ramrod-straight like wax dummies in a military museum: "*Army officer's uniform, early 1990s. Note service medals and commendation ribbons. In the period portrayed in this exhibit, more than 30% of the army's active duty officer corps was involuntarily returned to civilian life under a budget-dictated reduction in force, or RIF.*"

Into the vast silence following General Gilette's outburst, Colonel Hunt finally spoke. "Sir, it's clear that the Bureau is playing it close to the vest on this matter. We don't think they're giving us anything like complete disclosure. Our analysis is that they're onto a lead, and hope to bring this entire matter to a conclusion, then issue their report directly to the White House, thus scoring valuable points with the President and leaving us in a bad light."

"Thank you, Colonel, for that penetrating observation," the general said in a tone dripping scorn. "Now, please allow me to point out something to you. If the FBI finds Arnold Tubb and his coconspirators, and cracks this thing we've been trying to unravel for fifteen years, it's going to leak to the press. I guarantee it's going to leak to the press. Then we're going to have shades of MyLai all over again. Some people—some very important people in very high places—are going to start asking why the army covered it up for more than twenty years.

"The commanders who saw this thing all the way back in 1968, and decided that nothing would be gained by attempting prosecution at that time, are no longer here. Their judgment might have been faulty, but let me repeat: they are no longer here. We *are* here. We're the ones who will bear the burden if this ever comes out at this late date. The army that fought in Vietnam won't have to send spokesmen up to the Hill to sweat in front of a bunch of liberal naysayers who are always looking for new excuses to trim our budget. *We'll* be the ones who have to go into the meat grinder.

"Right or wrong, gentlemen, the decision was made long ago. If we don't get to the bottom of this now, before the FBI does, it's today's army that's going to be dragged through the mud. Do you *possibly* begin to see why some of us are upset about our failure to accomplish a goddamned thing right now?"

"Sir," Colonel Hunt said, "we've moved some personnel. Files are being screened. The plan to investigate every known associate of Tubb, and every VA-documented case of post-traumatic stress disorder, is going forward."

"Splendid," General Gilette snapped. "Following up on every case of posttraumatic stress that came out of Nam shouldn't take us more than twenty or thirty years, right?"

"Sir—"

"Let me outline for you what I plan to tell the secretary. I'm going to tell him that we have assigned additional personnel to the search for Tubb. I'm going to tell him we have under way a complete rundown on every surviving veteran from Baker Company's 2nd and 3rd. I'm going to tell him the incident of 6 April '68 is *not* going to come out. I'm going to tell him we're making good progress. I'm going to tell him we don't have any idea how Tubb or some of his cohorts got that data listing this tennis bum named Smith as a source of possible information on Wentworth and Green. I'm going to tell him it's obvious Smith doesn't know shit from apple-sauce about any of the true facts, and we intend to keep it that way."

The general paused and pointed a finger. "I'm going to tell him, gentlemen, that this is Wednesday and we'll have a progress report, signed by you two officers, by fifteen hundred hours on Friday. I'm going to tell him that *progress will be made by that time.*

"Gentlemen, don't make me a liar. I want results. Dismissed."

Washington

SEATED AT his desk in the J. Edgar Hoover Building, Deputy Director Ellis scanned the latest information. "This is splendid," he said.

Standing before him, Miriam Gonzales allowed herself a thin smile. "Yes, sir. There's no doubt that Maxwell's death out in Montana tends to verify the short list we still have going."

"This special agent McDonald. Too bad he couldn't take Maxwell alive, but judging by his report there was no chance of that. He has his new orders to remain with Brad Smith?"

"Yes, sir. Unfortunately, Smith went off on some excursion of his own yesterday while McDonald was in Missoula for debriefing and instructions. But he says Smith has agreed to take part in a tournament in Kansas City starting tomorrow, and he anticipates picking him up again there, if he has not already done so by this time."

"All right. Ask Mary to come in when you leave. I'm going to dictate a letter of commendation for McDonald's file. Meanwhile, where are we on our remaining suspects?"

"We have just two names left besides Tubb, sir. One is Raymond 'Buddy' Turner, in Omaha, and the other is this man Leventhal in Ann Arbor."

"I want both of them picked up no later than tomorrow noon. Coordinated moves, same time both places, or as close as possible. I don't want one of them to hear the other has been taken into custody, and run for it."

Gonzales nodded and made a note. "Now that Romanowski has started talking down in Knoxville, there may be more names."

"If there are," Ellis said, "we'll grab them, too." He heaved an expansive sigh. "I think we're very close to having all of this story, Miriam. The director is going to be extremely pleased."

"Sir, there is the ongoing problem with the army. There

have been two more official inquiries this morning already."

Ellis glowered. "For years we've tried to figure out the background for these seemingly random, senseless murders. The army has stonewalled us every step of the way. Well, now it's their turn to be stonewalled."

"Continue to tell them nothing, in other words?"

"Tell them," Ellis replied, "that we'll write when we have news."

Gonzales giggled before she could control herself. Deputy Director Ellis winked, held his nose with one hand, and held up the other like a drowning man. Then they both began laughing. This was going to be an FBI coup of the first order, and the fact that it was coming at the expense of the Pentagon only made it richer.

Langley, Virginia

COLLIE DAVIS and J. C. Kinkaid ran into each other in a Headquarters corridor.

"I guess Brad Smith is in Kansas City for that tournament?" Kinkaid asked.

"If not," Davis replied, "he must be on the way."

"Suppose the FBI will catch up with him there?"

"Probably. They know his playing schedule, and they aren't likely to underestimate him again and just assume he'll be a good boy because Reese McDonald said so."

"That was pretty neat, the way he went down to Oklahoma and checked that writer out without McDonald knowing anything about it."

Davis smiled. "Brad does something smart every once in awhile. But they'll watch him closer now."

"Some of that information in the report he sent you on what happened to Newberry was dynamite. It makes some things clearer."

"Too bad we don't have more information on the original incident."

"Well, you can thank the army for keeping us in the dark."

Collie Davis's smile was without humor. "It would be funny if Brad actually figured out a way to locate Green, wouldn't it?"

Kinkaid thought about it. "I suppose stranger things have happened."

"You would not exactly hear me weeping if he did. Maybe Green is the only man alive who could actually tell us what we don't know about Quang Xi, and all that crap that followed."

Ann Arbor, Michigan

EARLY EVENING twilight grayed the home office windows of Stan Leventhal, Ph.D. Under the bright yellow light of an old-fashioned lamp on the corner of his rolltop desk, Leventhal, forty-seven, pored over the working draft of a graduate student dissertation.

The page in front of Leventhal looked bloody with red ballpoint amendations and sarcastic questions scrawled savagely in the margins. Leventhal, known and feared in the history department as an uncompromising perfectionist, invariably lost his temper when confronted with shoddy scholarship like the work now in front of him. Leventhal was not the chairman of this student's committee, and his anger at the student's sloppy research and execrable logic extended also to his departmental colleague who chaired this committee and had pronounced this draft good enough to be circulated to other faculty members on the student's committee.

The student, Leventhal knew, expected to complete his dissertation and his orals this summer. There was absolutely no chance; Leventhal would block him until hell froze over, if necessary, to make him get this right.

Leventhal flipped a Xerox page, reaching the last in the

chapter on frontier attitudes toward Native Americans as revealed in the local press. His old-fashioned desk lamp gleamed on his balding forehead, glistening with a film of sweat. Tall, thickening, with his remaining black hair allowed to grow to collar length, he looked like a man who tried to live his academic specialty, the culture of the American frontier West. A wide black mustache with curving, upturned ends slashed across the middle of his face like a fence erected to separate his thick, coarse mouth from eyes that often looked driven and even haunted behind Benjamin Franklin glasses perched on the end of a bulbous nose. He was wearing Levi's, pants and jacket, and old boots. Some said that Leventhal had never quite stopped playing cowboy. But no one had ever said that to his face.

After a moment's thought, he scrawled one final note on the black bottom half of Chapter Four's last page: *Shallow nonsense. Not an original idea or insight anywhere. This chapt should be trashed and started over.*

As his pen stopped moving, a sound in the doorway of his small office room caused him to turn. His wife, wearing a pretty summer dress, heels, and a light sweater tossed over her shoulders, gave him a small wave of her hand. Five years younger than her husband, she was a pretty woman with fine, intelligent features, short-cropped dark hair, and a body she worked hard to keep in shape. There were more lines around her eyes and mouth than there should have been.

"I'm off," she said without expression.

"Be careful," Leventhal said, and started to turn back to his work.

"You're sure you don't want to go along?"

Leventhal swung his chair around to face her again. The irritation crackled in his voice. "I told you, Doreen. I've got all this work to do."

Pain moved behind her eyes. "It *is* summer term, Stan. You're supposed to be off this summer."

He looked at her with cold contempt, and said nothing.

She said quietly, "Becky will be disappointed. It isn't every day a granddaughter has her first birthday."

"My heart bleeds, Doreen. Go. Let me get back to my work."

For an instant Doreen Leventhal looked like he had slapped her. Then her expression went flat—dead. "I'll be back by ten."

Leventhal had already spun his chair back around and was reading another page. "Whatever," he said automatically, no longer really conscious she existed.

Some part of him heard the overhead garage door open, her car start and back out, the door close again. If he felt anything, it was relief to have his wife out of the house—to have no one asking anything of him. He knew he was a drone, cheerless, incapable of feeling much emotion of any kind, and he was aware that his marriage had become a barren cheerless tomb. He had tried for a very long time to explain to his family why he could not feel things the way he once had, and why he stayed inside himself. But they had never understood and he had finally given up. He had not mentioned it to anyone for years, and would never mention it to anyone again. He was functioning, teaching his classes, reading, watching TV. He felt no hope of ever doing more or feeling more.

Leventhal felt lucky to be able to function at all. The call last January, insisting that he be the one to go out and try to pry new information out of Kevin Green's widow, had been a terrible jolt after so many years of silence. He had imagined the group no longer existed—and then that call.

He had not wanted to do it. The veiled threats had made him do it. But he had made it clear that it was his last act for the old group. He had washed his hands of the whole affair.

The call the other day, however, had made all his nerves tighten painfully again. People were actually getting picked up—interrogated. He felt panic dancing in his nervous system. *Am I next? Do they have my name?*

But he had begun to feel slightly calmer about that. Mike had been true to his word—hadn't told anyone anything. Leventhal was in the clear. With any luck at all, he would never be identified as one of the old group.

He needed to work in order to keep his mind off the worry.

More pages of the would-be dissertation moved through his hands, more sarcasms and criticisms scrawled in the margins. Leventhal lost track of time.

The door chimes startled him. He felt a gust of fear. Was it them? Men come to arrest him—question him about all the things that had gone on over the years?

Shaking inside, he hurried through the quiet, unlived-in neatness of the living room, reached the front door, turned on the porch light, and swung the inside door open.

The man standing there was short, pale, almost hairless, slouched inside a lightweight jacket and trousers that looked far too big for him. Leventhal knew him instantly.

"Hello, Stan," the man said.

Leventhal recognized him. Something broke in Leventhal's brain. Reality changed. Snapshots kerchunged through his consciousness, freezing him back there again in splinters of time:

A dirt road. Smoke all around. Rossiter grabbing a kid—a small girl—by her hair and swinging her around. Awkwardly holding his M-16, shoving the muzzle into the girl's face. Blast. Blood and bone fragments flying everywhere.

Click.

Jacobsen and Irving bringing Morosco in. Morosco screaming in spite of the morphine or whatever, big white tourniquet wrapped tight around his upper thigh, only hanging shreds of cloth and flesh from the knee down.

Click.

Orientation lecture. Lieutenant standing up there behind a lectern, nervous and sweating, pipsqueaky voice:

"Men, remember what we are fighting for here. Always treat a prisoner humanely. Always be alert, but remember that innocent life must always be respected."

Click.

Jesus Christ! Helicopter right on fucking top of us! Explosions, concussion deafness, dirt flying, pieces of guys flying—

"It's me, Stan," the small man on the porch said. "Tubb. Arnie Tubb."

Leventhal had to swallow twice before he could speak. "What are you doing here? I told you! I'm through!"

"You've got to help me," Tubb said. "I'm broke. They're after me. We've got to get to Montana and talk to that guy Smith. He's our only hope. He knew where Wentworth was. He has to know where Green is, too. We've got to get to him there—make him talk." Tubb paused, hearing something in the darkness that no one else could hear. His eyes rolled with fear. "Let me in. Let me come in!"

Reality clicked in and out for Leventhal another few seconds. It was all smoke and terror in his brain. Then he came back, and Tubb was still standing there.

You could not turn your back on a man who had been there with you.

"Come in," Leventhal said, looking worriedly out into the dark. "Hurry."

Nineteen

June 20

An early flight from Oklahoma City to Kansas City Wednesday allowed plenty of time for checking in with the tournament sponsors and finding an old friend, Marv Fleck, to work out with later in the day. The things I had learned from Walt Newberry left me no closer to Kevin Green, and beyond the tournament starting on Thursday, I had no idea what my next step—if any—might be.

With all the top-echelon players in Great Britain for Wimbledon, I had hopes of struggling through a weak field at Kansas City and picking up a nice piece of badly needed change. As luck would have it, however, the area caught one of those early-summer high-pressure systems that can turn normal temperatures into a bake oven there, and my opening-round tournament draw on Thursday afternoon turned out to be a red-haired kid from Abilene with all kinds of ambitions that would be greatly facilitated if he could beat my butt off.

He started out like he was going to do just that.

With about 3,000 people scattered around the 7,500-seat stadium, Marshal—that was his name—opened with an ace and then won his first service at love with another. Maybe my mind wasn't in it. I started with a double fault, saved one break point, and then lost the next one to go down 0–2 before I had a good sweat up.

My knee felt good. Despite missing most of the practice I had originally projected for this event, I felt reasonably sharp. The sun, hot in a cloudless sky, beat down on my back.

More heat radiated up into my face from the pale green concrete court. Not a breath of air moved down here at the bottom of the bowl. I envied the man in the chair, with his nice dark umbrella for shade.

Marshal tossed the ball up for the first point of the third game, and here it came, a blur, wide into the alley. Didn't expect that—lunge, miss. His third ace. Some crowd roar of approval. I walked over toward the ad court and heard a single male voice stick itself out of the general noise: *"Wake up, Smith! We paid money for this!"*

That woke me up a little. I wasn't accustomed to people thinking I might be asleep at the switch, or dogging it. It was a point of pride. Whatever they said about me, they never said I dogged it. The lone, derisive voice stirred my juices a little—helped me start to focus.

Take a few seconds more to organize, Smith. Signal for a towel, wipe your face and arms, wipe the handle of this nice new widebody composite, toss the towel back to the kid, get into position. *Move your feet, move your feet.* Ready. On the far side, the kid tossed the ball high and slammed a bullet—wide again, backhand—I lunged but knew I wouldn't get it.

The ball made a yellow blur as it hit the line beyond my frantic reach.

"Out!" the linesman yelped.

I breathed. Bad call. Thank you, God.

Marshal looked over at the linesman—a kid little older than he was—with disbelief. "Out? Did you call that serve *out?*" His voice went up several decibels. "How could you call that serve *out?*"

The linesman stared straight ahead, trying to act detached the way he was supposed to, but his sunburned face got a little darker. A few ragged whistles of disapproval came from the stands.

Marshal, possibly hearing the whistles as directed at him—and maybe some of them were—whirled and started upcourt toward our umpire. "Are you going to overrule that chickenshit call?"

The umpire, a man who had been in the chair at other small matches I had played in the past, was good at his job. Beefy-faced and impassive behind aviator-style sunglasses, he pushed his PA mike aside and leaned over toward the kid, who had now reached a position just below him. "The call was 'out.' I agree with the call. Play."

Marshal put his hands on his hips and didn't budge. "The goddamned ball was clearly in! It was *in!* What is this? Some kind of Medicaid for the old guy over there?"

The whistling intensified, and individual voices started coming clearly out of the stands, telling him to get on with it, to quiet bellyaching, and so on. People in a crowd don't realize how the players can pick out individual voices. I don't know why some of them carry over the general hubbub, but they do. The noise can be so loud that it feels like waves rolling down over you; you can think your hearing has been numbed by all of it, and all you can hear is the pinging beat of your own pulse in your ears; then individual voices will come through loud and clear out of the general commotion, as if carried on a special wavelength:

"Grow up, Marshal!"

"You can do it, Smith!"

"Get back and serve! Get back and serve!"

"Shut up and play, you turkey!"

"Wake up, Smith!"

Marshal heard some of them, too, and started really losing it. "I demand you overrule the linesman!" he yelled up at the chair.

"The call stands. Play."

"I demand a new linesman!"

The umpire, whose name was Carmichael, leaned farther over the side. "The call was 'out.' The ball was out. Are you demanding we replace the linesman on that side?"

"Absolutely! Maybe you can find somebody that isn't going to give everything to grampa over there!"

There was some further discussion—if you can call quiet rationality on one side and a temper tantrum on the other "discussion"—and the crowd began to get into a real uproar. I walked to the back and toweled off again, pretending nonchalant indifference to the whole thing.

Since arriving here, despite my best efforts, I had been plagued by the recurrent thought that maybe I had just played my last card, and the search for Kevin was over. All I had left was the chance remark Barbara had made about a Slumgullion Mountain somewhere. I would call Lynette Jordon back in Elk City later today and hope she had come up with something through her newspaper files. But even if she chanced to find a mountain by that name, and could tell me where it was, there was only a slim chance that Kevin would be there. I was grasping at straws. It didn't feel good at all.

Given all that, my concentration for this match had been pitiful. But I had done a lot of shuttling around the country in the past couple of weeks, and given the price of airline fares today, my anemic checking account was going to need a major transfusion before the American Express statement arrived in another two weeks. Lose your first match in this little tournament, travel money and $2,000. Not enough. Win one match, travel money and $5,500. Better. Win two matches to reach the semis, and you were guaranteed winnings of $12,000. That would be getting somewhere.

I needed this match, and preferably the next one as well. I had to use this opportunity provided by Marshal's continuing tantrum to regroup and get my head on straight. I watched him, focusing.

He kept stomping around, yelling insults up at the chair. Finally the umpire had had enough. Unstrapping himself, he climbed ponderously down out of the chair, walked to the far end of the court, and leaned over a box railing to confer with a local bigwig named Adams, chairman of the tournament committee. I paced up and down my end, head down, still trying to psych myself up.

After more minutes, more complaining and conferring and whistling, a new linesman was trotted out and replaced the young man who had made the bad call; the young guy did a valiant job of maintaining his dignity as he walked off the court and out through the stadium door to the lockers.

The umpire climbed back up into the shade of his big umbrella. "Gentlemen? Ready? Resume play." He gave Marshal a long look through his dark glasses and then leaned closer to the PA mike. His voice echoed around the stadium, which had started to fill up. "Mr. Marshal leads Mr. Smith in the first set, two games to love. The score in this game, with Mr. Marshal serving, is fifteen-love. Second service. Play."

The kid got two balls from the ballboy at that end and came back to the service line. Glaring over at me, he bounced one of the balls several times. Sweat dripped off the tip of his nose. He looked up, looked down, bounced the ball four more times. He seemed to be having some kind of mental difficulty. It suddenly occurred to me that the delay might have cost him a lot more in terms of concentration than it had me. Suddenly I started to feel better.

He served a weak, looping second serve, and I got around on it, drilling it straight up the line for a winner. The crowd, definitely favoring me after Marshal's outburst, roared approval. I saw the fleeting expression of angry frustration on Marshal's face as he walked to the deuce side again. I detected a faint feeling of confidence in myself.

His next serve, at 15 all, came up the middle, and it was smoking. I stabbed and somehow got my racket in front of it, blocking it back deep and to his left. It caught him halfway in—no-man's-land—and he started to fling out a desperation backhand volley, then made the nanosecond decision to let it go because it might be out. It wasn't, hitting two inches inside the back line. The crowd noise came down on us with a *whump*. The kid looked up to heaven like he couldn't believe all this bad luck.

Back on the ad side again, he double-faulted, and all of a sudden I had him 15–40, two break points. The crowd noise began to become a felt presence that was in some other dimension, and my vision became so clear that it felt like I was seeing everything through a magic lens that magnified sight and slowed time.

Marshal had been coached some time or other to slow down when things started looking tough. He went back and toweled off, signaled for time with one upraised hand and knelt to retie one shoe, retrieved his racket and examined the strings, called for the balls and returned one of them for a different one, walked slowly up to the service line, gave me a glance, and started bouncing the ball endlessly. I waited, suddenly feeling very much alone, just me and him in a vacuum. The crowd noise was there but I didn't hear it. The heat was there but I didn't feel it. I had stepped through into some kind of emotional bell jar where nothing exists but the game.

He served. I knew it was a cannon shot, but it seemed to come in slow motion. I went wide, got low, had my racket prepared, and looped a return straight down the line. It hit well in, leaving the kid halfway to the net and staring as if he had been shot.

An adrenaline rush jolted hotly through me. *All right!* This was more like it. We were back on serve, and I had the full-voltage feeling you get when suddenly you are in the zone, your mind, body, and game all magical and taken out of the everyday world.

Changing ends, we passed each other behind the umpire's chair. I tried to catch Marshal's eyes and succeeded. He must have seen it, that feeling. His face, angry and impatient, changed to something else: worry.

He was right to worry. My knee felt good and warmed up, and he had no way of guessing that it might be just a little weak, even with the wonderful knee brace, whenever I went to my left.

The next game was nice, and I held at deuce. He rallied to win the next at love, but I managed to hold again. That made it 3–3. When he netted a volley to give me a look-in, I sneaked a desperation lob over his head from near the baseline to get up 30–0. He aced me again then, but my crosscourt return on the next serve caught him guessing down the line again, and there I was with two break points. He flubbed a volley at his ankles and I had the lead. After serving to go up 5–3, I lost to his next service game but then withstood his gangbusters net attacks on mine to win the first set, 6–4.

The second set, to my great amazement, was easier. Marshal seemed to have expended all his emotion on his outburst at the linesman and his kamikaze charges to the net in the deciding game of the first set. He had one more tantrum with the umpire, dragging it out endlessly, perhaps not so much because he was really outraged, but because he hoped it might distract me. Didn't work. I just stood there and watched from inside my magic emotional bell jar, knowing nothing he could do would hurt me today.

Thanks to the new widebody rackets, everything in the game today is power. People used to say I played with a certain degree of grace, whatever that means, and I am not completely comfortable with this new game where you whale hell out of every shot trying to blast the other guy off the court.

Midway in the second set, however, I was swinging out with such timing that balls were kicking chalk all over the place and it was the kid, not grampa, with his tongue starting to hang out. Toward the end—give him credit—he tried to change tactics, staying back on the fast surface and attempting to run me for a change. But by then it was too late; I was playing out of my mind, having the time of my life, and took him 6–2 in about forty minutes.

The applause was heavy when we walked off the court. Marshal was very gentlemanly despite his obvious chagrin and disappointment. I toweled off, gulped down half a lovely, chilled Coke, cased my rackets, and started offcourt still wrapped up totally in the moment.

Almost to the gate that led below the stadium to the showers, I happened to be waving up to the crowd and acknowledging applause when a face leaped out at me. Partway up, looking cool and impeccable in a white dress shirt open at the collar, his face shaded by the brim of a pale straw hat, sat none other than Reese McDonald. Our eyes met and he glared at me. So he had finally gotten here, and was hacked-off about my vanishing act back in Montana. I grinned and waved at him, and hurried to the showers.

Forty minutes later, McDonald looked sincerely horrified when I climbed up the bleacher stairs and plopped down beside him.

"You shouldn't be up here like this!" he protested.

"Why?" I demanded.

"It isn't . . . seemly."

"Oh. Sorry, Reese. I thought maybe you were anxious to talk."

He scowled and watched the conclusion of a point in a fine women's match going on below us. "It was hardly honorable, the way you ducked out on me in Montana."

"Sorry about that."

"You went to Oklahoma City. Why?"

"To see a friend."

"Who?"

"That's my business."

"You must tell me! I am to report your movements."

"Why?"

He seemed aggrieved by my insistence. "Isn't that somewhat obvious? Apparently someone believes that you know more about recent events than you have divulged. You have come under suspicion."

"Suspicion of *what*, for Christ's sake?"

His jaw set and he watched the tennis. Applause rippled through the crowd after a good point I hadn't seen. He didn't say anything.

"Suspicion of what?" I repeated.

"I have nothing more to say."

"How can someone suspect *me* of anything when I was the guy somebody else wanted to kill the other night?"

He sniffed. "That's for me to know," he said, "and you to find out."

It sounded so much like something Frank Burns would have said on the old *M*A*S*H* on TV that I almost laughed. "You're wasting government money," I told him.

He stonily refused to reply.

I clamped a hand on his knee, knowing that would irritate him because people like him hate to be touched. "If it will help any, here's my schedule. I'm going back to the motel now to rest. At seven, there's a cocktail party for players, press, and club members at—"

"I know your schedule," he cut in, piqued.

"Oh, good. Then you also know my next match is at two tomorrow."

"Of course."

"Wish me luck," I told him, still squeezing his knee. "If I can win that one, I can almost finish paying off last year's income taxes."

He looked at me with horror. "You owe back taxes?"

"Relax. You don't have to file any supplemental reports. The IRS already knows where I am." I let go of his knee and watched him compulsively smooth his fingertips over the wrinkle I had put in his pants. "See you around, Reese."

"I doubt that, unless I choose to show myself," he snapped, and grimly returned full attention to the tennis match.

I got up and left him sitting there.

* * *

I packed my gear and left the stadium, driving one of the
courtesy Buicks they provided each professional entrant. Despite myself, I looked in the rearview mirror about a hundred
times, trying to spot a car staying some discreet distance
behind me. It seemed that Reese McDonald was as overcon-
fident as he had sounded, and was not following me on a
minute-to-minute basis. Of course if our positions had been
reversed—and I had known that my prey stood to gain
$12,000 by winning another match tomorrow—I would have
felt reasonably confident about his immediate plans, too.

After I lost in the tournament, however—and I was sure
to lose sooner or later, given the field of young hotshots in my
bracket—McDonald would be a constant thorn in my side.
Any infinitesimal chance of looking further for Kevin Green
or his stalkers would be out the window. The thought was
depressing.

On the happy thought that my motel room telephone
might be bugged, I stopped not far from it and used a pay
phone to call our little weekly newspaper in Elk City. Lynette
Jordan herself answered.

"Lynette? Brad here."

"*Brad! Hey. Great. How did you do today?*"

"I eked one out. Listen. Remember that question I asked
you about the mountain?"

"*Sure. But it isn't a mountain.*"

"What did you say?"

"*I said, it isn't a mountain. It's a slide. The Slumgullion Slide. I found it mentioned in a tour book right away.
It's kind of famous. I just Xeroxed some stuff about it out
of our files and mailed it to you at the resort. It sounds like
a great place. What happened was, the whole side of a
mountain started sliding a few hundred years ago, I guess,
and it's still moving a few inches every year. It formed a
lake—*"

"Lynette," I interrupted, "hang on." Something—an old

memory—tickled at the back of my mind. "Where is this slide?" Then the memory clicked into place. I added, "It's in Colorado, right? It's somewhere around a town called Lake City, isn't it?"

"My gosh, Brad! If you already knew all about it, why did you ask me to go to all this trouble, looking it up and Xeroxing it for you?"

Lake City. Down in the San Juans somewhere. Now I remembered with crystal clarity how Kevin had talked about trips there with his parents when he was a kid—how good the fishing was there—how he intended to build a cabin there someday. Good God, maybe I really had stumbled onto something.

"Hey, Brad, you still there?"

"Lynette," I said, "remind me when I get back home that I want to take out ten more subscriptions to your paper, okay?"

"Huh?"

Twenty
Elsewhere

Wyoming: June 21

STAN LEVENTHAL'S old Volvo wagon, Leventhal at the wheel, left Casper behind in the midday heat haze and pounded out north into the vast prairie emptiness of Wyoming on Interstate 25. The change in tire sounds whapping on the concrete roused Arnie Tubb, who had been sleeping in the other seat, his head slumped against the window.

"Where are we?" Tubb demanded, his voice hoarse from sleep.

"North of Casper. On the way to Sheridan."

"How long till we get to Montana?"

"I don't know. Three hours, maybe. I don't know."

Tubb rubbed his eyes and peered out at the rolling scrubland they had entered. "Jesus, what a country. How could anybody live in this country?" Then he made one of his characteristic abrupt changes of subject. "Isn't it all the way across Montana, practically, to the Bitterroots?"

"It's going to be long after dark when we get there. We might have to stop short of there."

Tubb's voice went shrill: "We're not stopping till we get there!"

"It's a hell of a drive from here, Arnie, and we drove way too late last night."

"If you can't drive it, then I'll drive."

The thought of an erratic Arnie Tubb behind the wheel was far worse to Leventhal than the prospect of another fifteen hours of his own driving. "We'll make it," he said through gritted teeth.

Tubb jerked in his seat. "Look out there! What is that out there? That's antelope out there! A herd of fucking antelope!" He giggled. "I never saw no antelope before! Did you see 'em?"

"I saw them," Leventhal grated.

"Antelope! Son of a bitch!" Tubb reached for his cigarette pack.

"I told you we don't smoke in the car," Leventhal said sharply.

"Then stop the fucking car so I can get out and smoke!"

"I'll stop at the next rest stop."

Tubb's voice went shrill. "Goddamn it, you'll stop when I tell you to stop!"

Alarmed, Leventhal eased off on the accelerator. "All right, all right. Let me look for a decent place to pull off."

Tubb stretched. "I feel like shit."

"You smoke too much."

Tubb leered, a skull-grin. "What's going to happen? Am I going to get cancer?"

Leventhal felt his tattered nerves relax slightly as the immediate threat of another wild tantrum seemed past. The bastard was crazy—capable of anything. He scared Leventhal. If there had been a way to dump the maniac—turn him over to the police—Leventhal would have done it. But God, some of the others were sure to hear about it if he betrayed Tubb, and Leventhal knew what had happened to two members of the original group when the others suspected them of possible betrayal. It was a nightmare and it was never going to end.

Beside him, Tubb twitched and fidgeted around on the seat, his pack of Camels in hand. "Pull off here. There's plenty of shoulder."

"There's a pulloff up ahead," Leventhal said, despairing. "The sign said so. It can't be far."

"What's a pulloff? Who cares about a pulloff? Look at this

barren fucking country out here! I bet there's not a decent place to stop between here and Sheridan. Pull over now!"

"At least let me wait until there's a high spot or something, so it looks like we stopped to take a picture or something. Isn't there a lot less chance of some highway patrolman stopping to check us out if we're in a scenic spot, not just out in the middle of nowhere?"

Tubb's white, flabby face went slack. "Yeah. You're right. Okay. Step on it."

Leventhal obediently pressed harder on the pedal, making the speedometer swing back up near seventy. Tubb put his cigarettes back in his pocket and leaned forward, rocking in the seat. He had refused to buckle his seat belt. Leventhal always buckled his seat belt. They weren't alike in anything, he thought. He wasn't like any of the others. He had gotten on with his life—even finished the Ph.D., gotten married, built himself a faculty reputation. He could not imagine how insane he must have been when they formed the pact in the first place; if he had sworn himself to secrecy and told them then that he was putting it behind him, they would have let him go. Now he had been a part of it too long—contributing money when they demanded it, nothing else—and he knew too much.

Hot morning sunlight beamed through the passenger-side windows of the wagon, making the air-conditioning work hard. The sickly smell of Tubb's sweat filled the car. Leventhal cranked the blower control up a notch.

"How much *farther*?" Tubb demanded, whining.

"I'll stop up ahead there on that promontory."

Tubb kept squirming around. "Hurry it up. Hurry it up." Then he paused. "Don't go too fast. That's all we need, some asshole trooper stopping us for speeding. Not another car in sight for fifty miles, but go too fast and he's been hiding somewhere and he zaps your ass with a ticket." He paused again. "I like it out here," he said, making another of those unexpected mental jumps. "It's shitty but it's open. No rice paddies. No plantations. No jungle. No place to hide. Get them out in country like this and kill every last one of them." He giggled shrilly. "Remember what we used to say? How to win the war? Put the friendly Vietnamese on boats, take them out to sea. Pulverize the whole country and pave it. Then sink the boats."

Leventhal allowed the Volvo to slow as it started up the long, gentle climb toward a kind of brushy mesa ahead. This was Custer country, he thought suddenly. The egomaniacal fool had staged his troops up ahead, near a spot on the map called Kaycee. Custer country. The Little Big Horn. God, he had always wanted to see it. But not like this.

When Tubb showed up out of the blue the night before last, it had been a bad shock. Leventhal had begged him to take some money and keep going—at least ditch the stolen car and let Leventhal take him to a motel overnight until they could get something worked out. Tubb had gotten crazier then. The only safe place for the stolen car was in Leventhal's garage, he said. He wasn't going anywhere yet, he said. It was up to Leventhal to get him to Montana to confront someone called Brad Smith, he said. Brad Smith had been the most prominently mentioned name in all the papers stolen from that writer down in Oklahoma. Brad Smith had known where the copilot was. He had to know where the pilot was, too. They would go to Montana and find Brad Smith and get it out of him, Tubb said.

Leventhal had argued that it was crazy. That was when Tubb had pulled the old Saturday night special out of his pants pocket and started waving it around, almost out of control. God only knew where he had gotten it, but Leventhal's terror had shocked him into a brief flashback that made him sick at his stomach. By the time he got himself together again, Tubb was using his phone to call Henderson in Kansas and tell him the plan. That was when Leventhal knew he was trapped—had to go along, or end up dead.

Doreen had hated it when she came back and found Tubb

wolfing down peanut butter sandwiches in the kitchen. Leventhal had tried to make it look like a normal surprise visit by an old army buddy. Doreen hadn't taken that well at all, and she had frozen solid when Leventhal told her that Tubb would use the guest room overnight—that another buddy was desperately ill in Milwaukee, and the two of them would leave in the morning early to drive there and see him.

It wasn't like him to make a spur-of-the-moment trip, she said. Nothing he could say quite got the look of puzzled suspicion out of her eyes.

No help for it. For once, Leventhal was almost grateful for the conspiracy of silence that their marriage had become: Doreen turned her back on him and refused to say more about anything.

In the morning, at four o'clock, he had gotten up to find Tubb already in the kitchen, making more peanut butter sandwiches for the road. Leventhal carried his hastily packed overnighter out to the Volvo, and Tubb backed the stolen Olds Ciera out ahead of him. So nervous he was shaking all over, Leventhal followed the Ciera several miles to a spot of rural woods. Tubb's car veered sharply off the road, then crashed into roadside brush, vanishing. Leventhal stopped, thinking hopefully that maybe Tubb had hurt himself ditching the Ciera, wouldn't come out. No such luck. Tubb had hiked out with only a slight, oozing cut on his forehead.

Yesterday, that had been. An eternity ago.

They reached the top of the promontory. Ahead, the road stretched for what looked like a thousand miles of barren prairie fields. They had already put Casper out of sight behind them. Leventhal could not see another car anywhere, nor any sign of life. The fields on both sides were neatly fenced with wire. Seeing this, Leventhal was struck by a new sense of insanity. Who would fence such desolation? *Why?*

Tubb hopped out of the car, snapped his old Zippo open, and got his cigarette going. In his shapeless shirt and pants that were far too big for him, he looked like some mad, extraterrestrial child about to be incinerated by the unfamiliar sunlight. Leventhal could have wept. Where would it all end? Where would it all end?

Ann Arbor

SPECIAL AGENT IN CHARGE Tod Sandifer looked again at his watch and turned the ignition key to start the engine. "Here we go, boys," he murmured, switching on his left turn signal to pull away from the curb.

Beside him, Agent Howard Williamson put down the magazine he had been perusing and adjusted his suit coat over the shoulder holster. Sandifer pulled slowly out onto the residential street. In the rearview mirror, the car containing his other two agents nosed out to follow him.

It was just a block to the house. Sandifer drove sedately. He knew that at this precise same time, in Omaha, other agents were driving up to another place in a coordinated operation. The finding here last night of a car believed to have been stolen by the missing subject Tubb had moved everything earlier by one day, but Sandifer was fully confident that things in Omaha would be proceeding as smoothly as they were here, despite the speedup.

Ahead Sandifer saw the modest frame house he had reconnoitered twice yesterday and once earlier today. A delivery truck passed, going the other direction, but there was no other traffic on the street. Sandifer flicked on his turn signal again, braked, and pulled into the driveway. The other FBI car behind him came up swiftly to close the gap and rock to a halt right behind him.

Doors popped open. Men ran. Sandifer hurried to the front porch and hammered on the door, not yet aware that he was about to experience a great disappointment.

Omaha

BUDDY TURNER walked into his house to get lunch and found four men standing in the hallway, waiting for him.

"Mr. Turner?" one of them said politely.

"Yes?"

Two of the others grabbed his arms, shoved him painfully against the wall, and held him there.

"Mr. Turner, you're under arrest. You have the right to remain silent—"

Turner did not hear the rest. The cold clamp of handcuffs around his wrists made all his senses go haywire.

Kansas City

AN HOUR after finishing a light lunch, Special Agent Reese McDonald smiled smugly at his rowmates as he made his way past them to his seat in the stadium. He found his chair, sat down, and carefully arranged the creases of his pale lemon slacks. Reaching into the pocket of his stiffly starched madras shirt, he took out his aviator glasses, checked for possible specks on the lenses, polished them anyway, and fitted the temples over his ears.

The women's match below had gone to a tiebreaker, and was just concluded. Brad Smith's scheduled match would start a bit late. Neither he nor his opponent had shown up oncourt yet. McDonald checked his Seiko; it wouldn't be long. Linespeople were busy checking the height and tension of the net, while below the umpire's umbrella-shaded chair there seemed to be some sort of consultation taking place between three men and one woman McDonald recognized as tournament officials.

McDonald had checked the motel late last night to confirm that Brad Smith was in his room and sleeping. This morning, McDonald had arisen at six, had a brisk run before a shower and shave, and had indulged himself in a rare two hours of relaxation, perusing the latest edition of *Principles of Criminal Forensics*, before heading for the stadium to renew his surveillance. McDonald, as a result, felt relaxed and at ease about everything.

A few minutes passed. McDonald began to perspire. He hated perspiring, except when he was working out. Then perspiration was good.

McDonald watched for Brad Smith to come out.

The PA system loudspeakers around the stadium's upper rim suddenly buzzed to life.

"Ladies and gentlemen," a metallic male voice said, *"the schedule of afternoon play has been changed. The next match previously scheduled for this time has been canceled. Brad Smith, Elk City, Montana, has been forced by injury to withdraw. Jeremy Turner, Little Rock, wins over Smith by default. The next match will be in approximately thirty minutes. In that match—"*

Reese McDonald didn't hear the rest of the announcement. Feeling like he had been kicked in the stomach, he had already started a mad rush for the aisle, knocking roughly against people's knees and stepping on a few toes, drawing resentful looks and a couple of nasty comments. Once he reached the aisle, he ran.

His telephone call from the concrete labyrinth under the stadium confirmed his worst fears. The motel said Mr. Smith had checked out during the night.

Twenty-one

June 21

TAKING IT easy in the red Cherokee I had rented in Denver,
I crossed over Monarch Pass in light fog, found bright sunshine and only a few high, silvery mountain clouds in the sky
beyond, and reached Gunnison early in the afternoon. From
there I drove west a few miles, reached the east end of Blue
Mesa Reservoir, and turned south on Colorado 149.

The two-lane asphalt road took me through brush-
studded rolling terrain, mostly barren earth hills nearby on
both sides. The Cherokee deftly handled continuous road
curves as it climbed gently but steadily out of the sprawling
Gunnison Valley toward higher mountains, the San Juans, to
the south. Soon in more precipitous country, I drove more
slowly through twisting canyons, dramatically tall, jagged
brown rock formations all around, roughly paralleling the
Lake Fork of the Gunnison River. It wasn't long before a
road sign welcomed me to Hinsdale County, and a few more
miles to the south I rounded a sharp bend to get my first good
view of the taller, more jagged mountains up ahead. In the
bottom of a river canyon I passed a sign pointing to a distant
cluster of large, expensive-looking log homes sprawled across
a mountainside on my left, and then I drove past a couple of
gravel roads, lush green pastures, and a dark redwood motel
with bright yellow trim on my right. Just past the rise where
the motel sat, I could look down into a wider valley with high
mountains forming walls on the east and west, two much
larger mountains pressing their peaks against the brilliant
blue sky a few miles to the south, a cluster of small buildings

that included a grocery store and a little bakery on the right, the Lake Fork churning by on the left, houses scattered out on the flats beyond, and a glimpse of paved streets, many old trees, and a church steeple up ahead.

The sign "Lake City."

I slowed to get the lay of the land. A dusty Jeep Wrangler that had been on my tail for about five miles shot around me and hurried on down the curving road toward a gas station and store of some kind up ahead. Two more Jeeps came around the curve near the gas station, one of them pulling in and the other approaching me. The car that came behind the second Jeep had Texas license plates. In the next quarter of a mile I saw cars from Missouri, Kansas, and Oklahoma. I began to realize that Lake City might not be famous, but it was hardly undiscovered.

Driving around a couple of more bends in the road, I found myself headed down a tree-lined shotgun street with signs on the corners that said it was Gunnison Ave. I passed a white, green-roofed building on the right that looked like a school, then a block or two of pretty old rococo Victorian-style private homes, close to the street behind wrought-iron fencework. Beyond that I came into the downtown: motels, souvenir shops, a handsome old white frame courthouse with a flagpole and the caboose off a train in a tiny park in front, a motel, and the Lake City Cafe, with a side street looking west toward what turned out to be the real main drag, Silver Street. You could tell it was the main drag because the bank building was down there, and two blocks of small shops and eating places, and a small city park with nothing much in it except some swings.

I angle-parked in front of a store that called itself the Timberline Craftsman and climbed out on drive-stiff legs. A handful of tourists strolled along thick board sidewalks, peering into shop windows or just gawking at the mountains to the south, or the sheer gravel bluff that walled the city off less than two blocks to the west. The bright sun felt hot on my back. The air tasted like cold spring water. It was high here, almost 8,800 feet according to the map book. I instantly liked the place.

It was the kind of place Kevin would have liked, too, I thought. But that didn't necessarily mean he was around here, even though my wafer-thin theory said he might be. All I really knew was that I had to check it out, and if my wild guess wasn't accurate, I was out of leads and hope.

One of my first stops was the office of the local newspaper, the *Silver World,* where I found the editor in a relaxed mood because the week's edition was out and not much was going on. An extremely nice young man, he bought my phony name and my story about doing genealogical research which required that I find a long-lost cousin. He didn't have anyone named Kevin Green on his subscription list or in his files, and he had never heard of anybody by that name, which didn't surprise me. I had a lame story ready about how my missing cousin might have changed his name because of some problems with a divorce, and then showed him the old snapshot I had taken of Kevin in Vietnam. I provided as accurate a description as I could of the older Kevin I had seen in the grainy blowup off a television tape that the man calling himself Frank Simmons had shown me. My editor friend frowned over the picture, listened to my description, and drew another blank. Again it didn't surprise me, but it had to be tried.

Still attempting long shots, I asked about local tennis courts, and learned that the only ones around were in a middle-ritzy housing addition north of town. I wrote down its name on the theory that it was just possible Kevin would not have been able to give up tennis entirely, and if all else failed I might drive up there and scope out the regular players.

If all this sounds like straw-grasping, you have it right. I learned that the permanent population of Lake City—year-round residents—numbers in the hundreds. But in the summers, when all the seasonal cabins back in the woods are occupied, and the tourists trickle through, the head count on any given day is probably between four and five thousand. We were coming into the peak of the season, the editor said. So my search for a needle right now was in the biggest haystack Lake City ever became.

The rest of the afternoon was spent strolling around, ducking in and out of shops, and eyeballing everybody. I would have probably had a heart attack on the spot if I had actually looked up and found Kevin this way, and fortunately for my health I didn't.

Maybe, of course, he wasn't here at all. But I had to exhaust every reasonable possibility before I could tool back north to the arms of Reese McDonald and the certainty that if I hadn't found Kevin, some other people still might.

With evening coming on, I found a motel room in a strip of little cabins on the highway toward the south end of town. I read the local telephone book's white pages—which took about ten minutes—but naturally came up empty on that, too. Later I strolled down to the Lake City Cafe and had some trout amandine that blew me away, accompanied by two beers and followed by a cigar on the walk home. The nicotine, combined with the altitude, put me back in my tiny cabin a little out of breath.

My Calling Card call to the resort went right through, person-to-person for Ted Treacher. When he came on the line, he sounded nervous, worried, and relieved all at the same time. *"Brad, my man! What the hell! Are you okay?"*

"I'm fine, Ted. No problem at all. That's why I called. I figured you might be worried."

"Worried! That's not the half of it! I saw on ESPN that you had to withdraw in Denver because of an injury. The first thing I thought of was that damnable knee again! Is that what happened?"

"No. The knee is fine."

"Then what did happen? How are you? Where are you? What's going on?"

"I'm safe and sound, and nothing is wrong with me."

"Then what—"

"Ted, listen. This is strictly between you and me. No one else is to know anything. I mean *no one*. Is that understood?"

Ted's voice changed, lowering part of an octave with a wary concern. *"I'm not at all sure I like the way this is starting out, Brad."*

"Just between you and me, right? It's to go no further. Not to anyone, period. Agreed?"

He didn't speak for a moment. Then: *"Agreed."*

I briefly explained to him how Reese McDonald had picked me up again and how I had ducked out of the tournament. That decision had felt sacrificial to me when I made it—I was turning my back on money badly needed, and had never stiffed a tournament committee before in my life. It didn't feel much better telling Ted about it now.

"But Brad!" Ted interrupted. *"Why in the world—"*

"I'll explain as well as I can, Ted."

And I did. The Dave Wentworth part I left out. Some of the other stuff that I didn't think added much, I also left out. I made it clear enough that I thought Kevin Green was alive, and hiding somewhere—maybe here around Lake City somewhere. I assured Ted that I didn't feel in any danger because there was no way anybody could track me here, and promised that I wouldn't give more than a week to this; either I would have located Kevin by then, or I would have eliminated even the remotest hope of doing so.

"Have you got all that?" I asked finally.

"Yes, I suppose so," Ted replied after what seemed a long pause. *"But what if someone like your friend Collie Davis asks where—"*

"You don't know a thing. You've got no idea. That goes for anyone who asks, I don't care who it is."

Ted sounded dubious. *"Beth too?"*

"Beth too. Maybe especially Beth."

He hesitated again. He seemed to be having a hard time with this. It occurred to me that this might be because my plans sounded so amorphous and my faint hope so wacky.

Finally he said with some obvious reluctance, *"I would appreciate a call periodically, for my own reassurance."*

"I'll call every couple days, Mother." I hung up.

That was Friday. On Saturday I spent a lot of time wandering around town, staring at a great many more strangers, and striking up conversations with quite a few local shopkeepers about Lake City, the tourist season, the state of their business, and did they know anyone locally who looked at all like this old chum shown in a twenty-three-year-old picture. The merchants were uniformly pleasant, and by the end of the day, when I walked into a woodworker's shop at the far southern end of town, he greeted me with, "Hello there! I bet you're the man with the picture of an ex-soldier you're trying to locate!"

In the process, I learned a little about Lake City. The "lake" is San Cristobal, the one formed by the Slumgullion Slide. When I drove out that way on Sunday, it was easy to see the yellow mountainside dirt, marked by crazy-angled and fallen pines, which marked where the slow but inexorable earthen collapse continued. It's a beautiful lake. I didn't stay long to admire it because there were few places of business around it where I could go through my show-and-tell routine.

Lake City got to be there in the first place because of silver. It was a boom town at one time, with millions of dollars' worth of ore being hauled out. Most of that played out long ago, although some amateur prospectors still muck around from time to time, and not long ago the federal government refused to extend Wilderness Act protection to several square miles nearby despite the recommendations of its own experts because big-money mining interests protested, saying there was still a chance they could dig out millions more in minerals, provided they leveled a few mountains to mine it, killing off a few streams with toxic runoff in the process.

Somewhere in my wanderings around the area I was told that one of the mountains to the south was called Round Top, and another Red Mountain. One of the ridges nearby was, I was told, called Cannibal Ridge. When I asked, someone explained.

It seems that more than a century ago, when Lake City was little more than a small conglomeration of shacks, a man named Alferd E. Packer (yes, he really spelled his first name that way) led a group of silver-seekers over the mountains and into the valley despite warnings of a blizzard on the way. Sure enough, the blizzard came when the Packer party was camped not far south of the present Lake City. Nothing was heard from them for quite some time, and they were presumed dead from exposure or starvation.

Then, however, Packer wandered back to civilization looking surprisingly well fed. When questioned about the fate of the others, he told several different stories. When a search party finally located the winter camp, they found signs that Packer had not only killed the others but lived by eating parts of them.

The subsequent trial of "the Colorado cannibal" made sensational headlines at the time. The courthouse I had seen when I first arrived in town was the same one where the trial took place. Packer was sentenced to be hanged by the neck (according to legend) "until you are dead, dead, dead." This judgment was never served, Packer eventually was pardoned under circumstances I still don't understand, and he died peacefully while employed in some capacity by the governor of Colorado.

All of which I found interesting, as I picked it up, but none of which helped me at all in my search for Kevin Green.

The more I wandered around, the better I liked the place and the easier it was to believe that a man truly wanting to vanish could find no better place to have a new life. But by Sunday evening I had begun to feel any genuine hope guttering out. Even if Kevin was here, I might search for weeks and never catch a glimpse of him.

For Lake City was small, but it was not a dot on the map with a gas station and four houses. The woods were full of scattered cabins. Kevin might be in any of them, and I would never know.

Twenty-two
Elsewhere
Missoula: June 23

WRITHING INSIDE with humiliation, Special Agent Reese Mc-
Donald faced his temporary supervisor with an expression
which he hoped revealed none of his feelings.

"Nothing yet," the special agent in charge told him
coolly. "But he's certain to turn up at the resort again soon."

"He needs money," McDonald repeated dully. "He told
me so himself, and that's been verified. It was out of the
question for him to withdraw from that tournament."

The supervisor's eyes resembled cut glass. "Yes. Quite.
However, he did so."

It felt like a knife turning in McDonald's guts. "Yes."

"Go back to Bitterroot Valley," his supervisor told him.
"Ask questions, see if you can get information from anyone
about his likely present whereabouts. Call tomorrow morning
and let us know of any progress."

"Yes, sir." Eager to escape his disgrace, McDonald got to
his feet.

"Oh, Reese. Before you go." The special agent in charge
handed over two thin sheets of copier paper. "Look these
over. Keep an eye out. As you can see, one of these descriptions adds a bit to what we already had on Arnold Tubbs. The
other is on a man named Leventhal that we believe may now
be traveling with him."

Frowning, McDonald folded the sheets and put them in
his inside coat pocket. "I shall study them with diligence."

"It's within the realm of possibility that they might show
up here," his supervisor added. "Their coconspirators, some

of them, seemed to have an unholy interest in Brad Smith."
The special agent in charge paused and smiled, but it was one
of the nastiest smiles McDonald had ever seen. "Perhaps if
they show up and help you, you can keep track of Smith . . .
with all three of you watching."

Lolo, Montana

ARNIE TUBB slammed the motel room telephone down so
hard it made the table lamp rattle. "Still not there! Goddamn
it, where *is* he?"

"He'll show up," Leventhal said nervously. "All we have
to do is stay holed up here, and keep calling."

"But where is he? Why did he pull out of that tournament
in Kansas City? Goddamn it, what if he's onto something
right now? What if he's seeing Captain Green right while
we're sitting here, doing nothing?"

"All we can do is keep calling the resort and asking for
him," Leventhal repeated.

Tubb paced the floor, the movement making uneven gar-
goyle shadows on his face, now filled with lumps resembling
dumplings just under the surface. "We can't just sit here.
Somebody out at that place has to know where he is. If he
don't show up by tomorrow, we got to take the chance. We
got to drive on down there and start asking around in person."

Twenty-three

June 24

By Monday I had started to feel hopeless. I had told myself that the odds were against me, but had held out the same kind of hope that a man inevitably feels stirring inside when he buys a lottery ticket offering him something like a one-in-nineteen-million chance. It wasn't much of a chance, my emotions told me, but it was *some* chance—the only one I had.

But by Monday afternoon I was being forced to turn closer toward a face-to-face confrontation with reality. I had been in just about every shop and business in town. If anyone recognized the old picture, they didn't let on. I knew I should not be surprised. The old snapshot did not much resemble the grainy picture taken off the Denver TV station newscast that Simmons had shown me.

I had stared at what seemed like ten thousand strangers' faces. I had been through recent tax records and deed registrations at the old courthouse, and I had thumbed through every print saved by a local photographer who shot news for the *Silver World*. He had a small studio where he also shot old-time photos for tourists, and I had even gone through his display books of those pictures, hoping against hope.

I had been to most if not all the outlying cabin/residential developments, including Ball Flats (the area near the river that I had seen first when I came into town from Gunnison), San Juan Estates, San Juan Ranch, Wade Addition, Packer's Knob (which was about as far as one could get from the massacre site), and Riverside Estates (which wasn't on the

river). I had been up to the area's only tennis courts, a private
layout in one of the ritzier mountainside developments. But
except for a couple who patty-caked it back and forth for
awhile, I saw no one there.

After all of that, I felt a bit like I had once long ago when
I was married, and went with my bride to look for a house we
might be able to buy. There is a repetitive grind to house-
hunting that makes it far more tiring than the actual physical
effort ought to make it. You keep hoping, and you keep being
shown another pile of junk. You keep trying to think of how
you could afford to spend just a little more, and you keep
finding places you like that are still one additional step up the
ladder and out of reach. By late in the day Monday, it was a
house-hunting kind of fatigue and discouragement that had
begun to sink in.

Driving toward the north edge of town, I headed once
more for the ritzy tennis courts, another checkout in futility.
On the way, there was Beth in my mind again. It hurt a little.
No, hell, it hurt a lot. I missed her like nobody's business.
There had to be a way to fix things between us. But now the
dark feeling had grown that perhaps it was already too late for
fixing anything. We had both dug in our heels, intent on
winning our tug-of-war, and now both of us had been yanked
into the mud hole. Maybe it was really and truly over. The
thought made me sick. I forced my mind to the present.
Seeing a small grocery on my left, the west side of the highway, I stopped for a pack of cigarettes, which I began deplet-
ing at once.

I realized that my search for Kevin had become something like an obsession. There was a paradox here. The
deeper I got into this thing and the more bizarre it began to
appear, the more easily I could believe that someone could
leave Vietnam and vanish from the face of the earth. It was
the *why* that I had trouble understanding.

I had already known that it was common to live Vietnam
over and over again after coming back from there. Many of

the guys were hounded by dreams, driven by crazy ideas no "normal" person—for which read "someone who was not there"—could ever imagine.

I had been lucky. There were still the dreams now and then, but they had become rare now, after so many years. I had not had a flashback since about 1980. Of course my tennis provided me with two things most veterans never had: the money to pay a series of shrinks, and another overpowering obsession—the game.

My dreams now, when they were not of Danisa and those few months we had before she was murdered, were always of tennis.

Often they were of Wimbledon, the finals against Borg, when (miracle!) I had him out of position on match point, had a short ball at the net, and had only to make the simplest little cut dropshot for it to be all over. I was already seeing myself holding the big cup aloft, I think. I was already wondering how I could be so lucky. Already congratulating myself.

The instant I live over and over in this damned dream is seeing the ball tip the net cord and roll along it a full twelve or fifteen inches, then fall back on my side. And looking up for a nanosecond and seeing the shock in Bjorn's eyes, and the look that instantly followed it. Both of us knew in that moment that now he would recover and win it, no matter how hard I tried to think otherwise.

Some of the other dreams are wonderful wins or bitter losses: the match against Arthur Ashe in Fort Worth so long ago, or the semi against Brad Gilbert in the U.S. Open, or an incredible exhibition mixed-doubles match in Stuttgart, me and Martina against Billie Jean and somebody—for the life of me I can't remember—the usual mild competition of a match like that suddenly getting more serious, everybody really hitting out, trying to blast somebody, wild acute angle shots and impossible gets, everyone having a hell of a good time and playing at their peak. I have no idea who won that match. It doesn't matter.

If it hadn't been for tennis, perhaps my dreams would still be about Vietnam more often. If that is so, then it's another reason to be thankful for the years at the top in tennis.

Kevin could have had years like that, too. He could have been at the top. He not only had the body, the reflexes, and the strokes; even in college he had already had the disposition. There are all kinds in the top tier of professional tennis: the virtual recluses, the Hollywood-type phonies, the perpetual whiners, the kids manipulated by parents you wouldn't believe, the real bastards. The one personality trait they have in common is an ability to concentrate and handle pressure that you couldn't believe. Kevin had had that—had known he had it, had loved the game almost too much.

Then *why*? Why had he turned his back on the life he might have had at the top? Why had he vanished, and why was someone still looking for him?

It occurred to me for perhaps the first time that few people could possibly fully understand how quickly Kevin had become an obsession with me. It was not just anger and guilt about being tricked into giving away Dave Wentworth's whereabouts—and thus condemning him to a dirty kind of death. It was not old friendship, or the gallantry of his wife, Barbara, or any other single factor.

Maybe as much as anything it was the thought of all the dead—the ones I had known over there. Their names marched through my mind, and so did their faces: *Steiner, Jefferson, Kline, Murphy, Burnhardt, Fleischmann, Preodzic, Drinon*. And more came to mind, marching by me in uniform, or sitting under a tree in the intense, wet jungle heat; or lying in the mud, a part of their body blown away, while the guys came with the body bag: *Twillman, Vgzyl, Cooper*. Maybe there were enough of them that you could find rhymes. Maybe you could write a poem about them.

Wordsworth had written something about immortality.
Maybe I could write an ode about the opposite.

But I am over Vietnam. I never think about it anymore.
I was not chasing around like a crazy man, looking for a
needle in this Colorado haystack, because Vietnam is still a
black thing that sometimes stirs and rattles its coils in the
back of my mind. I was not looking for Kevin Green because
he was part of Vietnam for me, or because enough good guys
had died already, or because it was the ultimate obscenity to
me that somewhere, for some reason, men like Dave Wentworth were *still* dying because of Vietnam, somehow . . . or
because there had to be an end to it, there just couldn't be
any more killing, and if I could find Kevin and manage
somehow to save just his single life, it would be almost like
some kind of crazy vindication of my failure to die over there
like so many others did . . . like maybe I should have, too . . .
if I had been braver or something. None of that was involved
here. None of it.

Sure.

I reached the roadside marker that showed the way to the
residential area with the courts. Driving up the steeply twisting gravel road, I realized that I was probably too late to
observe anyone, because the sun was long gone behind the
ridgeline to the west, chilly night twilight already hanging
over everything this side of it.

I drove on up anyway.

Driving the twisty gravel streets past several huge "cabins" with warm electric light shining from their windows, I
reached the courts again. I saw a pickup truck parked on the
far side, and some big rolls of Cyclone fencing. Part of the
fence around the far gate had been taken down, and somebody had partly erected new fence in its place. On the court,
still whacking the ball back and forth despite the gathering
gloom, two boys of high school age were getting to balls that
my aging eyes couldn't track in the dark.

Standing off to the side of their court was the workman

from the pickup, I guessed, his hands jammed in the pockets of his Levi's, a baseball cap pulled low over his eyes. He seemed intent on watching the boys.

I pulled up, cut my headlights, and watched, too.

After a few energetic exchanges, one of the boys missed a backhand quite badly, losing the point. The workman, tall and very skinny, said something to him. The boy nodded, disgusted with himself, and went back to serve the next point. His opponent sent back another low screamer to my boy's backhand, and he netted it just as before.

The workman walked out onto the court in his clodhopper boots. As the boy retrieved the ball, the workman said something to him again. The boy replied and shook his head. The workman said something else and then reached for the boy's racket, which he handed over.

The workman held the racket back in a classic backhand position, talking all the while. Then he took a ball from the boy, bounced it, and stepped into a beautiful backhand, a real smoker that cleared the net by an inch and hit deep in the opponent's corner.

His movement out there made skyrockets go off inside my brain.

I sat quite still and waited until darkness forced the boys to quit their game. The workman came out again with a small sack of practice balls and talked to each of them as they practiced stroking a couple of dozen each. Then, after a brief confab, the boys scooted off, walking toward the distant houses.

The workman started picking up the practice balls and putting them back in his canvas sack. I got out of the Cherokee and walked over to the gate area he had under repair.

His expression—flat and utterly calm—did not change when I spoke his name.

"Hello, Brad," Kevin Green said quietly. "What in the world are you doing here?"

Twenty-four

"MY GOD, Kevin!" I said. "Isn't that *my* question? What are *you* doing here?"

His little smile gave me my first hint that this was not the Kevin I had known. He replied, "Why, I live here, of course. But my name isn't Kevin anymore. It's Ken. I'm Ken Givens now."

"*Why?*"

"Well," he said with the same unreal calm, "it's a long story."

"I've got time."

"It's a very long story."

"I've got time."

He turned his head and looked out across the gloomy vacant court toward the mountains to the south and west, indistinct now against a dishwater sky that had begun to spangle with a million faint stars. His face, changed by an unkempt gray stubble beard, was thin and deeply lined under the bill of his baseball cap, his cheeks sunken, eyes looking from dark sockets. He looked very little like the man I had known. I saw more clearly how his work clothes hung on his bony frame. Yet he looked strong and fit, as if hard work had melted every gram of extraneous tissue off his body, leaving only bone structure and the muscle necessary to move it. The blurry picture shown to me by Simmons had not revealed any of this detail. In person, Kevin did not merely look older. He looked old.

He continued to look off at the mountains as if he had forgotten me.

"Kevin?" I prodded.

He turned back. "No. Ken. It's Ken now. You have to remember that. It's very important."

"Why is it very important?"

He thought again for a few seconds. I felt a gust of scare that he would tell me to go away—refuse to say any more. I had no contingency plan for that.

Instead, he removed the baseball cap, revealing a fast-receding hairline that he mopped with a small towel. "Are you alone? Is anyone with you?" His voice went tight, suspicious. "You didn't bring anyone with you, did you?"

"No. I'm alone, and nobody knows I'm here."

He seemed to relax inside. He reached down to pick up the bag the practice balls had been in. "I don't live very far from here." Straightening, he pointed toward a battered old Ford 150 pickup parked on the tarmac across the court from where I had parked. "That's my truck. You could follow me." Then he smiled again. "I've got some leftover chili, dynamite stuff. What do you say?"

One of the taillights of his pickup was out. I followed him so closely all the way that I could see how it had been bumped by something long ago, and the red plastic cap shattered, leaving only a now-rusty lamp socket with nothing in it. His truck had a Colorado license plate and a heavy-duty back bumper and a broken chain-clasp on one side of the tailgate and deep-tread all-weather tires on the rear. In the back, along with another roll of Cyclone fencing and some wire-stretching and tying tools, he had chunks of firewood splinters and bark and a much-used red Stihl chain saw. Night had brought on cold, but I was sweating. Maybe it had been a mistake to let him get into his truck; maybe—unless I stuck to him like wallpaper—he would accelerate suddenly, whip around a couple of mountain curves, and lose me. And then maybe I wouldn't be able to find him again.

I needn't have worried. He drove sedately down the steeply twisting gravel road out of the housing addition, turned north on 149, and accelerated slowly, black puffs of bad-piston-ring smoke issuing from the rusty tail pipe. We drove north, away from the town.

I felt intense amazement and relief to have found him. He seemed physically well enough. But his mental condition was quite another matter. Puzzled questions piled up one on top of another in my mind as I kept the Cherokee close behind his pickup. Our brief conversation had felt unreal. I wanted to think that was because I had had so little hope left when I found him—had been so surprised. But closer to the truth was the baffling way he had reacted to me—my sense that we hadn't connected on exactly the same wavelength. He was the Kevin I had known, but he wasn't. Older, yes; but more than older—weather-beaten, with a vague air of stubborn self-reliance overlaying something delicate and fragile. I had sensed that a wrong word or action on my part might make him fly all to pieces. I hoped I was wrong about that, but didn't think so.

We drove two to three miles north, perhaps a bit farther, before he slowed and then turned left onto a narrow gravel road that led upward into a hillside forest of ponderosas and spruce, packed in so close on the narrow road that our head-lights made it look like a silvery tunnel. We came to an intersecting dirt road, studded with big rocks half washed out by winter erosion, and turned onto it, jouncing more slowly up the mountainside. A deer bolted out ahead of his truck, a tan flash in the headlights, and he braked sharply for it, then went on. The road, if you could still call it that, got worse, and I thought about going to four-wheel drive, but he was making it so I didn't switch over. There was no sight of habitation up here. The road had become so bad that the

constant pitching of the Cherokee would have thrown me out
from behind the wheel except for the seat belt.

His single brake light flared as his 150 humped up over
a particularly bad spot, and then he turned sharply to the
right, entering a narrow dirt driveway that I never would
have spotted in the waist-high brush. I followed through the
trees, a grove of densely packed aspen. We bounced up this
path for perhaps forty yards, taking two sharp turns around
house-sized piles of boulders, and then his headlights shone
onto the side of a small, cedar-sided structure with a metal
roof and rock chimney and a deck on the front that listed
sharply at one end with its underpinnings rotted away. All
around the small clearing I spotted piles of cut trees, little
mountains of logs, mounds of wood chips, a small piece of
equipment that I judged to be a log-splitter.

Kevin parked on the gravel-strewn dirt in front of this
shack. I pulled in behind him. He got out, climbed up on the
listing front porch, and stuck a key in the front door lock. I
hurried after him. He stepped inside the place and lights
flared on. I was surprised that electricity had gotten this far
into the wilderness.

I followed him inside.

"Be it ever so humble," he said with a touch of his old
irony.

The interior consisted of a single large room, bare stud
walls with rolled insulation stapled between them but not
covered by anything, open rafters overhead with a couple of
sheets of plywood laid across them to form a storage floor for
several beat-up old cardboard cartons, a small, utilitarian
kitchen in one corner, bunk beds—the lower bunk rumpled
and unmade—in another, a door into an alcove that must be
the bathroom. In the near end of the room where we had
entered, a sagging overstuffed couch and two folding director's chairs faced an iron heating stove that had a small stack
of firewood on the stonework supporting it. Some newspapers—the local weekly and copies of the Denver *Post*—had

been piled beside one of the chairs, mixed in with several
issues of *World Tennis* and *Inside Tennis*. In a corner stood
a TV cart with closed front doors, a small Sony color set on
top, with a cable leading to a wall plug for an outdoor antenna. Two small end tables, the brown plastic-covered kind
you buy in a flat box at Wal-Mart, completed the furnishings.
A cheap telephone sat on one, a puke-green plastic lamp on
the other. There were no personal effects—no mementos or
pictures—anywhere in sight. With the thick, plain brown
curtains pulled tightly shut, the place looked like someone
had camped here for a brief time, then deserted it, taking
every trace of themselves along when they left. I felt a small
chill. It was not that cold.

Kevin sailed his baseball cap at a wall peg near the refrigerator, scoring a hit beside a furry winter hat and a wide-
brimmed summer straw. "Make yourself at home. Whisky's
in the cabinet under the TV, glasses in the cupboard, ice in
the refrigerator. I need a quick shower." Without waiting for
a reply, he ducked in through the bathroom door, closing it
firmly behind him. In a minute or so I heard the gush of
water through exposed copper tubing in the far wall and the
spray hitting plastic in the shower.

Going to the TV cabinet, I opened up and found partly-
consumed bottles of Jack Daniel's black label, Windsor Canadian, and Smirnoff vodka. The bottles had a little dust on
them. I carried the Windsor to the kitchen corner, found a
large jelly glass in the cupboard, and poured myself two
fingers over an ice cube. I needed it.

The shower was still going. Rattling my ice cube gently
in the glass, I checked out some other drawers and cabinets
in the kitchen, and didn't learn much except that Kevin
seemed to like hot oatmeal, didn't use instant coffee, and a
family of mice had taken up residence somewhere under the
wood flooring below the sink, making frequent excursions
upward for provisions.

I was back in the living room end, messing with the TV

in an attempt to reduce the snow in a Denver newscast, when the door of the bathroom opened again and Kevin came out, barefoot and wearing a sweatshirt and jeans faded to gray. The way he had combed back his wet hair, making it cling to his scalp, made him look even more gaunt.

He saw what I was doing. "No sense trying, Brad. The picture doesn't get much better than that. We've got a couple of big mountains between us and the repeater site, and they only run a watt."

He walked to the kitchen corner, bent over to get some things out of the refrigerator, and started banging pots and pans around. "Got some potato salad and pita bread, too. Sound all right?"

"Sounds great," I said, fighting my impatience.

He put some things in the oven, started what sounded like an automatic coffeemaker, and slapped plates and silverware and a few other items on the small butcher-block table under the back window. He hummed tunelessly as he worked. *Be patient*, I reminded myself. *Just wait him out.*

He went back into the kitchen end and cocked his head, staring at the bottle of Canadian on the counter. "Don't mind if I do," he muttered, and poured a little into another jelly glass, plunking in two ice cubes last. Then he carried his drink into the living room part and dropped onto one end of the couch, extending a bare foot toward the center and facing my director's chair.

"So," he said.

I muted the newscast, which seemed at that point to consist of a male anchor telling the weather girl about a grade school he had visited earlier in the day. Kevin watched me with the same unreal detachment he had shown at the court when I first approached him. He seemed utterly at peace, as if no thought or feeling had ever bothered his mind.

He seemed so peaceful, in fact, that my good intentions about being cautious with him began to fade at once.

"Kevin—" I began.

"Ken," he corrected instantly.

"What's going on?" I blurted.

A frown flew by and vanished. "I suppose," he said, "you mean why am I here, why didn't I go back home after being released, and so on."

"Yes, and there's a hell of a lot of 'and so on'!"

He looked into some private space. "Well, I suppose there would be."

I tried to slow down. "How long have you been in Lake City?"

"Several years now."

"Maybe almost twenty years?"

He thought about it. "I guess it has been almost that long."

"What do you do here? What kind of work?"

He stretched and sipped his whisky. "Odd jobs sometimes, like fixing the fence around the courts up there. But I chop wood, mostly. It's a pretty good business. There are places you can cut trees for nothing, and then all you have to do is cut it into small enough pieces to fit in the back of the pickup, and bring it up here and saw it into firewood lengths and run it through the splitter. You can get sixty dollars a cord, delivered and stacked, from the summer people. That doesn't sound like much, but it adds up. A lot of nights get cold enough for a fire in the fireplace or the wood stove up here, even in the summer. The summer people like to have lots of fires. That kind of appeals to them. I cut and deliver to some of the year-round residents, too. The winters here are great, but it can get twenty or thirty below, and the humidity practically zero. I do some part-time rough carpentry for people, too; I have a card on the bulletin board down at the lumberyard, and they send work my way sometimes."

He paused to take another sip of his drink, then returned those blank, innocent eyes to me. "It doesn't cost a lot to live. There's another room I added onto the back of this place. You haven't seen that yet. I've got a big freezer in there. You can catch a lot of fish to eat, summer and winter, if you don't mind ice-fishing in the winter. And you can always get a deer, and some years an elk. My freezer is overflowing with good stuff. I make my own bread and watch for bargains down at the Country Store. In the summer there's a vegetable stand down on Gunnison Avenue and you can buy things there cheap and freeze them for the winter, too." He looked around. "The rent's cheap. I work part of it out sometimes, doing odd jobs for the owners downtown. I do a lot of the minor maintenance work up there at the estates where you found me awhile ago. It isn't necessary for me to be around town much in the summers, when there are a lot of outsiders around. That's good, too . . . I can pretty much stay out of sight."

I had begun to squirm inside, thinking he was going to filibuster all night. But his last comment gave me an opening I couldn't pass up. "Why is that important, Kevin—I mean Ken?"

He raised eyebrows in surprise. "Why is what important?"

"Not going to town much in the summer, when there are outsiders around. Staying out of sight."

He frowned. "It's, uh . . . ." He seemed to think about it, but he got a curious vacant look in his eyes for a moment. Then he came back. "It's just the way I am, I guess."

I hesitated, looking for the best way to press him, but he abruptly looked around toward the kitchen and jumped to his feet. "Gotta check the chili and stuff."

He clattered around out there for a minute or two, then padded back in, rubbing his hands together gleefully. "Almost ready. Hey, Brad, I guess you're still working at that club down in Richardson? You'll probably run into somebody you know while you're here. We get a lot of Texas and Oklahoma people in the summer. A lot from Dallas."

"No, I'm in Montana now."

"Montana? No kidding. Where? What are you doing up

there? Say, I've got some friends that are on the Lake City cable. I saw something about you on CNN or somewhere last summer. You went back to Wimbledon. But you tore up your knee and had to withdraw. You're not limping now. Has it healed up completely?"

I put down my glass and held my hands up in the form of a *T*, the sports official's signal for a time-out. He looked surprised again.

I said, "You were a POW in Vietnam."

His eyes instantly took on that curious, vacant sheen. The voice that came out of him sounded like a robot. "Yes. I was."

I began to get chill bumps on my arms. "They released you—when? In 1973?"

"Yes," he said in the same vacant tone, staring straight ahead.

"What happened then? You were checked onto an airplane, but when it landed in Hawaii you had vanished."

"Oh, no," he said very softly, in the voice of a child. "I landed in Hawaii. I got off the plane. But I knew. I *knew*. It was dark. We landed at night. Everything was real confused. I ducked behind a truck parked near the buses and then I just walked over to the fence. There was a gate. Nobody paid any attention. It was all very strange. Did I say we landed after dark? I just kept walking. I slept in a park. In the morning I stole some money and then I bought some real clothes and then later I had a little job and I saved some money and I got a new Social Security card and I flew home. To San Francisco, I mean. But I couldn't stay there. I couldn't go on *really* home. I knew what would happen to me if I did. I had to hide. Then I don't remember, exactly, but then I came here."

"To hide?" I asked carefully.

"Yes. To hide."

"To hide from who?"

The vacancy slip-shuttled behind his eyes again, and was gone. "Them."

"Who are they, Kevin? Why do they want you?"

He looked at me. His eyelids went up and down a dozen times, very fast. He got to his feet. His voice changed to a normal tone. He had gone somewhere else and now he was back here again. "Everything should be ready to eat by now, my man. Come and get it." He hurried barefoot to the kitchen and began rattling pans again.

I wasn't getting anywhere.

Twenty-five
Elsewhere

THE DEPUTY director strode into the meeting room and found Roger Magiris, Miriam Gonzales, and Dr. Cecil Kirby waiting for him at a table strewn with confidential reports. Deputy Director Ellis nodded curtly and started the meeting without preamble, directing his attention to Magiris. "Nothing new in the last hour or two on Tubb or Leventhal?"

"No, sir," Magiris said. "I'm afraid not."

"Have you talked to McDonald?"

"Yes, sir. He's back at Smith's lodge in Montana, and he knows Tubb and/or Leventhal may show up there in hopes Brad Smith has more information about this missing man, Kevin Green."

"McDonald understands how he's to proceed if he spots either of them? He isn't likely to blow somebody away like he did the last time?"

"That's right, sir."

"No word on Smith himself? His whereabouts?"

"I'm afraid not, sir."

Ellis set his jaw. "Dammit, I hope he's not dead in a ditch somewhere."

"We think the chances are better, sir, that he ran onto some hint of where Green might be, and is off checking it out on his own."

"We should have leveled with the sucker to begin with. I suppose we can hardly blame him for running around on his own, knowing as little as he does. He seems obsessed with the idea that Green is in danger, and it's up to him to find the man before somebody in the conspiracy does."

Magiris smiled thinly. "Given everything we know now, sir, it's not such a bad assumption on his part, is it?"

Ellis ignored the question and turned to Gonzales. "What's the status on filing of charges?"

Miriam Gonzales, looking tired and pale but still pretty in her red dress, glanced at a sheaf of handwritten notes. "Charges were filed late today in Knoxville on Michael Romanowski: the machine-gun charge, plus an ITOM."

"We can't make an Interstate Transport of Obscene Materials charge stand up in court," Ellis said.

Gonzales nodded agreement. "The U.S. district attorney says the same thing. But when the circumstances were explained to him, he agreed to file it. Tomorrow—now that Romanowski has told us all the rest of it—we'll file information for conspiracy and unlawful flight as well."

"What about the man out in Nebraska?"

"Based on Romanowski's sworn statement, on Raymond 'Buddy' Turner we've filed two federal handgun charges, two counts of murder, and a UFAP."

The deputy director jotted a note. "That holds Romanowski and Turner, then. The third one, Maxwell, is dead. So we're back to Tubb and Leventhal."

Magiris asked, "Has the army figured out yet what's going on?"

Ellis almost smiled. "No. Maybe the next time we file an INFODAT request with them about something, they'll remember how it feels and be a little more cooperative."

"The White House has now inquired, sir, I understand?"

"Yes. The director has an appointment with the President tomorrow at four o'clock. A complete dossier will be handed over at that time." Ellis actually did allow himself the smallest smile. "This is going to be a feather in our cap. I don't think we're going to hear anything more about budget reductions for awhile after the director hands this to the President."

Everyone shuffled papers for a moment. Ellis consulted a small notepad. "I've asked Dr. Kirby to come in with us for a few minutes because she's pulled together most of the information we have on one of our still-missings, Arnold Tubb. Dr. Kirby? Do you want to take over?"

Dr. Cecil Kirby was a small woman, dark-haired, with fine facial features behind overlarge eyeglasses. She glanced down at her notes and then raised keen hazel eyes to the others facing her.

"Tubb does not fit all aspects of the typical PTSD profile," she told them. "When he entered the army in 1966, it was as a volunteer. He had at that time completed two years of college work—accounting—with excellent grades. He comes from a middle-class family, and there is no hint of any emotional difficulty prior to his military service.

"Shortly after his good conduct discharge, Mr. Tubb first came to the attention of the VA. In his first postmilitary workup in the psychiatric section of the VA hospital in Oklahoma City, he was classified as schizophreniform with paranoid delusions, subchronic with acute exacerbation, moderately severe; it was theorized that the delusional thinking and bizarre behavior which resulted in his hospitalization stemmed from a recent significant psychosocial stressor, i.e., witnessing an attempted armed robbery at a supermarket, during which police exchanged gunfire with two robbers and killed both.

"Tubb was treated with chemotherapy and talk therapy, and after five months seemed greatly improved, with the result that he was released. However, less than six months later, he was again admitted to a Veterans' Administration hospital, this time in Baltimore, after a full-scale delusional episode in which he attempted to break through a guard gate at a military installation because voices told him to take over management of the arsenal before secret Vietnamese agents attacked from inside the compound. At this time, Tubb's diagnosis was altered to schizophrenia, paranoid type, moderately severe."

Kirby turned to the second and last page of her notes. "At that time, after initial treatment with chemicals that calmed him somewhat, Tubb told his doctor that he had witnessed a mass murder in Vietnam in the spring of 1968, and he would never be free of nightmares and flashbacks until he had—quote—taken care of every man involved, unquote. Attempts to elicit additional information so agitated the patient that further questioning along this line was discontinued, and his story attributed to his general pattern of delusional thinking.

"Over the years, Tubb has been arrested on many occasions. In the summer of 1980—and I believe this is new information just uncovered—he attacked two orientals on the sidewalk in downtown Baltimore, nearly killing one of them with a knife and seriously disfiguring the other. Judged criminally insane in a subsequent trial, he was first institutionalized by the state and then transferred on his request to the VA's long-term psychiatric incarceration facility near Silver Spring, Maryland. He was released in 1983, readmitted in 1985, released again in 1986, and readmitted still again in the autumn of 1988 after a psychotic episode on a New York City subway train.

"Sometime late last year, army investigators apparently finally were notified of his continued delusional talk about a massacre in Vietnam in 1968. Two investigators visited him. The army has not responded to our requests for copies of the reports on the interrogations that took place at that time.

"Shortly after this interrogation, Tubb was diagnosed as having non-Hodgkins lymphoma, acute lymphocytic type, poorly differentiated, Stage III, and transferred to Walter Reed Army Hospital for radiation and chemotherapy treatments. He had received two or three treatments when he walked away on Christmas Eve."

Kirby looked up from her notes as she removed her reading glasses. "I've given you this background to indicate the kind of man you're dealing with here. Let me summarize. He is delusional and unpredictable. He is capable of homicidal violence. He is not a stupid man, and his obsession tends to make him even more clever in some ways. Trying to guess his future course of action is quite impossible. I suspect that he committed one or more of the unsolved murders reflected in some of these files on the table. He is presently obsessed with finding the man you mentioned, Kevin Green. I have no idea why. Tubb is extremely, extremely dangerous. He is capable of anything."

Langley, Virginia

"YOU KNOW," J. C. Kinkaid said, "sometimes I get real tired of these all-nighters."

Thomas Dwight poured more coffee. "You might consider working for Kmart. They close at ten or eleven."

"Thanks, pal."

Kinkaid glanced at the third man who had just walked in, Collie Davis. "What's from Brad?"

"Nothing," Davis said gloomily.

"What's from the army?"

"Nothing."

"The FBI?"

"Nothing."

"Do you think Brad's partner out there really doesn't know where Brad is?"

"I don't know. It doesn't matter. He obviously isn't going to tell us shit, either way."

Dwight frowned. "I don't like the way this feels. All we know is that the FBI is rounding people up, but still doesn't have that crazy who walked away from the hospital last Christmas. That guy has to be hunting Kevin Green. Brad is out hunting Kevin Green again, too; I'd bet my paycheck on it. And we have no idea what's going on."

Collie Davis looked bleak. "And our charter says our hands are tied."

Dwight leaned back in his chair. "Don't you have some vacation time coming, Collie?"

Davis's eyes widened slightly. "Doesn't everybody?"

"Why don't you take a few days off? Maybe a change of scenery would do you some good. You might want to go to Montana and look at a mountain, or something."

Davis got to his feet immediately. "I assume you can get the paperwork processed?"

"Done."

"Then I'm out of here."

"Give us a call. Let us know how the vacation is going."

Davis walked out.

Near Elk City, Montana

ALONE IN the chill Montana night, Special Agent Reese Mc-Donald jogged south on the side of the two-lane highway, his breath forming great clouds of steam around his face. The headlights of an oncoming car appeared in the distance, and McDonald veered a bit farther off away from the pavement, moving from the gravel shoulder to the grassy berm beyond it. The car's lights came closer and became brighter and then were blinding for a second or two as it roared by, going in the opposite direction, leaving a hot ocean of fume-filled exhaust in its wake. McDonald jogged on southward.

This was an extra run today, one dictated not by his rigidly self-disciplined fitness program, but by sheer nerves and tension. Since losing Brad Smith in Kansas City—and having to go through the galling experience of *reporting* that fact—he had been a guest at Bitterroot Valley Resort, allegedly like any other tourist/tennis buff/golfer, but in reality doing nothing but watching while he hoped and prayed that

Smith would show up soon so at least a report could be phoned in that surveillance had been routinely resumed.

Brad Smith, however, had not cooperated. He was gone somewhere, and everyone around the resort swore they knew nothing of his whereabouts.

That frustration was galling enough. What made it worse was McDonald's virtual certainty that Smith's partner, Treacher, *did* know where he had gone, and simply wasn't telling.

Reese McDonald had no way of forcing someone to talk. Therefore, McDonald was stymied. All he could do was sit and wait—the most excruciating kind of duty imaginable, especially under the embarrassing circumstances.

The reports he had gotten over the telephone since his arrival back in Montana indicated that everything had gone wonderfully well in almost all phases of the operation, other than his dismal failure on Smith. God, this was the kind of screwup that could weight your file down through all the years remaining in a blighted career! McDonald would have done anything to track Smith. But what?

He thought about the descriptions of the two fugitives he was also to watch for. He would watch, but he didn't hold out much hope that they would be stupid enough to walk right in and present themselves to him. He felt more depressed.

Jogging on, he reached the curving roadway leading into the resort. Crossing the parking lot, he slowed his pace and walked the last fifty yards or so, checking his carotid pulse. It felt slightly irregular. Stress. He went into the lodge.

Climbing the stairs to his second-floor room, he carefully locked himself in and then dragged his suitcase out of the closet. Working the double security combination latches, he opened it and took out the tiny combination receiver-recording device tuned to the frequency of the electronic b~~ he had managed to place in the business office dow~ ~~pe-~~ ~~ization.~~

McDonald always felt extra nervous plantin~ cially ones like this one that had no court~

But he had been ordered to plant and monitor it, and he always followed orders.

Sticking the rig's tiny headphones into his ears, he squatted on the floor beside the open closet door and began playing back the last hour's conversations picked up below. VOX-operated, the equipment condensed time by recording only when sounds keyed the recorder. Updating took only a few minutes. Except for a titillating but useless bit of flirtatious talk between the assistant chef and a waitress he evidently was bedding, the new talk was of no interest whatsoever.

Disappointed again, McDonald reset the equipment, hid it back away in his locked suitcase, and closed the closet doors. Something would turn up soon, he told himself. It had to.

Lolo, Montana

MILES NORTH of Bitterroot Valley Resort, Stan Leventhal pulled up to the brightly lighted front of an all-night convenience store and cut the Volvo's engine.

Beside him, Arnie Tubb pulled his door handle to get out.

"Stay in the car," Leventhal said nervously. "I'll just get our cigarettes and be right back out."

Tubb, his sick-sweaty face ghastly in the bright fluorescent light streaming through the windshield, grimaced protest. "I want some beer!"

"I'll get some! Stay here. You know everybody in the world is looking for you."

Tubb muttered an obscenity but settled back in the seat.

Leventhal got out quickly and hurried inside. The cigarettes were in the back near the rear checkout counter. Looking for beer, he spied the refrigerators on the far left-hand racks that pulled over there, going behind high merchandise that blocked his view of the front windows of the store.
Pulling a beer out of the cooler, he noticed

the pay telephone right beside it on the wall, in the narrow hall that led to rest rooms. He felt a pulse of scared excitement. Tubb hadn't let him call home since they had left Michigan Thursday morning. He needed to call Doreen—at least make a stab at pretending his sudden absence had a semblance of normalcy about it.

This was his chance.

Ducking fast into the hall, he dug a quarter out of his pants pocket, slugged it into the telephone, and hurriedly punched in the zero-plus numbers. The AT&T chime sounded and he entered his Calling Card numbers. After a moment, the telephone back there in Ann Arbor began to ring.

"Hello?" It was Doreen. He had half expected her to be asleep, but her voice sounded brittle with nervous tension. He heard a little mechanical snapping noise on the line, too, but ignored it.

"Doreen? This is Stan. I—"

"Stan? Where are you? Why haven't you called? My God, the FBI was here—they're looking for you and that creepy man who stayed here that night. They've been arresting people all over the country—" Her voice stopped abruptly.

Shock sluiced through Leventhal's bloodstream. "Hello? Hello?"

A man's voice came on the line. *"Is this Professor Leventhal?"*

Leventhal dropped the receiver back onto the hook as if it had scalded him. Shaking, he hurried to the checkout counter with his beer and cigarettes. The clerk, a skinny teenager, said something to him. He didn't hear what the clerk said—smiled desperately and nodded as if he had. The clerk gave him change for his twenty.

Outside, Tubb grabbed the paper bag and pulled out one of the beers, which he popped immediately as Leventhal backed away from the store.

"What took you so long?" Tubb demanded. "What's the big fucking hurry all of a sudden? Hey! You look like shit, man."

"They've got the others," Leventhal blurted, wheeling onto the highway.

"What? What?"

There was no way to hide it. "I called home."

"You—!"

"Listen to me! Listen to me! Doreen said the FBI came. She said they arrested people all over the country. Then some man got on the line—probably an FBI agent."

"Jesus!"

"We're alone!" Leventhal groaned, driving as fast as he dared toward the motel on the outskirts. "The FBI must be looking for us, too—looking for this damned car! We're *ruined*, Arnie! Now it's just us, and they must have agents and police alerted everywhere!"

Tubb rocked backward and forward on the seat. "They got everybody? They got Buddy and Jack?"

"I don't know—I don't know! All I know is what Doreen said. She said it was the FBI. Jesus, they must have rounded up everybody!"

"Romanowski," Tubb bit off. "He must have cracked. They must have gotten him to talk. The bastard must have told them everything."

"We've got to give ourselves up," Leventhal groaned.

"What do you mean, give ourselves up?" Tubb shot back.

"We've got no help now. There's no one else. We haven't been able to find Smith, and we don't have a clue—we don't have a chance!"

"Are you crazy, man?" Tubb asked.

"What?"

"This don't mean we *give up*! This just means it's all up to us now! Now we *got to* find Green. He's the only one left that could tell 'em everything that happened—every bit of it!" Tubb stopped talking a moment, rocking violently, beer sloshing out of his can and onto his trouser legs. "Smith. He's our key. We got to find out where Smith is, and maybe he'll lead us to Green. That's our only hope."

"I've had enough," Leventhal protested, on the verge of terrified tears. "I'm quitting! I'm getting *out* of this thing right now!"

With a quick, violent motion, Tubb dug into his jacket pocket. His hand came up with the cheap, evil little revolver. He pointed it at Leventhal across the front seat. "You're not quitting me! You're not getting out now! You're in this with me to the end, motherfucker. Now, slow down and drive us back to the motel. I got to figure out what we do next."

Leventhal turned his attention back to the road with a sickening feeling of despair. He had been entrapped for years. Now the cage had shrunk to the dimensions of this car—to the black diameter of the revolver barrel pointed at his head.

Tubb was insane, he thought. Unless he could somehow escape from Tubb, or betray him—or kill him—he was doomed.

Beside him, Tubb jerked violently.

"What?" Leventhal asked, startled.

"I know what we got to do. I've *had* it, sitting up here and making phone calls. For all we know, he might be down there at his lodge right now. In the morning we're going down there."

Leventhal's nerves screamed. "How can we do *that?* There might be FBI all over the place, just waiting for us!"

"We can't just sit here anymore! We've got to risk it. Our time is running out. *My* time is running out. Just shut up, just shut up! We're doing it. Now, look. This is how we'll handle it."

Twenty-six

THE MEAL with Kevin was like *Alice in Wonderland*. He acted like it was the most normal thing in the world, the two of us eating leftovers together in a shack halfway up a mountain after all these years. There was something in him . . . something strange . . . that made me deeply uneasy. I decided not to press for additional information until we were through the meal. He talked quietly about his life in Lake City, about the local bakery, the recent refurbishing of the Baptist Church on Bluff Street, how quickly cut firewood became seasoned in the low humidity here.

"I guess at least you get to play some tennis regularly," I said at one point, fishing.

He looked up, his spoon of chili poised halfway to his mouth. "Tennis? Oh, no. Certainly not."

"But I saw you on the court up there—"

"That's a privately owned court."

Stranger and stranger. "Surely you play on it."

"I occasionally give the kids a pointer or two. They think I played college tennis in Kansas somewhere. But I don't ever play. I was only up there to fix the fence. I don't play anymore. That would be wrong."

He had thrown me again. "Why would playing tennis be wrong?"

"I just don't, that's all. Hey, your plate is empty. Want seconds? There's plenty."

My patience snapped. "Kevin, what I want is some straight talk."

His forehead wrinkled. "Ken. I'm Ken now."

"No, you're not. You're Kevin Green. We went to college together and you went to Vietnam as a helicopter pilot, and I came later as a grunt. You and I and your copilot, Dave Wentworth, drank beer together one night over there. Then you got shot down, or something, and were a POW. Then you were repatriated, but you walked away from the evacuation plane in Hawaii, and you've been hiding out ever since."

I paused, because every word I spoke seemed to hit him like a physical blow: his face twisted, his eyes darted furtively, a tic began jumping under his left eye. I didn't want to hurt him like this. I had no way of guessing whether I might even be doing psychological damage to him somehow. *Just stop and forget the whole thing—get out of here.*

But I couldn't take that way out.

"You're hiding," I repeated. "I don't know why, but somebody wants to kill you."

He flinched. "No."

"Yes. What happened over there, Kevin? Who are these guys that are after you? Why couldn't you ever go home again?"

His haunted eyes met mine. "It's just posttraumatic stress syndrome. No big deal. A lot of Vietnam vets have it. Haven't you ever read about it? I'm better than most. I can work. I'm earning a living. I don't have flashbacks . . . very often. Why have you come here? I thought you were my friend! Did you just come to give me a hard time?"

"I came to try to save your life."

"My life doesn't *need* saving! I'm getting along fine."

I had to escalate, break through some way—any way. "I saw Barb a week and a half ago."

Pain twisted his face. "You did?"

"Yes."

"How is she? Where is she? I suppose she's . . ." He paused, hanging up as if the word almost wouldn't come.

Then he squared his bony shoulders. "I suppose," he said more firmly, "she's remarried. And all."

"No."

Eyebrows raised. "No?"

"She's convinced you're still alive. She's waiting for you."

His eyes glistened. I had finally said something that broke through. He said huskily, "That's hard to believe."

"You have to go back," I told him. "If for no other reason than Barb. That's a wonderful woman back there. She loves you. She loves the hell out of you! Don't you owe her anything?"

"She's better off this way! She got the military benefits long before now, surely, and she has the privileges of an officer's widow. Hell, she's far better off than—"

"Bullshit! Kevin! *Dave Wentworth is dead.* He was murdered last month."

Kevin's face went slack with horror. "Dave? Oh, no."

"Somebody cut his throat. Somebody cut off one of his ears like a trophy."

He pushed back from the table so violently that his chair tipped backward, hitting the wood floor with a loud crash. He started toward the sink, then stopped and veered instead into the living room. For a second I thought he was going out the door. Then he turned back. Wringing his hands, he walked to the dark TV set and then to the potbelly stove. He knelt in front of the stove and popped the doors open. Pulling back the spark screen inside, he reached for a poker to stir some cold, half-burned logs in the stove's dense black interior. But then he just left the poker sticking out of the stove and put his hands on his thighs and knelt there and started to cry— silently, head down, tears dripping off his nose and chin, his whole body shuddering with spasms that were more terrible because of their silence.

I got up and went to the whisky and poured myself a stiff jolt, shaky enough that I sloshed some on the counter. I

downed half of it and shuddered. Such a fine brand: Old
Fortitude, 100 proof. I carried the rest of the drink into the
living room and sat in one of the director's chairs and just
watched him cry. Seeing it made me hurt more than I'm
capable of expressing.

"Kevin, what can I do?"

He seemed not to hear, the ugly sobs shaking him.

I went over and tried to put my arm over his shoulder.
"Listen, pal, just tell me what I can—"

With a violent motion he threw my arm off his back.

Helpless, I went back to my chair. Maybe this had to
happen, I told myself. Maybe this meant I had broken
through to him. Maybe it meant—*You don't know what it
means, Smith. You don't know anything. All you know is
he's hurting like hell and you can't make it stop. So shut up
all the psychobabble and drink your whisky. Maybe it will
make you feel capable or competent or something.*

After what seemed a long time, it stopped. It stopped in
stages, the shaking first, then some of the tears, then a slight
straightening of the slumped, crushed, kneeling posture in
front of the stove. Then he simply knelt there awhile, hands
still on his thighs, head down, looking at nothing. After that,
he straightened a bit more, sniffled, dug a bandana out of his
hip pocket, and loudly blew his nose.

"Sorry," he said.

"Kevin," I said. "What happened over there? What's
behind all this?"

Looking up at me from his kneeling position, he got
blank-eyed for a second or two. I knew he was having some
kind of a flashback. But then he looked normal again. He
climbed to his feet. "It's getting cold," he said in a perfectly
normal voice. "Let's get the stove going."

"Then you'll tell me what it's all about?"

"I'll tell you what I know."

* * *

I cleared the table, put things away, and stowed pots and dishes in the sink while he clattered around the stove and got a roaring fire going. The cabin, which had become quite chilly although I hadn't noticed it, began to warm fast. He got himself another touch of whisky and came back and slouched on the couch as he had before. His eyes looked inward as he started to talk. I kept my mouth shut, for once, and listened.

"The weather had been really bad for days. It wasn't supposed to be that bad, but it was. Dave and I and two other gunships had gone out three or four days in a row and couldn't see a thing down under the low stuff. When we took off that day—the bad day—it was drizzly, with low clouds, and we didn't think we were going to get anything accomplished that day, either.

"We'd gotten part of a message from Baker Company— the parts of Baker's 2nd and 3rd the big choppers had managed to put in a couple of days earlier. They were moving on a hamlet our intelligence had identified as a VC stronghold.

"Our radios were practically worthless for communications with ground units. Along with high atmospheric interference, the North Vietnamese had some kind of a noise machine they could get on our frequencies sometimes and really mess up communications. I think there might have been a sunspot eruption or something, in addition to all of that. So we had terrible weather and almost nonexistent comm, and combat units on a sweep where they needed all the help they could get, along with reinforcements, if the big choppers could get through the gunk and onto the ground.

"We headed out—four gunships including ours, and three of the big boys loaded with additional troops. There was a low scud layer, then a layer of almost-clear air a couple thousand feet thick, then a really dense cloud with rain coming out of it. We got airborne fine, and all of us headed north, flying in that little sandwich-layer of mist and rain that let you see all right.

"Getting close to the place where the hamlet ought to be right down below us someplace, we started being able to hear more on our radios from the ground. But there wasn't much of it, and it was chunks of stuff—orders to move some direction, calling a squad up closer, reporting fire, and so forth. The big black troop helicopter in the lead called down, trying to get more information, but got no answer.

"The 123rd hadn't been able to get up a small observation chopper to go with us, because there was a really big operation to the south and there weren't any extra units available. So we were stuck orbiting the battle site down below us someplace, Dave and me and the other gunships at about eight hundred feet, right on the top of the low scud layer, and the big guys up higher, about two thousand, everybody milling around, not knowing what was going on.

"After quite a long time, Colonel Starr, our on-site commander up in one of the Hueys, lost his patience. If we didn't find a way to put down soon, all of us were going to have to head back to base. So he ordered Dave and me to poke down into the cloud and see if we could feel our way through—find out if there was enough space under the bottom layer for the others to come down.

"It sounded like a dumb order to me—not the SOP way to do it—but I let down through the stuff. I felt like we might hit the ground before we came out. At no more than two hundred feet AGL, we finally came out enough to see the ground. It was still raining. What we could see were rice fields, a couple of small streams, some hills to the south, and a lot of jungle-type terrain. I could see right away that we had been orbiting several miles off from the hamlet, where the action was. Off to the west several miles I could see smoke coming up from something burning.

"Practically at treetop level because of the soup, we headed that way. When we got closer, I saw all the smoke was from the hamlet, everything on fire. That was okay combat doctrine in Nam, as you know: in a free-fire zone, with suspected VC activity, torch the place.

"I swung around closer, trying to get a total picture before hollering up to the colonel, and maybe find a target of opportunity. I saw at once that some of our guys had crossed the stream near the hamlet, and were out on a flat area between two rice fields a few hundred yards away. Not many, maybe thirty. They seemed to be making a slow sweep of the fields, moving toward dense trees and brush a few hundred yards on ahead of them.

"Going back over the hamlet, we saw bodies all over the little central square. You could see most of them were women and children. All the huts were on fire—most of them had already been reduced to smoking black piles of stuff. We saw some of our guys well on the far side of the hamlet—away from the ones across the stream. They were just sitting down and some of them were eating rations. It looked like they didn't even belong to the same group that had crossed the river, but I knew they had to be. I wondered why the command had been split that way. It didn't look like anyone was in charge.

"I flew back across the hamlet again. I spotted this wide drainage ditch. Dave began screaming and cussing, and I went around again, lower, maybe forty feet off the deck.

"The ditch was full of dead civilians. There were other dead civilians all around on the ground. I had seen some bad stuff, but nothing like that.

"Our course took us back across the little river. We went in over the troops on that side and we could see that they had a group of people—maybe a half dozen—standing out in the rice field, knee-deep in the water. Our guys were on the high ground thirty or forty feet from them, covering them with their M-16s. I saw the captain in charge waving and yelling something. The Vietnamese out in the field were holding their hands over their heads. They had what looked like ID cards in them. They were just standing there, hands up, showing those ID cards we issued to verified friendlies.

"As I came back around, I saw a puff from somebody's rifle. Then all the men started shooting. They mowed those civilians down like you'd cut weeds with a sickle. Then a couple of the guys ran out into the field and starting sticking their bayonets into these people. About the same time, from behind where the captain and his men were standing, just watching, a small boy of maybe five or six came out from where he had been hiding in some brush and ran right past the captain, down into the rice field, splashing along, running straight for where these few guys were still slashing and sticking at dead bodies. Maybe they were the little kid's family. I don't know.

"Then somebody shot the kid. He went over face-first. He wasn't very far into the field, it had all happened so fast. The captain ran over to the edge of the road and pulled out a sidearm, probably a .45, and shot the kid in the head, just to make sure.

"I had seen a lot, as I said. But I had never seen anything like this. Neither had Dave. He threw up, right there in the chopper. I flew on out past the rice fields and our few troops down there who had killed the civilians. I could see the captain with a radio in his hand, but it didn't seem to be working. He signaled the men with him and they headed on west, toward the denser trees and vegetation. The other part of his command just kept on sitting there, way back on the far side of the hamlet. I flew over that way. I think it was right about then that I called the commander and told him I thought they could bring the rest of the choppers on down if they went slowly and kind of felt for it."

Kevin stopped talking, stared vacantly for a moment, then seemed to come back to the present. The fire in the stove had burned down a little. He went over to slide the screen back and put in one more small split log. Then he closed the screen again, went to the kitchen, and came back with his whisky refreshed. He sat down and looked at me.

"That's it."

Baffled, I thought back to the reports Collie Davis had shown me. What Kevin had said dovetailed with much of what those documents, censored as they had been, also revealed. But something was missing.

"What about the VC ambush?" I demanded.

"I don't know anything about that."

"That captain—his name was Aldrich—took part of his command northeast of the hamlet. They ran into a VC ambush and virtually got wiped out."

Kevin's eyes glazed. His robot voice came out: "I don't know anything about that."

"It happened a couple of miles northeast of where you were. You had to have seen it."

The eerie calm returned to Kevin's expression. "I didn't see that."

"What," I persisted, more puzzled, "did you do after you called the other helicopters and told them it was clear enough to come down?"

"I don't know. I had done my job. I orbited the area for a while. They put more troops on the ground. The big helicopters took off again and headed home. Then we got ready to head home."

"Then what happened?"

"I had flown out farther, a bigger circle, looking for enemy. We were still real low, treetop. Separated from the others. We took some sudden small-arms fire and some rockets. We took some hits. I lost power and we started to smoke. I only had a few seconds. I put it down in a clearing not much bigger than my lot, here. We climbed out and ran, and the ship blew up. The concussion knocked the shit out of both of us, knocked us down. Then we looked up and we had North Vietnamese regulars all around us. We surrendered. They tied us up and marched us out of there."

"What happened later?"

"Nothing happened later. They put us in a camp. There were a lot of other guys there. A lot of them died. Then the commandant came out one day and said the war was over, we had lost, and Vietnam was going to return us to our side."

I studied Kevin's expression. It was unreadable. Whatever lay behind his eyes could not be guessed.

His story made sense, yet had told me nothing.

"You didn't see the ambush?" I said, repeating myself to be sure.

"No."

"Kevin, why in the hell—from everything you've told me—would anyone want to kill you or Dave or anyone else, for that matter?"

"I don't know. Maybe no one does."

"They do," I reminded him. "That's why you're here, dammit."

"There were . . . old grudges. I knew that even before we were repatriated. A few of the guys in the prison camp didn't die of mistreatment or sickness or something. A few of them were murdered by other fellow Americans in the compound. I knew if I came home, I would be next."

"Kevin, *why* would you be next?"

He gave me the same blank stare and said nothing.

"Kevin, what are you leaving out?"

"Nothing," he said with that same creepy calm.

We sat there looking at each other. I had seldom felt so stymied. There were holes in his story big enough to drop an elephant through. Either he wasn't telling me everything, or he really didn't remember everything—had shoved some part of that awful day back into a cobwebby recess of his unconscious. I had to learn the rest—somehow—if I was ever to be able to help him, get him out of here, keep him alive, take him back to his *real* life. But how did you unlock a hidden compartment when it was inside a man's skull, and possibly he didn't even suspect that it existed there?

I tried one more thing. "Kevin. Do you have a telephone here?"

"No. There aren't any lines out on this mountain. When people want wood or something, they leave a message for me down at the store. Why?"

"I want to call Barbara."

He flinched back. "No!"

"Then you call her. Let her know she hasn't been crazy, thinking you're still alive."

He drew back and looked at me like I was some slimy thing that had just crawled out from under a wet rock. "No! Are you insane? What good would that do? I'm never going back, and she can never come here or meet me anywhere else. Someone might follow her. *She* could be killed, too. No! It's out of the question! It's better this way—at least she can think I was a good soldier, not a criminal."

My nerve endings stung. "Why should she think you're a criminal?"

He blinked, almost flashed back to something, returned to the present. "No reason. I don't know why I said that."

I was getting nowhere again. I looked at my watch and saw with surprise that it was far past midnight. "I've got to be going."

Standing, he made no effort to keep me. "Can you find your way back to the highway?"

"Yes. I was paying attention."

He walked with me to the door and there held out his hand. "It was good seeing you again, Brad. But just forget you did. Tell no one. *No one.* You understand?"

I shook his hand. "I'm not leaving town just yet. I want to see you tomorrow."

"No, we can't meet again. This one time was risky enough. Just forget the whole thing, Brad. Please." He turned on an outside porch light and opened the door for me.

Stepping out into the cold night air, I glanced back at

him. There had to be more. I couldn't just walk away. "How about lunch tomorrow?"

"No. I don't go downtown. I take my lunch to wherever I'm working."

I pretended to give up. "Well, if you change your mind, I'll probably be at the Lake City Cafe around noon."

"Goodbye, Brad. Thanks for coming."

"Good night, Kevin."

He gave me a sloppy half-salute that almost looked like the old Kevin. I walked to my rented Cherokee, climbed in, got everything closed and buckled and started up, and backed out onto the "road." As I pulled away, I glanced back toward the shack. He was still standing in the open doorway, a skinny man, middle-aged now, his tall frame bent by the weight of things he had not told me and perhaps did not consciously know. I wondered what I would do now, because after coming all this way I did not intend to give up.

Twenty-seven
Elsewhere
Bitterroot Valley: June 25

SPECIAL AGENT Reese McDonald awoke promptly at 6 A.M., rolled out of bed at once, and walked into the shower. Twenty minutes later, he was shaved and combed and in his sweats for his morning run.

Going downstairs, he crossed the empty lobby and went out into the deep morning chill. Another beautiful morning, the sun brilliant on distant higher mountain elevations, flowers beginning to blaze in the resort beds. McDonald did a few stretching exercises, enjoying the way his muscles felt. Then, after a few deep breaths, he started off away from the lodge, across the parking lot, running well down the grassy side of the driveway, reaching the highway. He turned north, crossed the pavement so he would be running on the side of the shoulder facing traffic, and headed out.

Forty minutes later, sweat-soaked and blowing hard, he jogged back down the other side of the two-lane road, reached the resort driveway again, and slowed as he trotted through the parking lot, with its few guest cars. Automatically, he noted the various state license plates. The elderly Volvo with Michigan plates leaped out at him; it had not been here yesterday. *Was this the number they had given him to watch for?*

McDonald hurried up the steps onto the vast front porch. He entered the lobby quietly, knowing some of the other guests would be up and around by now. The only ones in the lobby were two older couples standing near the doorway of the dining room, waiting for its seven o'clock opening.

McDonald noted with casual distaste how fat both of the old men were. He wondered what their cholesterol count must be. People who didn't take care of themselves at any age irritated him, but to see older people in such condition was positively disgusting.

The disgust, however, was a moment's passing sensation. McDonald was in far too big a hurry to get up to his room and check his notebook.

Moving silently down the deserted upper hallway, he entered his room, ducked into the bathroom just long enough to get a towel for his face, and hurried back out to the small writing table where his locked attaché case was. He unlocked it, opened it, and unlocked the metal box inside that contained his notebook. He thumbed pages. Then his nerves tingled because there it was, in his neat, small-looped handwriting: *Mich Li No 456D788.*

Bingo.

Without hesitation, McDonald picked up the room telephone and accessed an outside line. He called the priority number and told the agent on duty what he had found. Yes, the car and plates both matched. No, he had not seen subject Leventhal, and no, he did not know yet whether subject Tubb was also here.

McDonald wanted very, very badly to go charging out of his room right away, find one or both of the suspects, and take them into custody. What a feat that would be, more than making up for underestimating Brad Smith those other times! But he knew better than to larrup off without reporting and getting instructions, especially on a Special such as this one. He also knew what the instructions were likely to be, and they did not surprise or even much dismay him: establish that they were still here and maintain a watch on them; do nothing to alarm them; his authorized firearm, the .38-caliber Browning in his suitcase, was not to be used in an attempt to take the subjects into custody except in the case of a pressing emergency, such as certain sign that they were preparing to leave and move on again.

Help would be on hand as soon as possible, and in no case later than 1200 today.

"Understand," McDonald snapped, and hung up.

He could smell his own sweat, and rapidly cooling off like this could lead to muscle cramps. But he had no time for his second shower of the day just yet. Locking things back up in good shape and pocketing the key case, he let himself back out of the room and went downstairs. He made it a point to saunter.

An hour later, still having seen nothing of either wanted subject, McDonald returned to his room. He quickly showered, shaved, and put on normal working clothes: a dark, immaculate suit, white dress shirt, and tightly knotted conservative tie. Going down to the main floor again, he casually approached the registration desk, where a middle-aged female clerk, identified by her name tag as Phyllis Eversol, stood behind the counter. She was the same clerk who had checked McDonald in, and they had exchanged pleasantries once or twice since then.

"Good morning!" Mrs. Eversol said with a big smile. "Another beautiful morning!"

"It certainly is," McDonald agreed. "I had a nice jog."

"You're certainly a demon for that running, Mr. McDonald! Is there something I can do for you this morning?"

He pointed over his shoulder toward the front. "I saw a familiar car out in the lot. I think some friends of mine must have arrived late last night or early this morning. I didn't know they were coming in today. The Volvo out there? Michigan plates?"

Mrs. Eversol glanced down at her registration card file. "Oh, sure. Mr. Brown and Mr. Henderson. They called and checked in late last night. Gee, after their long drive I bet they might still be sleeping. Do you want me to ring their room, or—"

"Not at all," McDonald cut in quickly. "Heavens no! Let
them sleep! By the way, are they on my floor?"

The woman looked at the cards. "No, actually they're on
three. Three fifty-six."

Reassured, McDonald slid a dollar bill across the counter.
"Thanks. You're a real dear. I'll just let them sleep, and we
can all get together later in the day. Oh, by the way, I don't
suppose Mr. Smith has returned?"

The dollar went into her dress pocket. "No, sir, not yet."

"Thanks again, Mrs. Eversol."

He walked away from the counter with a new spring in his
step. Brad Smith might still be among the missing, but being
instrumental in capturing these two men was far more important anyway. Now all he had to do was keep an eye on them
as best and cleverly as he could until help arrived. Oh, this
was wonderful luck!

Twenty-eight

June 25

DESPITE HAVING spent much of the night prowling my little motel cabin, trying to figure out what was going on with Kevin, I was awake again long before dawn on Tuesday, and headed north on 149 for Gunnison. The plan I had finally arrived at did not make as much sense in the morning light as it had in the dark of 3 A.M. But I couldn't think of anything better.

The evening with Kevin had frustrated and puzzled me as much as anything in my experience. He had been the same Kevin in some ways, but a stranger in others. The eerie feeling of detachment from reality that I got from him was not just normal change in a man as he grew older. Something had so profoundly altered his view of reality that he no longer functioned in precisely the normal dimensions. He had not told me everything. But I felt a spooky, intuitive certainty that he had not lied or held back intentionally; he simply *no longer knew part of his own past.*

I do not pretend to understand the human mind. But I know there are many ways the mind can protect itself from unacceptable past events. There can be self-protecting denial so strong that horrible memories are buried in the unconscious, and the sufferer truly no longer knows they exist. There are such things as screen memories—twisted symbolic recollections created by the mind to hide whatever really happened. A person on the edge of madness because of awful memories may suddenly experience something known as psychogenic amnesia, in which *everything* is forgotten and the memory banks are wiped clean.

Something like one of these had happened to Kevin. He was here in hiding because of something so terrible in his past that he no longer knew it. Yet it was *there*, tucked away, making him know without understanding that he had to hide forever.

I had imagined that everything would be made clear for me if I could find him before his pursuers did. But now I had no more idea of why he was marked for death than I had at the outset.

A therapist might be able to sift through all this, given time. But there was no time, and Kevin would never see a therapist anyway; pretending that everything was fine was a foundation stone of his craziness, so that the pretense at the heart of his sickness was the same pretense that would make voluntary therapy impossible.

My floor-pacing in the night and the smoking of an ungodly number of cigarettes had all been centered on trying to think of what I should do to help him.

The coldly logical thing to do was to contact the FBI and let them take it from here. He would be safe then, physically, at least for awhile. But maybe the Bureau knew the dread secret in his past, and simply hadn't told me about it; maybe it was a crime connected somehow with Quang Xi; at best, I thought, there would have to be charges of some kind filed because of his desertion from the army.

That left the CIA. Because of the old Vietnam background and the MIA question, they might get involved in a peripheral way. But I didn't trust people like J. C. Kinkaid and Tom Dwight, not entirely. How was I to know they wouldn't immediately turn Kevin over to the Bureau?

I was left with only two hopes: the feeble, intuitive trick I had come up with in the dead of night, and the one man I felt I could really trust: Collie.

I was in Gunnison when most of the stores opened at nine

o'clock. It's a nice small town in the valley with a number of motels and many touristy shops along its two main streets. I quickly learned that the stores handling sporting goods catered mainly to fishermen and skiers. Finding tennis equipment for sale was not easy. I was about to resort to Wal-Mart when I happened upon a small store with a wider variety of sports items, and located a couple of moderately priced Prince rackets that would be adequate for what I had in mind. I bought two cans of balls to go with them, along with some rubber-soled sneakers, and was headed back west, passing the cutoff for the small Gunnison airport, by a bit after ten—time enough to make my telephone call.

Parking beside an open booth close to the highway on the west side of town, I used my Calling Card to punch in the good number at Langley—the one you call when you're not the general public. My call went through to Collie's extension and I recognized the voice of the secretary who answered the line.

"Mary," I said, "this is Brad Smith. Is Collie in?"

"Hi, Brad. No, he isn't."

"Let me guess. In a meeting, right?" They were always in a meeting.

"No, actually . . ." Mary's voice trailed off. *"Can you hold one moment, please?"*

"Sure."

It was more like two. Then a familiar male voice came on: *"Brad? Kinkaid speaking."*

"Hey, J.C. I wanted to talk to Collie."

"Brad, he's, uh, taking a few days annual leave."

"Oh, shit."

"Not so fast. Actually, he's on the way out there to see you. Friendly, nonbusiness visit, you understand. He said he thought a few days at Bitterroot Valley would do him a world of good."

"So he's going to be showing up at the resort?"

"Right. Are you there now? Where are you?"

I hung up and stood at the phone a minute or two, thinking about it. I needed Collie *here*. There was nothing to do but get Ted Treacher involved.

I punched in another call and got Ted on the line. He sounded surprised and nervous. *"Brad! Where in the hell—?"*

"Hang on, buddy. I'm in a hurry here. Are you someplace where you can talk?"

"When Jeanne said it was you on the line, I came back to the office to take the call. Where—"

"Ted, listen. You're going to hear from Collie Davis, or he might just be showing up there. It ought to be pretty soon. When he shows, I want you to give him a message for me right away. All right?"

"All right, Brad." Ted sounded wary. *"What's the message I should give him?"*

I hesitated just a second or two, even though I had paced the floor several miles in the night, making this part of my decision. Was I sure that even Collie could be trusted—that the result would not be a swarm of feds grabbing Kevin and dragging him off to face charges? I had decided in the night—and redecided now—that sometimes you had to trust your instincts.

"Hello?" Ted said questioningly. *"Are you still there, Brad?"*

"Yes. Here's the message. Tell Collie I'm in Lake City, Colorado. Tell him I've located our man. Tell him I need to see him here, fast."

Ted mumbled the information, repeating it as he scribbled a note: *"Lake City, Colorado . . . found your man . . . get there as fast as possible."*

"Right," I said, and added the name of my motel on Gunnison Avenue. "Only one other thing, Ted. Nobody else is to know you've heard from me. You still know *nada*. Understood?"

"Of course." My partner sounded aggrieved. *"I've been*

*involved in a bit of your cloak-and-dagger before, you'll
remember. I know to keep my yap shut."*

"Okay, Ted. Great. See you later."

"Any idea, old chum, when 'later' might actually be?"

"Not yet. Soon, I hope." I hung up.

Back in the Cherokee, I drove west toward Blue Mesa and
the cutoff south to Lake City. It was a beautiful sunny day,
one that would get warm later down here in the valley. The
San Juans to the south loomed hazy-blue and beautiful, but
I felt no pleasure in looking at them today.

The last thing I wanted to do was betray Kevin. Bringing
Collie into it, and, *ipso facto,* the entire Company, was going
to look like a betrayal to Kevin, no doubt about that. I was
shattering his secret life. Maybe I had no right. Maybe I was
going about this all wrong.

But my interminable argument with myself in the night
had finally convinced me that Kevin couldn't go on as he was.
Two things could happen to him unless I interfered. He could
continue his crippled, hidden life until he died a lonely,
meaningless natural death, or he could be discovered by the
people who had done in Dave Wentworth. He deserved better. He deserved to be *free* again.

Would my dumb little psychological ploy with the tennis
gear break through his defenses so that both of us could know
what his mind had hidden from itself? I had no idea. It was
just the only thing I could think of, and my rationale for
it—if you could call something that was eighty percent guesswork and gut feeling a rationale—was that maybe by going
around all the stuff of the last two decades, I could break
through to the old Kevin Green again, and *he* would know
why he had spent half his life in hiding.

Maybe it would not work, and maybe trying it would turn
out to be another cruelty. But I had to try.

Twenty-nine
Elsewhere
Bitterroot Valley

FROM THE small, second-floor lounge area that overlooked most of the resort's three-story open lobby, Special Agent Reese McDonald could see the main staircase, the elevators, the front doors, and most of the lobby itself. Sitting on the end of a couch near the lounge railing, he pretended to read a newspaper and kept an eye out for one or both of his suspects, Leventhal and Tubb. He felt confident of recognizing them from the succinct descriptions he had read.

By 10:30 or so, McDonald was beginning to feel decidedly fidgety.

He was not worried about his suspects. From his perch here he could see the parking lot through the high front windows of the lobby, and the old Volvo hadn't been moved. He felt confident that his suspects were still here, probably still in their room on three. Situation well in hand. By the book.

What worried him was the other matter he should be working on. He had hurried so fast this morning that he still hadn't reviewed messages recorded by the listening device he had planted in the resort office. SOP was for the agent to review contents of the limited-memory recorder chip at intervals not to exceed twelve hours. Since he doubled whatever was expected of him, he had been checking the microchip device every six hours, maximum. He had intended to check the recorder promptly after his morning jog, then again a little after noon. Seeing the suspects' car had thrown him entirely off schedule. He was behind that schedule now by several hours, and he felt uneasy about it even though the deviation from plan in that regard seemed justified.

About 10:45, movement on the main staircase in the lobby caught his attention. His gut tightened. The two men just emerging into his view from the curve in the staircase matched the wanted descriptions perfectly: one tall, slightly bent, dark-haired, etc., the other short, very thin, bald, with a limp. Studying the two men over the top of his newspaper, McDonald was amazed to see that they hadn't even changed the mode of dress suggested in the bulletin. The taller man wore a tweed jacket and slightly baggy pants that looked professorial. The smaller man wore faded Levi's pants and jacket, just as described.

The men glanced around the lobby, then turned to their right and went in through the doorway to the breakfast room, going out of McDonald's line of sight.

McDonald carefully folded his newspaper, replacing the sections in their original order in such a way that it looked neater than when he had taken it out of the sales rack. He held the newspaper on his knees, waiting. He checked his Pulsar three times in the next four minutes before feeling confident that his subjects surely must be enjoying a late breakfast.

Walking to the end of the lounge area where another balcony provided a better view into the glass-walled dining area, he saw his men seated at a table well back in the breakfast room. They were just now talking to a waitress, giving her their orders.

Assured of where they would be for a few minutes, at least, McDonald hurried to his room, unlocked, went in, relocked and bolted, got out his miniaturized receiver and recorder, and stuck the tiny headphones in his ears once more.

There had been more than the usual number of calls, both in and out. One of the night clerks had made two surreptitious calls to her boyfriend, with whom she had been having trouble. One of their calls took more than five minutes to retrieve. The chef had called a supplier about late deliveries, Ted Treacher had called several internal departments to talk about details of running the resort, a plumbing firm had called twice to schedule repair at one of the condominium units, and a meat market in Elk City had called to say its delivery would be delayed until after lunch.

Listening to the calls, McDonald began to fret. His watch showed he had been gone from the balcony lounge more than fifteen minutes now. People usually took longer than that over breakfast, but his suspects might be in a hurry, have gotten swift service, and be wolfing their food down. How much longer were all these damned calls going to *take?*

In the coffee shop Arnie Tubb finished his coffee and put the empty cup on the plate bearing the wreckage of his French toast. "He still isn't back. How much longer can we sit around and wait? There's got to be something we haven't thought of yet. Some fucking way to find out where he is."

Stan Leventhal nervously chewed a bite of sausage that tasted like wood chips in his dry mouth. "Maybe no one knows where he is. Maybe this is a wild-goose chase. Maybe we should just give up."

Tubb's lumpy, misshapen face went red with anger. "Are you crazy? After coming this far?" He tossed his napkin down. "Pay the bill when you're done. I'm going back upstairs. Check with the desk again before you come up." He got up and limped out of the room.

Leventhal miserably finished his tasteless meal. Then, leaving a small tip, he went to the cash register to pay. He felt a stab of resentment again about how he was paying for everything—how Tubb had dragged him into this nightmare. The thought flitted through his mind that this was his best chance yet to escape the maniac. But the car keys had been left in the room.

"There you are, sir," the sunny girl said. "Five and five and one make twenty. Have a nice day!"

Leventhal pocketed the change and went out into the lobby, intent on what Tubb had told him to do. He walked straight to the desk, where a nice middle-aged woman was reading a newspaper spread out on the unoccupied registration counter.

"Good morning!" she said, beaming. "You look more rested now!"

"We both got some sleep," Leventhal told her. "Thank you."

"What can I do for you, sir?"

"I was wondering if Brad Smith has returned yet. We're so anxious to meet him."

"No, sir. I'm sorry. He's still out of town."

"Is he expected back today?"

"I asked that. Mr. Treacher said no, not today."

"Thank you." Leventhal turned away.

Up in their sunny room, he found Tubb pacing the floor. The room was thick with smoke from his chain-smoking.

"Anything?" Tubb demanded.

"No. They don't know when he'll be back."

His mouth twisted with rage, Tubb went to the nightstand and pulled the little Elk City telephone directory out of the drawer.

"What are you doing now?" Leventhal asked anxiously.

"I thought of one more thing we can try," Tubb said, flipping pages. "We got to try everything." He ran an index finger down the page. "Here it is. Good." He picked up the telephone, then put it down again while he thought about it. "I better be somebody good . . . lemme think . . ." He picked the telephone up again and dialed the number he had found in the book.

"*Frontiersman*," a woman's voice answered.

"Hello?" Tubb said, making his voice firm and friendly. "May I speak to your editor, please?"

"This is Lynette," the voice said cheerfully.

"Hi," Tubb breathed. "My name is Roscoe Tanner, and—"

"My gosh!" the youthful female voice broke in. *"Not the Roscoe Tanner!"*

Tubb almost smiled. Maybe it was going to be easier than he had imagined. He said, "You mean there are people around who still remember an old relic like me?"

"My gosh!" the girl's voice came back enthusiastically. *"I've always been a sports freak. I can remember seeing you on TV in the U.S. Open and everything else, Mr. Tanner!"*

"Why, how nice, not to have to explain myself," Tubb purred, winking at Leventhal.

"Gee, this is great, Mr. Tanner! What can I do for you? Are you in Elk City?"

"Yes," Tubb said. "I was driving through, and thought I would drop by to see my old friend Brad Smith. I know he lives around here somewhere. Could you possibly help me locate him?"

"Oh, sure. He lives out south of town here at a place called Bitterroot Valley Resort. He's a half-owner of the place. But he isn't there right now. Oh, what a shame! I'm sure he'll be sorry he missed you!"

"Do you have any idea where he is?" Tubb asked. "I know he isn't at Wimbledon this year, and if I could track him down before I head on to the West Coast—"

"I'm afraid you're out of luck, Mr. Tanner! He had to withdraw from a tournament down in Kansas City last week, and I'm not sure exactly where he is right now."

Tubb's teeth grated painfully. He very nearly slammed the telephone down in frustration. But he managed to keep his voice calm and neutral. "That is a shame. You have no idea where old Brad might be, then?"

"Well, let me think . . . Well, I don't know. I guess all I know is that he did ask me for some information about a place down in Colorado."

Tubb's stomach twisted into a knot. "Colorado, you say?"

"Yes. He called me, and I had looked something up for him. Let me think a sec . . . yes, here are my notes . . . I located a place for him. Lake City."

Lava spurted through Tubb's veins. "Lake City? In Colorado?"

"That's right. Maybe he went down there. I don't know. Have you asked his partner at the resort? Maybe you ought to call him. His name is Ted Treacher. I can give you the number."

"That's all right," Tubb said. "I can look it up. Thank you very much, ma'am."

"Hey, Mr. Tanner, if you're going to be in town, how about an interview? Where are you staying? I could meet you anytime. It would make a neat story for our readers."

Tubb gently placed the telephone back on its cradle.

Lake City, he thought, excitement building. He had never heard of Lake City, but suddenly he felt he *knew*. Smith had asked about it and now Smith was missing—no one knew his whereabouts. It had to be this Lake City place. He had to be there.

Tubb could think of only one reason why he would go there, telling no one.

He turned to Leventhal. "I was right. I know it. Smith knew all along where Captain Green was. I'll bet my life that's where Smith is right now—down there telling him what's been going on."

"Where?" Leventhal demanded nervously. "What are you talking about?"

"Hand me that map book," Tubb ordered. "We've got to find how to get to a place called Lake City."

"We don't know he's there," Leventhal moaned. "We can't just keep driving all over the country—"

"Shut up, goddammit! Just shut up! Get your shit packed. We're outta here."

* * *

Reese McDonald's knees, bent so long in front of the little recording device, had begun to ache badly. He had been listening to this routine stuff for almost twenty minutes now, and in another couple of minutes he would just have to reset it—lose whatever might be left in the microchip—and get back on duty watching the lobby. Closing his eyes in an agony of impatience, he listened to Ted Treacher call the newspaper about an ad. One more call was all McDonald could give time for. Then—

The next conversation started, Treacher's voice again.

"Brad? Where in the hell—?"

"Hang on, buddy. I'm in a hurry here. Are you someplace where you can talk?"

Tingling, McDonald lurched upright on his knees and grabbed for his notepad. The voices continued to spill out of the recording chip. He readjusted his little earpieces and strained to hear every syllable. It was Brad Smith, all right; he recognized the voice. *Say where you are,* McDonald prayed. *Just say where you are.*

Moments later, Smith did. Almost frantic with excitement, McDonald neatly wrote the name of the town on his notepad, tore off the sheet, and stuck it in his pants pocket. No more time for other calls, and they were irrelevant now. His fingers flew as he reset the machine, hid it again, and prepared to leave his room.

This was great, he thought. He could not have been more delighted. A quick check to make sure where his two suspects were—what they evidently planned to do with themselves for awhile—and then he could call Missoula to give them *this* gem of information.

Leaving his room, he imagined the reaction of his superiors. *"That McDonald is incredible! First he locates our two wanteds in the Special, and now he finds out where Smith is right now! He's a young man to watch, obviously a real comer!"*

McDonald reached the second-floor lounge area near the staircase. He glanced into the breakfast room and saw with some chagrin that his suspects' table was now empty. Turning to scan the lobby, he had his attention caught by something in the parking lot out front. He swung his gaze back, and what he saw made him go cold.

His two suspects—the tall one and the short, skinny one who looked so crummy—were just getting into the Volvo.

Stunned, McDonald started to turn back for a run to his room, and his Browning. But he saw in an agony of uncertainty that there wasn't time—already he spotted the puff of oil smoke from the Volvo's tail pipe as the engine was started.

He rushed down the stairs. By the time he reached the front doors, the Volvo had backed out of its spot and was pulling out of the lot and onto the long, tree-lined driveway.

McDonald could not let them get away. He had to follow—stop them if he could. *The special agent is resourceful.* Page 18. McDonald ran to his rental car, unlocked it, and threw himself in behind the wheel.

The Buick started eagerly and leaped away from its spot on the pavement. McDonald jammed his foot to the floor, careening onto the driveway on two wheels. Ahead, the Volvo had almost reached the end of the driveway. McDonald's car's engine screamed as he kept his foot on the floor.

The Volvo turned right—south—onto the two-lane blacktop road. McDonald reached the highway about five seconds behind them, and caught sight of them rounding a foothill curve and going out of sight a hundred yards or so ahead. The wheels of his Buick spun wildly as he floorboarded the accelerator again.

By the time he reached the curve in the road he was doing eighty. The car leaned heavily around the curve, which was sharper than it appeared going in. McDonald gritted his teeth and held the accelerator down.

Ahead, the Volvo was less than thirty yards in front now. The road had entered an ancient river gorge, steep hills on both sides heavily tree-covered, a small stream downrushing on the right. McDonald didn't see any other cars.

Surprise was his weapon, he thought grimly. Surprise and resolve. Just the ticket. Take a chance. Necessary. These two must not get away. A part of his mind could already see the same supervisor he had dreamed of only minutes ago, but this time the smile of approval had been replaced by a sneer of contempt. *"McDonald? Oh, Christ, isn't he the fool who let those two wanted fugitives get away in Montana, right after he flubbed a surveillance on someone else? Bury that file! I don't even want to think about fuckups like him!"*

Oh, that couldn't be allowed to happen. That must not happen.

Another phrase from one of the FBI manuals leaped into McDonald's head as he pulled his rocketing vehicle out into the left-hand lane to pull up alongside the Volvo. Something about courage—something about dedicated action—he believed in every bit of that, always had.

No time to think more about it or anything else, for that matter, right now. His car was up beside the Volvo. Glancing across, he saw the startled faces of the two men in the Volvo just as he swung his wheel sharply to the right, slamming his car into the front left side of theirs.

The ear-shattering clash of metal against metal almost threw McDonald out of control. He fought the wheel, skidding sideways, and managed to regain partial control as the Buick veered back right—he caught a glimpse of the Volvo behind him, out of control, hurtling off the road and down into the adjacent mountain stream with a horrendous splash—and then he spun again, hitting the highway shoulder sideways, going on around, bouncing over some rocks, sliding to a halt in a storm of flying dirt and gravel.

Slightly dazed, he wrenched his seat belt open and jumped out of the car. Through the dust cloud and smoke issuing from his own car, he saw the Volvo on its side in the shallow stream, a mammoth dust cloud still rushing around it from the wreck.

Afire with excitement, McDonald ran.

He reached the stream's edge nearest the overturned car. Splashing without hesitation into the icy water, he approached the car. "No one in there move!" he yelled. "You're under arrest! This—"

He got no further.

The door on the upside of the car wrenched upward. The little man, face and bald skull covered with blood, popped into view. *A revolver—!*

The little gun spat. Something hit McDonald a terrific blow in the chest. *Oh, God*— Pain came. It was overwhelming, far more terrible than anything in the world. He felt himself falling forward. His last thought was that his suit would be ruined.

Dazed with horror, Stan Leventhal climbed out of the top door of his smashed car in time to see Tubb, with amazing strength, grab the fallen man and drag him like a killed deer onto the wet rocks beside the stream. Tubb knelt beside the man, gun still in hand, and startled rifling his pockets.

Leventhal waded over, dizzy with panic. "You killed him! Oh, Christ, this is terrible! He must be FBI or something, and you—"

"Shut up, shut up," Tubb panted, pulling a slip of paper out of the fallen man's pants pocket. "What's this—" He read the words on the paper. Blood ran down out of the gash on top of his head, making the rocks turn garish red. He looked up, eyes alight with excitement. "Look at this! Look at this! Look what it says on this piece of paper!"

"You've killed him!" Leventhal groaned again. "Now everything is lost. We—"

Tubb lurched to his feet. "Shut up! Shut up! Nothing is lost, man! We've just had the break of a lifetime! You see what this says? It says, 'Lake City'! That proves it! Come on!"

He turned and stumbled toward the other man's car just up the stream.

"Where?" Leventhal cried. "What can we—"

"Come on! Come on! We can't stay here, you fool, and his car looks drivable!"

The crash, the shooting, the terror, and now this new madness all came down on Leventhal at once in an avalanche of overpowering despair. His legs refused to support him and he slumped to the wet rocks beside the body of the man Tubb had shot.

Tubb stared, then ran back two strides, his eyes wild and crazy. "Get up, goddamn you! Get up, or—"

"I can't," Leventhal wept. "I can't go on."

Tubb's eyes bulged. For an instant he hesitated, but then something new came into his eyes and he raised the revolver. "Get up!"

Leventhal knelt crumpled in the rocks. "No!" he cried out.

Tubb fired twice. Leventhal fell over sideways, partly covering the other body. Tubb turned and ran for the Buick. Moments later, smoke belched briefly from its tail pipe as he started the tortured engine. Then the Buick pulled out onto the pavement, fishtailing as it sped away to the south.

For three or four minutes it was still, the only sound that of the clear mountain water tumbling over rocks as it had for centuries, and around the smashed Volvo. A magpie darted out of the trees, swooped over the road, and disappeared on the far side.

A red Jeep came into sight from the north, slowly regaining speed after negotiating the hill curve. As it neared the wreck site, the Jeep slowed again, the driver and his passenger peering out anxiously at the wreck, seeing the bodies on the stream bank. The Jeep stopped on the shoulder. The driver, a teenage boy who looked very frightened, climbed out and walked around the front, then started slowly down toward the stream, gingerly approaching the bodies. Inside the Jeep, his girlfriend was talking excitedly to someone on the CB.

Thirty

My watch showed 11:45 when I rounded a familiar river-canyon curve and knew I was close to Lake City. Slowing, I watched for the gravel side road that cut off to the residential estates that had the tennis courts. I found it with no trouble and trundled up to the high ground. A brilliant sun threw angular shadows around the well-spaced mountain homes. Taking the side street that led to the tennis court, I saw with relief that Kevin's pickup was there. As I pulled up, I spotted him sitting on the tailgate of his pickup, eating a sandwich. Getting out of my car, I walked over.

Kevin looked surprised to see me, and not happy about it. "What do you want?"

"I came by to say goodbye," I lied.

"You didn't have to." He took another bite of his ham-and-cheese.

"I don't suppose you've got an extra one of those?"

"No," he said, and then added sarcastically, "I didn't expect a lunch guest."

The pickup sagged a bit lower as I sat on the tailgate beside him. "Is there anything more you want to tell me, Kevin?"

"Ken," he corrected sharply.

"Ken, then. Is there anything else?"

"No. There *isn't* anything else."

"I want to know why you have to go on hiding," I told him. "What happened over there that you haven't told me?"

He munched silently, pretending I didn't exist.

It was time to try my flimsy scheme. I sighed. "We had a lot of good times."

He didn't say anything.

"Remember the match with Pepperdine, when—"

"That life is over!" he flared. "That person is *dead!*"

"About Barbara—"

"Goddamn it, Brad! Leave me alone!"

I put my hands on my knees. "Okay, old friend. You win. I'll get out of here. But before I go, would you do me just one more favor? For old times' sake?"

He looked suspiciously at me out of the corner of his eye. "What?"

"Well, finish your sandwich, and—"

"No. Say it now. What do you *want?*"

If I said it, he would never do it. I got up quickly. "Be right back."

Hotfooting it to my car, I pulled out the two new Prince rackets in their pretty black covers, along with the paper sack containing the balls and the pair of sneakers. Hurrying back to where Kevin still sat on the tailgate of his truck, I saw the look of consternation and anger grow on his face.

"Hit a few balls with me," I said.

He drew back and looked at me as if I were dangerous. "Don't you ever listen? I don't play tennis anymore!"

"I know, I know," I said patiently. "Just hit a few balls with me. For old times' sake."

"*Why?*"

I shrugged, pretending confusion. "Call me a sentimental fool. But I remember how we used to play. After today I'll never see you again. It would make me feel a lot better if we just . . . sort of renewed things. Then I'll get out of here."

"You're crazy."

"Kevin. What can it hurt? For old times' sake!"

He raised one booted foot. "I can't even walk onto the playing surface with these things on, and besides—"

"I brought a pair of sneakers. See? Never been worn. We

used to wear the same size shoe. These will fit you, and I'm already wearing these old Nikes." I saw the protest forming on his lips and added hurriedly, "I'm not asking you to play, Kevin. All I'm asking is for you to rally with me five, maybe ten minutes. Won't you give me that? Something to remember? How can it possibly hurt you to humor me for five minutes?"

"Why do you want to *do* it?"

"I told you. To give me something to remember you by."

"That's stupid, Brad. That's ridiculous."

"What can it hurt?"

"What can it accomplish?"

"I remember when you were ready to graduate, the talks we had. The tips you gave me. All the times earlier when you helped me, and I was a smart-ass, but you helped me anyway. Then, after you were gone, did you ever know how hard I tried to live up to the trust you put in me? I screwed up— flunked out. But I never forgot. All these years I thought, if I ever could see Kevin Green again—if I could just get back on the court with him for a few minutes, it would be like . . . it would be like finishing things up with him, somehow."

Kevin studied my face. Clearly he thought I was mad. My excuse for getting a racket in his hands again was tissue-thin. But it was the only trick I had left. If he refused, or my trick didn't work, then I was finished and it would be up to Collie, or whoever he thought we should bring in.

Kevin said, "It's nice of you to be so sentimental, Brad. But I've got work to do here."

"All right," I said regretfully, making a big show of my disappointment. "I just thought—five minutes or so—" I started to get up.

"Oh, hell," he said suddenly. He hiked one boot up onto the back of his pickup. "Anything to get you out of here. Give me those shoes."

*   *   *

We walked out onto the empty court, unzipping the plastic covers of the rackets and dropping them by the net pole. Making a great show of being delighted, I peeled off the lid of the new container of Penn 3s and dumped them into Kevin's hand. "Take it easy on me."

He refused to smile. His expression brimmed with resentment. "Five minutes. That's all."

"Five minutes, right."

We took our positions to warm up. Kevin had the south court, so that beyond him lay the vast empty depths of the river canyon, and, far beyond that, the pale haze of Lake City's valley, with bare, beautiful, rust-colored Red Mountain far off, the evergreen of Round Top beside it, high wooded ridges well off to the east and west, and an intensely blue mountain sky with puffy little clouds speeding along in it. I took a moment to look all around—the scattered big log houses, distant to my left up the scrubby grass mountainside, the airy vacancy to my right where the land fell off into the canyon, with the road far below, a toy car tooling north on it, the jagged rock spires and cliffs to the north, with Uncompahgre Mountain's brutal promontory just visible to the northwest beyond lower rises still snow-spotted here and there in their dark green woods. I took a long, slow, deep breath. It seemed impossible to be here like this. Maybe my hope for this sentimental game would prove to be the most impossible thing of all.

I turned back to face Kevin, who stood at his service line, bouncing a ball, expressionless, unhappy, waiting for me. I grinned at him and signaled ready. He courtesy-served me the first ball. I looped it back to him, moving him slightly to his right. He went over for the ball, moving with the stiff, awkward gait of a robot, and got back a weak forehand. I moved in near the net and dropped a shot at his feet. With just an atom of his old spirit, he got his racket well down under the ball and scooped sharply upward, imparting heavy topspin. The lob went high over my head with a sound like a giant bumblebee and dived down well inside the backline behind me.

I laughed at him. "I see you haven't forgotten much!"

His face showed nothing. "Accident."

I walked back and he courtesy-served another. I made sure my return was not too heavy, and just within reach. He netted that one, shook his head in a hint of disgust, and sent over the third ball. This one I returned harder, and he got it back to my backhand. I reached it, careful not to overextend the bad knee, and he saw the crosscourt angle just in time to slip over there and hit a moderately decent return down the far line. I got to that one in turn, hitting back up the middle. We exchanged five more strokes on each side before my forehand clearly went long.

After retrieving the balls, I hit him a few. We did not talk, except for an occasional cry of "Nice one!" or "Great!," most of those coming from me.

With each rally I could see him beginning to forget himself, get into the tennis. He began moving better, with a return of some of the old quickness and grace. I began to sweat, loosening up. Without mentioning it, I walked to the centerline when it was my turn to start the next rally, and tossed the ball high for a medium-hard serve. It surprised him a bit, but he got it back. I stroked it crosscourt out of his reach.

"Fifteen-love," I called out.

Head down, he walked to the ad court without comment. I had him in a game.

This time, as I went through my usual pre-serve fidgets, he bent low—the old Kevin—and awaited my service. I hit a hard one. He blocked it back short and I flubbed the scoop return.

Only a part of me remembered why I had even set this up now. It was the old Kevin over there—rusty and badly off his timing, but still elegant and intelligent oncourt, with some of his old shot-making ability still very much in evidence. I

played at about sixty percent. We went to deuce on my serve
before I held. He changed ends with me, seemingly not
thinking about it at all, and hit a howitzer ace on his first ball.

"Mercy!" I pleaded, changing to the ad side.

It was a very curious little game. I was not hitting full-out,
and neither was he, most of the time. No one was worried
about the score. But as we moved, crosscourt to the backhand, return up the line, short ball back center, sharply
angled volley putaway, we both moved into some kind of
extra dimension where only the two of us existed, and the
game.

As we played, I reevaluated him. He had kept far more of
his old skill than I had first suspected. He had always been
a natural, doing without thought things oncourt that took me
years to learn. His smoothness was still there in flashes, and
all the intuitive sense of court angles and anticipated response. Once or twice I had the old, curious feeling that he
was reading my mind, knowing where I planned to put my
next shot before I was aware of the decision myself.

Both of us warmed up further, hitting out on some shots,
chasing down everything possible. He held service and so did
I. He double-faulted to give me a breaker. I tried to give it
back, but he suddenly fell prone to some of the kind of
lumbering awkwardness I had expected all along, as if he had
suddenly remembered who he was supposed to be now, and
where we were playing. After I won that game on his un-
forced errors, he held when I overran some shots and hit a
couple long on purpose, and then it was my serve again.

"Last game," he called across the net.

Had we played long enough? Had returning to the game
like this opened him to the things his mind had buried? I
didn't know. Caught in the lovely feeling of the play itself, I
prepared to serve.

I hit it as hard as I could, jamming him with it. He moved
nimbly aside and returned crosscourt. As I went for the ball,
I saw his movement forward to cut off my angle, so I went up

the line with it. He veered at the last moment and hit a lunging volley that nearly took my ear off and hit well in for a winner.

"Okay, okay," I called in mock surrender as I went back to serve again.

We moved back and forth, the pace changing and becoming almost balletic. The ball went back and forth slower, but with more elegant angles. I missed a volley and he hit one out on the side. It felt like we had entered a dreamworld, neither of us speaking, no one around, the mountains to the south for a craggy, majestic backdrop, little Lake City in the low foreground a few miles to the south. Kevin moved as if he had been playing regularly. We went to deuce but I lost the point at ad in. The same thing happened again. Then I flubbed a backhand and it was Kevin with the ad.

Glancing up from my ball-bouncing to look at him, I saw his skinny frame low, racket at ready, knees bent, swaying slightly, awaiting my shot. Work overalls and a sweatshirt, and a dirty baseball cap.

All the reality came back to me.

I double-faulted.

We walked to the side of the court, blowing and dripping a little.

"You did that on purpose," he said accusingly.

"Like hell I did!"

He gave me a you-lie look, then walked stiffly over to the back of his pickup. He sat down and began unlacing his sneakers, looking over toward me with a glad, gloriously alive look about him.

But then something suddenly moved behind his eyes. He stopped what he was doing, looked blank for an instant, and started to cry.

I hurried over and put an arm around him. "Hey. Hell. You were the winner just now, not me."

He shook me off violently. "Bastard," he managed through the sobs. "Bastard."

"What?"

"Dirty bastard!"

"Kevin, what are you talking about?"

Tears made white streaks in the sweaty dirt on his face. "You made it all come back, and I can't do that anymore. That isn't part of my life anymore."

"Why?" I asked urgently. "Why can't it be your life anymore?"

He took a sloppy swing at me, missing. The sobbing intensified, shaking him.

"Kevin—" I began.

He silenced me with a slashing gesture. "Because I killed them. I killed all of them."

"Killed who?" I managed. "What are you—"

"At Quang Xi, you son of a bitch," he choked. "When I saw what they had done to that hamlet and that family and I saw that fucking captain shoot that little boy, I flew out ahead of them, wanting to come back around and hose them down myself. And Dave was puking and we were right on the deck and I flew over the edge of the jungle ahead of them, and right down below us I saw the VC hunkered down, hiding, just waiting for our guys to get close enough to be clobbered. *Lots* of VC, rocket launchers, the works."

Kevin shuddered violently. "I could have come around and hit them hard. I could have gotten on the radio instantly and called a warning—yelled for help from on top. I didn't do anything like that. I was so mad. I was so mad at what that captain and that part of his command had just done. I just flew right on by, out another ten miles or more, and Dave there beside me, trying to clean up his puke.

"I flew about fifteen figure eights, telling the commander up above to hold off another five minutes or so, I would tell him when I thought they could safely descend.

"Then I watched from about five miles when that captain led his guys right into the VC ambush. The VC hit them with everything they had. I could see the shellfire and all the rest of it through the haze, and I didn't do a thing, I just watched it. And it wasn't until I felt sure that goddamned captain and those goddamned butchers with him had gotten theirs—it was only then that I called the rest of the command down."

Kevin turned to me. He had stopped weeping. His eyes looked like the blackened windowpanes of an abandoned house. "I killed our own guys as surely as if I had attacked them myself. I did nothing to warn them, nothing to help. That's why some of the guys who survived Quang Xi want me dead. Just like they killed most of the grunts that refused to take part in the massacre—the ones that stayed back on the other side of the stream."

He shuddered again. "I deserve to be dead. I let our grunts die. I'm a traitor and a murderer. Is it any wonder some of the survivors won't ever rest until they've shot my guts out, and taken an ear?"

Thirty-one
Elsewhere
Bitterroot Valley Resort

THINGS LOOKED normal enough to Collie Davis when he pulled into the resort parking lot at 3:45 P.M., but he knew something had happened the moment he walked into the lobby. A thickset deputy sheriff, in uniform, stood not far from the entrance like a bank guard; couples and small groups of guests scattered around the lobby had been conversing in hushed tones, and most of them looked up sharply as he entered, their expressions clearly denoting nervous curiosity. *What the hell?* His first thought was about Brad: something had happened to Brad—something bad.

His soft-sided bag in hand, Davis walked fast to the registration desk. The woman who came from the back to greet him looked pale and shaky.

"Collie Davis," he told her. "I called a reservation—"

"Oh, Mr. Davis!" the woman gasped. "Mr. Treacher said to notify him *the moment* you arrived! Please wait." She turned and fled into the back office area.

Davis leaned on the counter and surveyed the lobby. A few people were still watching him—avoided his eyes when he tried to make contact. His bad feeling intensified. The red-eye flight to Denver this morning and the connection to Missoula had left little time to call Headquarters, and his "unofficial" status required such calls to be made only in extreme emergency anyhow. He wished now that he had called regardless. Maybe they knew what had happened here. He fidgeted, found a cigarette, and lit it. Where the hell was Treacher?

Two minutes later, Ted Treacher bustled nervously out of the rear office area and shook hands with the fervor of a man thanking a lifeguard. "Jesus, man, I'm glad you're here. Brad said you would be calling—"

"What's happened?" Davis cut in brusquely.

Treacher took his arm. "Come back to the office."

Less than fifteen minutes later, Davis had the story: Brad Smith's call this morning saying he was in Lake City, Colorado, and the information should be passed on to Davis when he returned a call; on the heels of that call, a car wreck out on the highway south involving a guest named McDonald and a car listed as belonging to two other men who had just checked in at the lodge a few hours earlier. Two men found shot at the scene—the ambulances, wrecker, sheriff's department, and highway patrol—the arrival of two men who had already learned part of the story on their way in, and who identified themselves to Treacher as FBI. One of them was up in McDonald's room now, doing God only knew what, and Treacher had let the other one go to three and enter the room used by the two men who had been driving the car with Michigan license plates, the one wrecked in the creek.

A real mess, Davis thought, dismayed. He didn't quite have it all sorted out yet.

"Let me get this straight," he told Treacher. "Brad called this morning?"

"Yes. It must have been a little after ten. He said—"

"I know. He's found the man and he's in Lake City. Is that right?"

"That's right."

"Ted. Think. Did you tell *anyone* else about the call?"

"No!" Treacher drew back, offended. "I'm not an idiot, you know!"

"Could anyone have picked up an extension and overheard?"

Treacher's long face lengthened as he stroked his chin, thinking about it. "Jove, I can't imagine how. There are only two phones on that extension line, and both are in the office. I was right beside the other one. And my office door was open. I saw Jeanne hang up when she heard me pick up."

Davis glanced around the small, cluttered office. "These are the two phones you're talking about?"

"Yes."

Davis reached across and pulled the ivory touchtone instrument over to his side of the desk. Turning it over, he saw no sign of an external bug. He started unscrewing the earpiece cover.

"Surely you don't think—!" Treacher began.

"Ho, ho, ho," Davis muttered grimly, using his index finger to pry the microchip device out of the earpiece cavity.

"What's *that*?" Treacher gasped.

Davis turned the device over in his fingers. Gray, unmarked, it had only one very small slit in the side where it might be opened. He got a fingernail under the slit and it flipped back. A hearing-aid battery fell out.

"Oh, no," Treacher groaned. He leaned closer, eyes bulging. "Is it inoperative now?"

"Yes, but it's a little late, wouldn't you say?"

Treacher's eyes came up to Davis's face. "How did you know how to disable it so quickly?"

"It's the same unit we sometimes use." Davis pocketed the chip and started for the office door. "I need to make a call."

"You can use this—" Treacher began, then sat back, crestfallen. "Oh. I see. There might be more than one."

Davis went out into the lobby to the area where three public telephone stands were lined up against the wall. He put in the number from memory. It rang twice and was answered, and the extension call went right through.

"Mary, this is Collie Davis."

"Collie! Hi!" Unfailingly upbeat, she sounded glad to hear from him. *"How's the fishing?"*

"Mary, I need to talk to Mr. Dwight."

"Sorry, Collie. He's in a meeting."

"Get him out of the meeting."

There was a silence on the line. One did not call people out of meetings. Not ordinarily. The secretary needed a moment to realize that something not ordinary was going on.

Her voice sounded different when she spoke again. *"Hold."*

Davis waited, trying to sort out how bad some of this might be.

Thirty-two

June 26

The motel room telephone jangled at 10:30 Wednesday morning, but it didn't sound as jangled as I was by that time.

I snatched it up. "Hello!"

"Brad?"

"Collie, where the hell are you?"

"Gunnison. They tell me I can be down there in about an hour."

"Haul ass," I told him.

"What's happening? What are you doing?"

"Smoking cigarettes and watching *Captain Kangaroo*," I snapped.

"What?"

Obviously not a fan of the Statler Brothers. "Nothing," I said. "Just come on, man. I need you."

"You may not know the half of it, buddy. I'm rolling."

He hung up before I could ask what he knew that I didn't. I listened to the dial tone a few seconds before replacing my phone on the cradle and turning around to survey the messy wreckage of my room—unmade bed, copies of the Denver newspaper scattered around, ashtrays full of butts, the TV set turned on to CNN but muted, a bottle that had contained Jack Daniel's black label before I turned it into a dead Indian last night. My head still felt like a water balloon and my mouth tasted like somebody had buried something dead in it.

I paced the floor, something I had been doing a lot of lately.

Before my bush-league mind game with him yesterday,

had Kevin been conscious of the secret that had festered in his mind since 1968? Perhaps I would never know that. But I didn't think he had been fully conscious of it anyway; the violence of his grief and guilt when he told me about it made me believe he had shoved it out of awareness. Only playing tennis again—doing something he had loved as much as life itself before all this happened—had brought his mind back to what it couldn't look at year after year.

And he hadn't wanted to look at it again, ever. After his first outburst of passionate self-loathing, his rage had turned to me. If I had tried to stay with him another minute, he would have attacked me. In my own dimension of shock, I had mumbled something about seeing him later—lied again about leaving at once—and fled from there like the coward I am.

So much of it made an insane kind of sense now. Part of the unit on the ground at Quang Xi, cut off from most communications and reinforcement or fire support from the air, had been savaged by the VC for at least two days and nights. Entering the hamlet, something had happened. *What*, I probably would never know. Something. So the shooting had started, the executions, the fear-crazy, revenge-crazy retaliations against people who might have had nothing whatsoever to do with the VC.

Some of Aldrich's command had recoiled in horror when the slaughter began. Those were the ones Kevin had seen on the far side of the hamlet, taking no part in any of it. But some had gone along with Aldrich's orders—or had run wild in spite of them—and then followed him across the stream into the rice fields in search of others to kill.

A few of these had survived the VC ambush. A few of these few had never been quite sane again. Their revenge on some of the men who had refused to enter the hamlet or cross the stream had been exacted in later action in Vietnam: "death by friendly fire," unavoidable accident in the official records. They had avenged the Aldrich group against a handful of others in Vietnamese prison camps.

Some—those who had been murdered in subsequent years here at home—had been tracked down somehow and not only killed but mutilated in the way some grunts mutilated dead VC, as a terror-warning to others who might learn of it.

I could not be sure how they ever got Kevin's and Dave's names. But I think they must have seen his gunship in the area, giving no warning or help, and then one of them must have learned that a gunship had gone down, and determined the names of the crew, marking them for the ultimate retaliation.

All the years. All the madness. If I had not had my own time of nightmares and flashbacks, or known friends from over there who would never view reality in the normal way again, I might have discredited the evidence—refused to believe that such a thing could go on for so long. But here it was, and I could only wish that I did not understand it.

We begin our lives with a feeling of invulnerable safety. Many of us live to considerable age before something—a heart attack, perhaps, or an auto accident, or even complications after a surgery—confronts us with a jolting reality. Life is fragile. Fate is random. The world we live in teems with meaningless, often-violent accidents. For any one of us, at any moment, a blood vessel may burst, or a cell may go mad, or we may be struck down in a totally random drive-by shooting, or a little piece of cosmic stuff flying through space since the moment of creation may happen to encounter earth's gravity, and happen to survive its plunge through the atmosphere, and happen to kill you. In Vietnam, the reality of a hostile, uncaring, random reality became clear to most who were there. For many was added a confrontation with an ugliness and cruelty that's part of the human condition. The ones you see wandering the streets or drinking or drugging themselves to death are among those who saw all the mean-

inglessness and all the cruelty *in themselves* as well as everyone else, and will never be unafraid or secure in the kind of
la-la land they inhabited before they went to fetch Uncle
Lyndon his coonskin.

The ones who had killed Dave Wentworth, and still
sought Kevin Green, were no crazier than a lot of others who
came back; their craziness just showed itself—focused on a
single obsession—in a more striking way. So I could see how
it had all happened, even if it was mad. I had known just a
little of the madness myself once.

It was memory and unwanted understanding like this that
had haunted me through much of last night. Added to the
picture, however, was the feeling that I had started all this
intent on finding Kevin and helping him; but almost surely
what I had done instead was destroy what life he had
managed to build for himself. Not only did he remember now
what he had managed to bury somewhere in a dusty bin of his
mind; Collie—now that I had brought him here—would have
no choice but to report Kevin's whereabouts; and that would
mean the FBI would come, or the army, or both.

Either could take him away somewhere to face charges
that all the years might not dilute.

I waited.

At 11:35, Collie knocked on my door.

"You look like hell," Collie told me.

"Thanks."

He perched on the edge of the bed. He looked tired, he
had an uncharacteristic stubble of beard, and his slacks and
long-sleeved shirt were rumpled. "So where is he?"

"I don't know. But he's here. He lives out north of town,
does odd jobs, cuts firewood."

"So do you want to tell me about it?"

"Do I have a choice?"

"Not really. Not now."

Feeling like I was betraying Kevin's friendship, I told

Collie what I had learned. He listened with a face that grew longer and longer.

"Well, that explains a lot of things," he said quietly when I finished.

"What happens now?"

"I'm not sure. I think you can stop worrying about somebody finding your friend here, and doing him in. But that's about the only cheerful note I can strike."

"How can you say that?" I asked.

"The Bureau has rounded up several Vietnam vets. It isn't clear to us yet how they got their lead, but the ones being held, as far as we've been able to tell from our files, were all veterans in the Quang Ngai area at the right time to have been part of this. The Bureau isn't telling anybody anything yet. The Pentagon is having cats, from what we hear. We think the Bureau is preparing a report that tells a lot of the stuff you just told me, and clearing a number of vendetta murders occurring over the last ten or fifteen years."

"Did the FBI get all the guys who have been after Kevin?"

"No."

"How many did they miss?"

Collie looked glum. "I have no idea. I know this much: one of them, a college professor from Michigan, was found shot to death not far from your resort up in Montana. With him was the Bureau guy who worked with you before: Mc-Donald."

"McDonald is *dead?*"

Collie shook his head. "Alive, as of yesterday afternoon. Critical."

I didn't get it. "You mean they shot each other?"

"Probably not. I talked to the FBI guys at Bitterroot Valley. They didn't tell me much, naturally, but it's no secret that there's one more man out there somewhere, at least. Tubb, Arnold E. Walk-away from Walter Reed late last year. The FBI's all-points says he probably left the scene driving the rental car McDonald was using. He must have been trying to find you, thinking you could lead him to Kevin Green."

"Is there any chance he had a hint about my being here?"

"No. The FBI knows, though."

"God! How? Did you already—"

"No," Collie snapped. "I wouldn't give those guys the time of day. But I had to report your whereabouts when I got through to Dwight. There's nothing he can do, I think, but pass it upstairs, and upstairs they'll have no choice but to send something to the Bureau."

"What happens now? The FBI shows up here?"

"Maybe. Or maybe boys from the Pentagon. Or maybe both."

"And then?" I asked, certain I didn't want to know.

"I'm not sure about that, either. It's not our jurisdiction. But surely either the FBI or the army will take your pal Kevin into custody." He frowned. "Then nature will take its course."

"He didn't actually *do* anything, Collie."

"Right. But he could have done something. He let American soldiers walk into a VC ambush."

"He had just seen them wipe out a hamlet! And some of them murder a family that had *our* ID cards in their hands. How was he supposed to react? What was he supposed to do? Drop flowers? Fill out a report putting the fuckers in for the Bronze Star?"

Collie walked to the motel room door, put his hand on the knob, and turned back mercury-heavy eyes. "I don't know what he was supposed to do, Brad. But I know one thing: he was supposed to radio a warning, and he was supposed to blast the VC—not fly away and let our guys get hammered."

"It's all crap, Collie! It's all meaningless. It happened centuries ago. We've fought another war since then, one that the people approved of because it was nice and fast and made us look good again. Why can't all this old history stay dead?

Why does *any* of this have to be raked over again now, after all these years?"

"Let's talk philosophy some other day," Collie said, opening the door to leave. "Right now I need to go make my calls. I'm going to check into one of the other cabins here. I'll be back in about an hour. Try by that time to get your head on straight. He's a *traitor*, Brad."

When he came back, he said his information was that the FBI would have somebody in Lake City tomorrow, latest. As he had suspected, they already knew my location thanks to a tap they had placed on the lodge office telephone. The Pentagon had been informed, and no one knew the army's plans yet.

"What do we do in the meantime?" I asked, frustrated anger making my voice shake just a little.

"Nothing. Wait."

"What's the Agency's position?"

"We have no position. We're not in this."

"You're here."

"I'm resting up, using up some of my accrued leave."

"So the army and the FBI can fight over who gets the glorious credit for finding Kevin and putting him under arrest," I said bitterly.

"Sometimes I get tired of your Christly self-righteousness," he snapped.

I didn't say anything to that.

"Where," he asked into the strained silence, "are we going to have supper? And how early will they serve it? I haven't eaten today. I'm starving."

We strolled up Gunnison to the Lake City Cafe, two touristy types having a grand time.

"What," I asked Collie on the way, "is to prevent me from going and finding Kevin and warning him what's coming down? Why *shouldn't* I?"

Collie turned on me with a ferocity unlike anything I had

ever seen in him. "Because you're an American citizen, you son of a bitch, and he betrayed his country."

We went into the cafe. It was after the lunch rush, and only two of the battered old wood tables were occupied. Collie admired an antique map on one wall as if nothing in the world were out of kilter.

Thirty-three
Elsewhere

Washington, D.C.

AT EXACTLY 4:30 P.M., the secretary of defense, the director of the FBI, and the director of Central Intelligence were ushered into the office of the President of the United States, where both the President and his chief of staff awaited them.

The President looked strung out and angry, but he spoke with the kind of quiet good manners that seldom left him. He explained that he had now been fully briefed on the FBI's investigation of certain matters dating back to April 6, 1968. He said he had been fully apprised of the most recent developments, and exactly where things now stood.

"Now," the President said, folding thin hands together on the top of his immaculate desk, "I want to tell you gentlemen exactly what my position is on this matter. I want to be sure you understand that my instructions are to be carried out precisely—to the letter."

He paused and picked up a single sheet of bond paper on which a few lines had been typewritten. He scanned it, then gave his three visitors a long, appraising look.

"Here is how this matter will be handled," he said, and began reading.

Lake City

SAVAGELY TIRED, Arnie Tubb rounded the last mountain curve on Colorado 149 and squinted into the afternoon sunlight at the town of Lake City below him.

Just ahead, on his right, was a small cluster of buildings

that included a small grocery. Braking carefully, Tubb pulled off the highway and into the gravel parking lot.

Nudging the Buick in close to the railroad ties in front of the grocery, he cut the engine and climbed stiffly out onto the uneven rocks of the lot. The open public telephone stand was right in front of his car. A small telephone directory hung down on a thin length of chain.

Tubb picked up the thin directory and thumbed the well-worn pages back to the listing for motels and cabins. His eyes, sticky from lack of sleep, refused to focus on the small print until he rubbed them with the grimy knuckles of his right hand.

Tubb was operating on adrenaline and fanaticism now. He had stopped in Grand Junction at dawn and tried to force down a burger and milkshake—good energy food. But his stomach was getting worse with each passing day. He had no more gotten back in the car and on the road again when he had been forced to pull over, lurch outside, and vomit in the weeds beside the pavement. He couldn't hold anything down. His head buzzed continually. There had been tinges of red in his urine the last two times he peed. The damned cancer was all over the place now, eating into vital organs. It was too late for treatments. He had lumps in his neck, his shoulders, his armpits, his chest, his groin, his legs, his belly. His strength was almost gone.

It had been luck to find the scrap of paper in the pocket of the man he had killed back in Montana, Tubb thought. The scrap confirmed the information gotten from the stupid girl who had answered the telephone at the local newspaper back there. Smith was here. Green had to be here, too.

Tubb knew in the back of his feverish mind that he might be jumping to conclusions. Maybe Smith had come here, but by now would have moved on. Maybe he hadn't found Captain Green at all, but had only come here in another vain search.

Tubb could not allow himself to believe any of these

possibilities. If he could not find Smith—and Captain Green—here, he was at the end of his endurance. They *had to* be here.

If they were here—if Smith was here—didn't he have to be staying in a motel or cabin? And assuming no one knew his whereabouts, wouldn't he simply register under his real name?

Tubb's mind spun as he scanned the list of motels and rooms for rent. If Brad Smith had registered under a fake identity, Tubb might never locate him. But Smith had been confident no one knew he was in Lake City; under those circumstances, why would he register under a false name, denying himself conveniences like the use of a credit card?

He had to have registered under his true name.

For such a little town, the list of motels and cabins was dismayingly long. Tubb had to go into the grocery and hand over a five-dollar bill for quarters.

Back at the booth, he consulted the book again and punched in the first number, going alphabetically. Dizziness swept through him as he waited for the telephone at the other end to be answered. He knew how close he was now to the brink of collapse.

The first motel had no one registered by the name of Brad Smith. Neither did the second. Or the third. Or any of the first eight. Tubb's desperation intensified as he slugged in the next quarter. The sun was lowering in the sky, moving closer to the ridge of the San Juans that walled the valley to the west. Soon it would be dark and maybe another day would have been wasted, and maybe he would not wake up tomorrow.

He dialed the number. The telephone rang. No one answered through five rings . . . six . . . seven. *Come on! Answer! I don't have all night!*

"*Paragon Cabins, can I help you?*"

"Yes, I'm trying to locate a friend of mine, Mr. Brad Smith. Is he—"

"Yes, sir. Mr. Smith is in unit nine. Shall I ring?"

Tubb felt like hot acid had been injected into his veins. "No!" Then he quickly made his tone softer. "No, that's fine. I'll come down and find him. Many thanks." He hung up.

He limped back to the battered Buick and climbed inside. On the highway behind him, a red Jeep coasted down the incline in gear, and backfired loudly. The loud noise sent a wild shock through Tubb's nervous system. For an instant he flashed back—gunfire, mortar rounds coming in, the smoke, diving for the mud, seeing Davey Richmond stand up straight, his back arching, and the blood fountain from his mouth as he tumbled.

But just as quickly Tubb was back, sweat bursting from every pore, so that even the palms of his hands were slippery on the steering wheel of the car.

Now I will get you, he thought, starting the car. *Now you will tell me where to find Captain Green and I will get even for everything for all of us. Then if I die it doesn't matter because it will be over with.*

Tubb backed away from the store and pulled out onto the highway again. He drove very slowly and very carefully. It felt like his brain had different compartments in it, and each one was living a separate life. In one of them he was in Vietnam, in another he was having a chemo treatment, in another he was planning what he next had to do, and in still another he was standing off from himself, watching himself, issuing a reminder of how cautious he had to be now, how clever. There were so many different brain-rooms going all at the same time that he had to concentrate fiercely to see the tree-lined length of Gunnison Avenue.

At the far end of town he spied the motel—a line of tiny old-fashioned cabins near the highway—ahead in the next block. He drove by very sedately, seeing which unit Brad Smith had rented. At the next corner he turned around and headed the Buick back north again, pulling off the pavement into the dirt and gravel parking lot of a general store. He parked, turned off the engine, and sat watching the motel at a range of about one hundred yards. He had a clear field of view to the door of the little cabin that was Brad Smith's.

Tubb could make no mistakes now. He decided to watch and wait.

Thirty minutes passed. The sun sank lower and the first chill of evening soaked into the parked car. Tubb's teeth ached from the way he was gritting them against the cold that went to his very bones.

More time went by. Cars passed the store. A few pulled in, customers got out, went inside, returned with items. Tubb kept watch on the line of little cabins across the road and to the north. Once a car pulled up at another of the cabins and a man and woman got out with a small child. Tubb began to hurt—his stomach and intestines going into spasms—and he thought he might be sick again. Digging in the brown paper bag beside him on the seat, he got out his bottle of Gaviscon and chewed three tablets. You were supposed to chase them with water, but he knew he would throw them up if he drank water. He felt parched.

More time.

Then two men walked up the street on the far side, coming from the downtown area. Tubb watched them, squinting in the fading light. One was tall, walking with a very slight limp. The other was shorter, slender. Both wore jeans and jackets and hiking-style boots.

One of the men stopped at what must be cabin 6, unlocked the door, and went in. The second man—the taller one—went to the Smith unit, where he produced a key and entered.

Tubb's emotions rioted. He could not wait. He knew it was dangerous to act swiftly, without figuring out who the second man was, but there was no more time. It was almost dark and he felt too weak and nauseated to wait until morning.

Even if his guesswork proved to be all wrong and Smith

had not found Captain Green here, Tubb thought, Smith had to be taken. Smith had helped the FBI catch all the others. Smith not only had to talk. Smith had to pay.

Tubb started the car, backed out, pulled onto the street, and drove the hundred yards or so to the row of cabins. No other traffic was in sight, so he made a U-turn and pulled up almost directly in front of the Smith cabin. He jammed the gear selector in park and left the motor running. Rummaging in his paper bag, he got the revolver. He got out of the car and hurried to the door.

Thirty-four

THE KNOCK on my cabin door surprised me. Thinking Collie had either forgotten something or found the FBI waiting for him, I hurried out of the bathroom and opened the front door. "What—"

That was as far as I got. A filthy gnome of a man burst through the doorway, jamming a Saturday night special in under my sternum with enough force to drive me backward in pain.

He waved the revolver at me, then at the doorway. "Come on, you bastard. We're going someplace else."

"What is this?" I said, choking from the way his blow to my chest had knocked the wind out of me.

He stepped in close and jammed me again. "*Move*, motherfucker, or I blow your lungs out!"

Half-paralyzed, I saw in his crazy, red-rimmed eyes a willingness to do anything. Leaning against the wall, I fought for air.

"*Move!* I won't tell you again!"

I moved.

It was getting dark. A Jeep puttered by on the roadway, headlights already on. I glanced in the direction of Collie's cabin, but naturally he was nowhere to be seen. The little bald man moved behind me, painfully cramming his revolver muzzle into my body again, this time into the curve of my spine. "Inside."

He shoved me toward a beat-up late-model Buick sedan parked next to my Cherokee. Opening the passenger-side door with one hand, he gestured me inside. I ducked my head and climbed in. It just crossed my mind that he was being very stupid, giving me a chance by closing me in while he walked around the front of the car. But that was when I saw his sudden, violent movement, gun hand upraised.

I tried to duck by lunging to my left.

Too late. His revolver banged down on the top of my head and I felt bright, hot pain along with the ringing of a big brass gong somewhere inside my skull, and then it was hello darkness, my old friend.

Thirty-five
Elsewhere

Lake City

COLLIE DAVIS hung up his cabin telephone after returning the call that had come while he and Brad were out walking. It was the FBI, and they were staying at a place just a few blocks north on Gunnison, and they wanted to get with Brad right away. Davis had told them now was as good a time as any, and to come on down.

Starting toward the door to give Brad the news, he heard the sudden roar of a car engine being revved, then the nasty crunch of tires spinning in gravel. A sound like air-gun pellets loudly peppered the front wall of his cabin.

"Maniac," Davis muttered, cracking his front door to see who was playing destruction derby in the gravel parking area.

A late-model Buick sedan, filthy with road dust, most of the bodywork on its right side smashed and dented, was just pulling out of the motel parking area onto the blacktop pavement, heading south out of the cloud of pale yellow dust it had just created. One of its wheels spun an instant on the asphalt, howling.

Davis got only a glimpse of the occupants, but it was enough. Behind the wheel, a small bald man in a dark jacket. On the passenger side, slumped back against the seat's headrest, *Brad.*

Unconscious or worse, judging by the way his head rolled to the side as the car veered fully onto the pavement and headed south.

"Shit, shit, *shit!*" Davis ducked back into his cabin. It took him perhaps ten seconds to grab his Browning out of the compartment in his suitcase and scoop up his car keys off the rustic bedside table.

Running outside to his rented Taurus, he glanced south and saw that the Buick had already vanished around a slight turn in the highway, where it started to ascend into the foothills. He grabbed his door handle and almost broke some fingers, forgetting he had locked up. Getting the key in the lock and jumping inside took another few precious seconds. Backing out seemed to take an eternity.

Floorboarding the Taurus's accelerator, he swung onto the pavement and headed in the direction the Buick had taken. Startled faces looked up from an open-air vegetable stand as he rocketed past them, the Ford's transmission screaming in protest at such violent treatment. *All I need is for the town constable or somebody to arrest my ass for speeding.*

Reaching the curve where the Buick had vanished, he had to ease off a bit and allow the transmission to upshift. Then he poured power to the engine again, and it responded sweetly, the speedometer going up around seventy.

Ahead—well ahead, too far ahead—Davis could see the Buick nearing the outskirts of town, brake lights flaring brightly in the evening gloom, then swinging to the right and off the highway. He kept standing on the gas until he was almost on top of the place where the Buick had turned, seeing only at the last second that the intersecting road was gravel. He swayed violently onto the gravel, half losing it as the back end slewed around, then catching control again and pouring on more power. The guy in the Buick with Brad had turned on his headlights, which made two nice red taillight signals for Davis to watch for. He kept his lights out to avoid detection if possible.

The gravel road swung through a series of curves and came out in the deep canyon of a shallow river off to Davis's left. He was having a bad time seeing the road in the dimness without headlights. A pale cloud of whitish powder put in the air by the Buick ahead didn't help matters.

Sweat stung Davis's eyes. He was walking a tightrope, and knew it: get too close, and the bald man would realize he was being followed and possibly kill Brad, if he hadn't already done so; fall too far back in an overabundance of caution, on the other hand, and you could lose him altogether. Davis took several gravel curves in controlled drifts, and was rewarded with a glimpse of the Buick taillights well ahead. The bastard was driving like a maniac.

Which he probably was, Davis thought. Davis hadn't had time to see much, but he had seen enough to know that the driver of the car ahead fit the sketchy description he had of the conspirator who was still at large.

What did he want with Brad? Revenge? If so, for what? Far more likely, he had learned somehow that Brad might know where Kevin Green was. But how could abducting Brad help the loony in any way—abduction being far and away the best Davis could assume this was?

Sheer red rock walls closed in tightly on the road, which had begun to get worse, narrower and washboarded by traffic and erosion. Ahead was a tighter curve to the right around an outcropping of the hundred-foot rock face. Davis eased off a little and then swung wide into the turn. At the last possible instant he spotted the yellow glare of headlights just around the bend somewhere. Jamming his weight hard on the brake, he spun the wheel and felt for an instant that he was losing the Taurus altogether.

Dirt flew around the windows as the Ford skidded, swinging over jagged bumps in the dirt. Davis spun the wheel the opposite direction and got a semblance of control just as he went into the deepest part of the curve. A little Jeep, headlights yellow, poked its snout around the turn ahead of him. It immediately veered right as far as it could go without hitting the shoulder drop-off into the stream bed. Davis took the Taurus back right, overcorrecting as he regained full control and hitting the gravel shoulder nearest the cliff face. The right side of the Taurus brushed the rock wall with an ugly crunching sound, and then Davis was free again and speeding on into the thicker dust cloud left by the Jeep.

The dirt road narrowed and straightened out for several hundred yards, paralleling the rocky stream on the left. Davis didn't see any sign of the Buick's taillights ahead. Gritting his teeth so hard they ached, he floorboarded the accelerator again, making the Ford leap anxiously into passing gear as the tach needle swung into the red.

Another curve—Christ, it was almost impossible to see now!—and a side road right that was little more than a cow path back into what appeared to be a shallow box canyon, part of it fenced, choked with willows or some similar tree. As he roared past, Davis looked for dust in the air down there, but didn't see any. He wondered if it was too dark to see it if it were there. He had no time for speculation. Every ounce of his energy was funneled into the job of driving.

The roadway became narrower still and the canyon walls closed in on both sides, the stream much narrowed, marked by water rushing through a narrow rock ravine with such speed that its white water looked silvery even in this terrible light. No turnoffs here, Davis thought. The Buick had to be still ahead.

Up ahead he caught a momentary flash of pinkish-red light—the Buick, surely. He could get closer than this. He eased the Taurus a bit faster, feeling the back end slip and slide in minute losses of rear wheel bite. He didn't have time to glance at the instruments again, and maybe now he couldn't have read them in the gloom anyway.

The river canyon suddenly began to widen, and Davis drove out onto a broad meadow area, the stream off to the left somewhere behind a grove of aspen, a fence line along the right to protect perhaps as much as sixty acres of what looked like a cultivated field of some kind. The mountains seemed to have receded all around, were off in the dark where he couldn't pick them up now.

Ahead he saw the lights of the other vehicle flare for braking. He could not allow for much time if the bald man stopped; he might be stopping only to finish Brad off and dump his body in the ditch. Davis maintained speed.

The other car did stop, pulling off to the side of the road. Davis didn't know what the hell to do now, but he knew it wasn't a good time to count eenie-meenies. Flicking on his headlights, he tipped the high-beam switch and started braking hard as the lights came fully onto the Buick on the roadside less than a hundred yards ahead.

Only it wasn't the Buick.

It was a dark-colored Japanese 4 × 4 pickup, and a youthful man and pretty girl with flaxen hair had just clambered out onto the roadway, fishing poles in hand. They looked up and froze with alarm as Davis skidded the Ford to a halt on the shoulder behind their truck, fixing them with his brights.

Rolling his window down, he yelled at them, "Did you see a Buick sedan on this road somewhere?"

"You'd better be careful!" the boy replied hoarsely. "I've got a gun in the truck!"

"Did you see a dark-colored Buick back up the road?"

It was the girl who answered. "Yes, but we passed him when he turned off at Box Canyon."

"Shit!" Davis cranked the steering wheel hard left, pulled partway across the narrow roadway, backed around, and spun the wheel left a second time. The racket of his tires in the dirt and gravel was far worse than what the bald man had made back in town. The Taurus held a straight line, however, and pressed Davis lightly back in the seat as it accelerated.

Within ten or fifteen seconds he was going so fast that the car felt decidedly light on its springs, almost a projectile out of control. Davis did not ease off. He had screwed up. Maybe he had lost the trail altogether. Caution was the last thing he could afford now.

Thirty-six

FOR SOME period of time I knew nothing. When the first strands of consciousness began to return, everything felt jumbled—random jolts and forces throwing my body around, a sense of being tossed like a sack of feed. Nothing made sense.

Impression: roaring noises, and sounds like sleet hitting sheet metal. I was tossed sideways, then head downward. Roller coaster ride . . . something like that. My mind made up a little dream to explain things, but it wasn't a roller coaster at all. I was inside the bullet-shaped passenger compartment of one of those carnival rides that swings two cars up over the top of a big circular path, then lets them free-fall down to the bottom before jolting up to the top again on the other side of the curve. I didn't like the ride. I was riding with my father and he told me to hang on . . . not be a sissy. But then he turned into a skeleton face because he was dead, and I jolted down to the bottom of the swing again, pulling Gs, gravity forces crushing my chest.

Impression: bouncing around, my head on fire, feeling like all the parts inside had come loose. How had I not known my head was all full of gears and sprockets? Why had they all come off their spindles to rattle around loose like this?

A small bit of consciousness came back. I remembered somebody . . . sometime . . . coming into my house. But it wasn't my house and they didn't come all the way in . . . they stuck a gun in my midsection. But who was that? Where was I now?

More impressions: fragments of sense messages bouncing around: the pain in my head, sticky stuff on my face, the taste of vomit, vertigo, disorientation, occasional flashing lights, some white, flashing by fast, others close to my eyes, pale green and red, jouncing, that constant roaring sound.

I was in deep green water, trying to fight my way to the surface. The confusion overwhelmed me. I began to sink, my arms over my head, the pale green of the surface high above me fading again, going out.

I do not have a vast storehouse of experience about being knocked out. It happened to me once when I was about eight or nine, and fell off the roof of the porch of our home. That time I experienced an instant of sickening free-fall, then the crunch and rush of branches as I hit the middle of a big wisteria bush by the steps, and then a sharp, severe pain as my head banged off the second step. I was in blackness then only a minute or two before finding myself conscious again, confused, with my mother crying over me and my father yelling that he had told me never to climb out of my bedroom onto that damned porch roof. I remember thinking that I felt too shaky to be bawled out, and far preferred my mother's fright to his anger.

There were two or three other times in my life. Another came in high school, when a gym teacher decreed that since I had won my weight division in the junior class's required physical education boxing segment, I had to fight the senior class champion in my weight category. Most of us hadn't liked boxing much, and our matches had been polite sparring bouts, lots of flash and footwork, and tippy-tap for points. But the senior class kid, a redhead, came out with his chin ducked down in his shoulder, feinted with his left, and hit me with a haymaker right. The next thing I knew, I was sitting in the middle of the gym-pad "ring," the coach holding smelling salts under my gushing nose.

At those times, and the others that are of no consequence either, my return to consciousness seemed to come instantly, as if a switch had been thrown. But this time it was different. A part of me knew I was in a car, and some senses told me when the car noise finally stopped. But then I went under again, and had only the vaguest impression of being pulled by someone, hands under my armpits, and then dragged. It felt strange to be dragged. I knew I was being dragged not very far—tumbled out of a seat and into weeds and then manhandled a step or two. The next thing I knew, something was hurting my arms and shoulders.

Then something started slapping my face. It stung.

"Wake up, goddamn you!"

I woke up. A hand slammed across the side of my face, making my head jerk back and bang painfully into something hard behind me.

I was sitting up—slumped back against a post would be more accurate—and it was almost dark; we were in the country someplace in the last shadows of evening. My head roared like a bonfire. There was brush all around, the remnants of an ancient, tumbledown fence running through the brush, and I was propped up against one of the rickety posts that still stood firm and straight in the ground, the wire that it had once held long since rusted or fallen away. Trees around. Distant mountains or cliffs, maybe, hard to tell.

Leaning over in front of me, crazy eyes like coals, the bald man. Behind him in the high weeds, the gray bulk of a car with the front door swung open.

Everything came back to me.

"Are you awake?" he rasped. "Say something, damn you, or I'll hit you again."

I tried to move. The movement wrenched my shoulders. I realized that my arms were wrapped behind me, around the weathered old fence post, and my wrists had been lashed together with cord or something that had already made my fingers go cold from lack of adequate circulation.

The bald man seemed to sway back and forth as if he were drunk. Or maybe it was my confusion. He leaned closer. The hot wave of his breath stunk like something that had died. "Where is he?"

"Wha—?" I mumbled.

He swung again. His hand, made into a fist this time, hammered the left side of my face, making me rock against the fence post. It hurt.

"Where is he? This is the last time I'll ask nice."

"Dunno who," I said thickly. A slender little thought darted through my mind. I thought I knew who he was asking about, but it was very confusing. I was also scared.

"Captain Green," Baldy said. "Where is he? I know you know."

I licked sandpaper lips. "Don't know anybody . . . Green." I was practically becoming an orator here, I thought. I was almost up to whole sentences.

He hit me again. I felt my nose start to bleed.

"Tell me!"

"Don't know."

All this time he had had that ugly little revolver in his left hand. Now, muttering an obscenity, he straightened up and dropped the gun into his jacket pocket. With his right hand he rummaged in his pants and came out with something he quickly unfolded. A knife, maybe a Buck, with a four-inch blade that shone dull in the faded light.

"You'll tell me easy, motherfucker, or you'll tell me hard." He stepped up closer to me, painfully grabbing my hair with one hand and jerking my head to one side. His other hand moved. Sheer fire lanced the left side of my head. *My ear—godalmighty—!* Blood trickled hot on my neck as he stepped back a half-pace, eyes totally maniacal.

"I didn't take much," he said, with a crazy, shrill giggle. "See?" He held up a tiny pale chunk of something in his bloody fingers. "I can just whittle and whittle, motherfucker, until you finally tell me. I know how to do it real good. Does it hurt? Do you want to tell me where he is?"

I don't know what I might have said. Whatever it might

have been, I didn't respond quickly enough to suit him. He moved against me again, his knee jamming painfully into my chest so hard that I felt the old post behind me sway back and creak as if it was about to break off at the ground. Then, instantly, the incredible hot pain seemed to slice through the entire side of my head.

I think maybe I cried out.

He stepped back again, his fast breathing making his lungs sound like the air in them was bubbling up out of deep water. His teeth gleamed in the darkness. *He was enjoying this. He was having fun.* That was when the terror really struck deep into my intestines.

"Just the top part." He giggled again. "See?" He held up a larger pale chunk of my ear between bloody fingers. "Nothing much, see? Does that hurt maybe a little, motherfucker? You want me to just keep cutting? *Where is he?*"

He looked so happy, and the blood coursing down my face and neck felt like it was a lot, very warm and streaming down, and the pain made yellow stars dance in my vision against the gloom around us.

I managed to say, "I don't know. I haven't found him yet. I think—"

"You lie!" he snapped. "All right! All right! I can just keep whittling away."

"I'm telling the truth."

He moved, but this time he staggered around behind me. I felt him kneel down in the weeds. I felt his blood-slippery hands grab one of mine.

Panic gusted. "What are you doing?"

He began to hurt me. I felt the knife blade cutting in. "Just getting me a different piece," he crooned, sawing with the knife blade.

"Jesus *Christ!*" I cried out. The fence post groaned and cracked with my convulsive movement.

The sawing stopped. My left hand was on fire with the pain. He got unsteadily to his feet and lurched around in

front of me. He danced a little mad dance, holding up the
bloody first joint of my little finger. He turned and tossed it
on the ground where he had tossed the pieces of my ear.
"We'll just keep trimming and whittling," he crooned.
"Trim and cut, saw and slice. You know what, motherfucker?
I bet you're going to tell me where he is *long before* this pile
I've started over here is as big as the pile left where you're
sitting. You wanna bet, motherfucker? You wanna tell me
now?"

Something desperate in me brought up the lie. "He's . . .
in town. I can . . . take you there."

"No! You tell me! Now!"

I shook my head, making blood splatter. "Can't—don't
know the way."

He lurched around behind me again. I felt him kneel
down.

What I expected to accomplish, I will never know. It was
probably sheer animal terror—a convulsive heave without
thought of any kind.

What I did was dig my heels into the soft earth in front
of me and lurch back with all my remaining strength. He
started to react. The old, rotten fence post groaned loudly
and then snapped off at the ground, throwing me backward.
My body and the broken post hit him and went right over on
top of him. He yelled. The rope holding my wrists slipped off
the muddy bottom end of the post. I rolled, arms still tied
behind me, and managed to get to my feet as he scrambled
around in the weeds for his knife.

Back in high school, before I knew tennis was my game—
about the same time I learned the hard way that boxing
certainly *wasn't* my game—I played on the football team for
two years. All I could do well enough to be of service was
punt. I was a decent high school punter. And there he was,
on his knees right in front of me.

Stepping into it, I tried to punt his skull clear over the
mountain. I didn't—he ducked marginally at the last instant

and the connection of boot against chin wasn't solid—but it knocked him over backward. The momentum of the kick tossed me into the weeds again, too, but desperation made me scramble up fast. I saw him starting to move again—come to his knees and plunge a hand into his jacket pocket. *The revolver.*

Turning, I stumbled around the front of the Buick, trying to use it as a shield. On the far side I saw slender aspen, more weeds, a downhill slope where he must have driven up here; out maybe two hundred yards, the lights of a car.

I ran for it, careening along with my hands still tied behind me. But fear is a wonderful strength-giver. The first shot behind me sounded well back when I hit the aspens and darted down between them, making for the headlights I could see below.

Partway down, I stumbled over something and went sprawling, face-first into loose dirt that half filled my mouth with mud. I scrambled up fast. Another shot sounded behind me, and this time I heard something whir nastily past my shoulder. Ducking around a big spruce or fir, I stumbled around a couple of pale white fallen boulders and half slid, half fell down the shale declivity beyond them. Down below I could see a dirt road and a ditch in the headlights of a car that seemed to be just pulling up there.

I made for the lights, falling again, hearing another gun-shot—no whirring sound this time—and tumbled down into the roadside ditch. I got up and started toward the head-lights. It occurred to me that the headlights would help Baldy, but I was beyond rational thought.

The driver's side door of the car ahead popped open. There was just enough light left for me to recognize Collie. If I was ever more glad to see anyone in my life, I don't know when. Or how that would be possible.

I stumbled toward him, awkward with my hands tied.

Something banged behind me—another gunshot—and the windshield of Collie's car exploded.

"Brad!" he yelled. *"Down!"*

I took a nosedive into the gravel roadside. Rolling, I saw Collie behind the opened door of his car, his arms resting on the top of the door to support his two-handed grip on a pistol that looked a lot bigger than the popgun that had been shooting at me.

Fire burst from the muzzle of Collie's pistol. It flared four times, four shots very close together. I turned and looked over my shoulder, back at the way I had fled.

I was just in time to see the bald man stand up very straight, to see the little revolver drop from his fingers, and then to see him crumple over like a sack whose contents have just been removed.

Collie ran by me, going like a halfback. I knew he was checking Baldy out. I let my neck muscles relax, and my face drooped down into the gravel and dirt at the roadside. The pain was extraordinary.

Footsteps crunched gravel. Collie knelt beside me. "Brad? What did he do to you? Jesus Christ! *Jesus Christ!*"

About that time I passed out.

Thirty-seven

June 27

COLLIE WALKED into my Gunnison hospital room at ten o'clock Thursday morning with a plastic bag in hand and found the nice young doctor still arguing with me.

"If you're this man's friend," the doctor told him sharply, "you'll talk sense to him."

Collie glanced at my bandage-swathed head and lumpy wrapping on my left hand. "Doctor, I've never been very good at talking sense to this man, but I might try. What do you have in mind?"

The doctor, whose name was Bonner, looked back at me with an angry expression, the overhead light making little lightning-bolt reflections on the lenses of his eyeglasses. "Mr. Smith has had a concussion. Our tests indicate no permanent brain damage or internal bleeding, but he should stay in the hospital through the weekend as a safety precaution. We've stitched his other injuries, but he should be evaluated by a plastic surgeon in Grand Junction without delay, if that mutilated ear is ever to look half-right again. The loss of part of his finger is less worrisome. But his total medical picture *definitely* suggests further observation at the very least."

Collie absorbed this information, then turned to me. "What do you say about it?"

"I'm leaving," I told him.

"The doctor, here, doesn't think that's smart."

"I'm leaving," I repeated. "Now."

Collie turned back to the doctor and shrugged. "I tried, Doctor."

"I can't be responsible!"

"Please sign the papers," I said. "You might as well. I'm leaving one way or the other."

Dr. Bonner got up from the edge of my bed and started for the door, his mouth set tight. "I think you're a damned fool, sir."

"Doctor, thanks for all you've done." I swung my legs out of the bed. "Collie, are those clean clothes for me?"

"As clean as I could find in your motel cabin," he said, and tossed the plastic bag on the bed.

I pulled off the hospital gown and rummaged around for underwear. "What's happening in Lake City?"

"Let's talk on the drive back."

"No," I said, getting to my feet. "Let's talk—" A wave of dizziness almost dropped me to my knees. I hung on. "Maybe you're right," I said, fighting to clear my head again.

Lake City has a pretty new community clinic that everyone is very proud of, as well they should be. The only problem is that the clinic has no doctor. When Collie had hauled me in there late Wednesday after a stop at the sheriff's office to alert someone, the nurse-practitioner took one look at me and said I was going to Gunnison's hospital in the ambulance. I weakly protested that I didn't need an ambulance, then passed out again. When I next woke up, I was in the back of the ambulance, rocking and swaying north on 149, she had temporarily patched my head and hand, and a male paramedic was perched beside me in the steel compartment, watching an IV drip into my arm.

At Gunnison's hospital they did my repair work on a more permanent basis, scrubbing and disinfecting and stitching here and there, and taking some X rays. Then they gave me something strong and I was out for the night. Collie's telephone call had been the first thing I knew this morning, and he had not been any more informative then than he was at the hospital while I dressed.

In his car, headed back, he tersely answered my questions.

"The bald guy who chopped me up?"

"Dead."

"He was the one everybody was still looking for?"

"Yes. Tubb, Arnold. Late of Baker Company and all the VA hospitals in the world, more or less."

"What about Kevin?"

"Two guys appeared last night not long after I sent you off north in the ambulance. They're talking to him now, I imagine."

"FBI?"

"No, the FBI arrived earlier, about the time Tubb decided to take you out and make hamburger out of you. When I brought you back to town last night and they heard the story about Tubb, they had a bit of a hassle clearing everything with the sheriff. But they were anxious to get on with things, so they called in with a report and then went on out to talk to Kevin late last night. One of them was out there until this morning, finishing up with him."

I didn't want to think about what "finishing up with him" might mean. I said, "They found him that easily?"

"They found the real estate man who rented his cabin to him. The Realtor led them up. Then this morning the Pentagon types were to get their turn."

"So they're taking turns," I said bitterly. "I hope there's enough Kevin for everybody to get their share."

Collie turned left at the intersection of 149 and started south across the water of Blue Mesa Reservoir toward the barren, humpy hillocks to the south. He seemed amazingly unconcerned, and that wasn't like him.

I asked, "Have you talked with either of the FBI agents since they first went up to Kevin's?"

"One of them, yes. I told him I was going to pick you up at Gunnison this morning. He said they'll need a statement from you. After that they plan to leave."

I sat up straighter. *"Leave!"*

"Leave."

"Why? Where are they going now? When will they be back?"

"They won't be back."

"That doesn't make any sense!"

We started up a long, curving uphill part of the road that led away from the level of the reservoir, with its handful of fishing boats making gnat-specks on its sun-bright vastness. Collie didn't reply for a moment, paying attention to the job of passing a rickety camper shell on the back of a venerable Ford F-150.

Once we were around and in the clear again he said, "The FBI boys were hot to trot when they arrived last evening. But by the time I got back from taking you to the clinic, they had called in to report and gotten new instructions."

I studied his profile, trying to read him. "Which were?"

"There were some questions they said they needed to ask. But they said Kevin Green isn't wanted for anything that they know about, and all they needed to do was clarify the Tubb episode with him, get some background, and then talk to you. They got a statement from me, of course, about Tubb, same as the sheriff did. That part has all been straightened out." He reached for a cigarette, and his eyebrows tilted the way they often did when something struck an ironic chord in him. "It seems Mr. Tubb was seriously deranged and was killed when an unidentified federal agent attempted to apprehend him."

"But that doesn't help Kevin," I said.

"Well, not in terms of their having to get a statement from him."

"And once they start taking his statement, the story about Quang Xi will all come out, and they'll have enough to hang him."

"Not so," Collie said as we came to a straighter stretch of the road that aimed arrow-straight toward the misty San

Juans. "I talked to the one agent again this morning before I left. The one who came back to town. Nice fellow. Name's Steed. Ever hear of him?"

"No. What did he say?"

"Me either. Anyway, he mentioned—quote—information about Vietnam, unquote. He didn't seem to care about that. He said he had been instructed last night that none of that was of any concern to the FBI; all they cared about was the series of murders stateside. He said, with Tubb dead and some other people in custody, their case is about all wrapped up."

"But what are they going to do with Kevin?" I insisted impatiently.

"Nothing."

"But—!"

"Did that blow on the head mess up your other ear, too, Brad? I *told* you: the FBI is just waiting to talk to you, and then they're ready to truck on out of town. They say they'll be finished here."

"I don't get it."

Collie didn't answer me.

Back at the motel in Lake City we found one of the FBI men, the one named Steed, sitting in his car waiting for my arrival. Middle-aged and affable, he expressed concern about my health and asked if he could ask a few questions at once, as he and his partner planned an early departure. Collie went off to his own cabin unit and I took Steed into mine. He started a small recording device and deftly went through a chronology of events with me, starting all the way back when somebody calling himself Frank Simmons planted the bug in my telephone.

He was very concerned with getting dates right, Steed was, and he made notes to back up the recording. He did not ask anything about Kevin, or why anyone had been after him. He did not ask why Dave Wentworth might have been killed.

His whole intent seemed to be in defining my role, and the timing of events.

I was still waiting for him to get to what I felt sure he would consider the good stuff when he closed his notebook and turned off the recorder. "I think that will do it, Mr. Smith. Thank you very much."

"That's all?" I blurted.

Our eyes met for a moment. There was knowledge in his. He knew exactly what I was thinking.

He said, "That's all. Yes. Thank you again."

I hotfooted it down to Collie's. "He didn't ask me *anything* about Quang Xi, Kevin's role there, his bugout in Hawaii—any of that."

Collie shrugged again and picked up a note. "I had a call from the head man on the Pentagon team. Name's Steadman. He wants to know if we can meet him out at the Crystal Lodge, where he's staying. Do you know where that is?"

"I ought to. It's the fanciest place around here, down south on the highway a couple of miles."

Collie sighed. "It figures. The Pentagon always seems to have more money than anybody else. Shall we go down there and continue this gay mad whirl of social activity?"

When we met Steadman in the restaurant at the Crystal Lodge, he allowed as how he would like to have "a few words" with each of us separately, and he would like to talk to Collie first. He obviously knew Collie's connection. They went off together and I had two cups of coffee, and then Collie was back in surprisingly short order.

"Your turn," he said with a slight smile. "One-eighteen."

I went down the redwood deck and found the room overlooking the swimming pool. Steadman was gracious, almost courtly, inviting me in and offering me more coffee, which I refused. He was wearing civilian clothes, jeans, and a sweatshirt with an owl and the words *Lake City* on the front, but he might just as well have been wearing his uniform. Civilians just didn't talk that way, or stand that ramrod-straight, or carry themselves with quite such an air of authority. Muscular, an inch or two taller than I, he appeared to be about forty, with streaks of gray in close-cropped dark hair. Women would have found him interesting, partly because of his very pale gray eyes, which felt like they were boring right into you. Not army, I guessed, but more likely marines.

"Good of you to help us, Mr. Smith," he told me, giving me a cruncher of a handshake. "I remember many of your great matches on television. I was assigned in London the year you lost to Borg in the finals at Wimbledon, got to see that from the stands. Hell of a match."

I smiled. "Only one thing could have made it better, from my standpoint."

He appeared momentarily nonplussed. "What's that? Oh. Yes. Of course. If you had won. Sorry you didn't."

"I am too, Colonel. Tell me what's on your mind."

To my mild delight, he didn't even notice the "Colonel," which told me I had perfectly guessed his rank. Frowning at me, he asked, "Are they going to be able to fix that ear?"

"They think so, yes."

"Where did all the facial cuts and bruises come from? Did he do all that?"

"No, only part. I fell down a lot trying to get away."

"How about that hand?"

"Well, the fingertip won't grow back, but it won't bother me much."

He scowled. "Might be better all around that the man is dead. It looks like the VA will have to pay for his funeral, however. Parents dead, brother and sister won't take responsibility."

"Colonel," I repeated, losing patience. "What about Kevin Green?"

"My associate is up there with him now, tape-recording a statement. We should be finished by noon, and be ready to depart right after lunch."

"Where will he be taken?" I asked.

Steadman's eyebrows raised fractionally. "Where will who be taken?"

"Kevin, of course. Kevin Green, the man you've been trying to find ever since he bugged out of a hospital airplane in Hawaii in 1973!"

Steadman tented his fingers. "You're quite mistaken if you think we've been actively searching for Captain Green."

"Have it your way," I said, hearing the bitter edge in my own voice. "You've got him now. All I want to know is what happens to him next. I think I've got a right to know that much."

Steadman's light eyes did not waiver. "Why, nothing is going to happen to Captain Green, Mr. Smith. Not at this late date."

His words so surprised me that I just sat there for perhaps a minute, wondering if I had heard him correctly. I couldn't read his expression. I was back in never-never land.

I said, "Are you telling me that the Pentagon has found a man who deserted—technically speaking—after failing to do his duty in combat—after you paid all those benefits to his assumed widow—and now *you're not going to pick him up*?"

"The case is very old," Steadman said calmly.

"But hell! I would think the army would want to sue him for some of the benefits his wife received, if nothing else."

"The benefits she received while he was a POW? You certainly can't say he didn't earn *those*. As to the payments she received for the short time he was listed as MIA again after his bugout in Hawaii—I assume you know all about that—they were hardly very substantial, nor were the death benefits she received when he was declared KIA. A small amount to lose in order to have this thing behind us once and for all."

"But my God! What about—"

"The military was concerned about murders, Mr. Smith.

Some in Vietnam, under combat conditions: deaths by friendly fire, but falling into a pattern linking the deaths to earlier duty in the Quang Ngai province. There were also bizarre killings in later years, back here in the States. *These* interested us. They interested us greatly. Now . . . as a result of a direct presidential order which opened certain FBI files to us only yesterday . . . we believe those murders have been solved. Our area of interest has closed."

"What about what Kevin did at Quang Xi? Charges—"

"What good end would be served, Mr. Smith, by persecuting a man who might have made a mistake under the pressures and confusion of combat?"

"I—!"

"How," Steadman cut in, maintaining the same inexorably calm tone, "can we even be sure, at this late date, that his recollections are accurate? What advantage would there be in prosecuting a man shot down in combat, held in captivity, and obviously suffering from posttraumatic stress disorder?"

"Am I hearing what I think I'm hearing? The army isn't going to charge him with *anything*?"

"What good end would be served?"

"But what about everything else that happened at that hamlet? What about the VC ambush, the—"

"I'm sorry, Mr. Smith, but I don't know what you're talking about." Steadman reached into his pocket and dug out a pipe and tobacco pouch. Stuffing tobacco into the pipe's bowl, he gave me an innocent, engaging, amazing smile of total placidity. "I have examined *all* the files . . . the unclassified files . . . on this case. I spoke only yesterday with higher authorities about the matter. These were *very* high authorities, Mr. Smith, and I can assure you that nothing untoward ever occurred at a place called Quang Xi. There was never an ambush, and there was certainly never a massacre. It was a very small operation, and it was a very long time ago, and the books on the incident have long since been closed. And they will remain so. Now, if you will, allow me to ask just a few questions. I believe we will be close to having our business here concluded."

Thirty-eight

THE REMAINDER of the interview with Steadman took less than thirty minutes. Then, feeling dazed by the suddenness of it all, I found myself shaking hands with the other Pentagon investigator, back from his work with Kevin; hearing Steadman say they would spend the afternoon processing reports and be on their way in the morning; driving back toward our motel with Collie.

"I don't know whether to be happy for Kevin or mad as hell for all the other guys," I told him as we pulled up in front of our place.

He gave me a sideways look. "I have made up a brilliant and original aphorism that I think you should take to heart in this case. Here it is. Never look a gift horse in the mouth."

"Kevin is clear. That's wonderful. But it's just another case of the army sweeping something under the rug for political reasons."

"What choice is there? Vietnam is *over*. Let it stay dead."

"You're a little younger than I am, Collie. You weren't over there."

He flushed, and his words showed that he could never understand where I was coming from. "Brad, I said it before: your pal Kevin was a traitor."

"The circumstances—"

"Damn the circumstances! Two wrongs don't make a right. He had a duty and he didn't perform it."

Furious, I put on a thick, bogus German accent: " 'I vass

only following orters.' Is that it? Stand by and witness slaughtering innocents, and then use the Nuremberg defense?"

His eyes kindled with impatient anger. "That's bullshit and you know it. Vietnam wasn't Dachau. We weren't Nazis."

"No. But you can't understand how that war screwed people up."

"And you can?"

"Thousands—maybe hundreds of thousands—of guys came back screwed up—posttraumatic stress syndrome. And yes, I do know. I was a hell of a lot luckier than most, but I was pretty crazy for awhile after I got back and Elizabeth dumped me while I was still getting treatments for the damage that shell fragment did."

Collie looked sincerely puzzled. "So?"

"I was a little crazy. I know how many came back a lot crazier."

"You got over it."

"No thanks to the policy of the government of the United States."

"What's the *point*, Brad?"

"The point is that thousands and thousands of guys went over there and fought a lousy war and came back as stressed-out and crazy as any of the veterans who might have been on this insane search for Kevin. A lot of them have never been helped at all. You see them on the streets in every big city in the country. You see their names in drunk tanks and drug raid lists. The country shouldn't have ignored all those guys, Collie, goddammit, *that's* the point. The country shouldn't have turned its back on them just because it was an unpopular war. The amazing thing to me, now that I think about it, is not this insane vendetta Arnie Tubb and a handful of old pals carried on for years; the amazing thing is that there aren't a lot more vets just like them. And now—sure—I'm glad for Kevin, he's going to go free. But the country is doing it again with him, with Quang Xi: sweeping it all under the rug, more garbage out of sight, out of mind. The real story of all this isn't Dave Wentworth or Kevin Green. It's how this country fucked over all the guys who came back from Nam with their minds in pieces, and maybe abandoned some guys over there when we fled—and how our government is *still* pretending none of it happened."

Collie looked at me awhile. "So that makes Kevin innocent?"

"No. Yes."

"We'll never understand each other on this one, Brad."

"You're right," I told him. "We never did and we never will."

Dense gray clouds had begun to trundle in from the southwest, already obscuring Red Mountain. It was going to rain. I felt drained and ready for a nap. But I was far too upset—outraged and overjoyed at the same time.

I told myself to concentrate on the good news for Kevin. He was free.

I had to see him.

The rain, light and breezy, had set in before I reached the shack. To my great relief, I found Kevin's pickup in front, and a wisp of woodsmoke over the chimney pipe. I hurried through the drizzle to the front porch and knocked. He opened at once. He looked very tired. He didn't smile as he invited me in.

"They told me about your near-thing," he told me, dropping into one of his chairs near the stove. "I'm glad you're okay."

"I'm more than okay," I told him. "I'm beginning to feel pretty good about you, actually, old pal, old sock. You're a free man at last, after all these years!"

"They aren't going to charge me," he said in a dull, unemotional tone.

"Right. When you call Barbara, it will be the greatest

thing that ever happened to her. When are you going to call her?"

"I'm not calling her."

"What did you say?" *

He shook his head slowly, the way a stubborn child will do when he is not going to budge, no matter what the playground bully—or Mom or Dad—threatens him with. He repeated dully, "I'm not calling her."

"Hell, Kevin! Talk sense! Didn't the investigators make it clear? You're not going to be charged with anything. You're home free, man. Vietnam is finally *over* for you. Whatever happened over there is buried, and they're going to keep it buried. The guys who might have been after you have been picked up, and they'll be in prison a long, long time, if not for the rest of their lives. There's no cloud left for you, Kevin. You don't have to hide anymore."

He looked up at me with eyes that suddenly blazed with bitterness and rage. "You dumb shit!" he burst out. "Don't you understand *anything?*"

I stared at him, afraid I knew what might be coming. "Understand what?"

His voice dropped to a whisper. "I can't call Barbara. I can't ever go back."

"Then she can come here. Man, the way she loves you, she would—"

"No, no!" he broke in, slashing the air with his hand.

"Kevin," I said, baffled, "what are you saying?"

"The army can say it's over. The army can say I've got no one left to fear—"

"Is that it?" I cut in. "Then, hell! Keep your new name, the one you've used all these years. Barbara won't give a shit about that. If you feel a need to remain anonymous—"

He shook his head. "It isn't over. No matter what you or the army or anyone else says. It's never going to be over."

It was as I had feared and refused to expect. I said lamely, "But there's no one after you anymore."

He finally met my eyes, and I wished that he hadn't. His pain was like nothing I had ever seen.

He said, "It doesn't matter if anyone is after me anymore. Not guys who were over there, and crazy to get revenge, and not the army or anyone else. That's not really the issue. Maybe it never was the issue."

"What *is* the issue?" I asked quietly.

"I saw those dead civilians. I saw those children. I saw the VC, waiting. I did nothing. I never told anyone about the massacre. Instead, I was a traitor. I caused our guys to die just as surely as they killed those innocent people. It doesn't *matter* what the army says, or what *you* say, or what anybody *ever* says. I . . . let . . . our . . . guys . . . die. Nothing can change that. Nothing can take away my knowing what I am, for having done that. *Nothing.* I'm not fit to live a normal life with Barbara or anyone else."

I saw, then, and dropped onto the chair facing his. "Kevin, some of this guilt of yours is bullshit and you know it!"

His teeth grated audibly. "Is it? Is it? What do you know?"

"Those guys staged a massacre. Then you let them get blasted. There was no single fault. It was a double fault, Kevin. Theirs, then yours." I paused, trying desperately to find a way to get through to him. "But this kind of a double fault isn't like in tennis, Kevin! They don't add up. *They cancel each other out.* It's behind you. It's done! You've been given a second chance, and now you'd be crazy not to move on—grab life again!"

He flung himself to his feet and rammed around the room, waving his arms as if trying to attack invisible demons. "Move on?" he repeated with vicious sarcasm. "Put it behind me? Goddammit, Brad, don't you see I can never put it behind me or move on beyond it because what's wrong isn't out there—*it's inside me: what's wrong is me.*"

Listening to how his voice shook with self-loathing, I

began to understand more fully. It was worse than I had anticipated. I had been a fool not to see it before, to imagine that the signing of a few papers in Washington somewhere could heal his life. I saw now that Tubb and the others had been wasting their time, seeking him out for death. In one way he had died in Vietnam a long time ago.

I stayed awhile, of course, trying to talk sense to him. He did not and could not budge. Finally I realized that it might be better to let things soak for awhile, try later.

"I have to get back to town," I told him, getting to my feet. "I'll check in with you again tomorrow. Does that sound all right?"

He stood, surveyed me with lifeless eyes, and held out his hand. "Don't come back, Brad. I really don't want to see you again. I mean—I appreciate everything you tried to do. But I just don't want to see you again. All right?"

He would not be moved. Baffled and depressed, I drove back to town and found Collie Davis packing his bag.

"Leaving already?" I said, dismayed.

He tossed some underwear into the bag. "Called Dwight. We agreed maybe I've had enough annual leave right now and it's time to get back to work." He grimaced. "Seems like there's some fun in El Salvador again and they need an extra body."

I sat down. "Got a cigarette?"

He gave me one and lighted it for me, studying my face. "I judge things did not go swimmingly with your friend up on the mountain."

I told him about it. He finished packing while I did so, and did not comment when I was through.

"I guess you can go home, too, then," he said finally.

"It all feels unfinished, Collie."

He closed his bag and hefted it to the floor beside the door. "Not at Langley, it doesn't. There's an analyst some-where who's probably feeling transported about now. I imagine he's going to be busy the next few days, closing about twenty-five old files that have nagged his ass forever."

"The story will leak," I said. "The FBI will see to that."

"Nope. The FBI will keep quiet, on orders. So will the military."

"Are you so sure of that?" I demanded.

He looked at me. "Does the Pentagon need an old scandal that will make it look stupid—stir up some of the old bitterness about Nam?"

"Of course not. But the FBI—"

"Does the White House need something like this to come out now, the year before a national election, when the press is sure to make it look like there's been a cover-up?"

I thought about it from this angle, and my surprise mixed with the general disappointment. I am always amazed at my naive ability to be disappointed by some of our institutions and the people who run them.

I said, "Maybe you're right. Maybe it will never come out."

"It won't. Trust me."

I didn't say anything.

He said, "No good purpose would be served."

We looked at each other.

I said, "Collie, I don't think you believe in that kind of expediency any more than I do."

"What I believe doesn't matter. I follow orders. Or I turn it in."

I walked with him down to the office, where he checked out. Going back to his car, he stopped and looked out toward the Lake City Cafe, and beyond that, the American flag whipping in the after-rain breeze. You could see the old white frame courthouse and the high, wooded ridge to the east.

He took a deep breath and stretched. "I like this place. I'm going to come back here someday when I really am on leave."

We shook hands.

"Don't feel bad," he told me. "You found him. You saved his life. You did good."

"Did I?" I said. "So long, Collie."

He got in his car, backed out, and drove away.

Thirty-nine

July 1

THEY WERE putting up some bunting around a temporary platform in the small city park off Higgins Avenue when I went back to the Missoula hospital to be looked over by a plastic surgeon (ear) and orthopedic man (finger). They examined and poked and prodded and pronounced everything good. The plastic surgeon said he could give me a nice new plastic top for my ear, and if I let my hair grow shaggy over it, no one would ever notice. The orthopod said the stump of my little finger was healing just fine.

Before leaving, I asked if Reese McDonald, boy FBI wonder, was still in-house. They said he was, and I looked him up.

Getting out of the elevator on two, I made my way to the nurses' station and asked for McDonald's room number. The nurse on duty gave me a mildly hostile once-over.

"Mr. McDonald's visitors are restricted, sir."

"Maybe someone gave you my name? Brad Smith."

Her expression changed marginally from hostile to businesslike. "Of course. I should have known." She pointed. "Two-eighteen. You are limited to ten minutes."

The room was near the end of the hall, on the south side. The solid wood door was closed. I tapped lightly and went on in.

The draperies on a south wall of glass had been pulled open, and the room had a splendid view out over a graveled lower roof to an open field beyond, sun-drenched under a flawless blue sky, and far off in the distance the white brilliance of Mount Lolo's peak. Propped halfway up in bed, Reese McDonald held an FBI operations manual and a box of Kleenex on his bed tray. His upper torso tightly wrapped in multiple layers of bandage and tape, he looked shaky and even paler than usual, and almost frail. But now at least both of us knew he would live. He was freshly shaven, and every hair was in place. His rimless eyeglasses popped blinding sunlight reflections at me as he turned.

"Mr. Smith," he said, expressionless. "Please come in."

I was already in. I walked toward his bed, feeling an impulse to say something really neat and important about being glad he had made it, or something. He reached for a tissue and carefully wiped the white tips of his fingers before touching his manual to close it with a small marker where he was leaving off. Dreadful, I suppose, to leave a finger mark in a book. I felt my poetic impulse drain away.

"So how are you?" I asked.

He blinked several times, frowning. "My condition has been upgraded from serious to good. Earlier it was critical. Despite a certain light-headedness, which the doctors attribute to the lingering aftereffects of the anesthetic, I feel quite well, actually."

"The pain pills make you woozy, too," I pointed out.

His lip stiffened. "I am taking no pain medication."

"I heard they had your whole chest opened up. Don't you still hurt?"

"Of course. However, in view of the complexity of the surgery, I would classify it as nominal."

"Too much for most guys," I said, "but about right for you?"

His forehead wrinkled. "Please?"

"Nothing. So when do you get out of here?"

"Another two weeks, they say. I predict five days."

"That soon?"

"I heal rapidly, and have a higher pain-tolerance level

than most. I rank in the top eight-tenths of a percentile in that regard, actually."

"It figures."

He studied me. "You're all right?"

"Never better." Two could play, I thought.

He frowned. "I have been informed that the case is closed."

"That's what I was told, too."

"I am somewhat puzzled about certain aspects."

"Really?"

"Yes. Perhaps you could fill me in on a few details?"

"I'm afraid not," I told him, straight-faced. "Need to know, and all that sort of thing—you know."

He seemed vastly disappointed. I didn't stay long. As I walked out of his room, I glanced back and saw that he had already placed a clean tissue over his fingers and was again engrossed in his manual.

That same evening I had dinner at the lodge with Ted Treacher and Lynette Jordan. Avery Whitney came by and joined us as well, his stunning young live-in pal, Melody, at his side.

Melody moued and murmured about my "terrible injuries." Lynette, narrow-eyed, apparently had figured out just enough to suspect that she might have caused me real trouble when she told "Roscoe Tanner" where I could be found. I pretended innocence. Avery said I looked peaked after my "fishing accident," and ought to get some rest. He said I ought to invite Beth up for the July 4 doings in town. I told him I would think about that. We had a pleasant evening.

The next morning's mail brought a letter from the lady in question. It was really very sweet but very clear about everything. She always did have a way with words, my Beth. Formerly my Beth.

Forty

AFTER THE surgery I was behind on all my work at Bitterroot Valley and we were at the peak of our season. But I couldn't let go yet. Not quite yet.

I drove into Lake City late in the day. It was a different town with so many cars on Silver Street and all the tourists. But it was still very nice.

Too late to look for Kevin that night, so I checked into a motel on the north edge of town and got up very early the next morning to get out to his place and catch him before he went to work for the day. I just needed to see him—see that he was all right, and tell him I was fine. That, I thought, would make things stop feeling so unfinished between us.

When I got to his old cabin out on the wooded mountainside, however, I found a Hall Realty Co. For Sale sign at the edge of the driveway, and no sign of life. Kevin's pickup was nowhere to be seen, and when I peered in through a side window of the cabin, I saw that the kitchen shelves were bare, and nothing on the shelving near the stove.

Back in town, at Hall Realty, I talked to a man.

"Ken?" he said. "I don't know. He left Lake City."

"Left," I said, absorbing it.

"Two or three weeks ago. Rented a small U-Haul and headed out. We owe him a half month's rent rebate, but he said he didn't know where he was heading—would let us know. I don't think we'll ever hear from him, to tell you the truth. He always was a strange one, wasn't he?"

* * *

I treated myself to a Kitchen Sink omelet at the Lake City Cafe and headed north again. Maybe I would hear from Kevin one day, I thought. Maybe some fine afternoon I would be playing in an exhibition somewhere and look up in the stands, and there he would be. But I couldn't really believe that.

Dave Wentworth was dead, and so was poor, mad Arnie Tubb, and God only knows how many others—some killed by "friendly fire" over there in Vietnam because they had seen too much or had refused to participate blindly in a slaughter no more insane than most of the things that happened in that war. A tiny clique of the wounded, driven by ghosts they could not exorcise, had been found and would go to federal prisons or the psych wards of VA hospitals, and there would be no more ritualistic murders in the name of revenge or loyalty or the "honor" of a military unit filled with good guys in over their heads, and a handful of animals who had disgraced them. The secret would stay buried along with its dead.

It would be fine to think this put an end to it, and that something good had been accomplished. But only one little piece of a very large and nasty secret had been laid to rest. No help would come for any of the other shattered men walking around this land of ours, pushed aside and forgotten, considered at best a nuisance. And whatever had been done, ultimately none of it had helped Kevin Green in the slightest, either.

Being listed as KIA was appropriate for him; his journey to that war had resulted not in his physical death but in something more terrible. For him, like so many others, Vietnam had shown him horrors about others—and himself—that could never be gotten over.

I don't pretend to understand how any of the others were ruined. But Kevin was a different matter; Kevin I thought I could understand. He would never leave that war behind him. He could never return to the identity he had had before.

He would never be free, regardless of what I had tried to persuade him. Driven to a terrible decision made in a single moment of shock and confusion long ago, he had discovered something he could not abide.

Because for Kevin, what he had found there in the deeps of himself really was a Boojum, you see.